THE PROMISE OF RAIN

Donna Milner lives in British Columbia with her husband. Her first novel was the acclaimed *After River*, which was sold all over the world. *The Promise of Rain* is her second novel.

Also by Donna Milner
After River

THE PROMISE OF RAIN

Donna Milner

Quercus

First published in Great Britain in 2010 by

Quercus

21 Bloomsbury Square
London
WC1A 2NS

A CIP catalogue record for this book is available
from the British Library

ISBN 978 1 84724 952 4

10 9 8 7 6 5 4 3 2 1

Typeset by Ellipsis Books Limited, Glasgow

Printed and bound in Australia by Griffin Press

In memory of Hazel Huckvale,
who planted the seed

My mother died on the same day as Marilyn Monroe, August 4th 1962, and just like the movie star her body would not be discovered until the following day. There was no mistaking Mom's presence when she was alive. True to form, her death was not without drama. It would force my father to return to our family. Even though for the entire eleven years of my life he had come home every night to our two-storey wartime house in South Vancouver, a large part of him was not really there. I was used to his absence; I was not used to hers.

Over time I would come to believe it was that very absence that woke me so abruptly, in the dark hours that morning. More likely it was simply a gust of wind rattling my bedroom window, or the rain pounding against the glass. I can't be certain. I only know that when my eyes snapped open I felt compelled to leave my bed and creep out into the narrow hallway between the two bedrooms. I stood in the shadows at the top of the stairs, my heart racing, listening to the silence of the house before I started down, pausing at the turn to listen once more.

Downstairs, I made my way to the open door at the end of the hall and peered into my parents' bedroom. The familiar fragrance of my mother's Evening in Paris perfume filled my nostrils as I scanned the room, my eyes adjusting to the dim light. My breath caught at the image of a figure in the corner. But it was only a dress hanging on the closet door. The room, like the rumpled bed, was empty.

I stepped over the clothes strewn on the floor and ran my hand down the soft material of Mom's dress. Even without her in it that Kelly green dress looked like her. It was her favourite, the one she called her knock-'em-dead, Sunday-go-to-meeting outfit, and the only one she kept on a padded hanger.

The day the Eaton's truck delivered it she had called me into her room the moment she'd slipped it on. Leaning into the mirror, she applied lipstick and dabbed powder across the small bump on her nose, then tilted her head and studied the effect. Satisfied, she pushed aside the books, discarded nylons and half-full ashtrays on the dressing-table and stepped back to pose before the mirror. 'What do you think, Ethie?'

I thought she was perfect no matter what she wore. But something about that dress made her hazel green eyes even brighter, her thick auburn curls shinier, and the smattering of freckles, which the powder could not erase, seem even more exotic. 'You look beautiful,' I told her, 'just like a movie star.'

Her reflection smiled back at me. She leaned down and pulled me into her arms, enfolding me in perfume, new green dress and all. 'Oh, Ethie,' she sighed, 'it's so nice to be called beautiful. Especially by my favourite girl.' She released me and whirled around to look at the back of the dress, which clung to her rounded bottom.

Even then I think I knew the purchase of that dress was punishment for some transgression of my father's. Whenever she was angry with him, Mom's solution was to flip through the catalogue and order something they couldn't afford. Dad looked after the finances in our house. Everything we needed, including the weekly groceries, was charged and he paid the bills at the end of each month. Before she went to work, the only money my mother had control of was the monthly family-allowance cheque, ten dollars for each of her children. Somehow

Dad believed that thirty dollars should cover anything extra.

'It *is* a special dress, isn't it?' Mom asked, her expression saying she was pleased with it. I grinned and nodded, but I was pretty sure she wasn't expecting an answer. 'It's a classic,' she said, then knelt and hugged me again. 'And I'll keep it nice,' she promised, 'so you can have it when you grow up.' Every time she put the dress on I imagined myself wearing it one day. But, as things turned out, I never would.

I caught a movement in the shadows and spun around. But all I saw was the tangled red curls and startled face of an eleven-year-old girl wearing an undershirt and panties staring back from the mirror. With blood pounding in my ears I turned away and tiptoed out of the room. I checked the living room and the bathroom at the other end of the hallway. Both empty. Then I turned towards the kitchen and I saw him – my father sitting alone in the dark staring out of the kitchen window. I stood frozen in the entryway. Somehow I knew this was not the time to do my little dance of distraction that I often used to entice him back from wherever he disappeared to when he went into one of his trances. I shrank back into the shadows and watched the ember glow of his cigarette move slowly from the saucer on the table up to his lips.

A flash of headlights splashed across the window, lighting up his silhouette. Without moving his eyes from the street, he took the cigarette stub from his mouth and crushed it into the overflowing saucer. I ducked back down the hall and into the living room, where I pressed against the wall by the front windows and pulled back a corner of the sheer curtains.

Outside, a black and white car pulled up to the kerb. The wipers stopped. Light-filled droplets covered the windshield, obscuring the shadow of the occupants. At the same moment the car doors opened, the bedroom curtains in the house across the street parted, then were yanked shut, leaving a small gap.

Mrs Manson. The neighbourhood watchdog, Mom called her – when she wasn't calling her a busybody. And, like me, what she was busy doing right then was spying from her peephole while two policemen climbed out of the car in front of our house.

My father's chair scraped away from the kitchen table. I rushed out of the living room and fled back up the stairs. Breathless, I sat down on the step above the turn and leaned forward to listen.

The knock at our front door that would change our lives forever was gentle.

'Howard Coulter?' The voice saying my father's name after the door creaked open sounded so young. Younger even than Frankie's – my oldest brother who was twenty. Like the knock, the voice sounded too gentle, too kind, to belong to a policeman.

There was no response from my father. After a moment of silence an older, deeper voice asked, 'May we come in, Mr Coulter?'

Suddenly a hand gripped my shoulder. I turned with a jolt to find Kipper leaning over me, his slack mouth opening to form a word. I lifted my finger to my lips. He smiled back at me, mimicking my shushing gesture. I patted the step beside me and he slumped down. Even though he was three years older, my brother, heavy and pear-shaped, was shorter than I. He reached up and put his stubby arm around my shoulders, not understanding this game but thrilled to be a part of the conspiracy. We must have looked a strange pair, sitting there in the morning shadows, me in my underwear, twisting a long corkscrew curl of hair, and my grinning fourteen-year-old brother wearing blue teddy-bear pyjamas and a brown pork-pie hat.

That narrow-brimmed felt hat was like a part of Kipper. The only time it was not on his head was when he slept. It hung on his bedpost every night, ready to be donned the moment he woke. He had inherited it from Dad – a birthday gift from Mom – years ago. Dad had never worn it. Kipper was never without it.

Down in the foyer the too-young voice repeated my father's name, and I felt a pang of fear at the sympathetic tone. Leaning forward, I strained to peer around the corner. Another hand gripped my shoulder and Frankie, shirtless and barefoot, pushed his way between Kipper and me. His sandy-blond hair, usually combed back in a perfect ducktail, stuck straight out from the sides of his head like wings. I could smell the Brylcreem left over from his date the night before. Without stopping he said, 'Go back to bed,' and rushed down the stairs, zipping up his blue jeans.

Kipper rose and turned to go up to his room, always ready to obey Frankie without question. I usually did too. But not this time. I stood up and followed him. Downstairs my father – looking shrunken and small in the shadows of the unlit entry – stood motionless, his hand frozen on the knob of the open door. In the half-light beyond him, the rain poured down on the two police officers on the front porch.

I knew he was different. By the time I was six years old I knew my father was not like other fathers. Other fathers didn't sit and stare at the wall a few inches above the top of their television set. They didn't disappear regularly into a silent world, or get lost on long treks through the Vancouver rain. Sometimes my father would be gone for hours, whole days even, on those journeys from which he would return watery-eyed and drenched to the skin, but somehow lighter in spirit as if his black mood had been cleansed, like the city's air. I knew other fathers played catch with their sons. I watched with envy when they swung their daughters up on to their shoulders to piggyback them around their yards. I knew they could see their children. I wasn't always sure my father could.

The year I started school Mom allowed me to run to the top of Barclay Street when it was time for him to return home from work at the sawmill. Every evening I waited in anticipation while my handsome father, with sawdust scattered through his thinning brown hair, climbed off the bus. And every evening I saw that split second of confusion in his pale blue eyes when he saw me standing there. It would fade just as quickly when he said, 'Why, hello, Ethie.' He would place his hard-hat on my head and hand me his humpback lunch pail, which reeked of metal and sardine sandwiches. I would walk home swinging it in one hand, while clinging to his with the other, pretending he was happy to see me.

I understood early the cause of my father's detachment from the world. Or, at least, I thought I did.

'The war.' It hung in the air of our home like a phantom. It lurked behind my father's vacant eyes, and at the bottom of the whiskey bottles above the fridge. Sometimes it cried out from his nightmares at dead of night, waking the household with its thrashing insistence. Mom kept a broom beside their bed for those episodes. Once, not long after he had returned from the war, she made the mistake of reaching for him as he struggled against the horrors that haunted him in his sleep. A flailing arm had caught her squarely between the eyes, breaking her nose, and my father's heart, she said. So, for the last seventeen years whenever he started fighting his nightmares beside her, she had jumped out of bed to grab the broom and poke him with the handle. Only when she was certain he was fully awake would she climb back into bed. I would lie upstairs in my room listening to her crooning to him in her off-key voice until I fell back to sleep. The following day my father's eyes would be empty, drained, waiting for the next rainfall to revitalize them.

'It's the war,' Mom confided, in hushed conversations to visitors, in an effort to explain his sudden withdrawals. I heard both her and Frankie use those words in reference to my father's absences so many times when I was very young that I believed 'Thewar' was a person. But I soon learned it was nothing more than memories. Memories that my father shared with no one.

Even though our home in Fraserview, like all of the look-alike veterans' homes in that South Vancouver neighbourhood, was commonly referred to as a 'wartime house', the war was seldom mentioned there. Never when my father was at home. It lay in wait, a dark spectre, in the corners of our lives, ready to emerge without warning and grasp my father in its silent grip, until only his long walks through a weeping city could send it away. By the time I entered primary school, I found myself praying for rain whenever I noticed the light fading from my father's blue eyes.

It was never long before my prayers were answered.

'No one would complain about the weather in Vancouver if they'd ever lived in Tahsis,' my mother often said. 'It was like living in a car wash.'

Before I was born, after my father returned from the war, our family had lived on the north-west coast of Vancouver Island. Mom said she suspected Dad had searched for a job in the location with the highest rainfall, and Tahsis was it. I'd seen pictures and heard Mom's stories of the remote logging town, but I found it hard to imagine living in a place where the only way in or out was by boat or seaplane.

I once heard Aunt Mildred, Mom's sister, suggest that the emergency flight from Tahsis to Victoria during a thunder storm on the day my brother was born was the reason for Kipper 'being the way he is'. I remember being startled by her words. I glanced up from the living-room couch. Beside me Kipper sat listening to me read from the book on my lap, while he fidgeted with the brim of his hat. When I stopped he tugged it down over his eyes and sighed heavily.

In the kitchen, Aunt Mildred sat at the table, her back to me, still wearing her raincoat. She must have found our house too cold, or was afraid of getting cat or dog hair on her expensive clothes. At any rate she always left her coat on, as if she was going to leave at any moment, whenever she visited, which was mostly when Dad was at work.

Across the table Mom raised her eyebrows. She stared at her sister over the rim of her teacup. 'I've told you before, Down's syndrome is not an accident of birth,' she said, with a sigh. She put her cup down and propped her elbows on the table before she went on. 'Kipper's destiny was decided the moment he was conceived. Heaven did not have a last-minute change of heart.'

'Unfortunately,' my aunt muttered.

'Mildred!' My mother's voice hardened with warning.

My aunt was silent for a moment. But she couldn't resist getting in another word. She never could. She clicked her cup noisily into her saucer, sniffed and said, 'All I'm saying, Lucy, is that that boy belongs in an institution. The longer you leave it, the harder it will be. It would be better for everyone. Besides, he would be happier with his own kind.'

'We are his kind,' Mom said tightly. Then she glanced past my aunt and caught my eye. She smiled. 'And he's happy with us, thank you very much.'

That was true. Most of the time.

Kipper's real name was Christopher Adam. 'After St Christopher,' Mom said. Although she wasn't Catholic, she thought it appropriate to name her son after the patron saint of travel, 'given someone was watching over me on that stormy trip into Victoria Harbour'.

She told me I was responsible for his nickname. 'As soon as you could walk you used to toddle behind him everywhere calling his name. "Kipper" was how it came out.' The name stuck. Except for Aunt Mildred, everyone called him that.

In return he had given me my nickname. Unable to wrap his tongue around the *l* in Ethel, I became Ethie. A fair exchange, and a favour for which I will be eternally grateful.

Who but Lucy Coulter would name a baby girl Ethel? When I was old enough to complain about it she explained that she had wanted to call me Lily, but Dad would not allow it. 'It was the only time I can remember your father digging in his heels over anything.'

Just before I was born Aunt Mildred gave our family her old black-and-white television set. It was Mom's first TV. The first show she watched on it also happened to be the first episode of *I Love Lucy*. No one but my mother would take all those firsts as a sign that, if she had a girl – and she couldn't name her Lily – she would name her after Lucy Riccardo's sidekick, Ethel. Every time the television show came on Mom would chirp, 'Here we are, Lucy and Ethel,' as if I needed to be reminded where my name had come from. And every time I would bury my face in one of the sofa cushions and moan. If Kipper was there, he would pull his hat over his eyes and moan with me.

My brother took on the emotions of those he loved. Especially mine. When I laughed, he laughed, loud, barking imitations of joy. If I cried, he would howl too, with gulping sobs and red-splotched eyes that leaked huge tears of grief. His mirroring of my emotions was so immediate, and so grand in scale, I often only realized how I was feeling after I'd seen him react. In time I learned to curb my outbursts, knowing they could trigger one of Kipper's asthma attacks.

With Dad he was completely different. He was quiet and at peace around him, regardless of Dad's state of mind. Mom believed that of us all Kipper had the deepest understanding of our father. Often, when he sank into one of his about-to-disappear moods, my brother would squeeze his short wide body next to Dad's thin frame in the overstuffed chair in the living room. With his arm around Dad, Kipper would rhythmically pat his bony shoulder while they sat in silence in front of the television set as if they were one person.

Last week the rains had come hard. During the first days of August Mom clipped out articles from the *Daily Province* reporting the record number of automobile accidents to match the record rainfall. All along our street, children's faces moped behind rain-streaked windows while gutters filled and storm sewers ran over. Confined to play inside, they felt cheated out of their dwindling summer holidays. Their mothers felt the same. They sat in our kitchen drinking coffee and swapping stories about how their husbands always sensed the change of weather before it arrived. They felt it in the throbbing pain around metal lodged deep in muscles. They felt it in ragged and uneven war wounds long healed over. And they felt it in bones aching with memories of the windswept beachheads and frozen battlefields of Europe. Mom added nothing to the conversations. Unlike many of the fathers on our street, Dad had returned from the Second World War visibly unscathed. No wounded-in-action medals were stored with a mothballed uniform in our basement. No embedded German shrapnel foretold the coming weather. Unlike his neighbours, he welcomed the rain.

At the height of the summer storm, on Thursday afternoon, Dad had taken his leather bomber jacket from the hall closet. It was at least two sizes too large for him, the faded brown leather cracked and brittle from years of rain. Still, the ancient flight jacket was the one our father always wore on his walkabouts. He had pulled it over his shoulders, lifted the sheepskin collar, and slipped out of the front door. While the rest of us breathed an inner sigh of relief, Kipper had grabbed his yellow rain-slicker and followed him. Frankie jumped up to stop him, but Mom waved him back. When the rain let up later that day Dad and Kipper returned, cold and wet, but both declaring their hunger.

As they sat down at the dinner table Kipper removed his soggy hat. Tufts of fine hair, more orange than red, stuck up every which way on the top of his head. My father smiled wistfully at him and called him 'my people-sorter'.

'Yeah, people-sorter,' Kipper parroted.

I think we all stared at Dad with the same questioning look.

'People-sorter?' Mom prompted.

'Yes,' Dad replied, in his slow, quiet voice. 'He sorts people into two groups. Those who are comfortable with him and those who aren't.' His shoulders lifted ever so slightly. 'I figure that tells you pretty much all you need to know about a person.'

I glanced at Kipper. An errant pea fell from his spoon and joined the droplets of stew on the table around his plate. Unconcerned, he shoved the overloaded spoon into his mouth. With a dribble of gravy hanging from his thick bottom lip, he chewed open-mouthed, then swallowed and grinned at my father.

Frankie glanced down at his wristwatch, wiped his mouth and jumped up. 'Gotta go,' he said, ruffing up Kipper's damp hair. 'Maybe I could get you to sort out my girlfriends,' he teased, then rushed out to yet another date.

'Okay, Frankie,' Kipper called after him, while Mom rolled her eyes.

As the rest of us finished eating, I thought about my father's words. There was no denying that people reacted to Kipper when they first met him. I had seen it at one time or another with the kids in our neighbourhood. There were those, my friends, who accepted him, and those who didn't, who either teased or ignored him. One way or another there was always a reaction. What startled me was that my father was aware enough to notice it.

Years later, when Frankie and I spoke for the first time about that August night in 1962, we found we had different memories. He didn't remember Kipper and me on the staircase or ordering us back to bed. He only remembered arriving in the living room to find our father at the open front door, the rain blowing into the hall. He had switched on the light. 'Dad?'

Dad turned slowly and blinked as if he was just waking.

'What's going on?' Frankie asked, ushering the two policemen inside and closing the door.

'It's your mother.' Dad's voice was low, oddly flat. 'There's been an accident.'

'Is she okay?' Frankie demanded, his question directed not at our father but at the two officers.

The shorter one, whose smooth-skinned face matched his too-young voice, glanced at his partner, who nodded, encouraging him to continue. 'No,' he said quietly. He removed his dripping hat, looked down at it, then back up. 'I'm sorry, your mother—'

'She's gone, Frankie,' Dad whispered.

'Gone?'

Kipper, who had followed me downstairs, grabbed my hand. A tiny whistle rose from his throat as he sucked air into his asthmatic lungs. Dad's eyes flickered to where we stood behind Frankie, but registered no awareness of our presence. He ran his hand through his uncombed hair and said the unbelievable: 'Your mother's dead.'

There was a ringing silence while the blunt words sank in. Then the screaming started. A chorus of howling, animal pain relayed between Kipper's open mouth and mine. I could see Kipper gasping for air with each echoing cry, his eyes, wide with horror, searching mine, and his fists pounding against his hat in an attempt to mimic my hysteria. But I couldn't stop.

It was Frankie, not my father, who came over and knelt down to put his hands on my shoulders. 'Ethie, stop,' he said, quiet but firm. 'This isn't going to help anything.'

I tried hard to gulp back my tears while he held my shaking body. Struggling to swallow my sobs I lifted my undershirt and wiped my face.

Frankie turned to Kipper. He reached up and pulled his hands away from his head and placed them by his sides. 'Look at me,' he said, holding Kipper's face between his hands. 'It's time to be a big boy now.'

His chest heaving, Kipper nodded and squeezed his hands over his mouth, the tears and mucus running down between his fingers.

'Deep breaths.' Frankie inhaled, long and slow, and waited until Kipper did the same.

Then he stood up and, with an arm around our shoulders, pulled us against him and faced the police officers. 'What happened?' he asked.

That's where Frankie's and my memories diverge completely. I remember nothing of the explanation he swears they offered while Dad stood there looking dazed. Perhaps I was in shock too, lost in my mind's vision of my mother's green Hudson crumpled up on some rain-slicked street, or perhaps because the explanation made no sense. I only remember Frankie's next words reaching me as if they were coming from a hollow tunnel. 'No, wait,' he said. 'That can't be right. There must be a mistake.' I came awake to the hope in his voice.

The older police officer looked down at something in his gloved hand. 'I'm sorry,' he said. He turned the card around and held it up.

Frankie's shoulders slumped a second before I, too, recognized our mother's name leaping out from the driver's licence.

Sitting in the back of the patrol car Howard tried to concentrate while the baby-faced officer in the front passenger seat spoke. Around midnight, he explained, the owner of a houseboat in Coal Harbour had noticed lights in a sailboat moored nearby. He'd called the marina to report what he believed was a break-in.

Howard still couldn't make sense of it. What did a sailboat have to do with Lucy? He had never been on one in his life and was certain she had not either. While the uncomfortable officer related how the police had boarded the vessel and discovered the bodies, Howard allowed himself to believe that it was all a huge mistake. But the moment he spotted the green Hudson in the marina parking lot he felt the sour bile of false hope rise in his throat.

Focusing on putting one foot in front of the other, he followed the officers down the ramp and through the maze of floating walkways. The rain had let up. Overhead, seagulls dipped on the wind, begging insistently for alms. The morning seemed too bright, the light too harsh as the rising sun shone through the breaking clouds. The first rays bounced off the water and reflected from the polished wood of a boat moored at the end of the dock. A small crowd of people milled about in front of its hull. Hushed conversations ceased as Howard and the officers approached.

A man in a business suit – looking out of place among the casually dressed bystanders – strode back and forth in front of a uniformed officer who was jotting down notes. 'Bloody hell! Bloody hell!' the man muttered as he paced. Then his eyes connected with Howard's and he stopped short. 'What-the-Christ – more damn people to come and gawk?' he barked.

The officer glanced up from his notebook. 'The husband of the other victim,' he explained.

'Bloody hell,' the man repeated, subdued now.

The young officer with Howard leaned closer. 'That's Jeremy Telford,' he whispered. 'He owns the boat.'

The name was vaguely familiar.

Ahead the older officer stopped. He turned to Howard. 'Are you ready?' he asked.

Howard nodded. Following his lead he reached up, grabbed a stanchion and pulled himself onto the deck. Two more policemen flanked either side of the open hatchway in the cockpit. They avoided Howard's eyes as he climbed down the wooden ship's ladder to the cabin.

Below, except for the sound of the waves lapping on the hull, and the boat creaking against the dock, it was eerily silent. The vents and portholes were cranked open. Too late. Howard was suddenly dizzy, not from the motion of the boat, or from the perceived trace of gas in the stale sea air, but at the sight of two empty wineglasses on the galley table. And the navy blue jacket tossed in the corner of the booth. Lucy's raincoat.

Outside, the boat owner's voice cried in anguish, 'God, we were getting ready to host a major art show next week. We were going to celebrate tonight.'

Up on deck one of the officers muttered under his breath, 'Looks like she had a different idea of celebration.'

The officer with Howard frowned, then gently urged him forward. 'In there,' he said.

The door to the front berth was open. A shaft of light from the overhead hatch illuminated the white sheet draped across the cabin bed. Howard had thought he was ready but as the edge of the sheet was lifted nothing had prepared him for the slamming blow that hit him squarely in the chest at the sight of Lucy's body. Or for the way she lay curled up next to her friend, Marlene Telford. Now he realized why the name of the distraught businessman out on the dock was familiar. He had never met him, but the man must be Marlene's husband.

He shook his head, his numb mind straining to make sense of it. At his feet another empty wine bottle rolled on the cabin floor. The red stain on the teakwood testified to its spilled contents. The world was askew. Lucy here? Drinking? Lucy didn't drink. Even what she was wearing made no sense, the old pants and baggy shirt she usually wore to clean the house. What could have caused her to go anywhere dressed like that? Lucy would never be caught in public without changing and putting on her makeup.

Still, even without it, even in death, she was beautiful. Her auburn curls lay spread out on the pillow beside the wild frizz of Marlene's grey-streaked mane. The freckles on Lucy's milk-white skin took on a pink tone against the black linen of her friend's blouse.

He reached over to brush her cheek and noticed the damp hankie balled up in the centre of her relaxed palm. Struggling to stop his knees buckling, he nodded and turned away while the officer pulled the sheet back over her face.

He placed the package on the car seat. This was what it came to, his wife's possessions in a brown-paper sack. He unfolded the top of the bag. The sweet musk of Lucy's scent wafted into the interior of the car. He closed his eyes and inhaled. Saliva trickled into the back of his throat. He needed a drink. He had been fighting it ever since he'd woken in the early hours of the morning to find himself alone in their bed.

His chest tightened at the image of Lucy lying curled in the foetal position on the boat, her friend's arm around her, as if comforting her. He opened his eyes and tried to recall how she had looked the last time he saw her. Yesterday morning. Had she been upset about something? He vaguely remembered her cooking breakfast in her housecoat while she teased him and Frankie that they could buy her something nice with all the extra money from their overtime shifts. Had that been yesterday or another morning?

Lucy had once accused him of never looking back when he left. 'It makes me feel like you forget me the moment you walk away,' she said. 'There's no worry that you'll ever turn into a pillar of salt,' she added wryly.

If only he had looked back yesterday morning.

He refolded the paper bag, then gripped the steering-wheel and stared out over Burrard Inlet. The irony struck him like a blow. His mind whirled with memories of the first time he had laid eyes on these waters, the limited glimpse through the mist before he had shipped out to an unexpected war. He had looked back at her then. Always had, until his return to the same pier four years later, an old man of twenty-four, weighed down with a burden of guilt too heavy to share. Not even with Lucy. Some day, he had promised himself over and over, some day he would tell her, confess everything. But in seventeen years he had never found the courage.

He slumped over the steering-wheel, burying his face in his arms. Moments later someone knocked on the window. Howard lifted his head to meet the concerned eyes of the young police officer. He gathered himself together, wiped his face with his sleeve and wound down the window.

'Are you all right, sir?' the officer asked.

Howard swallowed. 'Yeah,' he managed.

But he wasn't all right. He hadn't been all right for a long, long time.

5

27 October 1941: Canadian Pacific Trainyards, Burrard Inlet

The screech of steel on steel jarred Howard awake. Rubbing the back of his neck, he leaned over to peer out of the window. A heavy grey mist obscured his first view of Vancouver as the train rumbled to a jerking stop. Around him, soldiers in various stages of sleep stirred.

'We're here, men,' Brigadier Lawson called from the back of the car. The officer, a veteran of the Great War, stepped over the outstretched legs and sleeping bodies curled up in the aisle. Every inch the career soldier, from his perfectly groomed moustache to his spit-polished boots, he made his way through the compartment acknowledging his men before he moved on to the next car.

The word on the train was that the troop commander was less than happy about this posting. Before he was promoted to brigadier, Lawson had been assigned the task of assessing all Canadian units for 'combat readiness'. Apparently he had rated both the Royal Rifles and the Winnipeg Grenadiers, the battalions who now filled the troop cars, as class C: not ready for combat. If the rumours were true, Howard wondered what their commander would make of the four hundred or so reinforcements – of which Howard was one – recently added to bolster the two battalions. Many had never fired a gun.

He nudged his seatmate, who woke with a start and jumped

up all in one motion. 'Destiny awaits, my friend,' Howard said, grabbing his kitbag and helmet and joining him in the aisle. He wouldn't be sorry to leave the stale smoke-filled air of the crowded car. As he followed Private Gordy Veronick, Howard smiled: even pushing through the jostling bodies his childhood pal managed to swagger. Lucy had once described him as 'all muscle and panache', an affectionate label, which Howard thought was particularly apt. A good four inches shorter than himself but built like a bulldog, dark-haired and olive-complexioned, Gordy was his best friend, had been since they were six years old.

Growing up with three older brothers, the youngest of whom was four years older than he was, Howard had sometimes felt like an only child, with five parents instead of two. So when his mother told him that a six-year-old boy who had lost his parents in the flu epidemic was moving in with his grandmother on the farm next to theirs, he was excited about the prospect of having someone his age to play with. The first time the boy showed up in their yard Howard had tried to make friends with him.

The moment his mother and Gordy's grandmother disappeared into the farmhouse Gordy's eyes hardened. 'Howie? That's a sissy name,' he scoffed, and strutted away.

Howard had kept his distance for the rest of the summer. But in the one-room schoolhouse he was unable to ignore him. At the end of the first day Gordy sought him out in the schoolyard. Perhaps he picked on him because Howard was the tallest in the class, perhaps because he was their neighbour, or because he had three older brothers and Gordy had no one. Whatever the reason, he circled Howard like a bantam rooster, then stopped and held up his fists. 'On your mister,' he ordered.

'On your mister?' Howard repeated.

'Come on, chicken, put up your dukes.' Planting his feet wide apart, Gordy shadow-punched the air. His boxer's stance looked so comical to Howard that he burst out laughing. Before he knew it he was on the ground, a whirlwind of arms and legs on top of him trying to pin him down.

As he and Gordy wrestled in the dust a crowd gathered around, egging them on. Just when Howard gained the top position, someone yelled, 'Hey, Howie's clobbering the orphan.' The chant spread through the onlookers. *Orphan. Orphan.*

Gordy stiffened, then squeezed his eyes shut. But not before Howard saw them fill with tears. He let go and rolled off him. 'He's got dirt in his eyes,' he announced, getting up. 'He can't fight.'

He leaned, down, grabbed Gordy's hand and pulled him to his feet. As he led him away, he said, 'Wanna come to Miller's pond with me and catch pollywogs?'

Gordy swiped at his eyes with his shirtsleeve. 'Yeah,' he said. A few steps later, he added, 'I coulda cleaned your clock, you know.'

'Yeah, I know.'

Ever since, Gordy had been Howard's closest friend. They did everything together, which included enlisting with the Winnipeg Grenadiers.

Now, climbing down from the train, Gordy halted abruptly on the bottom step. 'Aah, just smell that salt water, fellas,' he called.

It was Howard's first scent of the ocean. He wasn't sure if he loved or hated it, but there was no denying the thick odour.

'Smells like sex,' someone said, echoing his thought.

'Yeah, like a woman ready for loving,' another answered.

'Or just fresh from it,' Gordy retorted, and laughter rippled through the disembarking troops.

Howard chuckled. A light rain misted his face as he joined the men on the ground. He pulled down his wedge cap and watched officers down the length of the train impatiently waving off the remaining soldiers.

'Step lively!' The command was relayed down the line to the stream of uniformed men.

'Fall in!' The troops scrambled to obey.

'Right turn! Forward! March!'

'Well, there's one thing we know how to do,' Gordy muttered. This time no one laughed.

Howard fell into step with the rows of men moving towards the pier. The crunch of thousands of boots on gravel carried across the rows of tracks in the stationyard.

Approaching the end of the train someone from the ranks ahead shouted, 'Eyes right!' and Howard turned his head with the rest of the troops.

She stood on the bottom step of the last car. The midnight blue cloth coat did not disguise her shapely figure. Shoulder-length hair – a mass of untamed curls – framed a freckled face. Even in the grey light Howard could see her green eyes scanning the troops as they filed by. *Lucy!* What in God's name was she doing here? Shocked, he lost concentration and bumped into the Grenadier in front of him.

'Easy, chum,' the startled soldier muttered. 'Ain't you ever seen a lady before?'

Howard regained his step, his mind racing to make sense of his Lucy here in Vancouver. The last time he had seen her was at the embarkation point in Winnipeg two days ago with his three older brothers. Like every other soldier saying their good-byes to family and loved ones in the crowded station, he had hung on to her until the last minute. With Gordy tugging him backwards towards the troop car, she had called after them, 'Now, you two look after each other.'

'Don't you worry. I'll take care of him, Luce,' Gordy shouted, over his shoulder. 'I'd rather face Hitler himself than have to answer to you if anything happened to our boy here.'

The moment Howard was on the train it had started to move. He pushed his way to a window but couldn't find her face in the waving crowd. Now he wondered how she had boarded the train. And why. As his column marched past Lucy he caught her eye. She jumped down and, with two battered suitcases banging against her legs, ran to catch up to his group.

'Jesus, Lucy. What're you doing?' he said, out of the side of his mouth, when she reached him. Ahead, soldiers rubbernecked to catch a glimpse of the beautiful girl trying to keep step with them.

'Now, don't be mad, Howie,' she puffed. 'I knew if I told you I was coming you'd try to stop me.'

'How did—' He turned his head and raised his eyebrows at the grinning face to his left.

Gordy shrugged. 'Don't look at me,' he said, leaning forward. 'Hello, Luce. Fancy seeing you here.'

'Hi, Gordy,' she said with a smile, then looked up at Howard. 'No, I didn't tell him. I knew he couldn't keep a secret from you. Your brothers helped me. They boosted me onto the train.'

'They were in on it? Didn't anyone think to tell me?'

'Would you have listened if I'd said I wanted to come?'

'Hell, no!' Howard glanced at her, then forced his eyes front. He struggled to control a grin at the determination on Lucy's face while she marched along with her head held high and her chin out. He couldn't help feeling a twinge of pride in her tenacity.

'I don't know where you're heading off to, but I'm going to be as close to you as I can while I wait for you to come home. I'll stay here in Vancouver with Mildred.'

'Mildred!'

Lucy's older sister had always treated her more like a daughter than a younger sister – a daughter whom she thought needed her constant supervision. She had never bothered to disguise her disapproval of Howard from the day she had met him.

'It'll be all right,' Lucy said, her voice softening.

So Mildred knew as well. Everyone except Howard. Lucy must have acted fast. But, then, life was fast these days.

A few months ago Howard and Gordy had been delivering blocks of ice to the kitchens of Winnipeg housewives. Canada had been at war for almost two years. All around them young men – either through patriotic duty, or the promise of a steady pay cheque – were rushing to enlist. All three of his brothers were stationed at the Air Force Training Center, forty miles north of Winnipeg. As the youngest son he had been designated to stay at home with their widowed mother. Like his brothers, he had grown up knowing that both his parents had served in the Great War, she as an army nurse and he in the infantry. As the new war in Europe escalated, Howard had felt the pull to follow in his father's footsteps. Recruitment posters taunted him from every store window. Yet, although his ailing mother had urged him to do so, he would not leave her. Then two months ago she had passed away. Three weeks after the funeral, when he had settled her affairs, a grieving Howard had enlisted. Unlike his brothers, he preferred to keep his feet on the ground. Like his father, he chose the army. Gordy signed up the same day.

While they were at the training centre in Portage La Prairie, a commanding officer, Lieutenant Colonel Sutcliffe, of the Winnipeg Grenadiers, had requested volunteers to reinforce the battalion. The tall, thin-faced officer, whose dark eyebrows matched his thick moustache, made his way down the rows of recruits, who, to a man, had stepped forward. His piercing eyes inspected each volunteer, the rejected falling back with disappointment etched on their faces. When he reached Howard, his bushy eyebrows arched as the staff sergeant, reading from a clipboard, informed him that Private Coulter had yet to complete basic training and had had no instruction in weapons.

'Never fired a gun, soldier?' Sutcliffe asked Howard.

'No, sir . . . I mean, yes, sir. I've shot my share of prairie dogs on my family's farm.'

'You still live with your folks?'

'No, sir, my parents lost the farm in the drought.' Howard didn't bother to mention that less than two years after they had lost the farm his father had suffered a heart-attack and died.

The officer narrowed his eyes. 'How old are you, soldier?'

'Twenty, sir.'

'So the last time you fired a gun was when?'

'Seven years ago, sir.'

'When you were thirteen? At gophers?' Sutcliffe shook his head. 'Did you ever miss?'

'Not without meaning to, sir.'

A hint of a grin lifted the officer's moustache. He turned to the sergeant. 'This soldier is accepted,' he said, and moved on.

Two weeks later Howard and Gordy had boarded the train in Winnipeg with the rest of the Grenadiers, their final destination unknown.

Now as they neared the pier Howard sensed Lucy struggling beside him. Every muscle in his body twitched to reach out and help her. He forced himself to keep his eyes ahead.

The dark waters of Burrard Inlet came into view. An unexpected surge of apprehension rose in his chest. He had never been on a boat of any kind, much less a ship the size of the grey hulk looming over the dock. As the first soldiers filed up the gangways of S.S. *Awatea*, Howard's company came to a halt in front of the warehouse sheds stretching along the wharf.

With a sigh of relief, Lucy set down her suitcases on the dock. 'I'll wait here until you sail,' she said, rubbing her hands.

'Lucy, listen to me,' Howard said. 'I want you to find a cab and go to your sister's now. We don't know when we'll ship out.'

'Private Coulter! Fall out!'

Howard stepped forward, causing Lucy to move aside. Behind her Brigadier Lawson, his swagger stick tucked under his arm, glared at Howard. 'Is this your girl?' he demanded.

'Wife, sir.'

Lawson glanced from Howard to Lucy. An expression of sadness passed briefly over his face and was immediately re-placed with a scowl. He leaned forward until he was inches from Howard's face. 'Soldier,' he growled, 'you have until the second to last man is on the ship's gangplank to say a proper goodbye. And, by God, you'd better be the last man up that ramp.'

'Yes, sir!'

The brigadier dismissed him, then strode away.

Howard reached out and Lucy flew into his embrace. She threw her arms around his neck and his lips met hers. While his troop mates hooted and cat-called from above, Lucy's lips moved to Howard's cheeks, to his eyelids, until they were both covering each other's faces with hurried kisses. Finally, Howard buried his head in her hair. Even now he was overwhelmed at the scent, the feel, the essence of his wife. His wife of seven days.

He had known her all his life. Well, almost. They had met in grade school, after her father had bought Hamm's drugstore in town. In the small two-room school it would have been impossible to miss any new student, but Lucy's arrival caused a division in the fifth- and sixth-grade students. There were those who were intimidated by her easy confidence, flashing green eyes and wild red hair, and those attracted to it. Howard and Gordy were somewhere in the middle. For some reason she chose to attach herself to them. It wasn't long before they had accepted her and for the next few years the twosome became a threesome. Then puberty hit. They all moved on to high school where other girls took notice of the boys. Like Gordy, who was beginning to strut around like the cock-of-the-walk, Howard found he didn't much mind the attention, and found himself playing to it.

One day when they were both sixteen Lucy caught him sitting on another girl's desk at lunchtime. On the way home from school that afternoon she accused him of letting her comparison of his watery blue eyes to those of the current heart-throb, Henry Fonda, go to his head. 'You've turned into a swell-headed flirt,' she pouted.

'What?' Howard teased. 'Are you jealous?'

Lucy hugged her books to her chest and stuck out her chin. 'And what if I am?'

Howard grinned. 'Here,' he said. 'Let me take those.' She passed them to him, and he carried them to her door, the universal sign that she was his girl.

Soon he noticed a change in Gordy. Ever since Howard's family had left the farm and moved into town, Gordy had stayed with him on weekends and even on many school nights. But no longer. One Friday night Howard cornered him before he could get on the school bus. 'What's going on?' he asked.

'I'm busy.'

'Yeah? Doing what?'

Gordy kicked at the ground.

'Look,' Howard said, 'if this is about Lucy, nothing's changed. We're still—'

'She's your girl now. You don't need me hanging around.'

Howard studied Gordy's face. 'Hey, look, no girl's going to come between us.'

Gordy stared back, his eyes challenging. 'Yeah?'

'Yeah. Just say the word.'

'Nah.' Gordy grinned and punched his shoulder. 'She chose. That just leaves all the other girls for me.'

Lucy's family was not quite so quick to accept their changed relationship, in particular her sister, Mildred, whom Howard heard refer to him as that 'ragamuffin' boy after she had seen him kiss Lucy good night on their front porch.

Lucy's indignant response carried out to him through the open window: 'That *ragamuffin* boy helps support his family by delivering the *Winnipeg Tribune* every day before school and the *Star Weekly* on weekends.'

Walking away, Howard had found himself smiling when she added, 'And some day I'm going to marry him.'

Like her family, he soon learned that Lucy was a force to be reckoned with. But when the time came to enlist and she tried to convince him to stay at home, to work for her father and learn the family business, as much as he loved her he stood firm. 'I couldn't visit my parents' graves if I stood by while Germany ran roughshod over Europe again,' he told her. 'I'd have too tough a time facing myself in the mirror.'

A month later, when he confessed that he had volunteered for a mission overseas and would be leaving soon for parts unknown, she had insisted, 'Then we'll get married before you go.'

Neither of her parents could deny her. Mildred had fallen in love with a physician at the hospital in Winnipeg where she worked as a nurse. They had married and moved to Vancouver. Howard wasn't sure if he was relieved or sorry her sister wasn't there to object when they said, 'I do,' in front of the munici-pal clerk at City Hall.

Now they clung to each other in the drizzling rain of an unknown city, the scent of mothballs wafting up from his damp woollen tunic. He released her, and took a step back. Placing his hands on her shoulders, he searched her face. Unrepentant green eyes flashed at him. 'Lucy . . . what can I say?' He wiped moisture from her cheeks. How could he be angry with her? 'Why didn't you tell me?'

'I wasn't going to risk you saying no.' She sniffed. 'I made up my mind to come, and I didn't want to waste what time we had left arguing. Let's not do it now.'

He pulled her back into his arms, sneaking a glance at the thinning group waiting to board. 'Go to your sister's,' he mur-mured into her hair.

'No.' She stiffened in his arms. 'I'm going to be here when you sail.'

Howard stepped back. 'That's crazy,' he said. 'I have no way of knowing when that will be.'

'Then I'll wait until you find out.'

'Damn, Lucy, don't be so stubborn. Our departure time is secret. I may not find out until the minute we sail.'

'Then I'll wait here until you do. You'll not be sailing off to heaven-only-knows-where without me here to wave goodbye. And that's that.'

'It may not be until tomorrow,' he said.

Lucy shrugged.

'Lucy . . .' he pleaded, then spotted the last group of soldiers making their way to the gangway. 'I've got to go.' He pulled her into his arms once again for a final kiss. Forcing himself to release her, he bent to retrieve his gear. 'Find a taxi,' he said, backing towards the ship.

He stepped onto the ramp behind the last soldier. Nearing the top he glanced back over his shoulder. On the dock below Lucy stood unmoving between her two suitcases, exactly where he had left her.

'*Go,*' he mouthed.

He stepped on board to the cheers and jeers of the soldiers milling around on the crowded deck.

Gordy leaned against the rail beside the gangway. 'Aren't you the lucky sod?' he said, when Howard joined him. 'What a send-off.'

Howard dropped his kitbag at his feet. 'Yeah. Except now she won't leave the dock until she finds out when we sail.'

'Then I'd say she's going to get a trifle wet.'

The rain was heavier now and Lucy's hair hung in matted curls around her face. She pulled a kerchief from her pocket and tied it under her chin. Before long it, too, was plastered against her head.

'I'm going to check out the ship,' Gordy said, 'see if I can find out when we're leaving.'

'Thanks.' Howard pulled off his cap and strapped on his steel helmet without taking his eyes off Lucy. Rain dripped from the rim while he thought about ordering her to leave. He opened his mouth, then clamped it shut. Fat lot of good that would do. Overhead, the cry of gulls competed with the wrench of cranes loading cargo into the holds of nearby ships. Above *Awatea* the cranes were motionless.

After what seemed like hours Gordy returned and joined him at the rail. 'This tub's meant to hold five hundred passengers, not two thousand,' he said. 'We're packed in like sardines in a can. You won't believe where we have to sleep. Hammocks are strung up everywhere – even in the galley.' He looked down at the pier. 'She still here? Sorry, I couldn't get official word, but the rumour is we're waiting for our heavy equipment to arrive. It's supposed to be loaded some time today. The best guess is we sail in the morning.'

'Good enough,' Howard said. He cupped his hands around his mouth and yelled down to Lucy, 'Tomorrow morning.'

'What time?' she called back.

Howard shrugged his shoulders. 'Go now. You can't stand there all night.' When he saw that she wasn't moving he pointed to the warehouses beyond the pier. 'At least get under shelter.'

'Private Coulter!'

Howard spun around and stood at attention. The stern-faced selection officer from Portage la Prairie, Lieutenant Colonel Sutcliffe, now commanding officer of the Grenadiers, was glowering at him. 'Soldier, do you know how many men I've lost from this company on the way here?' he asked.

Howard had heard that at least twenty soldiers had missed the train and some had actually disappeared during stops across Canada. But he answered, 'No, sir.'

'Too many, and I'm not about to lose another.'

'Yes, sir.'

'If I grant you a pass to leave the ship for a few hours, do I have your word you'll return?'

Howard couldn't believe his ears. 'Yes, sir!'

The commander handed him a slip of paper. 'You have until no later than twenty-one hundred hours to take care of your problem.'

Howard took the pass and snapped a salute.

Before Sutcliffe turned to leave he muttered, 'You might want to tell her to be here tomorrow at seven hundred hours.'

* * *

In the back seat of the taxi Howard wrapped a shivering and soaked Lucy in his arms. Outside, a canopy of black umbrellas bounced above the crowds jostling along Vancouver's downtown sidewalks.

The cab stopped at a red light on the corner of Granville and Georgia streets. Howard watched pedestrians flood all four crossings, while the traffic waited at the intersections. 'You'd never know there was a war on,' he said, as throngs of shoppers hurried in and out of the Hudson's Bay department store.

The drive to Lucy's sister's house on Vine Street took twenty minutes. After the taxicab pulled away, they stood at the gate and looked up at the imposing three-storey Victorian home.

Howard whistled. 'I'd say they might have room for you.'

'Now, you be nice,' Lucy scolded, as they went up the porch steps.

The last time Howard had seen Mildred he had been a skinny boy of seventeen who stood barely eye level with her. Hauling fifty-pound ice blocks had filled out his upper body, and at five foot eleven, he was now a good three inches taller than the woman who opened the door.

Howard supposed that, like her sister, she was beautiful. But unlike Lucy, who was soft and rounded, Mildred was sharp and angular. Her brown hair was rolled back in the latest style, emphasizing her high cheekbones and the frown lines etched between her brows. At twenty-eight, Howard thought, his new sister-in-law was already becoming matronly.

He was surprised when she did not recognize him – she glanced blankly from him to Lucy. At the sight of her sister, though, she let out a startled cry and pulled her into her arms. Then she ushered them both through the door. Howard was encouraged by what he believed had been a softening in Mildred's eyes at the sight of his uniform.

'You two look like a couple of drowned rats,' she said, helping Lucy out of her coat. Her gaze flickered to her sister's waist. 'You're not . . . ?'

'Mildred!' Lucy snapped. 'Of course not. And, for your information, Howard and I are married.'

'So I understand. You two are just full of surprises.'

'You never told her you were coming?' Howard whispered to Lucy, as they crossed the wide hall.

'How could I?' Lucy whispered back. 'I didn't even know if your train was headed east or west.'

In the living room Mildred waved them to the couch, then sat straight-backed on the matching chair before them. 'Now, what's this all about?' she asked.

For the next fifteen minutes Lucy spoke without interruption. She told her sister about the death of Howard's mother, his joining the army, their marriage, and now this secret mission. 'But the minute this war is over we have plans,' she said, sitting up straighter. 'When we get back to Winnipeg, Howie's going to study to become a pharmacist and we're going into business with Dad.'

While she spoke Howard sat next to her, feeling awkward and out of place in the high-ceilinged room with its formal furniture. His damp uniform itched, and he fidgeted with his army cap while he struggled to control the desire to scratch.

'I'm going to wait in Vancouver until Howard returns,' Lucy concluded. 'I'm hoping to stay with you and Sidney for a while – just until I get a job and a small place of my own.'

'Nonsense,' her sister interrupted. 'You'll stay right here with us for as long as you need to.' She gave Howard a tight smile. 'It's not as if we don't have plenty of room.'

Her last words carried a trace of sadness. After three years of marriage, she and her husband, a surgeon at the Vancouver

General Hospital, were still childless. According to Lucy, she was bitterly disappointed at not having conceived. Well, she would have her sister to mother again, Howard thought, surprised by his relief at her offer.

'There, that's settled then,' Mildred said, with a note of finality. She stood up. 'Now let me get you two some dinner before Howard has to go back to the ship. You must be starved.'

Lucy let herself be led out of the room, and Howard took the opportunity to scratch himself before he followed.

'Good luck, son.' The cab driver's gravelly voice reminded Howard of his father. Taking a taxi twice in one day was an unheard-of extravagance, but it had been worth it to spend a few more minutes with Lucy.

Mildred's husband had still been at the hospital when it was time for Howard to return to the ship. Since she did not drive, Mildred had called for a cab, promising that she and Sidney would bring Lucy to the pier in the morning.

Back at the docks, Howard watched the vehicle's tail lights disappear. The rain had stopped. Still, he pulled up his collar and thrust his hands into his pockets. A prairie boy, used to the bite of honest cold, he felt chilled by the dampness of the west-coast air. Like a thief, it crept through his clothing right to the marrow of his bones, robbing him of every ounce of warmth. He shivered and turned towards the warehouse sheds lining the pier. And even though he knew that almost two thousand men were aboard the ship on the other side of those sheds, he suddenly felt a deep loneliness.

Before he reached the pier he heard the commotion. A rumble of angry voices carried to him through the night. Howard quickened his pace. When he rounded the corner between the sheds he was startled to see a crowd of soldiers, most of whom he recognized as Grenadiers, gathered on the docks below *Awatea*. Above, at the ship's rail, two officers stood with machine-guns trained on the mob.

'Howard!' Gordy broke away from the group he was with and hurried over.

'What's going on?' Howard asked, when his friend reached his side.

'We've jumped ship.' His words ran together in the rush to explain. 'The living conditions on this tub are impossible. This boat used to be a luxury cruise ship in New Zealand before she was turned into a troopship. But the only ones who will see any luxury are the officers. The boys are packed cheek-by-jowl in a hell-hole, while the officers have cabins, a private lounge and dining room. And tonight while they all ate high-off-the-hog, we were served tripe and onions. We're protesting.'

Howard tried to ignore the pang of guilt he felt about the roast beef and Yorkshire pudding still warm in his stomach. 'Looks more like a riot,' he said, pointing up to the machine-guns.

'You think those are loaded?' Gordy scoffed. 'Hell, they couldn't afford ammunition for training, so what makes you think they'll waste it on our sorry asses? Anyway, we just want some concessions. We heard some of our flyboys headed to England walked off their ship in Halifax last week and they got looked after. We're negotiating.' He nodded to Colonel Sutcliffe, who was trying to make himself heard over the shouting. 'So far they've transferred a hundred and twenty Royal Rifles to *Prince Robert*, our escort ship,' he grunted. 'Fat lot of difference that'll make. Now we're being accused of mutiny and desertion. Shit, Howie, we're the peons in this man's army. Come on. If enough of us—' A fresh roar of disapproval drowned his words.

In the confusion beyond him two soldiers backed away from

the edge of the crowd. They ducked between the warehouse sheds and disappeared into the shadows. Watching them slip away, Howard felt the tug of temptation. For an instant he imagined himself leaving, taking Lucy and heading home. He turned to Gordy. 'I figure a fella gave up the right to pick his battles when he enlisted,' he said. 'At any rate, I sure didn't sign up for a skirmish over grub and sleeping arrangements. I don't think you did either.' He began to push through the crowd. A few soldiers joined him as he climbed the gangway. Halfway up he glanced back at Gordy, who shrugged, then followed.

On board they stood together at the railing, watching the negotiations below. After the threat of court-martial was withdrawn, and promises of improved conditions were delivered, the grumbling men trickled back on board. Once the gangplanks were secured Howard threw his arm around Gordy's shoulders. 'Come on,' he said. 'Show me the hell-hole.'

Gordy had not exaggerated. The cramped quarters already reeked of sweat and damp uniforms, reminding Howard of woollen socks worn too long. He also recognized the pungent stench of mothballs. Most of the Grenadiers' uniforms, like his, were from the last war. The inside of his tunic was stamped '1918'. Even his underwear was Great War issue. He would be glad when they exchanged these scratchy clothes for the new uniforms they had been promised on departure.

Below deck, hammocks were strung in every conceivable overhead space. They hung so close together that Howard was sure if one man moved they all would. Still, he didn't mind. Growing up the youngest of four boys in a two-bedroom farmhouse, he was used to tight sleeping quarters.

He sat down at a mess table beneath the hammock Gordy indicated and leaned down to unlace his boots. He would sleep tonight.

He felt, rather than heard, a rumble. *The engine?* He sat up and listened. He was certain the ship's engines were idling. Hurriedly he retied his laces and bolted from the mess hall. He pushed his way up a companionway and on deck he rushed forward to the rail. Out in the dark waters a tugboat waited, her lines attached to the ship. Howard hurried to the port side and peered over the shoulders of the other men crowded there. The wharf itself seemed to groan as *Awatea* inched sideways. With the deep blast of the horn Howard's fear was confirmed. They were leaving.

On the docks below, longshoremen untied thick ropes from their pilings. The gap of dark water widened between the ship and the pier. Then, with her engines idling, S.S. *Awatea* seemed to take a breath before she moved slowly forward.

Beyond her bow, Howard could see the white wake streaming behind the tugboat ploughing out into the inlet with *Awatea* in tow. In the dark waters ahead, HMCS *Prince Robert* was approaching the narrows. When the escort ship disappeared into the mist under the Lion's Gate Bridge, he walked to the rear and stood at the railing while the two vessels crept out into the harbour and dropped anchor. He didn't need to hear the speculation going on around him to figure out why the plans had changed: after the near mutiny on the pier, anyone else thinking of leaving the ship tonight would have to swim.

In the distance, city lights twinkled through the heavy mist, and Howard shuddered. He felt hollow. As he said a silent goodbye to Lucy, he tried to ignore the ominous sense of foreboding that filled the empty space inside him.

6

If I closed my eyes real tight. If I didn't move a muscle. If I didn't cry. If I was good – if I was good – then the words my father had spoken would not be true. Curled up in a tight ball under my blanket, my clenched fists wrapped around my knees, I tried not to shiver. I squeezed my eyes tighter and searched for my mother's face in the flashing lights behind my eyelids. I tried picturing her as she had been yesterday. I couldn't remember. The days of last week were all mixed up in my head.

In the summer, when there were no classes, the days all seemed the same. It was easier to keep track of time during the rest of the year. When I was in school, Mom worked two days a week. Every Thursday and Friday morning she took Kipper with her to her job at Marlene Telford's art shop on Granville Street.

Marlene? Now I remembered yesterday morning.

Kipper and I had slept late. After bolting my corn flakes I had called goodbye to Mom. I heard her saying something behind the bathroom door about going downtown to Marlene's. But I was in a hurry. I rushed Kipper out of the house, worried that I might miss the first song of Bible School at the new evangelical church on Fifty-first Avenue. Each day at exactly ten o'clock we sang 'I Will Make You Fishers of Men', and the teacher picked someone to wear the straw hat and carry the bamboo fishing pole. Then he took a Polaroid picture of the chosen fisherman, who got to keep it. Maybe it would be my turn at last.

Kipper and I had joined the two-week Bible School, which promised 'cookies and crafts' with my friend Ardith Price. Kipper loved the songs. He mostly liked 'Onward Christian Soldiers'. He marched on the spot, singing the words in his loud, monotone voice, a few beats after everyone else.

At the end of the first day, the teacher took me aside and said that perhaps it would be better if I left Kipper at home next time. I felt a guilty relief at his words, because lately – and I sure wouldn't ever tell my mother this – I had felt a gnawing resentment at having my brother tag along everywhere I went.

But instead of keeping him at home, Mom's eyes had narrowed when I told her what the teacher had said. 'We'll just see about that,' she exclaimed. 'They can keep him out of regular school, but you can bet your breeches they're not going to keep him out of Bible School, if I have anything to do with it.'

The next morning she came with us to the church. I didn't know what went on in the minister's office, but when Mom came out she told me to take Kipper and join the other kids in the church basement. The teacher never again suggested that Kipper shouldn't come. But he had never chosen him, or me, to be fishers-of-men either.

Now I wished I'd waited for my mother to come out of the bathroom yesterday. When we returned from Bible Class, Irene Manson's teenage daughter, Mary, was at the house. There was a note on the pad by the wall phone and a frozen tuna casserole thawing in the sink. Later, both Frankie and Dad had grinned as they read Mom's familiar slanted handwriting explaining that she was going downtown for the afternoon and then to Marlene's to play cards. 'I see she didn't say poker,' Frankie laughed, after Dad paid the sitter and she left. We all knew why. Mom wasn't about to let her secret vice be made known to the neighbourhood gossip – Mary's mother, Irene.

Only days ago Frankie had teased Mom that some day the police were going to break down Marlene's West End apartment door to raid the illegal gambling ring.

'We only play for pennies,' Mom had retorted, playing along with Frankie's teasing. 'No one loses more than a dollar a night.' Still, she swore us to secrecy over her weekly poker sessions. As far as anyone else – except our neighbour, Dora Fenwick – was concerned, it was bridge she played on Wednesday nights. She wanted neither her sister nor the ladies of the neighbourhood to know about her clandestine activity. The games were never over until long after my bedtime, so I hadn't worried that she wasn't home when I'd gone to bed last night. Or given much thought to the fact that it was Saturday, not Wednesday.

Now I threw back the covers. Even though Frankie had told me to stay in bed, I climbed out and crept downstairs again. I could hear him talking quietly on the telephone in the kitchen as I slipped into Mom and Dad's room and crawled into their bed. I pulled the sheets and blankets over my head and buried my face in Mom's pillow. I could smell her. Everything was all right now. She couldn't be dead.

Dead? Dead was the awful-smelling seagull Kipper and I had found on the beach last week and buried in the sand. Dead was my goldfish that Frankie had flushed down the toilet after I found it floating upside-down in its glass bowl. Dead was our old dog Pepper. 'Heaven wants him,' Mom had told us, when we buried our black cocker spaniel's limp body, wrapped in a faded baby blanket, in the backyard. 'He belongs in heaven now.'

But my mother didn't belong in heaven. And I was going to be so good from now on that heaven would just hold off.

Today at Bible School I would take Jesus Christ as my saviour, as the teacher had encouraged us to do at the end of class each day this week. I had resisted going up to the front, like my friend Ardith had a few days ago, to kneel down while the minister's hand forced Jesus through my head into my heart.

Afterwards Ardith told me that she could feel the heat of Jesus Christ in her heart. 'Now I can ask him for anything,' she said. 'And when I die I'll enter the Kingdom of Heaven.'

I didn't know about that, I just didn't want my mother to go there. Soon I'd be able to ask Jesus for favours, too.

I was running out of smell. I shifted the pillow to a new spot and breathed in my mother's sweet scent again.

Someone tugged at the blanket. I peeped out to see Kipper standing there. I pulled back the covers and he climbed in. He placed his hat on the night table, then snuggled down beside me.

I bit the inside of my lip. *I won't cry. I won't cry.* Any moment now Mom would come driving down the street, saying, 'Home again, home again, jiggety jig,' as she did every time she pulled up to the kerb in front of our house. I promised myself that next time I wouldn't groan as she repeated the nursery rhyme. It was impossible that I would never again hear her say those silly words. Wherever she had been all night, whatever had kept her from home, the police were mistaken about what they had told my father. They had to be wrong. Adults could be wrong.

Like Frankie had been wrong about the baby crabs. 'They will die,' he'd told me, when I came home from Birch Bay last Sunday with dozens of tiny black crabs scratching at the sides of my bucket. 'They need the ocean,' he insisted. 'They need salt water.' Now, a week later, the crabs were still alive in our old sandbox. Every day I poured table salt into a jar of water and took it out to the back yard to dump over them. I sprinkled goldfish food into the puddles of water in the little home I had made for them with shells, rocks and barnacles from the beach. It even smelled like the beach. But the crabs were getting kind of soft and limp. Maybe I should take them back to the ocean and set them free. Yes, that's what I'd do. Today was Sunday. If it didn't rain again I'd ask Dad if we could go to Birch Bay this afternoon. Mom loved the beach.

I woke to sunlight seeping through the crack in the curtain. A woman's voice came from the kitchen. Mom was home! I threw back the covers and leaped out of bed.

Everyone stopped talking when I rushed into the kitchen. I looked from Dad to Frankie, sitting hunched at opposite ends of the table, to Aunt Mildred and Uncle Sidney standing at the counter. Sweat glistened on my uncle's bald head. Even the short tufts of hair above his ears looked damp. He removed his glasses and concentrated on cleaning them while I searched their faces.

'Mom?' I choked.

My father raised his head. His mouth opened and closed. I turned from him to Frankie. Slumped over his coffee mug, his shoulders rounded, my brother's red-rimmed eyes seemed tired, old, as empty as our father's.

'Sweetheart,' my aunt said, and knelt down to reach for me.

'No.' I stepped back, pushed myself against my father and sobbed into his chest. He lifted an arm and placed it over my shoulders.

Behind me Aunt Mildred sighed and stood up. 'Go upstairs

and get dressed, dear,' she said. 'You're coming home with Uncle Sidney and I.'

My aunt often asked me to stay at her house, and most of the time I liked to go. Whenever I went I was sure to get new clothes, dolls or comic books. Treats I seldom got at home. Today none of that mattered. I shook my head, holding tighter to Dad.

'I think it's a good idea that you go for a while,' he said quietly.

'Is Kipper coming, too?' I asked, standing back and wiping an arm across my face.

Aunt Mildred reached into her handbag and pulled out a cotton hankie. 'I don't think my house is the place for your brother,' she said, passing it to me. 'I wouldn't know how to take care of him.'

With Kipper, our aunt was one of those people in the second group. She mostly ignored him when she visited, and he had never stayed overnight at her house.

'Then I'm not coming either.' I backed away, then ran from the room.

'Let her go,' I heard my father say wearily behind me.

Upstairs I pulled on pedal-pushers and a T-shirt, then my sneakers. I made my way downstairs to the basement, out of the door and up the concrete stairwell.

Outside in the backyard the air smelled of wet dirt and grass, and earthworms rising in the overgrown patches of soggy lawn. Two robins hopped away, not bothering to take wing as I passed. They resumed their search for breakfast when I stopped by the old sandbox where the crabs sat motionless in their makeshift home. I knelt and picked up a stick to poke at them. Tiny bubbles foamed below their raised eyes. Claws lifted and reached listlessly for the stick and their legs began to move. They were still alive.

I stood up and stepped onto the rain-soaked sand. I lifted my foot, then brought it down again and again, methodically grinding the crabs under my heel until every one was crushed and broken in the bottom of the sandbox.

7

The kitchen door opened and Frankie came outside. Squatting in the sandbox with my arms wrapped around my shins, I watched him walk down the porch steps. At the bottom he pulled a crumpled pack of Player's cigarettes from his shirt pocket. He tapped one out and brought it to his lips with shaking hands. He had to strike the match three times before it ignited. He leaned against the side of the house, took a single puff and then, holding the cigarette between his fingers, stared at the smoke curling up from the glowing end. When he brought it back to his mouth he glanced up and saw me. In no hurry, he walked over and sat down on the edge of the sandbox beside me. We both studied the mess at my feet, while his cigarette burned down.

'I didn't know you smoked,' I said.

'I don't.' He held up the pack. 'Dad's.' He took another puff, then bent over and ground out the unfinished butt in the sand, his slow, steady movements so much like our father's. Looking at his profile, the grim set of his jaw, the tiny lines at his eyes that hadn't been there yesterday, I saw for the first time why Mom always said he was a carbon copy of Dad.

A sandy-blond curl fell onto his forehead as he straightened. He pushed it back, then stood up and brushed the wet sand from his jeans. 'I guess we should go back inside,' he said, with a sigh. He held out his hand and I let him pull me to my feet.

We came up the side porch steps in time to hear Aunt Mildred, in the kitchen, demanding, 'Did you hear me, Howard? I asked what Lucy was doing on a sailboat.'

A sailboat? I stopped and turned to Frankie. And that was when I saw it: out on the street, parked behind my aunt's new shiny black Volvo, my mother's green Hudson.

'She was with Marlene Telford,' Dad answered. 'The boat belongs to Marlene's husband.'

'Marlene!' Aunt Mildred snorted. 'I still don't understand.'

I didn't either. I'd thought Mom had been in a car accident.

'Carbon monoxide . . .' Dad started, but his words stopped as Frankie reached past me and pushed the door open.

In the kitchen my aunt and uncle were standing at the counter, exactly where they had been when I left. Still hunched over his coffee cup at the table, Dad looked bewildered as we entered.

'Go ahead, Dad,' Frankie said encouraging him to continue. 'Ethie should hear this too.'

I heard Aunt Mildred's sharp intake of breath.

'The police believe it was carbon-monoxide poisoning,' Dad said, his hesitant words directed at the table. 'From a faulty gas heater. Somehow neither of them had thought to open the vents.'

'But why was she there in the first place?' Aunt Mildred asked.

My father winced at the harshness of her voice.

Yes, why? I waited for him to answer. He swallowed; his eyes went to the top of the fridge and back to the unlit cigarette between his nicotine-stained fingers.

'I wish I knew,' he said. 'It was a freak accident. I don't know what else to tell you.'

'Carbon monoxide is deadly,' Uncle Sid interjected, 'but painless. They would have just drifted off to sleep. Although I'm surprised they didn't notice each other getting drowsy.'

'They were drinking wine,' Dad said.

'Ah,' Uncle Sidney offered, as if that settled it.

My aunt's eyes widened. 'Lucy was drinking? I find that hard to believe.'

I did too. The only time I knew my mother to have a drink was the glass of wine she seldom finished with Christmas dinner.

The toilet flushed in the bathroom. The door opened, and a moment later Kipper appeared, still wearing his pyjamas – and his hat. Wordlessly he searched our faces. Then he walked over to stand beside Dad.

Aunt Mildred gathered her purse and gloves from the counter. 'We'll go over to Forest Lawn now and pick out the casket—' Her voice caught. She hesitated for a moment, then continued, 'We'll make the arrangements. You don't have to worry about the expense. Sidney and I will take care of it.'

'That's not necessary.' Dad sighed.

'We want to,' Uncle Sidney said gently.

While they droned on about funeral arrangements I tried to sort out the confusion of unanswered questions. Why had Mom and Marlene gone to a sailboat? Mom's note said they were going to play cards last night. Had she lied? I'd always believed Mom was like Kipper – that she didn't know how to lie. I thought about what Uncle Sidney had said. Hearing that my mother hadn't been hurt, that she had just gone to sleep, should have made me feel better. But it didn't.

I closed my eyes and tried to imagine her face. I couldn't. Panicked, I looked up at Frankie. 'I can't picture her face,' I cried. Tears blurred my eyes as I turned frantically from him to Dad. 'I want to go see her.'

I felt my aunt's hand on my shoulder. 'I don't think that's a good idea, honey,' she said. 'We can get out the photograph albums at my house and you can go through all the pictures of your mother.'

'No!' I jerked away and went to Dad. 'I can't remember her face. I want to see her before she goes to heaven.'

'I want to see Mom, too,' Kipper chimed in, his lower lip quivering.

Aunt Mildred ignored him. She glared at my father. 'Surely you're not considering this?'

'Maybe it's not a bad idea,' Frankie said.

'Nonsense. This child is traumatized enough.'

'Well, actually, dear,' Uncle Sidney said, 'there's no evidence to suggest that viewing—'

'No-o,' Aunt Mildred moaned.

Dad held up his hand up. 'Stop,' he said quietly, almost apologetically. Pulling Kipper closer, he looked from my brother to me. 'You can't see your mother today,' he said, 'but maybe tomorrow. Or at the funeral you can see her to say goodbye.'

'Howard!' Aunt Mildred cried. 'I can't believe you'd consider that. And surely you're not bringing them to the service.'

'Of course they'll be there,' he answered. 'She's their mother.'

'The boy? You'll take the boy? I'm sorry, Howard, but think about that. He'll just howl through the whole ceremony.'

'If you can't cry at a funeral,' Dad said, 'then I don't know where you can.'

Moments after Aunt Mildred's Volvo had pulled away from the kerb someone knocked on the front door. Dad answered, to find Mrs Manson standing on the porch. 'Is Lucy home?' she asked, not bothering to disguise that she was straining to see over his shoulder into the house. Dad turned away and let Frankie deal with her.

For the rest of the day friends and neighbours, most of whom

I could see my father didn't even recognize, trickled in and out of our house. They brought casseroles and pound cakes with nervous offerings of sympathy.

8

Mom once took a tally of the population of the twenty-three houses on our block. Except for the Fenwicks' next door, all the homes on our street were built by the government after the war to house the growing families of returning troops. Each family had to have at least two children to qualify for the sub-sidized housing. According to Mom's numbers, which didn't include Frankie, whom she said could hardly be counted as a child any more, seventy-six children lived on Barclay Street. Yet all that day it was strangely quiet. Even though the rain had stopped, none of the usual hockey or baseball games were played on the road. No one jumped rope or played hopscotch on the sidewalk. Even the kiddie park across the street was empty. Except for Kipper.

After all the neighbourhood women had gone home, leaving their husbands in the living room with Dad, I sat out on the front porch. I leaned against the railing and watched Kipper twirling on the swing, then letting go to spin in circles. Some time later the front door of the house next to the park opened and Mr Manson came out. He headed across the street in the evening twilight carrying a bottle wrapped in a brown-paper bag.

As he came up to me he nodded back at the park. 'That seems like a good way to get dizzy,' he said. I stood up and let him into the house to join the other men sitting in the shadows of what now felt like the unfamiliar territory of our living room.

In the kitchen Frankie was leaning into the open refrigerator with a perplexed expression on his face, trying to rearrange the array of food on the shelves. He glanced up as I came in and sat down at the end of the table. 'Have you eaten?' he asked.

The melded odours of our neighbours' cooking made my stomach lurch. Or perhaps it was because I had just noticed that the whiskey bottle was missing from the top of the fridge. 'I'm not hungry.'

Frankie's eyes followed mine. His jaw hardened. He shoved the last dish into the fridge, as if he was forcing the final piece into a jigsaw puzzle, then closed the door before it could fall out. 'You have to eat,' he said, but there was no conviction in his voice.

Before I could argue we both noticed Dora Fenwick walking across the lawn to our side porch. Her son Danny followed a few reluctant steps behind.

Mrs Fenwick was Mom's closest friend. She and Danny lived in the old farmhouse next door with her mother. Danny and I were the same age, had grown up together and, until last summer, had been best friends.

As they came up the steps, Frankie strode over to open the kitchen door. Mrs Fenwick, her eyes swollen, looked momentarily startled before she stepped inside. Danny hung back on the side porch, his head down. I could see his scalp beneath his flat-top crew cut as he studied his feet through his new Buddy Holly horn-rimmed glasses.

'Baked spaghetti,' Dora Fenwick said, with a forced smile. She placed yet another casserole dish on the counter, pulled my brother into her arms and hugged him, murmuring something into his ear.

Frankie muttered, 'Thanks,' coughed and stepped back. 'I'll get Dad.'

She nodded. Nervously tucking strands of short dark hair behind her ears, she turned to me. She must have sensed that if she took me in her arms I would break into little pieces. Keeping her distance, she pulled a tissue from the sleeve of her sweater and pressed it to her eyes, then turned to Danny. 'Are you coming in, honey?' she asked him.

Pushing his glasses back on his nose, he shook his head. 'I'll wait here,' he said. Then he surprised me by asking, 'Do you wanna come out?'

I got up from the table. Just then Dad walked into the room. He and Mrs Fenwick embraced awkwardly, then stepped apart. 'I'm so sorry, Howard,' she said, sitting down in the chair he offered. 'Is there anything I can do?'

'No. No,' Dad said. He brushed a hand through his hair. 'I think her sister will manage to herd us all in the right direction.'

She nodded with understanding. 'I can't believe this. I was at work all day yesterday and today.' While she blew her nose Dad sat down in the chair I had just vacated.

'My mother said that Lucy . . .' She hesitated for a second, then continued, 'She said Lucy came over looking for me yesterday morning. But then,' she added, with a choked laugh, 'the way Mother's memory is, these days, that could mean last week.'

A strange heat flooded my chest at hearing her talk about Mom yesterday. It already hurt to hear someone say her name. I slipped outside, leaving the kitchen door open, and sat on the porch steps. Without saying anything, Danny dropped down beside me. The only sound on the street was the creaking of Kipper's swing.

In the kitchen Dora blew her nose again. After a few moments of silence, Dad cleared his throat. 'Was there something bothering her, Dora?' he asked, in a voice so low I had to strain to hear. 'Did she seem upset lately?'

I sat up straighter. *Upset? Mom? Was that why she was in the bathroom yesterday morning? Why she went to see Marlene?*

Danny squirmed on the step beside me. 'Let's go over to the park,' he whispered.

I shook my head while inside his mother assured Dad that as far as she knew nothing unusual had been worrying Mom.

Then it struck me. Maybe it was *my* fault. Maybe she was upset because she realized I'd started to resent Kipper.

Someone knocked at the front door. 'I'll be going now,' Dora said, her chair scraping away from the table. 'Call me if I can do anything.'

Dad opened the kitchen door for her. As they came out on to the side porch Danny jumped up. His mother looked down at us, her eyes softening. 'Would you like to come and sleep over at our house tonight, Ethie?' she asked.

Startled, I glanced sideways at Danny. His face was expressionless. When we were younger, when Danny and I were friends, the Fenwicks' house was like a second home to Kipper and me. We had slept over on many weekends and summer nights.

'If that's okay with you, Howard?' Mrs Fenwick added.

Dad nodded. 'If she wants to.' I thought he seemed relieved.

'Kipper, too?' I asked.

Danny's mother smiled. 'Of course Kipper too.'

I went upstairs and gathered our pyjamas. I avoided the living room when I came down because I still didn't understand what Frankie had meant when I'd asked him earlier why those men just sat there with Dad saying hardly anything. 'They're all veterans,' he said, with a shrug. 'I guess there's a bond between them that's beyond words.'

9

Howard had never seen anything like it. Squeezed in at the ship's rail, he jostled shoulder to shoulder with the other soldiers vying for a better view. Directly below, on the lower decks, heads and flailing arms protruded from *Awatea*'s port side. The noise from the cheering troops all but drowned the ukulele music accompanying the bronze-skinned hula girls on the wharf. Coins and banknotes, along with the odd pack of cigarettes, rained down on the dancers. A boy in a red flowered shirt rushed about gathering the bounty and tossing it into a large wooden bowl on the pier.

An exotic floral perfume carried up on the sea air from the dancers' thick orchid *leis*. Polished coconut shells cupped full breasts and long, dark hair flowed with the same rhythm as the swaying grass skirts. The graceful movement of arms and hips was so fluid, so sensual, that it made Howard ache for Lucy.

Embarrassed at his arousal he leaned closer to the rail. Like the other soldiers on deck he wore only his new tropical uniform shorts and a short-sleeved undershirt. The troops had been ordered not to display any badges or insignia that identified them as Canadian. That made sense to him. The British Empire and Germany were at war, after all, and although the Canadian infantry had yet to enter into armed combat, troop deployments were top secret. Everyone was confined to the ship while they took on fuel.

'Ain't you gonna give the girls a little something?' Gordy nudged him, then threw down another silver fifty-cent piece.

'You're such a sucker for a pretty face,' Howard said, 'but I'm a married man now, remember? I've got to watch my pennies.'

'Come on, cheapskate. Fifty cents.'

Howard reached into his pocket, pulled out his loose change and tossed the coins down. 'There. Happy?'

'Don't worry,' Gordy teased. 'I won't be telling Lucy.'

'You'd better not.' Howard laughed. He was only half joking. Over time he had come to the conclusion that it was a bad idea to test Lucy's jealous streak. Throwing money to swivel-hipped beauties was not something he wanted to explain to her.

He pulled out the cigarette pack rolled up in his sleeve. Even though he didn't smoke he accepted the rations the army doled out. He'd grown up with the notion that you never turned down anything that was free: you didn't know when it might come in handy. Out of boredom he had tried one or two cigarettes, but couldn't see himself getting hooked on the foul-tasting things.

He flipped the pack over the side. When the boy scurried over to retrieve it Howard saw he was not a boy at all but a man. He shoved the cigarettes into his pocket, then glanced up and gave a mock salute. Howard touched his fingers to his forehead.

The Hawaiian music and dancing continued until the ship's engines rumbled and the lines were cast off. At the first blast of the horn the hula dancers on the dock removed their *leis* and flung them up to outstretched hands. Howard reached out and caught one. He smiled and waved at the girl who had tossed it to him. 'Throw it on the waters as you leave,' she called. 'It means you will return.'

Caught up in the moment, Howard blew her a kiss.

'Whoa,' Gordy said, eyeing first the girl and then the *lei* in Howard's hands. 'Don't know if I'll be able to keep that little tidbit from Lucy.' He cocked an eyebrow, then reached over to finger the purple and white orchids. 'On the other hand . . .'

Howard jerked the *lei* out of his reach. 'Oh, no, you don't,' he said, with a smirk. 'You're not going to manipulate me into giving this to you.'

'What? You don't want your best pal to come back?'

Howard hung the flowers around his neck. 'Get your own,' he said, but by then the ship was moving away from the wharf. As the waving girls on the dock grew indistinguishable in the distance, Howard and Gordy edged through the crowd to the back of the ship. They climbed up to sit on the metal locker below the gun turrets. With tugboats manoeuvring her along, the troopship inched forward, passing within yards of a Japanese freighter. Having read the reports about Japan's new war-minded prime minister, and the increasing tension between the States and Japan, Howard guessed that the Asian passengers crowding *Lisbon Maru*'s decks must be Japanese nationals heading home.

A group of soldiers approached the rail. They stood and watched the Japanese ship as *Awatea* slipped by her. Suddenly one young man lifted his hands to the sides of his face and pulled his eyelids up into tight slits. 'Japanese father.' He pulled his eyelids down. 'Chinese mother.' Then, stretching them in opposite directions, he jeered, 'Poor baby.' The passengers on the freighter could not have heard the words, but the crude gestures were obvious.

'Jesus!' Gordy said, pushing himself forward.

More embarrassed than shocked by the childish joke, Howard grabbed his friend's arm and held him back. He had seen Gordy start fights over less. 'He's just a boy,' he said. The soldier grinned at them, then moved off.

Gordy settled back beside Howard. 'Everyone knows that some guys fudged their ages,' he said, 'but how in Sam Hell could any recruitment officer have believed that snot-nosed kid was more than sixteen years old?'

Howard shrugged. He glanced over at the receding *Lisbon Maru* just as a man at the ship's bow lowered his camera. Their eyes met. Even in the growing distance between them there was no mistaking the hatred smouldering in the Japanese man's glare. With a shiver Howard turned away. Once again, the sight of the American fleet lined up in Pearl Harbor awed him. It occurred to him that *Awatea* – like the man on the dock – was dwarfed by the battleships and destroyers looming there.

After they had passed out of the harbour the tugboats released their lines and veered off. *Awatea* and her escort, *Prince Robert*, headed due west. Howard moved over to the rail and tossed his *lei* overboard. Watching the circle of flowers disappear beneath the foam of the ship's wake did nothing to dispel his growing sense of foreboding.

Two hours later everyone was mustered on deck. 'Guess we're finally going to learn our destination,' Gordy said, as they waited for the announcement. Rumours over the last five days at sea had them heading everywhere from Singapore to India and even to the battle in the African desert. Given the tropical uniforms with which they had been issued any of those destinations made sense to Howard. But over the wind and the growl of the engine Brigadier Lawson announced from the bridge that it was to be their duty to 'defend the Gibraltar of the Pacific'.

His voice crackled over the ship's speakers. 'Men, we are *en route* to shore up the British garrison in the colony of Hong Kong.'

Audible groans sounded among the Grenadiers. Howard could hardly blame them. Many of the experienced soldiers had just finished fifteen months of guard duty in Jamaica and were itching for action. He thought he didn't care one way or the other. He had joined the army because his country was at war, he told himself. It was as simple as that. He would go where he was told. Yet, secretly, he had to admit that a good part of the reason had been a boyhood notion of the call to adventure. Now that it looked as though the chance to prove himself in combat was lost, he found himself torn between disappointment and relief.

That night the ship was on blackout. Portholes were darkened and kept closed. Driven by heat and the fetid air of the enclosed quarters, Howard unhooked his hammock, rolled it up and took it above deck where he found that many others had had the same idea. He returned to the spot at the stern and set up his hammock under the ship's guns. He crawled in, grateful – and surprised – that, unlike some of the boys, he had experienced no seasickness. He found he liked the feel of the wind on his face as it rocked his hammock, and drifted into sleep lulled by waves crashing against the hull as *Awatea* ploughed west through a moonlit ocean.

Under Lawson's orders, training continued during the voyage across the Pacific. The troops spent hours, in alternating shifts on the crowded decks, doing everything from mortar and Bren-gun drills to rifle cleaning. Howard didn't mind. It helped to pass the time.

Lectures on what to expect while on duty in Hong Kong filled the rest of the daylight hours. Officers took turns talking about everything from the history of the colony to tropical diseases – including venereal diseases. They shared reports from British intelligence regarding the nature of the Japanese soldier – reports which mostly dismissed as insignificant the four to five thousand Imperial Army troops gathering along the border of the Hong Kong territories.

Howard had seen the cartoon caricatures in newspapers back home, depicting bucktoothed Japanese trembling behind thick spectacles. He thought about the man on the deck of *Lisbon Maru*, the hatred on his face, and wasn't so sure. It seemed Brigadier Lawson wasn't so sure either, Howard thought, listening to him warn his men not to discount the soldiers of the Imperial Army.

Even though the brigadier insisted that training was carried out every day they were at sea, some of the ranks found the energy at night to join in the illegal poker game running in a storage room on the lower deck. Men popped in and out as their pockets allowed. Howard went down the first few nights and watched Gordy play. A great deal of money was changing hands and he wondered if tempers would flare, but everyone seemed to take their losses and winnings in their stride.

'Ay?' a Royal Rifle taunted Howard one night as he stood behind Gordy. 'You going to play dat game or what, Wheat-head?'

Howard's sun-bleached hair had earned him the nickname among the Grenadiers. But when he heard the French accent, he wasn't quite sure whether he should be offended or feel complimented. He studied the grinning Québec soldier, then pulled out a ten-dollar bill. He felt a twinge of regret as it left his hand but decided that the camaraderie among the men was worth the few dollars he might lose. Anything to alleviate the boredom of the long nights.

Twelve days later, when the ship pulled into Manila Harbor

in the Philippines, Howard was five hundred dollars richer and smoking a dozen cigarettes a day.

Like the rest of the men, Howard was starting to get restless. After a total of seventeen days at sea they had yet to set foot on land. But, as in Hawaii, they were confined to the ship. A few hours later, after they finished taking on fuel, they sailed out of the harbour with the British cruiser HMS *Danae* accompanying them.

'So, why do we suddenly need a second escort, eh?' Gordy wondered aloud, as he threw his ante into the pot that night.

The poker players around him began to speculate about the likelihood of war with Japan. 'That'll be the day,' a Royal Rifle scoffed, adding his stake to the pot. But many were convinced that when they reached Hong Kong they would have to fight their way off the ship. Howard thought they sounded eager to do just that.

While the debate went on he kept his silence, privately wondering about the empty cargo holds below. The military equipment had not arrived in Vancouver by the time *Awatea* had pulled anchor and sailed out of English Bay on the morning after the near mutiny. The word on board was that the transports and gun carriers were loaded onto a freighter, which was only a few days behind. Howard hoped the rumour was true.

In the early hours of 16 November, twenty-one days after they had boarded *Awatea* in Vancouver, Howard and Gordy stood at the rails watching the dark mass on the horizon turn into land. 'There she is my friend. Hong Kong,' Howard said. 'Holiday or hell. Guess we're going to find out.'

They approached the colony just as the rays of the rising sun lit the mountain and hills along the ten-mile length of the island. When they entered the harbour between it and the mainland, hundreds of sampans bobbed in the water around the ship's hull. Howard was amazed they didn't collide, but the strange-looking craft with their rectangular sails moved deftly out of the way. Expressionless faces stared up from the crowded boats as Awatea passed.

'Look at that.' Howard pointed to the roofs of palatial homes showing amid the lush green vegetation on the island's peaks and hillsides.

'Whoever thought two prairie boys would end up in Paradise?' Gordy laughed.

As they got closer Howard noticed what appeared to be thousands of huts clustered on the shores and docks of both the island and the mainland. The flimsy shelters, constructed of everything from corrugated tin to bamboo and paper – looking like a brisk wind would blow them away – were a stark contrast to the opulence of the hillside homes.

Awatea tied up on the mainland while planes circled overhead. 'I sure hope that isn't the entire air force,' Howard said, watching the four antiquated push-prop planes.

On the wharves below, representatives of the British garrison stood to attention in the morning sun. Howard whistled. 'Glad those boys are with us,' he said, pointing out an East Indian Regiment. Not a muscle twitched or an eye moved among the tall, dark-faced troops. He couldn't imagine a more regal, or fierce-seeming group of men, all cut from the same cloth, identical in height and stance, in their crisp khaki uniforms and tan turbans.

Awatea's gangways were lowered. An army band on the docks struck up 'Rule Britannia', and Howard watched as Major General Christopher Maltby, the British commander of the Hong Kong garrison, and his officers boarded the ship. In tropical uniforms and carrying full battle order equipment, the troops of Canada's C Force – some, like Howard and Gordy, having been issued their rifles only last night – waited impatiently on deck while their commanders met the British officers in the ship's lounge.

'The Brits do love a military parade,' Gordy said. 'And now, boys, we'll be able to give 'em one.' Howard, too, was relieved they would march to their new quarters with real rifles and bayonets instead of the wooden ones they had trained with in Canada.

Oddly enough, the men had again been instructed to remove any badges or insignia identifying them as Canadian Army. While they waited to disembark the band played 'The Maple Leaf Forever', and shouts of 'Welcome, Canada' rippled through the gathering crowds below. So much for secrecy, Howard thought.

At noon, to the music of the Royal Scots pipe band, the troops began to disembark. He wasn't sure he had any ancestral Scottish blood flowing with the Heinz 57 mixture in his veins, but Howard couldn't help feeling a patriotic shiver at the sound of the bagpipes. Finally, he joined his company as they assembled on the mainland wharves. Encouraged by the cheering of the crowds along the way, and with the strange sensation that the earth was moving under his feet, Howard forced his sea legs to keep time with his troopmates'.

In the humid afternoon heat the procession made its way up Kowloon's main thoroughfare. During the two-mile march to their new barracks Howard peered down the shadowed side-streets. A chaotic disorder of rickety three- and four-storey buildings, fronted with Chinese-character signs and bamboo scaffolding, stretched as far as he could see. The narrow streets teemed with people jostling past food stalls, wicker cages of squawking chickens and squealing pigs. Strange cooking

odours, pungent with unknown spices and rancid fat, assault-
ed Howard's nostrils. Still, there was something compelling
about this bustling city. He felt a sudden thrill, a mixture of
excitement and apprehension.

Along the route, rickshaws pulled by bare-chested coolies
wove deftly through gaps in the column, flashing grins at the
passing soldiers. Old women, stooped low under bamboo poles
laden with heavy baskets, waited without expression for them
to pass. Asian pedestrians and shopkeepers watched from sidewalks and shop windows while throngs of white people waved
Union flags and shouted greetings. Howard noticed a few
Oriental faces that either ignored them or cast them furtive
glances, but for the most part everyone seemed ecstatic at the
appearance of reinforcements to the ten thousand troops who
now made up the garrison.

From the lectures aboard ship Howard knew that the population of the small colony had swelled to almost two million
with refugees from mainland China fleeing from the Japanese.
But as the colonists cheered them into the gates at Camp Sham
Shui Po, he wondered what difference two thousand new troops
could possibly make.

10

I first saw the girl on Monday morning. The bed in the Fenwicks'
upstairs guestroom was right next to the window. Without
lifting my head from the pillow, I had a clear view of Barclay
Street. The road was so narrow that if two cars were parked on
opposite kerbs there was barely enough room for a third to pass
between them. The houses, crowded together on either side, all
looked the same except for their colour – Mom always said the
government must have had only three shades of paint. The
homes alternated – brown, green, grey, brown, green, grey – all
the way up the street. The Fenwicks' whitewashed old farmhouse, which had a fenced yard that contained tangled
overgrown gardens, stood out like a sore thumb. A carpet of
struggling lawn stretched in front of the others, broken only
by the concrete sidewalks leading to identical front porches,
and by the swings in the kiddie park across the street.

The small park was not really a park at all but an extra wide
space of adjoining lawn between the Mansons' house and my
friend Ardith's. Years ago some of the fathers in the neighbourhood had got together to put up a set of swings and a slide.
No one used them much any more, only the few toddlers left
on our street and sometimes Kipper. The rest of us played our
games of childhood on the road.

I squinted at the reflection of the morning sun in the
Mansons' front window. The harsh glare blinded me momentarily, but not before I saw Mrs Manson's face peering out. She,

too, was watching the park – and the girl who stood all alone in front of the swings. Even if she hadn't been a stranger, I would have noticed her. Her clothes, a white blouse tucked into a dark pleated skirt, looked too formal for a summer day. Her ebony hair was cut in a square bob, and long bangs hung to her almond eyes. She was Oriental – Japanese or Chinese. I couldn't tell the difference. There were no Oriental families in our neighbourhood. The only Chinese people I knew were the owners of the greengrocer's store down on Victoria Drive, and Mr Fong, the vegetable man.

Until a few years ago, almost everything we needed was delivered to our door. The milkman came every second morning. The vegetable man and the McGavin's bread man both showed up once a week. During the day, when we were younger, the delivery trucks were sometimes the only traffic on our street. If we were playing out on the road we would step aside, indignant at the interruption.

The vegetable truck came on Wednesdays. Mr Fong was the oldest man I had ever seen. He spoke few words, but his dark eyes always wrinkled even deeper with a smile whenever he climbed out of the cab and saw Kipper and me waiting with Mom's list. We would follow him up the steps into the back of his truck. I loved the warm smell of garden soil, vegetables and fruit coming from the wooden bins inside. Mr Fong would hand us wicker baskets to hold while he filled them with the order. Every now and then he would put a spotted banana in our pockets.

One summer day, when I was seven, his truck came lumbering down the street as we were playing double-dutch out on the road. My friend Ardith and I were at opposite ends of the long skipping ropes while a line of girls took turns jumping in and out to the chanting of our singsong rhymes. When Mr Fong's truck approached everyone groaned and moved to the kerb where they stood with hands on hips. The truck came to a shuddering stop in front of our house, the cab door opened, and Mr Fong climbed down slowly from the driver's seat.

As he made his way to the back of the truck I felt an impatient tug at the end of the rope and allowed myself to be pulled back out onto the street. The rope started to turn once again. At the first words to the next skipping rhyme I saw the smirk on Ardith's lips, the challenge in her eyes as she sang, 'Chinky, Chinky, Chinaman . . .'

It was a verse that we had often repeated, but for the first time I connected the words to Mr Fong. Still, they tumbled out of my mouth and everyone else's.

> 'Chinky, Chinky, Chinaman
> Went downtown,
> Turned around the corner
> And his pants fell down.'

Mr Fong stopped on the steps of his truck and waited for the rhyme to end. Then he turned. His eyes met mine. I saw his sadness and felt my face redden. But it was too late. I looked away.

For the rest of the summer I stayed inside whenever he made deliveries. Soon after, a large supermarket was built a few blocks away and, one by one, the deliverymen stopped coming. More than five years later, I still felt a flush of shame when I remembered that day. I wondered if my mother ever knew. I hoped not.

At the thought of Mom, my chin quivered.

'Are you coming downstairs?' Danny asked, from the other side of the bedroom door.

'Yeah,' I answered, but I remained curled under the covers as his footsteps retreated. Leaving me alone. Just like the night before. After we arrived at his house, I think he was relieved when I went straight to the guestroom. I had crawled into bed while he took Kipper into his room to play Snakes and Ladders. When Mrs Fenwick poked her head in to check on me I pretended to be asleep, but I didn't think it was possible that I could sleep, or laugh, ever again. I had lain alone in the dark, resenting Danny and Kipper every time a muffled burst of laughter came from across the hallway.

Danny was one of the few neighbourhood kids who never teased my brother. And he hadn't seemed to mind him tagging along with us when we used to hang out together. Then one day last summer, cutting through the bush on our way home from the swimming-pool, I had given in to curiosity and Danny's dare to show him 'mine' if he showed me 'his'.

Afterwards, I swore Kipper to secrecy. But I should have known. The minute we got home and Mom asked about our day, he blurted, 'I can't tell. I promised Ethie.'

Mom took me aside. 'Don't make your brother break his promise,' she said.

Her reaction was less dramatic than I expected. She said it was natural to be curious, but for the time being it was best to keep privates private. I don't know if she ever said anything to Danny's mom, but from that day on he avoided me.

Now, as his footsteps echoed down the stairway, I glanced once more at the girl standing in the park. With a sigh, I sat up and pushed the covers back. Kipper was already up. When I heard him go downstairs earlier I had stayed in bed. I wanted to stay there forever. Last night I hadn't wanted to go to sleep; this morning I didn't want to get up.

Reluctantly, I rose and got dressed. Downstairs I passed the door to the enormous living room. Danny's grandmother sat in the shadows staring at nothing, her mind in another place – like my father's, but her retreats were caused by old age. I said a meek hello, but she didn't move.

In the kitchen Kipper stood at the counter wearing an apron over his jeans and T-shirt, his hat pushed back on his head. He flashed a proud smile at me as he dipped a slice of bread into a bowl of egg mixture.

'Who's hungry?' Dora Fenwick asked, from the stove. She flipped a piece of golden-brown French toast onto a plate, then reached over and let Kipper transfer another dripping bread slice into her sizzling pan.

I felt a pang of guilt when I realized I *was* hungry. 'No, thanks,' I mumbled. I left the kitchen and went to the bathroom.

After I'd washed, I grabbed a brush and tried to run it through my hair. The bristles became snarled in my knotted curls. The more I tugged and pulled the worse it got. With the brush still hanging from my head I sank down in the corner, wrapped my arms around myself and sobbed as I rocked back and forth. Who would do my hair now? Who would cook our meals? Look after Kipper? Who would take care of us?

'Ethie?' Danny's mother called from the other side of the bathroom door. 'Can I come in, honey?'

I tore a handful of toilet paper from the roll and blew my nose, then reached up to turn the doorknob.

Mrs Fenwick slipped in and closed the door behind her. She took my hand to help me up, then led me over to sit on the edge of the bathtub. She sat down beside me and began gently to untangle the hairbrush. I tried to sit still while she worked.

'It hurts awful bad, huh?' Mrs Fenwick asked, after a few moments.

I swallowed, then nodded. I knew she wasn't talking about

my hair. The hurt was inside, where I was bruised and sore. The ache had crept into my stomach yesterday where it had lain like a hot stone all day and last night while I tried not to fall asleep. How could I sleep or eat when my mother would never ever do those things again?

Never. It was impossible to imagine. Never is for ever and ever, Amen. My stomach burned at the thought. So how could I feel hungry?

'I wish I could tell you everything's going to be okay,' Mrs Fenwick said. 'I wish I could make the hurt go away. But I can't. A part of it will always be there, but one day it will go to a different part of your heart, a stronger part, and it will be easier to carry. Until then I'm here if you need me.'

I didn't believe the ache would ever go away. But I sniffed back tears as Mrs Fenwick brushed my hair, starting at the bottom and gently working her way up. 'We'll give you some French braids after breakfast,' she said. She patted my knee and stood up. 'And it's okay to be hungry,' she added.

After breakfast she washed my hair in the kitchen. As she rubbed shampoo onto my head I looked out of the window above the sink. The girl I'd seen earlier was still standing in the same spot in the park, staring across the street at our house. Curious, I wondered if she had a crush on Frankie. Girls were always calling him on the phone or showing up at the door asking for him. Maybe she was watching for him.

Was he up yet? Was Dad? Suddenly I was anxious to go home.

Half an hour later I looked into the mirror at my tightly plaited hair. Lately I had avoided letting Mom braid my hair because I hated being told I looked like Pippi Longstocking. I touched the still wet French braids. I liked the way they lay neatly against my head, then fell to my shoulders instead of sticking straight out like Mom's crazy braids did. 'Thanks,' I murmured. 'We'd better go now,' I told Kipper.

While I waited for him to lace up his runners I went outside to the veranda. Yesterday Barclay Street had been deserted. This morning a few kids had migrated back outdoors. Down on the road Wayne and Rob Ellis were riding their bikes in slow figures of eight. Debra Martin and Ardith Price bounced a lacrosse ball on the sidewalk.

Danny came out and stood by the door. He had changed a lot in the year since we used to hang out. He was taller than me now. With his new flat-top crew cut and Buddy Holly glasses, I guess he thought he was pretty cool. And I was just . . . Well, I was just a girl.

He squinted, an old habit that even his fancy new glasses hadn't cured. 'Do you want to, uh, maybe hang around today?' he asked, adjusting the dark frames on his nose.

'No,' I said, and headed down the steep steps. His mother had probably forced him to ask me.

'Are we going to see Mom today?' Kipper puffed behind me, trying to keep up with my hurried descent.

'I don't know.'

The laughter from the kids in the street stopped as we came out of Danny's yard. I veered off the sidewalk to avoid Ardith and Debra. Two days ago Ardith was my friend. Today she looked as if she was scared of me.

Kipper stopped right behind her. 'Hi, Ardie,' he said. She caught the hard rubber ball and held it to her chest. She mumbled hello to him, then tried to smile at me but it came out funny. 'Are you going to Bible School today?' she asked.

'No,' I snapped. 'Are you?'

'I dunno . . . maybe.'

'Yeah, well, see ya.'

'Hi, Wayne,' Kipper called.

'Hey,' Wayne answered, concentrating on steering his bike in the opposite direction.

'We're going to see our mom today. Before she goes to heben.'

Wayne put one foot down on the road and stopped his bike. 'Yeah, I heard, I . . . uh . . . I'm sorry,' he stammered. He was looking at neither Kipper nor me but at some point between us.

I grabbed my brother's hand and pulled him away. 'I told you I don't know if we're going – and it's heaven. Heaven! Not heben.'

'Sorry, Ethie.' Kipper sniffed, sounding dangerously on the verge of tears. 'Heben,' he repeated. 'Heben.' He looked at me for approval.

I was already regretting having gotten angry at him and tried to smile. 'That's okay,' I said. Before we turned into our yard I glanced over to the park.

The girl was gone.

11

I suppose if I'd really thought about it at the time I might have come to the conclusion that indirectly Kipper was responsible for everything that happened back then. If it hadn't been for him, Mom and Marlene would never have met. The year I started grade one, Mom was still fighting her losing battle with what she called the 'closed minds' that were keeping Kipper out of school. She began teaching him herself. The first week of September that year they went shopping for art supplies and came home with new paints and brushes for Kipper, and a job for Mom at Marlene's Art Supply on Granville Street. It was the perfect job, because Kipper could go with her. While she worked in the front of the store, he spent his day in the studio at the back with Marlene's art students.

I liked Marlene Telford. She wouldn't allow Kipper and me to call her Mrs Telford, insisting instead that we call her by her first name. A few times, when Mom couldn't get a sitter on Wednesday nights, we had gone with her to Marlene's West End apartment near Stanley Park. We sat at the kitchen table, me with my home-work books and Kipper painting, while the women played cards in the living room. All of Marlene's friends knew my brother from the art store and made a big fuss of him, kissing him, pinch-ing his cheek and calling him their handsome Picasso.

They were so different from our mother. While Mom always wore a dress when she went out, or to work, they wore pants or long flowing skirts and baggy shirts. And unlike Mom, who would never go out of the door without her lipstick and rouge, none of them wore makeup.

Frankie called Marlene a beatnik. I didn't know what that meant, but I did know that he liked her too. Aunt Mildred did not. Whenever she referred to her she called her 'Lucy's bohemian friend'. 'She wears anti-establishment like a suit of clothes,' I once heard her say to Mom, 'yet her husband is a big-shot art dealer. Easy to be critical of the system when you're rich.'

Mom had laughed. 'Marlene is just Marlene. She's one of the most authentic people I know.'

'Authentic?' Aunt Mildred had snorted. 'Next thing you know she'll have you wearing black leotards and turtle-neck sweaters, haunting coffee houses and reciting Jack Kerouac poetry.'

'Hmm, sounds groovy,' Mom teased, and even Aunt Mildred had to smile.

The Monday morning edition of the *Daily Province* was on the front porch when Kipper and I came home from Danny's house. A photograph of a smiling Marilyn Monroe posing in a bathing suit filled half of the newspaper's front page. The headline read, *'Star's Death A Mystery'*.

I grabbed the paper and flipped through, searching for something about my mother. Kipper slumped on the top step and watched the discarded pages fall to my feet. I almost missed it, but on page twelve of the second section my mother's name leaped out from a small article in the top corner.

Carbon Monoxide Claims Two Victims
City police have confirmed the accidental death of two Vancouver women, Lucille June Coulter and Marlene Agnes Telford. Their bodies were discovered in the early hours of Sunday morning aboard a sailboat in Coal Harbour. Cause of death is believed to be

carbon-monoxide poisoning. The boat's owner, Jeremy Telford, proprietor of Telford Galleries, and husband of one of the deceased, could not be reached for comment.

Marlene Telford? I had heard the conversations yesterday – even remembered Dad saying 'they' – but hadn't connected the meaning until that moment. The night before I had lain awake searching for a reason, for someone to blame, and I had blamed Marlene. It was her husband's sailboat, after all. Just as my mind, numbed with this new information, registered the truth that she was dead too, the front door swung open and Frankie stood squinting in the morning glare. His eyes red and swollen, he looked as if he hadn't slept all night. He glanced down at the mess on the porch. 'I see you've already got the paper,' he said.

He bent over to help me pick it up. As he did so, our cat Ginger streaked past us onto the porch, her tail in the air. Kipper scooped her up and nuzzled his face in her fur. 'You hungry?' he asked, as he stood up and carried her into the house.

I followed him and Frankie inside. I stopped short when I saw Dad lying on the living-room couch beneath the spare grey blanket from the linen closet. Shocked, I looked at Frankie, but he was already in the kitchen, his back to me, placing the mish-mash of newspapers on the table.

Kipper went to the counter and filled the cat dish, then took it and Ginger out onto the side porch. I sat down across from Frankie. 'Why is Dad sleeping on the couch?' I whispered.

Frankie shrugged. 'He just can't face the empty bedroom, I guess,' he said, concentrating on sorting the papers.

'Frankie? Do you think, umm . . .' I stammered, '. . . do you think Mom was mad at me, that it was my f-f-fault?'

Frankie dropped the pages he was holding. 'No. Of course

not,' he said, studying my face. 'Why would you even think something like that?'

'Dad said – he said she was upset about something. I thought – I thought maybe it was because I didn't take Kipper with me everywhere—' I choked on the sobs rising in my throat.

'Ethie, no.' He knelt down until he was at eye level with me. 'Mom is – was, very proud of you. And of Kipper. What happened had nothing to do with either one of you. It was just a horrible accident.' He reached out for me and I fell forward into his arms.

'But why was she on a boat with Marlene?' I murmured into his shirt, already damp with my tears.

'Maybe she just needed a break, some private time with a friend. I don't know.' He sighed. 'We'll probably never know. And it'll only drive us crazy trying to guess.'

At that moment I looked over his shoulder to see Aunt Mildred coming through the open front door. Her eyes softened as she saw us huddled in the kitchen. Then she turned towards the living room. 'Howard!' she gasped.

Frankie released me and stood up. We went into the other room just as our father pushed back his blanket. He still had on the same clothes he'd worn the day before. With a bewildered expression he swung his feet to the floor and slowly sat up.

Aunt Mildred clicked her tongue. 'Just look at this place,' she said, surveying the room. Last night's dishes and glasses were scattered everywhere. Ashtrays, spilling over with butts, and empty liquor bottles littered the coffee-table. 'What would your mother think?' she asked, then headed into the kitchen.

'She would think that we miss her,' Frankie said, behind her.

Aunt Mildred's shoulders sagged. She took a deep breath,

then pushed the window open. 'It stinks in here,' she muttered.

For the first time I noticed the unwashed dishes overflow-ing in the sink. I rushed over to the counter to start cleaning up.

'Who did your hair?' Aunt Mildred asked.

I blushed, mute with guilt for having let Mrs Fenwick braid it. For having stayed overnight at her house. For eating break-fast.

Coming in the side door Kipper announced, 'Danny's mom did.' Then he added proudly, 'And we made French toast.' Ginger jumped from his arms, made a beeline across the room and, back arched, wound herself around our aunt's leg.

Aunt Mildred shrieked and leaped back. 'Scat,' she hissed, shaking Ginger from her foot.

Kipper retrieved the fleeing cat and went into the living room. Aunt Mildred's lips pinched together. She placed her purse on a chair, then joined me at the sink and started to remove dirty glasses.

Frankie came up behind her. 'Please, Aunt Mildred,' he said, his voice polite but firm, 'we'll clean up.'

'But I just want to . . .' She replaced the dishes in the sink and faced him. 'Look,' she said, 'let's just get through the next few days. The funeral is set for Thursday. I came over to pick out an outfit for your mother.'

'We can take care of that,' Frankie insisted.

She squared her shoulders, went back to the table and picked up her purse. 'I'll come back tomorrow at ten,' she said. 'I'm going to take Ethie shopping for something decent to wear to the service since your father insists on her going.' Her eyes darted towards the living room. 'But I'm beginning to believe your father is in no condition to make decisions.'

Frankie accompanied her to the front door. 'If any of you

need anything,' she said, as he held it open for her, 'just make a list and I'll pick it up tomorrow.'

Frankie kissed her cheek. 'We'll be fine, Aunt Mildred.' But as he reassured her, I heard the lie in the flatness of his voice and realized he didn't believe it. Neither did I. How could we be fine ever again?

After Aunt Mildred had left, Dad sat on the edge of the couch, his head in his hands, his fingers squeezing his temples. He looked smaller, diminished somehow, as if a huge chunk of him had gone with our mother – and there weren't many pieces left to lose. I thought about my aunt's words. Was that what she'd meant when she'd said Dad was in no condition to make decisions? The truth was that, except for money, it was always Mom who made the decisions in our family's day-to-day lives, Mom who smoothed the rough spots. Watching my father sitting there, only partially with us, a wave of panic flooded me. I wondered, without her to prop him up, would he sink even deeper into his silent world?

Kipper sat on the couch beside him. Stroking Ginger with one hand, he patted Dad's shoulder with the other. From somewhere far off, a tiny noise – the hiss of steam escaping from a kettle – sounded. It grew until I recognized the shrill animal-like screams rising from my father's abdomen. 'A memento from the war lurking in his intestines,' Mom had called it, whenever he had one of these flare-ups.

He pushed himself up and rushed to the bathroom.

'I've made coffee,' Frankie called after him.

He came into the kitchen while I was wiping the top of the stove and picked up the coffee-pot from the back burner. Struggling to control the tremor in his hands, he poured a cup of thick black coffee, then eased himself into the chair at the end of the table.

At the sink, Kipper was up to his elbows in soap suds. 'We're cleaning up,' he announced.

'Yes, I see.' Dad attempted a smile. He took a sip of coffee and winced.

'Sorry, I never made coffee before,' Frankie said, wiping down the table.

'I've tasted worse,' Dad said, and took another gulp to prove it. He put the mug down and picked up a pack of cigarettes from the window-sill.

Frankie slid a clean ashtray across the table and sat down at the other end. 'Dad?' he said, absentmindedly pushing the dish-cloth over the same invisible spot on the table. 'Did you hear what Aunt Mildred said about, uh, an outfit for Mom?'

'No.'

'She wanted to pick something out. I told her we'd take care of it.'

'Yeah,' Dad said. 'That's one decision that isn't your aunt's to make.' He inhaled deeply on his cigarette. As the smoke seeped slowly out of his mouth, he said quietly, 'It will be her green dress.' He stared out of the window.

Frankie waited awhile. Then, shaking his head, he pushed himself away from the table, came over to the sink, grabbed a towel and started drying dishes. Aunt Mildred was right about that one. We needed to get through the next few days. Numb our brains and keep moving. If anyone knew how to do that it was our father: he had become a master at sleepwalking through the obstacles of life. But, then, Mom had always been there to clear the way.

For the rest of the day he gazed out of the window while my brothers and I cleaned the house in mute silence. After the dishes were done I dusted and wiped down every surface inside while Frankie and Kipper mowed the front lawn. Later that evening, when I was upstairs in my room, I heard Frankie go out, and the house felt even emptier. I climbed into bed, with the scent of lemon oil and vinegar heavy in the air. I inhaled deeply, trying to let the smell of Mom's cleaning spray bring her into my mind. But I still couldn't see her face. I cried into my pillow until I heard Kipper's spongy breathing. I lifted my head and, vision blurred, saw him standing by my bed, his pigeon chest rising and falling with each raspy breath.

'Where's your puffer?' I asked, wiping my face.

He took a laboured breath, reached into his pants pocket and pulled it out. He stuck it in his mouth, pressed it down with one hand and held something up with the other. As he exhaled he squeezed out the words, 'So you can 'member her face.'

Kipper missed nothing. Yesterday I had complained that I couldn't see Mom's face and here he was with a photograph of her. Grateful, I sat up and reached for it. While he inhaled his medicine I looked down at the snapshot of Mom and Kipper taken at Marlene's art shop.

After he had gone back to his room I slipped it under my pillow and fell asleep with Mom's smiling face fresh in my mind. I woke late on Tuesday morning, forgetting for a brief moment that everything was changed, and had to go through the pain of remembering all over again. Remembering that I would never see my mother's face again, except in photographs.

The sound of the bathroom door closing downstairs broke the silence of the house. I got out of bed. Down in the living room, Dad's blanket and pillow were still on the empty couch. The sound of splashing came from the other side of the bathroom door. In the kitchen, the coffee-pot sat on the counter, coffee grounds spilled next to it. I opened the fridge and stood staring at shelves filled with other people's dishes. I wasn't hungry. I closed the door. I sat down at the end of the table and looked out of the window just in time to see Aunt Mildred's car appear at the top of our street.

Shopping! I was supposed to go shopping with her today. About to jump up, I glanced across the street at the park. The girl I'd seen by the swings yesterday was standing in the same spot looking at our house. When my aunt's car pulled up to the kerb, she headed up the sidewalk.

Behind me the bathroom door opened and my father entered the kitchen. Trance-like he came over to the window and peered outside, his face ashen, as though he had seen a ghost.

12

17 November 1941: Camp Sham Shui Po, Kowloon

Her name was Feng Shun-ling. Howard first saw her the morning after he had arrived in Hong Kong. Driven by the restlessness induced by sleeping in a motionless bed after a hammock and the suspicious itching that had woken him in the middle of the night, he rose early. Outside, in the solitude and chill of pre-dawn, he lit his first cigarette of the day. The clanking of a lonely bell buoy sounded from somewhere across the harbour.

He leaned against the compound fence and gazed out over the bay. In the patchy morning fog, fishing-boats were setting out to sea, their lights twinkling. Below the camp, debris left by the receding tide littered the mud flats. The briny scent of seaweed and decay wafted up on the damp air. Dragging on his cigarette he heard scuffling behind him. He spun round and saw two old women, ancient and bent, shuffling down the road on the other side of the fence. Fascinated, he watched their slow progress as they made their way on feet so tiny it seemed impossible they could hold up the frailest of bodies. Behind them other dark figures emerged from the mist. They came from every direction, a silent ragged procession of men, women and children. When they reached the edge of the banks above the bay, they ignored the coiled wire barricades and slipped through invisible holes to disappear over the side.

In the gaunt faces of those passing close to the fence Howard recognized the desperation of hunger. And in many the blankness of acceptance. A few cast covetous glances at the cigarette in his mouth. Instinctively he reached into his pocket, then realized the futility of trying to offer the few that were left in his pack. There were just too many people. Feeling the shame of abundance in the face of blatant poverty he dropped his, unfinished, to the ground and crushed it under his heel.

Not wanting to seem like an intruder in whatever was unfolding before him, he started to back away. Then he saw the girls.

They came down the road arm in arm. The younger girl, guided by the older one, walked slowly with her head bowed as if she was studying the black fabric shoes they wore. A man carrying a crude, shovel-like tool walked protectively beside them. As the trio drew closer to where Howard stood, the youngest girl saw him. She gave a startled cry, then buried her face in her companion's shoulder and clung to her. The taller girl turned her oval face and looked straight at Howard.

The wide brown eyes that held his were so dark they appeared ebony in the morning light, as black as her hair, which was pulled into a tight knot at the back of her long pale neck, emphasizing the unexpected beauty of her face. Like her companions she wore a grey tunic and baggy pants. The shapeless garments did nothing to hide the sharp angles of an emaciated body, yet her rounded cheeks and full lips mocked the ravages of hunger. She held Howard's gaze for a brief moment, then her lids, heavy with lashes, fluttered down. She pulled the young girl even closer, holding her tightly and murmuring soothing sounds of comfort as they passed.

When they reached the banks at the end of the road, she wound her way fluidly through the coiled wire until, like magic, she was on the other side. Then she helped the others – who, Howard was now convinced, were her sister and father – to step through.

He knew he was staring but couldn't pull himself away.

As if she felt his scrutiny, the girl glanced back. Howard felt another jolt of voyeuristic guilt at observing the naked sorrow in her dark eyes before she followed her family down a hidden path.

Minutes later they appeared on the mud flats below. Removing their cloth shoes, they tied them together and hung them around their necks, then walked barefoot past the crowds already scouring the shores. When they had distanced themselves from the others, the girls waded through the shallow tidal pools, parting seaweed with sticks they had picked up along the way. Every once in a while the older girl bent down, scooped up some object and stored it, with handfuls of seaweed, in the cloth bag tied to the younger girl's back.

Nearby, the man plodded along, stopping every now and then to poke at the sand with his shovel. When he suddenly began to dig – with a speed Howard was astonished at – both girls ran to help. They squatted opposite each other and, with bare hands, scooped out sand until the man reached down to pluck an elusive clam from the hole. The treasure was stored in the cloth bag and they moved on.

Along the expanse of the tidal flats others performed similar routines. In the wake of this moving army of scavengers everything was stripped bare, the slick sand and mud marred only by footprints.

Howard kept his eyes on the taller girl. Even from a distance she was easy to spot. Although most wore similar shapeless garments, there was something about the way the girl moved that set her apart. Unlike the others who scurried along, hunched over, darting back and forth as if in fear they might miss something, she moved with purpose. Her head remained bowed, her eyes downcast, but she walked with the regal posture of someone used to a better life.

'What're you looking at?' Gordy startled Howard out of his reverie.

He nodded at the beach. 'They look like they're starving to death.'

Gordy lit a cigarette, and they stood in silence. Both had experienced the hunger of the depression years, yet it was difficult to comprehend an existence so meagre that seaweed would become sustenance. Finally Howard turned away. On legs still wobbly with the phantom motion of the sea, he headed for the mess hall.

'Howie, wait,' Gordy called, and gestured towards the barracks. 'Before we eat you've got to see this.'

Howard shrugged and went back with him to their hut. There was no rush. The newly arrived troops had been confined to camp for the day.

Inside soldiers milled about in various stages of undress.

'Get a load of that,' Gordy said, indicated the mosquito-draped army cots at the end of their row.

Howard recognized two British soldiers he had met last night. Peter and Dick – he couldn't remember their last names – wearing only their skivvies, lay with eyes closed, as if still asleep, while Oriental men shaved their lathered faces. Last night the two machine-gunners, of the Middlesex Regiment, had bragged to their new roommates about the Asian servants who showed up each morning. For two Hong Kong dollars a week, which translated to about sixty cents Canadian, they performed duties from cleaning uniforms to polishing boots, making beds and shaving. Howard shivered as he watched the skilful barbers.

That would be the day when he let any hand other than his own near his throat with a straight razor.

'Looks like you guys are living the life of Reilly here,' he said. 'Seems more like a holiday camp than a military one.'

'Yeah, a paid holiday in Paradise, mate,' the soldier named Peter said, not bothering to hide the sarcasm in his words. 'Hong Kong, blimey. You boys may as well get used to what we already know – you'll see no action on this duty. But, then, you'll win no medals either.'

Both scenarios sounded fine to Howard. It was not a sentiment he cared to voice, though, especially here, in close quarters with two hundred Grenadiers champing at the bit to see action. Still, something about this carefree lifestyle unsettled him. 'You don't think the Japanese will attack?' he asked.

Dick took the towel from the hands of his barber and wiped the soap residue from his face. 'Not a friggin' chance.' He swung his legs over and sat on the edge of his bed while his servant shuffled away. 'It would be the same as attacking the whole British Empire. Besides, the Japanese have bloody poor eyesight. They can't fight at night and their pilots are too short-sighted to dive-bomb. The little yellow buggers wouldn't dare pick a fight with us.' He stood up and pulled on his shorts. 'We've kept an eye on them, watched them through binoculars up near the border. Scruffy lot, lazing around camp looking half asleep and as starved as the refugees. No, they won't be giving us any trouble.'

His servant returned bearing a tray. Dick picked up a cup of tea and toasted the group of half-dressed Grenadiers gaping at him. 'Still, there's some benefits to this posting. Might as well take advantage while you can, eh?'

Later, at breakfast, the two British soldiers sat across from Howard and Gordy at the mess table. Listening to them banter,

Howard felt an immediate affinity with them. Like himself and Gordy, they were farm boys and childhood pals. They had enlisted together, too, determined to be in the same regiment. Yet unlike Howard and Gordy, who had no physical similarities, Private Peter Young and Private Dick Baxter looked like brothers. They were both slightly built and no more than five foot eight. Even their hair was identical, close-cropped to above the ears, then left to grow wild on top. The only difference was the colour: Peter's was a dirty blond and Dick's a gingery orange to match the freckles that all but covered his elfin face.

'A bit of a nuisance, that,' he said, nodding at Howard unconsciously scratching a spot on his arm. 'Those little beasties must love the taste of fresh Canuck blood.'

While they ate, they advised their breakfast companions to dismantle their cots and paint the metal frames with coal oil. 'While it's drying hang your mattresses outside in the sun,' Peter said, through a mouthful of sausage. 'Bedbugs hate light and heat.'

The tide was creeping slowly over the mud flats when they returned from the mess hall. Anything still above water was stripped clean, the silky wet surface shining in the rising sun.

At the back door of their hut, Gordy bent over to scratch the back of his calf. 'Let's go check the quartermaster's shed for some of that coal oil before it's all gone.' As he straightened, the family Howard had seen earlier appeared at the top of the bank behind the barracks. Howard heard his quick intake of breath before Gordy moved, hypnotized, towards the fence. With his hands on the post he called out, 'Hallo, there. Speaky English?'

The younger girl shrank back and hid her face in her sister's shoulder. With a disdainful glance over his shoulder the father hurried his daughters along the road.

'Wait,' Gordy called, 'I just want to talk . . .' His voice trailed off as he watched their retreating backs.

'No need to worry, mate.' Peter came up to the fence beside Gordy and threw his arm around him. 'There's plenty of Suzie Q downtown who'll be happy to chat with you.' He winked at Howard. 'Not to mention a few other favours. Come along with us tonight. Dicky and me'll show you colonial boys the ropes. You don't have to go chasing after refugees to have a good time in Hong Kong.'

Confined to barracks the night before and all of that day, Howard, like most of the regiment, was more than ready for his first four-hour pass and to see the sights. In the muggy heat of evening, he took his first rickshaw ride. He and Gordy leaned back in the contraption, which felt dangerously close to tipping over, as a barefoot coolie hoisted the long wooden shafts to his hips and trotted into the heavy traffic. Ahead, Peter and Dick rode along in similar fashion.

Howard laughed at the sight of other soldiers from the base urging their drivers to race down Nathan Road. The grinning coolies speeded up, deftly weaving past automobiles, buses and bicycles, oblivious to the honking and frustrated shouts. As they jostled down the thoroughfare, Gordy leaned forward and bribed their driver with double the fare if he pulled ahead of the rickshaw in front of them. When they arrived at the moneychanger's in the lead, he paid the man twenty-five cents.

'Don't be daft,' Peter scolded, climbing down from his rick-shaw. 'The fare's ten cents.'

'Twenty-five's only two bits,' Howard said, waving the driver away.

'Still, you'll spoil it for us. Our pounds don't get the same rate of exchange your Canuck dollars do.'

'Ah, come on, buddy,' Gordy said. 'What's the big deal?'

'It's what they're used to.'

'Okay, okay,' Howard said. 'Just let us change our money and we'll buy the beer.'

'Yeah, and that's ten cents, too. Don't be paying any more.'

'All right.' Howard laughed, pulling Gordy inside. 'We're not here to destroy the economy of Hong Kong.'

Moments later they came out, grinning over the stacks of money they'd received in exchange for their poker winnings.

'Keep that hidden,' Dick said. 'There's pickpockets and thieves everywhere. And too right, you blokes can buy the beer.'

Even distributed through all the pockets of his uniform, and tucked in his puttees above his boots, Howard's wads of paper money still bulged. For the first time in his life he felt the heady power of wealth, tinged with the fear of losing it. Following their self-proclaimed tour guides through a maze of narrow alleys and streets, he kept double-checking his pockets.

The thriving nightlife of the colony was like nothing he had ever seen. Even Winnipeg, which had awed him the first time his parents had taken him there as a boy, was nothing compared to this. Neon lights, in English and Chinese characters, glowed over darkened storefronts. As exotic as Kowloon had seemed when they'd marched through it the day before, at night the city, like any other, showed a seedier side. The cobbled side-streets still bustled with hordes of people, moving haphazardly in all directions, oblivious to the beggars who sat on their haunches with their hands out. Raw sewage ran in the gutters of narrow alleys. The smell of spices mingled with the stench of decay. Sleeping bodies – which at first Howard mistook for bundles of discarded clothes – lay curled up in the shadows. Women with glossy black hair stood in open doorways. 'Hey, wanna party, so'diah? Happy, happy time.' The singsong invitations followed the foursome. 'Fifty cent short time. One dolla' long time.'

'Not tonight, sweetheart,' Peter called back, then winked at Gordy and Howard. 'No need to take chances. There's a chap at the Sun Sun Café. If you're interested in that sort of thing you can pick a nice clean bird from the display in his catalogue. All examined by – and don't say I said it – one very reputable army doctor.'

'I'm married,' Howard said.

'Well, I'm not.' Gordy laughed.

After a night of pub-crawling and with bellies full of ten-cent beer, they arrived at the Sun Sun Café and Dance Parlour. Upstairs, exotic Asian and Eurasian dime-a-dance girls filled the room, dancing with soldiers and sailors or each other. Others sat giggling at crowded tables and lounging at the bar. Brilliantly coloured silk dresses, slit to the thigh, exposed ivory legs in various poses. Embroidered dragons wound up to mandarin collars to meet powdered and painted faces.

The smoke-hazed room smelled of spilled beer, incense and one too many perspiring bodies. Music blared from the Wurlitzer jukebox in the corner. Above the din, uniformed men vied for the attention of the girls and each other. At the far end of the bar a group of well-dressed businessmen, white and Oriental, huddled together, distancing themselves from the military clientele.

Following their new chums, Howard and Gordy pushed their way across the crowded dance-floor. When their beers were served the four soldiers leaned back with their elbows on the bar to watch the action.

Gordy said something, but his words were swallowed in the racket.

Howard put his hand to his ear. 'What?'

Gordy shouted, 'None of these dames can hold a candle to that little China doll outside the camp this morning.'

Howard might not have agreed with his friend's choice of words but he certainly agreed with the sentiment.

The next morning when Howard woke, Gordy's cot was empty and made up for the day. He had a feeling he knew where his friend was. He rose and dressed. Except for the banknotes in the soles of his shoes and tucked inside his puttees, he left the bulk of his Hong Kong dollars in his kitbag inside his locker. Glad to be away from the coal-oil stench, which clung to the metal beds, he joined Gordy outside at the fence. They stood together smoking and watching the beachcombers on the mud flats below.

Late last night the seriousness of the refugees' plight had been made all too clear to them. As they had left the Sun Sun Café, a heavy truck had rumbled to a stop a few yards away. 'The death squad,' Dick muttered, when two men jumped out of the cab. With black cloths wrapped around their mouths and noses, the men retrieved what Howard had thought was a bundle of rags from the alley. Together they hoisted it up and tossed it into the back of the truck where it landed, then slid down a growing pile of lifeless bodies. Only then had Howard realized that the lingering stench beneath the exotic odours of the city, the underlying foul odour of decay, was the smell of death.

He could even detect it out here.

Leaving Gordy at the fence he went to the mess hall. His appetite had gone but he drank a cup of coffee. Before he left he took the three hard-boiled eggs from his tray and shoved them into his pockets.

The beachcombers were abandoning the mud flats with the incoming tide when he returned to the hut. Gordy was still at the fence searching the faces of the returning refugees when Howard joined him. They almost missed her. After slipping though the barricades at the top of the bank the family had stayed well over on the far side of the road. It was only after they had passed that Gordy spotted them. 'Wait! Wait!' he yelled. He thrust his hand, which held three Hershey bars, through the fence. 'Look. Chocolate. A gift.'

The girls hurried along, but their father showed signs of slowing. Gordy pulled his hand back and ran alongside the fence until he was a little ahead of the group. He thrust the bars out again, calling, 'Here – Hershey bars for you. Please, take.'

The man stopped. Encouraged, Gordy offered his other hand through the fence. 'Name's Gordy Veronick, pleased to meet you,' he said, with a grin so wide Howard was certain that even the most suspicious would be unable to resist him.

The man approached the fence and, to Howard's surprise, shook Gordy's hand. 'My name is Feng Guo-ren,' he said, sur- prising Howard again, this time with his English. 'Thank you for your gift.' He snatched the chocolate and retreated after his daughters.

'No! Wait!' Gordy cried. 'I want to talk to you! I want to ask your daughter—' Defeated, he watched the family scurry away. 'Jeez, I just wanted to ask her out to the picture show.'

Howard thrust the eggs at him. Gordy grinned, grabbed them, then bolted down the fence. He caught up to the family and, keeping pace with them, held out the eggs until he reached the corner posts at the edge of the base.

Just when Howard was certain it had been a waste of time, the father stopped again. Leaving the girls on the other side of the road, he walked over to the fence. An animated conversation, which Howard could not hear, continued for a few minutes. Finally the eggs were passed through the wire. The man returned to his daughters. He spoke briefly with the older girl, who came to the fence. Another brief conversation took place, between her and Gordy, before she nodded, then returned to her sister and father.

Gordy stood motionless, watching them disappear down the road. Then he thrust his hands into his pockets and, with shoulders hunched, head down, headed towards the barracks.

Howard ran after him. 'Well? Is she going to the movies with you?' he asked, trying hard to keep the note of envy out of his voice.

Gordy nodded. Uncharacteristically mute, he kept walking.

'Well, uh, that's swell,' Howard said to his back.

Gordy stopped, then turned around, his face a mask of indignation. 'Jesus H. Christ, Howie,' he choked out. 'He sold her to me. Can you bloody believe it? Sold me his daughter's services for three Hong Kong dollars a week!'

13

Aunt Mildred and I returned from our shopping trip early on Tuesday afternoon. She gathered up the Woodward's shopping bags from the back seat of her car while I rushed up to our door. The hot summer air smelled of freshly cut grass and the sweet williams blossoming under our front windows. I breathed in the perfume of Mom's favourite flowers and the hot stone thudded back into my stomach.

Inside, Frankie was leaning against the kitchen wall, his back to us, speaking quietly on the phone. At the table, Kipper sat with his paint pots and art supplies spread out before him. He looked up from the painting he was working on and saw me. 'Ethie!' he squealed. He dropped his brush, jumped up, threw his arms around me and snuggled his head into my shoulder. 'I missed you.'

Aunt Mildred sighed and asked, 'Where's your father?'

Frankie turned from the wall phone and waved at the living room. He knew she had not addressed Kipper. She rarely spoke directly to him. More often she talked around him as if he were not even in the room. It had annoyed our mother no end. 'Don't speak about Kipper as if he's not there,' she would insist, whenever anyone made that mistake in front of her. But with Aunt Mildred it made no difference. Whenever she did speak to Kipper it was usually to criticize him. Only last week he had been standing with Mom on the front porch when her sister was leaving. 'Close your mouth, Christopher,' Aunt Mildred said, after she'd hugged Mom goodbye. 'You look like you're catching flies.'

He grinned up at her. 'That's because my tongue is bigger than other people's,' he said, with the honesty that only Kipper could pull off. 'And,' he added proudly, 'I have an extra chromosome.'

Mom laughed. 'Well, now you're just bragging,' she said putting her arm around his shoulder.

Everything she learned about Down's syndrome Mom had passed on to the rest of us, most importantly to Kipper. She wanted him 'armed' with information, as she put it, and from her smile that day as my aunt huffed off I knew she believed it had paid off. Later I heard her telling Dad how the truth had won that skirmish with her sister.

Our mother never pretended Kipper was the same as everyone else. She wanted him to know his differences. Not limitations, she would say, just differences. When he was old enough to start grade one she refused to accept the excuses she was offered when the authorities would not admit him to the school system. From 1954 to 1958 she was given the run-around each time she tried to register him. The school board left it up to the principals; the principals left it up to the teachers.

'He'll never learn to read and write,' one teacher after another told her. 'We would just be babysitting him. It's not fair to the other kids in the classroom.' Their minds were more than made up, Mom told them accusingly, time after time. They were closed, tighter than the school doors, to Kipper. Closed to the possibility, she said, that the other kids might have something to learn from him.

So Mom taught him herself, she, and he, proved them wrong. By the time he was ten Kipper could read, not smoothly but he could sound out many words. He could print as well. But the best thing he could do was paint. And what he painted mostly was houses, all shapes and sizes. The homes in our neighbourhood may have been similar but in Kipper's bright watercolour paintings each one somehow resembled the families that lived inside it. They looked as if they might start breathing, especially our brown two-storey home. The living room and kitchen windows on either side of the front door were like eyes beneath a steep roof forehead. The door and the three steps up to the porch looked like a mouth, and the open upstairs side windows like ears. He painted our house in various colours, depending on his mood and the season. Marlene, who loved his paintings, framed each one and had included some in her last art show. Two had even sold. To celebrate his windfall, Kipper insisted on taking us all out to dinner at King's Drive Inn on Kingsway for hamburgers and milkshakes, our father's favourite treat next to sardine sandwiches.

Kipper kept on painting. Marlene kept on framing. Our walls were running out of space. I even had one of his paintings of our house, in shades of pink, hanging above my bed. Aunt Mildred never mentioned the art that decorated our walls, and she paid no attention to the painting my brother was working on at the table before she went into the living room to talk to Dad.

I stayed in the kitchen peering over Kipper's shoulder as he sat down again. I was surprised to see not the beginnings of another house but a brilliant blue sky filled with a multitude of variously shaped clouds. 'What's this? Where's the house?'

'Mom doesn't lib in a house now,' he said. His tone told me he was trying hard to be brave. 'She libs in heben.'

I swallowed the lump rising in my throat, and with it the impulse to correct his pronunciation.

Just then I heard my aunt telling Dad she would take Mom's

outfit for the funeral home. Frankie heard, too. He said a quick goodbye to whoever he was talking to, hung up the wall phone and hurried past us. I moved to where I had a view into the living room. My aunt stood by the television set in the corner with her arms crossed, waiting for a response from Dad who sat slumped in his chair. He opened his mouth, then closed it as Frankie came in and stood beside him. 'We'll take care of that, Aunt Mildred,' Frankie said.

'But—'

'I was just speaking with Forest Lawn,' he said. 'The coroner is releasing her . . .' He saw me watching them. 'Dad and I will go over to the funeral home tomorrow. We'll take whatever is needed.'

'All right, then. Just let me know when you're going and I'll meet you there.'

'Thank you,' Frankie said. 'But I think we need to go alone first.'

'Oh, well, I, uh, I . . .' she sputtered. Then she, too, noticed me. 'Ethie, take your new clothes up to your room,' she said, holding out the bags. 'And take your brother with you,' she added, as I reached for them. 'I need to speak with your father.'

Disappointed to be taken away from his painting, Kipper clomped upstairs behind me. In my room, I tossed the shopping bags into the corner. 'Mary Jane shoes, that's what she bought me,' I wailed, as he came in. 'Baby shoes, and lacy baby socks. And white gloves!'

Kipper stood looking down at the bags.

'I won't wear them.' I pouted, and threw myself across my bed.

And then, as clearly as if she were standing in the room, I heard my mother's voice say, 'Birdie's gonna come and poop on your lip.' I sucked in the bottom one. The last time I had heard her use that silly expression was just over a week ago, when I'd lost one of my favourite shoes at Trout Lake. The small swampy lake was only a ten-minute drive from our house. Mom often took us there to cool off on hot days. The last time we went was the day before it started raining. When we returned to our blanket after a swim I found my towel and one of my shoes missing. My mother comforted me as I cried over the lost sneaker. Those plaid runners with yellow laces were my favourite shoes, my only shoes, except for a pair of ratty old canvas ones. We searched the area but found nothing there, or at the lost-and-found in the beach house. As we packed up to go home Mom told me to leave the remaining shoe on the shelf in the changing rooms. 'Why?' I demanded.

'Whoever took the other one might find it,' she said. 'No sense two people walking around with just one shoe.'

I sulked all the way home. I could still hear Mom trying to tease me out of it with her bird-poop threat. But it wasn't Mom's voice I was hearing now: Kipper was teasing me with her words. I rolled over to see his grinning face. I pushed myself up and reached into my pocket. Then, as the adults talked quietly downstairs, Kipper and I sat on the end of my bed looking at the photograph of our mother.

During the days before the funeral I kept that snapshot with me and pulled it out every time I started to forget her face. Still, everything I did and everywhere I went, my mother's not being there was the only thing I could think about. Without her, our house was strangely quiet. Everyone who came with food, or to sit with Dad in the living room, spoke in hushed tones or whispers. Even the phone, which rang every few minutes, seemed to ring softly. I spent most of my time cleaning up, trying to keep our house tidy in fear that Aunt Mildred would drop in unexpectedly and get mad at my father again.

I guess Kipper was thinking along the same lines. Late Wednesday afternoon, the day before the funeral, I was in the kitchen scrubbing one of the endless casserole dishes to return to the neighbours when I heard him shriek, then an explosion of footsteps racing to the basement door. I had never seen my father move so fast. He threw the door open and bolted down the steps. Frankie and I followed on his heels. We pulled up short at the turn in the stairway where Dad stood gaping down at Kipper, standing in a sea of suds, his arms full of foam, his face full of panic. Beside him the washing-machine swished and chugged, pumping out billowing white waves. Thick suds covered the entire floor and bottom step of the stairway. Cloud-like puffs floated in the air; a large clump had landed on Kipper's pork-pie hat and sat there like a pom-pom. Above him Ginger crouched on the window-ledge surveying the scene.

Frankie rushed down to pull out the washing-machine's plug, Dad and I behind him. Wading through the sea of froth, Dad stifled a choke, which turned into a laugh. On the other side of the machine Frankie was chuckling. Kipper looked from him to Dad, his panic-stricken expression turning into a grin. 'Oops,' he said. 'Too many bubbles.'

Dad and Frankie burst into hysterical laughter. Momentarily confused, I stood mute until Kipper flung his armload of suds at me. Then we were all scooping up and tossing handfuls of foam at each other as tears rolled down our cheeks.

After we regained control of ourselves, our clothes wet and soapy, we began to mop up. While we worked Kipper told us he'd been trying to help by doing the laundry. Frankie asked, 'How much soap did you put in?'

Kipper pointed to the shelf above the washing-machine where a large Tide box lay on its side. 'One,' he said proudly. 'I read it on the back.'

'One cup?' Frankie asked.

'Oh,' Kipper said, reality dawning, 'one box.'

The clearing up of Kipper's well-intentioned if messy mistake turned out to be fun. I suppose that was because it gave us something to do together, something else to think about besides Mom. I'm sure some of the tears of laughter we shed were for her, but during that time we somehow forgot our sorrow for a little while.

And then Aunt Mildred appeared at the top of the stairs and spoiled everything.

14

'This is exactly what I warned you about,' Mildred said, to Howard's back, as he stood at the kitchen sink rinsing the soapy film from his hands. 'How can you possibly look after these children once you go back to work?' *If you can't do it while you're at home.* He heard the implication in her voice as clearly as if she had said the words aloud. He wiped his hands on a dish-towel and turned to face her. His sister-in-law stood as if braced against the table, her black purse hanging from folded arms. Did the woman never sit down in their house?

'It's only suds.' He sighed.

'This time,' she said. 'Maybe next time it will be fire or . . .' She continued to outline the litany of tragedies that could occur in a heartbeat of inattention. Her words melted into a drone as Howard's gaze strayed to the window behind her.

Ever since yesterday morning he had found himself con-stantly checking the street for the phantom vision he had seen in the park to materialize once again. A vision that could not be real. Was he starting to hallucinate? Or were his nightmares catching up to him in the daylight? There wasn't enough alcohol in the world to drown remorse.

'Are you listening, Howard?' Her shrill voice cut into his thoughts.

He forced himself to look at her, to bring her face into focus.

'Did you hear me?' she repeated. 'I asked what your plans are.'

'I don't know,' he said slowly. He didn't know anything any more. His mind was a clutter of confused questions and images, real and imagined.

'Well, you're going to have to start thinking about it – and soon.'

As she spoke a dull ache began to build between Howard's shoulder-blades. It crept up his spine to the base of his neck. A searing mushroom cloud of pain exploded inside his skull. With a will of their own his hands reached up to rub his throbbing temples while he stared down at the yellow linoleum floor. From downstairs came the sudden bark of Kipper's laughter, followed by Ethie's muffled response. In the hallway the basement door opened, then closed. Howard lifted his head and asked quietly, 'Do we really need to talk about this now?'

Mildred uncrossed her arms, shifting her purse to the other side. 'I don't want to make an issue of this before my sister is laid to rest, but do you even remember what we talked about yesterday? Have you given my proposal any thought?'

Howard remembered. He knew what she wanted.

'Just consider it, Howard,' she insisted. 'She's almost a teen-ager, a young woman. Who will guide her through those years? Who will buy her first bra? Teach her about her changing body? You? Frankie?

'And Christopher,' she continued, without waiting for an answer. 'There are places for people like him, homes, residential schools, where they know how to look after him, keep him safe. Really, it should have been done a long time ago. But now that Lucy's gone I – well, there just isn't any other choice.'

'We'll manage,' Frankie said, walking into the kitchen.

'And how will you do that?' Mildred's voice grew noticeably softer as she addressed her nephew.

'Dad will take his holidays for the next few weeks, then I'll take mine,' Frankie said. 'After that we'll figure it out. Maybe we'll go on opposite shifts at the mill, I don't know, but we'll make it work somehow.'

'And give up your night-school classes?'

'For a while.'

She turned to Howard. 'Are you really going to stand by and let your son, through some misguided sense of loyalty, do this?' she demanded. 'Are you going to continue to allow him to reject our offer to pay for his university tuition? Or do you want him to work for the rest of his life in a mill?'

'It isn't Dad's decision,' Frankie interrupted, a warning edge to his voice.

'It's a senseless sacrifice he's making, Howard,' Mildred pleaded. 'If Ethie lived with us, if Christopher was in an institution, there would be no reason for Frankie to be tied down. Our offer still stands. All it would take is a word from you.'

Howard shook his head in an attempt to clear the cobwebs, or her words, because the odd thing was that her harsh reasoning made some kind of sense. 'Give us some time,' he said wearily. 'I'll think about it. We'll talk about it. Just not now.'

'Fine,' Mildred said, then reached into her purse and brought out a brown manila envelope. 'This is information on residential schools and homes in the city,' she said, placing it on the table. 'And this . . .' she said, reaching into her bag again. 'Sidney was able to pull some strings to get an early copy of the coroner's report.' She was looking down at the white envelope. 'He would not let me open it. Said it was up to you to share it with us.' Reluctantly she held it up. 'I'm hoping that will happen.'

When Howard made no move to take it she placed it on top of the manila one. 'When you're ready,' she said.

After Frankie had closed the front door behind her, he turned to Howard. 'You're not considering . . .'

Howard's mouth was dry. He swallowed. 'I don't know,' he mumbled. 'I just don't know.' He went over to the table and picked up the two envelopes. Holding them by the edges as if they might burn, he walked out of the kitchen.

Behind him Frankie swore under his breath.

In the hallway Howard steeled himself at his bedroom door. Every time he had to go in there he felt the same wrenching sorrow. He still couldn't bring himself to sleep in their bed. He took a deep breath and opened the door. Inside, dust motes danced in the sunlight streaming through a gap in the curtains. Someone had made the bed, but Lucy's belongings still littered the room, and her scent still hung in the air.

As if he was making his way through a minefield, Howard went over to his dresser and opened the top drawer. He dropped the envelopes onto the other papers stored there, then closed it. With his hand still on the knob, he stood motionless for a moment, then changed his mind. He pulled the drawer out, reached inside and retrieved the manila envelope, the one containing the information about residential homes. Without opening it he ripped it, and the unread contents, in half, then tore them in half again and dropped them back into the drawer.

He picked up the white envelope. He turned it over, hesitated for a moment, then opened it and cautiously removed the coroner's report. The muffled sounds of the house, the ticking of the bedside alarm clock, receded as he read and reread the report, trying to make sense of the technical jargon.

There were no surprises. It was just as the police had suspected. The coroner's report concluded: 'Accidental death due to incomplete combustion of a faulty kerosene space heater resulting in the release of carbon monoxide ...' But a single statement in the report leaped out at Howard. 'Alcohol count in the subject's blood was at such an extreme level that it is likely the victim was unconscious at time of death.'

Although the report was what he had expected, he hadn't been prepared for the hammering blow he felt at the impersonal words. Lucy drunk? It was inconceivable. He sank down on the vanity stool and lowered his head. He closed his eyes and pressed his palms to them. After he removed them, through blurred vision, he noticed something caught in the bottom drawer of Lucy's vanity dresser. Leaning forward, he removed the slip of paper, then sat staring at it until he realized what it was. He reached down and slowly pulled the drawer all the way out. Inside, a shoebox lay tipped over on its side. Half of the box's contents, a jumble of newspaper clippings, similar to the one in his hand, lay scattered on top of the neatly stored stationery in the bottom of the drawer. He picked up a handful. This was typical Lucy. It was her habit – a habit that verged on obsession – to cut articles from the daily papers to share with whomever she thought might be interested. Almost every night Howard would be greeted with holes in sections of the *Daily Province* if she had got to it first. But these clippings were not recent. They were browned and brittle with age. He dropped them, grabbed another handful and sifted through them. Each one was dated during the war. Why had he not seen them before? Why had she secretly hung on to this connection with a past he was trying to forget? Had she saved them all this time hoping for a day that would never come now? The day when he would be able to share those lost years?

She had known. Of course she had known that he had returned to her carrying something far worse than the latent parasite in his bowels. Yet in all these years she had never pushed, never asked what had happened over there. He squeezed his eyes shut. God, why hadn't he told her the truth?

The bedroom door opened. 'Dad?' Ethie called.

He jerked back, dropped something on the floor, then shoved the rest into the drawer, at the same time leaning over to retrieve the paper that had fallen. Before he put it with the rest and closed the drawer, he noticed it was not a newspaper clipping, but a yellowed telegram. A telegram, dated twenty-one years ago, declaring his safe arrival in Hong Kong.

15

19 November 1941: Hong Kong

19 NOVEMBER 1941 17:46
MRS LUCY COULTER
455 VINE ST
VANCOUVER BC CANADA

**ARRIVED WELL AND SAFE WILL WRITE SENDING
ALL MY LOVE.**

HOWARD

Howard reread the too-short message. Permission to cable home came with restrictions. He signed the back and handed it to the clerk, who acknowledged it with a quick nod before moving on to the next anxious soldier.

Outside the telegraph office, Gordy waited impatiently, unconsciously shifting his weight from one leg to the other.

Howard rushed down the steps. 'Done,' he said, noticing the relief in his friend's eyes. He had been startled earlier when Gordy had suggested he accompany him that evening. 'I tagged along with you and Lucy enough,' he argued, as if it was a debt he were repaying. But Howard heard the plea behind his insistence. Gordy nervous at meeting a girl? He wouldn't have believed it if he hadn't seen it with his own eyes. He hardly recognized his childhood chum. This was not the cocky, brash friend whom he had grown up with. As boys they had been inseparable until he and Lucy had started dating. It struck Howard that he was about to get an insight into how it felt to be the odd man out.

They joined the steady stream of people on the sidewalk heading to the Kowloon pier. At the bottom of Nathan Road they darted across the wide avenue, dodging buses and other honking traffic. In the back of his mind Howard wondered if the girl would even show up. Perhaps her father had accepted the chocolate, the eggs, intending to take his daughters and disappear into the masses, along with Gordy's three dollars. It would be understandable if he had.

Earlier, Howard couldn't help asking Gordy, given his indignation at the idea of a father selling his daughter's services, why he had agreed to it. 'You don't think I'm going to let some other palooka get his hands on her, do you?' But for the rest of the day Howard had sensed his friend's nervousness.

Approaching the line of passengers waiting for the Star ferry, Howard experienced his own apprehension, and felt a surge of sympathy for Gordy. But there she was, standing by the turnstiles. She waited with her head held high, her hands folded over a cleaner version of the tunic outfit she had worn on the mud flats. Her hair, though, was not tied back but hung loose, an ebony cascade that framed the oval face and dark eyes. A questioning expression flickered across her face – there, then gone – as she saw them coming towards her. Howard wondered if she was surprised by his presence but she said nothing when they stopped in front of her.

Again Gordy shifted from one foot to the other as he hurriedly introduced Howard. The girl nodded a silent greeting. She offered neither encouragement nor discouragement as

Gordy lifted his hand, then lowered it, obviously unsure if he should take hers or offer his arm. Finally he plucked up some bravado and placed his arm around her shoulders to guide her through the turnstiles.

They moved with the flow of passengers towards the wooden benches on the ferry as it groaned and pulled away from the dock. After they had found seats Howard noticed there were no other white people on the crowded lower deck. He also noticed women standing. He and Gordy jumped up at the same moment to offer their places. Shun-ling followed them to the side where they squeezed in at the rails. Discomfited by the closely packed bodies, especially the girl's – she stood pressed between him and Gordy – Howard stared out over the busy harbour.

Across the water the sun's dying rays dissipated behind the looming mountains rising abruptly from the sea. A crimson sky backlit the cluster of dark peaks, towering cliffs and steep shore-lines that made up the island of Hong Kong.

Shun-ling said something, her soft voice lost in the throb of the engine and the busy water traffic. 'Pardon?' Gordy leaned closer.

'Fragrant Harbour,' she repeated, above the din. The two sol-diers raised their eyebrows. The smell of the murky waters reminded Howard of rancid garden compost.

'Chinese meaning of Hong Kong,' Shun-ling explained. 'Fragrant Harbour.' She pointed out the peak rising above the brightly lit city of Victoria. 'You must take tram to top. Beautiful view,' she said.

Other than her demure greeting when Gordy had introduced them, this was the first time Howard had heard her speak. He leaned closer to catch the musical lilt of her words as she named the smaller islands and pointed out the local landmarks.

Gordy seemed to lose his nervousness as Shun-ling took on

the role of tour guide. 'Is Hong Kong your home?' he asked. 'I mean, were you born here?'

'No. We lived in small village near Nanking.' She hesitated for a moment, then said, 'Until Japanese come . . .' Her last words disappeared on the wind. Neither Howard nor Gordy asked her to repeat them. She remained silent for the rest of the ten-minute ferry ride.

As busy as Kowloon had been, the city of Victoria, crowded along the shores on the island side of the harbour teemed with humanity. The clacking of a multitude of wooden sandals on the pier's boardwalk competed with the hum of traffic and the cries of rickshaw drivers calling in broken English to potential customers. The scent of sandalwood and incense mingled with the odour of the overcrowded harbour. Taking in the sights and sounds as he made his way down the busy street, Howard could not help thinking that back home two soldiers escorting a beautiful Chinese girl might cause a stir or, at least, turn a few heads. Here they were not even noticed, just part of the mêlée swarming the causeways and sidewalks.

He found himself mentally composing a letter. *Imagine two million people, Lucy! More than double the entire population of the province of Manitoba!* It was hard to believe, let alone describe. On one hand Hong Kong was a cosmopolitan metropolis complete with modern buildings and stores more impressive than any he had ever seen. On the other, ancient temples with curled roofs crowded in beside rabbit warrens of fragile structures. And everywhere, on the bustling streets and in the darkened alleys, there were beggars.

At the first street corner an old woman squatted with her hand out. Howard stopped and pulled change from his pocket. The coins disappeared into a tattered sleeve. Suddenly other skeletal fingers were clawing at his arms, tugging at his uniform. A growing crowd, all pleading with words that needed no interpretation, pressed against him, pushing him backwards along the sidewalk in their scramble to get his attention. A passing Englishman batted at them with a rolled-up newspaper. 'Don't be encouraging them, you silly arse,' he shouted, 'or we'll all be swarmed.'

Gordy and Shun-ling pulled Howard into the street where they wove through the gridlocked traffic.

'If you want to give alms,' Shun-ling said, when they were safely on the other side, 'best you let me. I do it so no one see.'

Howard nodded. The incident had left him shaken and ashamed. It certainly wasn't something he planned to include in a letter home. People had gone hungry during the depression, but in all the time he'd lived in Winnipeg he'd never seen anything like the desperation in the eyes of those beggars. Neither had he seen shop windows like those they hurried by, all mockingly displaying expensive merchandise within arm's reach of starvation.

In front of the Harbour Hotel a street photographer, his camera mounted on a tripod, snapped pictures of passing pedestrians. Well, there's one thing that's just like home, Howard thought. When they were within the photographer's view range, he reached over Shun-ling's shoulder, grabbed Gordy's arm to pull him closer and grinned for the camera. The flash bulb went off and Howard took the numbered ticket from the photographer's outstretched hand, wondering what in the world had possessed him. His recent encounter with the beggars? Or perhaps the memory of him and Gordy mugging for a street photographer with Lucy on a downtown Winnipeg sidewalk on the day they had received their uniforms. Whatever it had been, though, it was worth it: when he passed the ticket to Gordy he was rewarded with a shy smile from Shun-ling. The first he had seen on her face.

'Now,' Gordy said, pocketing the photographer's ticket, 'dinner. Where should we eat?' He stopped in front of the hotel. 'Here?' he asked Shun-ling.

She shook her head and continued walking. Howard peered in at the brightly lit window. They might be invisible on the street but he was certain that if the three of them entered the busy hotel dining room heads would turn. Inside, men in white dinner jackets and officers in dress uniforms sat at linen-covered tables with ladies decked out in formal evening wear. Shun-ling's shabby outfit marked her as one of the city's poor.

Following her, they veered off the main thoroughfare into a dark side-street. In the dim light they wove through a maze of narrow alleyways until Shun-ling stopped in front of a shop window. Inspecting the rows of roasted ducks hanging in the yellow light, she said, 'This good.'

Inside they found an empty table at the back of the crowded restaurant. Howard sat down and looked around the smoke-filled room. Again, he and Gordy were the only white people to be seen. The chatter of foreign words and clicking of chop-sticks carried on, as the waiters pressed between the tables balancing huge food-laden trays over their heads. Gordy glanced at the array of strange dishes strewn on a nearby table, and asked Shun-ling to order.

The waiter appeared and placed a white teapot and glasses on the table. Shun-ling exchanged quick words with him and he disappeared again. After he left she poured the steaming tea into the glasses. When it appeared that no one else was going to begin a conversation, Howard said, 'You speak very good English, Shun-ling. Where did you learn?'

'My father. He was teacher.'

'And your sister? Does she speak English as well?' he asked.

'My sister, Shun-qin, does not speak,' she said, staring at her hands, which were folded in her lap.

'She doesn't speak English?'

She lifted her head, allowing her eyes to meet his. 'Not English. Not Chinese. She does not speak.'

'Oh. You mean she's mute,' Gordy said. 'Can't talk.'

Shun-ling turned to him. 'No. Not *cannot*. *Does* not. My sister does not speak. Not since Japanese come to our village.'

Howard saw the pain in her dark eyes. He remembered a *Life* magazine article about the reign of terror during the siege of Nanking in 1937. But to relate those brutal reports to reality in the form of a person sitting before him made the atrocities even more horrific. He did not know how to respond. Shun-ling returned to studying her hands until the waiter slid three dishes and three sets of chopsticks onto the table as he scurried by.

'I'll starve to death if I have to eat with those,' Gordy said.

Howard winced.

'I will teach,' Shun-ling said. Moments later, when the steaming platters of food appeared, she took Gordy's right hand. Her long elegant fingers held up his palm then gracefully placed the chopsticks in position. With movements so purposeful, so fluid that Howard thought her hands appeared to be boneless, she expertly guided his friend to reach over and pick up a slippery white morsel from the grey sauce in the first dish. His hand slowly lifted. She released her hold. 'Something that swims,' she said, as he managed to transfer the food to his mouth with a triumphant grin. Taking her own chopsticks, she used them to point to each of the equally unidentifiable dishes. 'Something that crawls, and something that flies.'

Howard had to take her word for it. Her explanations left him no closer to knowing exactly what he was eating – and he wasn't entirely sure he wanted to – but whatever it was, every flavour-filled bite certainly beat mess food.

While he and Gordy competed to master the awkward chopsticks Shun-ling watched their progress with the trace of a smile. She ate slowly, chewing each piece delicately. For every three pieces she took from each platter, Howard noticed, she ate only one. He caught Gordy's eye over her head and by unspoken agreement they both took less on their plates. By the end of the meal more than half of the food remained. The waiter reappeared to gather the platters and spoke briefly to Shun-ling. When he returned with the bill he placed a box wrapped in brown paper in front of her.

Outside, they followed Peter and Dick's directions and found their way to the Empress Theatre.

'Pretty snazzy,' Gordy said, taking in the elegant marquee. 'I'll bet Hollywood's got nothing on this.' Inside, they found three seats together in the balcony. The smell of ginger and sesame oil wafted from the package on Shun-ling's lap while 'Britain at War' newsreels played out. Watching the black-and-white images of bombers taking off over the English Channel Howard wondered if his brothers had been posted overseas yet.

When the main feature, *The Grapes of Wrath*, started and Henry Fonda appeared on the screen, Gordy whispered, 'Don't he look like Howard, eh?' He repeated it a number of times until someone shushed him from behind.

After the show a number of the women streaming out took a second glance at Howard and whispered behind their hands.

'See? I told you, you look like him.' Gordy elbowed his side.

Except, perhaps, for the nose and square jaw, Howard could not see the resemblance, although Lucy had often remarked on the similarity. Uncomfortable, he stepped away from the life-size poster of Henry Fonda as the idealistic young share-cropper, Tom Joad, looking up at the sky with the pain of the world in his blue eyes.

Shun-ling studied the poster, turning from Howard to the actor's face and back again. 'It is eyes,' she said. 'You have same eyes. Kind eyes.' Her fingers touched his arm for less than a second, a touch as light and feathery as a whisper, barely there then gone, but as they made their way towards the ferry pier he felt the heat from it radiate up his arm.

Along the harbour a night market had been set up on the boardwalks where vendors hawked everything from paper fans to silk robes. Soldiers and sailors, as well as British and Asian civilians, wandered among the stalls, inspecting the wares and bartering in broken English. Howard couldn't help comparing the city's almost carnival atmosphere with the devastation of London shown in that evening's newsreels. No blackouts or food rationing here.

Suddenly Gordy stopped walking. 'Excuse me, you two,' he said, 'but I gotta go see a man about a horse. Too much tea.' He gesticulated at a nearby hotel and set off towards it.

While they waited for him to return Howard and Shun-ling continued to browse among the stalls. One of the vendors held up an embroidered red dress. 'You buy for you girl,' he called.

'She's not—' Howard said, then noticed Shun-ling watching him. Her dark eyes sparkled with playful challenge. He laughed. 'Shun-ling,' he said, 'help me pick out something for my wife.'

'Oh – you are married.' She stepped closer to the stall to examine the folded silk garments.

Howard wondered if he had imagined the note of disappointment in her soft voice. He picked up an elaborate orange cheongsam. 'How about this?' he asked.

'Wrong colour,' Shun-ling said. 'Maybe too fancy.'

'Oh, I think Lucy could pull it off.' Howard refolded it and put it back down.

Shun-ling fingered the mandarin collar of a white and blue floral dress.

'That one much less,' the vendor said of the simple garment. Looking at Howard, he added, 'The same blue as you eyes.'

Shun-ling stroked the cotton material. 'This one better,' she said. 'Wear more.'

Howard pulled a green silk dress from the pile and unfolded it. 'What about this one?'

While Shun-ling haggled over the price Gordy returned. 'For Lucy,' Howard said, showing him the dress.

'I can just see her strutting her stuff in Winnipeg in that little number,' Gordy said.

As the vendor placed Howard's purchase in a paper bag, Gordy reached for the orange cheongsam. Holding it up to Shun-ling he asked if she would like him to buy it for her. Her face fell. 'You want me to be happy-time girl?'

'No. Oh, no, no, wait.' He laid it down. 'I just wanted to buy you something pretty.' Awkwardly he touched her shoulder. 'Listen,' he stammered, 'I don't want you to be anything. I don't need you to shine my shoes, shave me or wash my clothes. You don't have to do anything. Just friends, okay?'

Behind her Howard cocked his head down at the stall.

Gordy turned. 'Say, how about this one?' he asked, picking up the blue and white cotton dress Howard had indicated. 'Would you let a friend buy it for you?'

She looked longingly at it, then nodded.

Back in Kowloon she tried to dissuade Gordy from escorting her home, telling him her sister was frightened of all men except their father. 'I will be safe,' she said. 'I have nothing to steal, except this.' From the way she clung to the packages containing her dress and the left-over food Howard doubted anyone could have snatched them from her fingers.

Still Gordy insisted. He wouldn't come inside, he said, 'but I have to at least see you to your door. I couldn't leave you alone in these streets and be able to sleep tonight.'

Howard took his leave of them on Nathan Road. Instead of hailing a rickshaw he walked the few miles to camp, the bag containing Lucy's dress tucked under his arm. Back at the barracks he sat outside on the steps and lit a cigarette. Blowing out the match he noticed someone squatting in the shadows against the building. He recognized the man as one of the servants who shaved soldiers inside the barracks in the mornings. Did he sit there all night waiting?

Howard held up his pack of cigarettes. Smiling, the man approached, took one, put it between his lips and leaned down. After Howard lit it he motioned the man to sit next to him. He ventured a few questions, but his companion shook his head. No English. They sat smoking in silence. Howard gazed up at the brilliance of the starry sky. He thought of Lucy under the same stars then realized it was probably daylight at home. What time would it be? What might she be doing? He reached into his breast pocket and took out his pocket diary, opened it and removed the photograph tucked inside. He studied it for a few moments, then showed it to his companion. 'My wife,' he said, with pride.

'Ah.' The man nodded, the universal language of appreciation.

'We were childhood sweethearts,' Howard said.

'Ch . . . ch . . .' He attempted to imitate the sounds, then gave up.

'Yeah, childhood sweetheart,' Howard repeated, to her smiling face. His Lucy. She was his everything. 'I'm one lucky guy,' he said, more to himself than to his companion. God, he missed her.

So why was it that he could still feel the heat on his arm where Shun-ling had touched him?

16

It wasn't right that the sun was shining that morning. I believed the whole world should be crying. Heavy raindrops should soak the earth, splash up from the pavement, run down the windowpanes like endless tears. But sunlight streaked into the living room. By ten o'clock our house was already stifling, the air thick with summer heat. Outside, fluffy white clouds, eerily like those in Kipper's painting, floated in a bright blue sky. The sound of our neighbours' unsynchronized lawn sprinklers seeped in through the open living-room windows along with the smell of wet grass and sun-baked asphalt. The smells of summer. Smells that usually meant all the kids on our block were outside playing. I looked out at the lonely street. Where was everyone? Probably hiding in their houses so they would not have to see us leave for Mom's funeral.

I sat on the couch to wait for my aunt and uncle to arrive. My anger at the sunshine spilled over to include almost everyone and everything. I was angry with my aunt for making me wear the stupid white Mary Jane shoes and silly outfit, angry at all the kids on our street who still had mothers, and angry at Jesus, who I would never let into my heart now. Most of all I was angry with myself for going to Bible School last Saturday because if I'd stayed home that day maybe Mom wouldn't have gone out.

Beside me, Kipper sat fidgeting with his hat. His jacket sleeves were a little short and white socks showed at the bottom of his pant legs, but the outfit Mom had bought him for the art show was still like new. He tugged his hat down onto his forehead, then lifted his eyebrows to move it up and down, which he did unconsciously whenever he was nervous.

'Stop it!' I snapped. I kicked the back of my shoes against the couch and looked at Dad for a reaction. He sat hunched in his chair, wearing the suit Frankie had magically produced for him. At the expression on his face I instantly regretted my outburst. But my father wasn't focusing on Kipper adjusting his hat, or my heels slamming against the bottom of the couch: he was staring at my hands.

'No gloves,' he said, in choked whisper. 'Please take them off, Ethie.'

Relieved, I tugged off the white gloves my aunt had bought and stuffed them between the cushions.

My father's fingers tapped on the arm of his chair and sweat glistened on his forehead. Frankie stopped pacing. He reached into his pocket and handed Dad a handkerchief.

I had never thought of my brother Frankie as anything other than an adult. Dad's protector. Mom's best friend. He had always seemed like a grown-up to me, like a younger version of our father. The version in old pre-war photographs. But as I watched him resume pacing, his chin quivered and I saw the boy he must once have been. 'You look really handsome,' I blurted, then felt foolish. He must have been pretty much used to being told so, but not by his little sister. And not on the day of his mother's funeral.

One side of Frankie's mouth lifted in an attempt at a smile, but it looked more like a grimace. He leaned down and touched my cheek, a gesture so gentle and unexpected that my eyes filled. 'Thanks, Sis,' he said.

I bit the insides of my cheeks and rolled my eyes back, a trick

Mom had once told me would ward off unwanted tears. But one escaped anyway. I jumped up and went to the window to stare out at the sun-drenched street again.

The scent of Sweet Williams floated up from the flowerbed beneath the window. And with the perfume came a vision of Mom kneeling in the garden cutting a bouquet. *She sticks her nose into the colourful array, inhales deeply, then offers them to me. 'Isn't that the most heavenly smell, Ethie?'*

Ever since Kipper had given me Mom's picture on Monday I had gone from not being able to see her face to seeing her everywhere. Whenever I went into the bathroom I could see her in the medicine-cabinet mirror. *She puckers her lips and applies a coat of ruby lipstick, tilts her head slightly to the side, smiles at the effect, then turns and, with exaggerated gestures, dabs colour onto my lips.*

When Kipper first came into the living room wearing his suit I'd seen her adjusting his bow tie, as she had before they went to Marlene's art show to sell his paintings. *She tightens the bow, then pats it down, beaming at him. 'My handsome fella, you're going to knock 'em dead.'*

Earlier that morning, as Mrs Fenwick had braided my hair, I'd imagined my mother standing there. *She smiles and reaches up to twirl a strand on my forehead. 'There was a little girl, who had a little curl . . .'*

And as I stared out of the window I saw my mother standing with one foot on the running board of the car parked at the kerb. I blinked and our old green Hudson sat alone and empty on the street.

Although she always said she'd bought it for Dad, that car was really Mom's. And the reason, Frankie said, why Aunt Mildred had insisted on picking us up for the service in a limousine. 'She's petrified of us showing up in Mom's "gangster car".'

Mom's gangster car. That was what he'd called it from the day she'd brought home the green 1947 Hudson – mostly because of Aunt Mildred's horrified reaction to where she'd bought it.

I was nine the day Mom spotted the announcement for the police auction in the *Daily Province*. She'd clipped out the article and placed it on the table in front of Dad at suppertime that night.

Money was a touchy subject with Dad. It was the only thing he seemed to pay attention to in the running of our lives. He would spend a tense weekend every payday organizing white envelopes and paying the monthly bills. Any mention of money seemed to pain him. 'An old-fashioned notion, left over from the depression,' Mom would mutter, but she usually avoided talking about finances. Except when it came to the issue of a family car. Our father insisted he didn't mind taking the bus to work and that an automobile was a luxury we could do without.

We were not the only family on Barclay Street without a car, but when Mom read the article about the upcoming auction she decided it was a sign that the time was right. She started her campaign on Dad. His lack of interest in the article did not put her off. Every night that week she reminded him of the coming auction, her stories of bargains growing wilder. When Dad told her he couldn't afford to take the day off, she said that was fine: she would go on her own. His eyebrows rose. 'A woman at a police auction?' he asked.

'And why not?' she countered.

'Right. Why not?' he admitted, a smile playing at his lips. Then he added, 'Except that we can't afford it.' His claim that he was broke fell on deaf ears: there were bargains to be had and she meant to have one. Finally, on the morning of the auction before he left for work, Dad fanned open his wallet to reveal a single twenty-dollar bill. She plucked it out before he could say anything.

I sat on her bed and watched her getting dressed. She rolled silk stockings up her legs and attached them to a frayed garter belt, pushing a nickel through one of the suspenders to replace the missing tab. She surveyed her closet, then pulled out a plastic-covered hanger and winked at me. 'A special dress for a special occasion,' she said. Her stockings might have had runs in them and a coin helping to hold them up, but when I saw that Kelly green dress slip over her head I knew this was serious business.

In the early-morning drizzle Kipper and I huddled under a bent black umbrella with her at the bus-loop on Victoria Drive. I remember the warehouse on Water Street in shades of black and white. Grey light spilled in from the large sliding doors. Naked lightbulbs hung from the ceiling on long cords, their white glare absorbed by the black walls and grease-stained concrete floor. The air smelled of dust and oil. And men. Just as my father had predicted there were no other women.

Kipper and I trailed behind Mom as she joined the crowds inspecting the vehicles. She walked around each car as if she knew what to look for. She opened doors to peer inside, kicked tyres, and if the hood was raised, she inspected the engine. She paid no attention to the curious stares and appreciative glances. She appeared unaware that she was the only woman in sight, and certainly the only one there with children in tow.

When she was done we stood together at the back. While we waited for the auction Mom kept us entertained by guessing the occupations of the men. She nodded at the huddled groups comparing notes. 'Car dealers,' she whispered. Anxious young men trying to look casual were 'boys looking for their very first car', and older ones in suits nervously checking their watches were 'businessmen sneaking a morning off work to check out the bargains'. According to Mom, every profession, from penny-pinching teachers to antiques collectors, was represented. Workmen in grey overalls and policemen in blue uniforms were easy to spot. All the men, whoever they were, pretended she wasn't there. Still, I noticed many stealing glances at her while she whispered her appraisals to us.

When the hands on the clock behind the wire cage on the wall said exactly ten, the crowds parted. The auctioneer approached the first car. He pulled the numbered card from the windshield and, with his hand on the hood, started the auction. The bidding opened at one hundred dollars. I had a sinking feeling when I thought of my father's twenty-dollar bill in Mom's purse.

Before I knew it the auctioneer's palm had slammed down on the car's hood. 'Sold!' he yelled. 'For one hundred and seventy-five dollars!'

He moved to the next car. Once again, the songlike string of words came out of his mouth, until finally he took a gulp of air and announced, 'Sold!' He auctioned off car after car in the same way.

The bidding rose higher as he moved along. If Mom was surprised by the prices she gave no sign and waited calmly. Then he came to the dark green 1947 Hudson. The dust-covered sedan was surely the oldest car in the warehouse, and the one she had spent the most time inspecting. When the auctioneer placed his palm on the arched fender Mom sprang into action. Grabbing Kipper and me, she pushed her way through the crowd, squeezed to the front and stood in full view of the auctioneer. With the two of us gathered to her like armour, she waited, ready for battle.

There was no response at the call for an opening bid of fifty dollars. The auctioneer took a breath and said, 'Do-I-hear-forty-who-will-give-forty-dollars?'

'Five dollars!' my mother called.

Laughter came in muffled spurts, then rippled through the warehouse. Even the auctioneer fought with a smile playing on his lips. Choosing to ignore her bid, he repeated his call for forty dollars. A second voice called, 'Ten!'

The last murmurs of chuckles stopped. Heads turned to locate the second bidder. I followed the direction of the auctioneer's gaze to where one of the car dealers stood slouched against the wall, a toothpick hanging from his lip, a grey snap-brim fedora pushed back on his forehead. Apparently unconcerned with the progress of the auction, he concentrated on the clipboard he was holding.

I looked up at Mom. She had located the competing bidder as well. With her eyes narrowed and firmly fixed on him, she called, 'I bid eleven dollars.'

There was no laughter this time. The entire warehouse was silent, as if holding its breath. The dealer lazily raised his head. His gaze travelled across the room to where my mother stood, in all her defiant glory. Their eyes met. He eyed her up and down, the toothpick moving slowly from one side of his mouth to the other. 'Twelve,' he challenged.

'Thirteen,' she called, without missing a beat.

As if they were the only two in the room, and he had all the time in the world, Mom's opponent eyed her.

'Going once!' the auctioneer sang out.

With their eyes locked in a defiant staring contest, neither Mom nor the car dealer flinched.

'Going twice!'

Her back straight and her chin held high, Mom did not blink.

Without taking his eyes off her the car dealer raised his pen. I saw the corners of his mouth lift with a hint of a grin. He was enjoying this. I looked from him to the auctioneer, who had all but stopped the auction while he waited for the dealer's response. The dealer, still locked into Mom's stare, touched the brim of his hat in a two-fingered salute, then made a slight bow towards her. Slowly he shifted his gaze to the auctioneer's questioning eyes and shook his head.

A palm slammed down on the hood. 'Sold for thirteen dollars to the lady in green!'

All eyes were on Mom as she strode over triumphantly to re-trieve her ticket from the auctioneer. And everyone saw – how could they not? – the coin fall between her legs. Horrified, I watched the nickel from her garter belt bounce on the concrete with a clink and roll across the floor.

Mom had always said that even if you only have a penny in your pocket you should walk like you had a million dollars. And that was exactly what she did as her nickel found its way to the feet of the startled car dealer. Her head held high, she took the receipt from the auctioneer, then strode back to us. 'Well, now,' she said, 'we'll just let these gentlemen get on with gentlemen's business.' Then, taking our hands, she marched through the parting crowd to the back of the room to pay for her new car. The sound of shuffling feet, coughs and throat-clearing carried on for a few seconds before the auction resumed.

But Mom was not finished yet. After she paid she was told she must remove the vehicle from the warehouse as soon as the auction was complete. She had never driven a car so it was arranged that someone would park it on the street until Dad could pick it up. It was a young police officer who climbed in and turned the key. Nothing happened. He pumped the gas pedal and turned the key again. Nothing. He climbed out and, with Mom peering over his shoulder, lifted the hood. The car was missing a battery.

Like a wet hen with her feathers ruffled, Mom marched back to the counter, indignant that Vancouver's 'finest' would sell an unsuspecting woman a car with no battery. Even though the rules were that cars came 'as is', Mom argued and complained and shamed them. She kicked up such a fuss that a new battery was provided, which cost the Vancouver City Police Department fifteen dollars, two dollars more than she had paid for the car, as she was always quick to point out whenever she told the story.

She sat triumphantly behind the steering-wheel after she had telephoned her sister, while Kipper and I bounced around in the back, raising clouds of dust from the cloth seats.

Aunt Mildred arrived, more embarrassed than impressed by Mom's purchase. 'For heaven's sake, Lucy, if you needed a car why didn't you ask us to lend you money to get a decent one? Who knows where this has been?' Our aunt's indignation did not end there. A police reporter for the *Daily Province* had attended the auction. The next day a photograph of Mom standing with her foot on the running board of her thirteen-dollar car, looking like some wild-haired and beautiful huntress standing over her kill, appeared in the paper.

'Lucy! How could you?' Aunt Mildred wailed.

But Mom was proud of her purchase and enjoyed telling the story of how she went downtown to a police auction with a twenty-dollar bill, bought Dad a car and came home with change. Her story got better with each telling. She always said she got such a good deal because she outbid the car dealers. She claimed innocence when Dad teased her that it might have had something to do with the effect she had had on the men at the auction.

I suspected he might be right because I saw the look she gave that car dealer, the look that could stop unruly children or grown men dead in their tracks, the don't-you-dare-say-another-word look. I had also seen that identical challenge in the steely-eyed glares of the army of men standing behind her.

After Frankie started work at the mill the first thing he bought was a second-hand Studebaker. It was a few years newer than the Hudson but, according to Mom, had far less character. Frankie argued against this: the girls all thought his blue bullet-nosed coupé was sexy. When Dad began to travel to work with him, Mom learned to drive and took over the Hudson. Either Frankie or Dad was always tinkering with it. 'It's held together with hay-wire and a promise,' Frankie teased her. 'One day it's just going to sigh and give up the ghost.' But there it was now, parked out on the street as if it was waiting for her to jump in and drive it away.

A black limousine pulled up behind it. 'They're here,' I said, my heart pounding. Even though I had insisted I wanted to go to the funeral, I was suddenly scared.

'I need to go pee.' Kipper jumped up and ran to the bathroom.

The limousine's door opened and Uncle Sidney and Aunt Mildred climbed out.

I watched them make their way to the porch. Everything my aunt wore was black, her dress, her hat and shoes, even her stockings.

Frankie opened the door before they knocked. Dad pushed himself up from the chair and I moved over beside him. 'Are we all ready?' Aunt Mildred asked, from behind the black net veil covering her face.

'Ready,' Kipper called, from the hallway. He came around the corner wiping his hands on his pants.

Behind her veil I saw my aunt's eyebrows rise when he joined us in the living room, but she said nothing and waved us forward. Like condemned prisoners we filed out into the bright sunshine. When Kipper came out onto the porch, Aunt Mildred snapped, 'Take off that ridiculous hat.'

Confused, Kipper reached up and held onto it, looking helplessly from her to me, his eyes filling.

With a flash of burning heat in my chest, I realized exactly what my mother would have done. And what she would have expected of me. Squaring my shoulders, I put an arm around Kipper. 'It's all right,' I said. 'Leave it on.' I guided him forward. 'He's wearing it,' I said, as we passed my aunt. 'Mom gave him that hat.'

17

It wasn't until years later that I would come to understand that death was no stranger to our father. He was all too familiar with its raw truth. He knew the way it looked, sounded, smelled. He'd lost both his parents before he was twenty. He had become a man with the first battlefield explosion when flesh, bone and blood had landed on his helmet.

He knew it cut just as deeply long after the Grim Reaper had staked his claim, when he had returned from the war to learn of the death of his three brothers. All lost, all disappeared on bombing missions over the English Channel, less than six months after they had arrived in Britain.

Yes, he knew death. But even Frankie would remember watching Dad hunched over in the back of the limousine on the way to our mother's funeral, and feeling afraid that the unexpected blow of her death had hit him with such force that he might never straighten again.

Memory is often fickle, coming in fits and starts, vague at best. But my memory of that day is all too clear. The air inside the back of the limousine was thick with the musty smell of leather. The rusty brown seats, the same colour as my father's bomber jacket, were cracked and faded, not by rain but perhaps by thousands of mourners' tears. That animal scent would for ever after remind me of the journey from our house to Forest Lawn.

I was squeezed in on the bench seat with my father and

brothers. Directly across from us, Aunt Mildred and Uncle Sidney sat at opposite ends of an identical leather seat. We rode in silence, each lost in our own thoughts as the limousine drove slowly down Kingsway. I stared out of the window, wondering how the world could look so normal.

The traffic around us slowed, making way for the black funeral car to pass with its cargo of bereaved. *Relieved it's not them, not their turn.* I remembered Mom once voicing that thought as she pulled over with the rest of the traffic to allow a funeral procession to claim the road.

We passed Boundary Road and the dense forest of Central Park. And I realized I would never walk those paths again while she talked about how the prairie girl in her would always feel overwhelmed by the huge and magnificent trees in the middle of the city. Everything, everything was Mom. How could the world still exist without her in it?

Too soon we were on Royal Oak, creeping through the massive wrought-iron gates of Forest Lawn Cemetery. We wound along the narrow road and through acres of flat stones marking graves in the manicured lawn. Beside me, Dad's jaw clenched at the sight of one lonely grave surrounded with floral wreaths and a pile of earth.

The chapel sat on the highest knoll, next to the overflowing parking lot. We pulled up directly in front of the marble steps. No one moved until the driver got out and came around to open the door. Standing outside, our eyes adjusting to the glare of the day, I think we all became momentarily confused. But Aunt Mildred propelled us forward, herding us up the steps.

Inside, the heavy perfume of lilies filled the foyer. Kipper looked around. 'It's a church,' he said, removed his hat and held it against his chest.

The four of us stood huddled together while neighbours,

friends and strangers streamed into the already crowded chapel. Some touched Dad's shoulder or arm lightly as they passed, murmuring quiet words. A man came to usher us, with Aunt Mildred and Uncle Sidney, down a hall and into a dimly lit room at the front of the chapel. A large window covered with sheer grey curtains separated us from the other people, and from the flower-covered casket.

I sank down onto the tapestry-covered pew next to Dad. Kipper sat on his other side, one hand patting Dad's knee, the other clutching his hat. Beside me Frankie sat ramrod straight, staring ahead. I pressed close, as if I could burrow into him.

The faint sound of sniffling and blowing of noses carried in from the chapel. I peered through the curtain, over the top of the flowers and into the crowded room. All the seats were full, and many people stood at the back. I recognized Mrs Manson, with her husband and children, in the front pew. Behind them, more of our neighbours' faces came into focus. The Prices, the Blacks and the Johnsons. Ardith, Mary, Susie. Everyone from Barclay Street was there. But the others? So many. I recognized some ladies from Marlene's art shop, from their card night. Among them I spotted the tear-stained face of Dora Fenwick, Danny sitting beside her.

The soft organ music, which I had only just noticed, came to an end. Behind a wooden podium the minister, a stranger, cleared his throat. How long had he been there? He started speaking. I tuned out the unfamiliar voice talking about things that had nothing to do with my mother. Finally the sermon ended and the organ music started again. A few brave voices joined the minister's as he sang, 'There's an old rugged cross . . .'

A moment of silence followed the hymn, broken by a fresh round of nose-blowing and coughs. 'The next hymn was one of

Lucy Coulter's favourites,' the minister announced. 'Number eighty-seven in your hymnals.'

How would he know Mom's favourite? Who would have told him? Aunt Mildred? Dad? Would Dad even have known?

The sound of paper rustling filled the silence as everyone searched for the hymn. Frankie nodded at the first bars of organ music. Then Kipper jumped up. Marching on the spot, he sang out, 'Onward Christian so-o-oldiers', his loud voice filling the small room. Frankie and I rose together to sing with him. When Uncle Sidney joined us, Aunt Mildred sank back into her seat, her head in her hands. Dad sat staring at a place none of us could see.

After the final chorus, when everyone was settled back in their seats, the minister announced that the family wished to speak. Removing a piece of folded paper from his breast pocket, Frankie leaned forward. 'Dad,' he prompted. When there was no response he reached past me and nudged Dad's arm with the paper. 'The poem,' he whispered.

But our father was beyond hearing him. Frankie heaved a sigh and stood up. He gave Dad one last glance before he squared his shoulders, then went through the door into the chapel. The minister stepped back, allowing him to take the pulpit.

'This is not easy,' Frankie began, smoothing the paper before him, 'but I have a promise to keep.' His voice cracked, he swallowed and began again. 'Anyone who knew our mother knew she loved poetry. Poetry of all kinds. Good and bad, silly and serious. She was as apt to repeat Byron as Ogden Nash, or a simple nursery rhyme at the most appropriate, or inappropriate, moment.'

Chuckles of agreement floated to us from the pews, and a few heads nodded. 'She particularly loved this William Wordsworth poem, if for no other reason than it contained her name. Mom never denied her vanity,' he added, with a half-smile, then took a moment to allow the murmurs to die down. 'It was her desire that . . .' he glanced towards Dad '. . . that some day it would be read at her funeral. None of us ever imagined that "some day" would come so soon.' His jaw tightened and he blinked a few times. 'Before I honour her request, I would like to say that, while the sermon today was heartfelt,' he turned to the minister with an apologetic smile, 'it was not my mother. It was not about the strong, spirited woman who would fight for her beliefs, her children, her husband at the drop of a hat. She is . . . was a woman with a fiery temper that rivalled her red hair, who loved a good tear-jerker movie and the TV show *Name That Tune*, even though she was tone deaf. A woman who played poker instead of bridge.' He looked up at the ceiling and whispered, 'Sorry, Mom.' He cleared his throat. 'She encouraged her children to be the best they could be – who believed that there are no "ordinary" people because everyone, she always said, was extraordinary in some way.' He took a deep breath. 'She was many things to all of you, I am sure. She may not have been the best housekeeper in the world, or even the best cook, but God knows, her children know, she was the best mother.' He lowered his head and smoothed the paper again. 'This is for her,' he said. Then, in a strong, clear voice, he began to read:

> *She dwelt among the untrodden ways*
> *Beside the springs of Dove,*
> *A maid whom there were none to praise,*
> *And very few to love.*
>
> *A violet by a mossy stone*
> *Half hidden by the eye!*

Fair as a star, when only one
Is shining in the sky.

She lived unknown, and few could know
When Lucy ceased to be;
But she is in her grave, and, oh,
The difference to me!

He took a moment, then raised his head and added, 'The line "And very few to love" makes no sense in reference to our mother because everyone who knew her loved her. And, yes, what a difference, a huge difference, her absence will make to us all.' He carefully folded the paper and, replacing it in his breast pocket, left the pulpit.

Outside, I stood between Frankie and Kipper while the crowd filed past us. Comments on how wonderful she looked made me angry. Didn't these people know my mother at all?

'Just like Marilyn Monroe,' a woman whispered to her companion. 'Such a waste.'

I looked up at my father, but he hadn't heard. Once again, even though his body was standing with us, he wasn't there.

Then a strange thing happened. The veil lifted from his eyes. Shaking his head as if he didn't believe what he was seeing, Dad took a step towards two men approaching him. I'd never seen either before. They wore identical blue jackets but the shorter man's sleeve was pinned up at the elbow where his right arm should have been. The taller man offered Dad his hand.

'Ken Campbell,' Dad said, his voice a jagged whisper.

'We read about Lucy in the Legion newspaper,' the man said, folding Dad's outstretched hand in both of his. 'Of course we had to come.'

18

20 November 1941: Hong Kong

'I think Lawson's trying to kill us,' Ken Campbell moaned, throwing himself, splayed, onto the army cot next to Howard's. The metal frame shook under the assault of his six-foot-three-inch body.

Howard removed his steel helmet and grinned down at the radio operator. The size and bulk of his fellow Grenadier was in stark contrast to his cherubic face, which was still covered with dirt. But there was nothing infantile about Private Campbell. Howard had seen his brute strength during the day's manoeuvres and was glad they were in the same platoon.

'Guess our commander doesn't think those Japs are gathering along the border for a campfire sing-along,' Howard said, unbuttoning his sweat-stained uniform.

'Decoys,' the British machine-gunner Peter Young retorted from his bed, where he was sipping tea. 'If there's an invasion – and that's not bloody likely – Major Maltby says it'll be a naval assault.'

Most of the British soldiers within hearing distance muttered their agreement. Some of the Canadians, however, supported their own commanding officer's view that the major thrust would come overland from the north. Early that morning Brigadier Lawson had announced that they would begin immediately to familiarize themselves with the lie of the land, both on the mainland and the island. Training exercises would be intense, he promised the troops, but anyone with the energy and inclination at the end of the day would find the issue of evening passes to be liberal.

Howard's aching muscles were testament to their first day of manoeuvres. Yet, as exhausted as he was from climbing up and down the torturous hillsides under a glaring sun, he was unable to resist when Gordy invited him to join him and Shun-ling again for the evening.

'Hey, Campbell,' Gordy called, heading for the showers, 'come along with us to the Sun Sun tonight.'

'Nah,' Ken said, pushing himself up. 'I'm headed over to the cinema with Black and Richards. I'm a married man, you know.'

Shun-ling stood outside the camp gates wearing the blue and white floral dress. Looking shyly pleased with herself, she blushed and lowered her eyes as they approached.

'Wow, hubba-hubba.' Gordy whistled in appreciation. 'You'll be the prettiest girl on the dance-floor.'

She lifted her eyelids. 'First we go please to Kowloon? Then after, up to Peak?'

'We're in your hands.' He laughed, holding up his arms in surrender.

Howard's rickshaw followed theirs, weaving through traffic, down cobbled back-streets, and away from the bustling commercial area to an older part of town. In the shadowed alleyways cloth banners hung above the doorways of curio shops and smoking parlours, the black-painted characters undulating with the slightest breath of wind. Overhead, laundry stretched across open windows and rickety balconies where entire families sought relief from the late-afternoon heat. Black-haired children sat between the rungs with feet swinging, while their parents lounged in wicker chairs fanning themselves. On one crowded balcony, four storeys above the street, a group of teenagers leaned on a balustrade, which looked as if it might topple under their weight. They called down greetings to the 'soldiahs' in the rickshaws below, giggling behind their hands when Howard returned their waves.

The friendliness of the Chinese amazed him. Everywhere they went they were greeted with exuberance, treated like heroes come to keep the colony safe. He hoped they could live up to it.

Their rickshaws slowed and came to a stop in front of a narrow shop. The minute the drivers had been paid they padded away, swallowed into the shadows. The glow from an Rx sign in the window cast an orange aura around Shun-ling's profile as she led them inside.

An overhead bell tinkled with the opening and closing of the door. The interior of the shop looked like a miniature version of Howard's father-in-law's drugstore back home. He recognized many familiar products on the tightly packed shelves, from Bayer aspirin to rubber enema hoses. But the man locking the glass display case on the wall behind the counter appeared nothing like Lucy's father. Instead of the white pharmacist's jacket, he wore a floor-length black robe. A matching round satin cap sat on his head and a long, braided queue hung like a rope from beneath it.

He pocketed the key somewhere in the folds of the robe, then turned around. His round face broke into a smile. 'Feng Shun-ling,' he cried.

'Ah Sam.' She acknowledged him with a bow and they chatted in Chinese for a few moments.

As she introduced Howard and Gordy the man's eyes appraised them. He acknowledged each with a slight bow, his arms crossed, his hands lost inside the wide sleeves.

Shun-ling continued to speak. When she stopped the shop-keeper nodded. 'I see,' he said. 'What you gentlemen need will not be found here.' He waved his hand to dismiss the Western drugs, then stepped out from behind the counter. 'What you require for your affliction, *Cimex lectularius*, those nasty little nocturnal beasts, warrants the skills of an apothecary,' he said, speaking not only in perfect English but with a British accent. He beckoned to them, and led them through the maze of shelves. His long braid swayed with each step he took while he continued to explain the scourge of bedbugs over his shoulder. Behind him Howard raised his eyebrows at Gordy, wondering if he had told Shun-ling about their problem. His friend shook his head and shrugged.

In a darkened corner Ah Sam pulled up a bamboo curtain to expose a wall of tiny wooden drawers, each with a different symbol carved into it. On the shelves above, a multitude of jars and bottles held powders, dried leaves, herbs and roots, shrivelled frogs' legs, dried lizards and unrecognizable animal parts.

'How is your honourable father, Shun-ling?' Ah Sam asked, taking down a jar of green powder and expertly tapping tiny amounts into two small vials of oil.

'He is well, thank you,' she answered.

'Why does he not visit me? I miss our chess games. And,' he added, with a chuckle, 'our philosophical debates.'

'My father is a very busy man.'

Ah Sam arched an almost non-existent eyebrow, but let the comment go. He corked both vials, then lifted a burning candle from the counter and poured wax over them. 'And your sister?' he asked, setting the bottles aside to let the wax harden.

'Shun-qin is the same.'

He reached under the counter and pulled out a tin box the

size of a book. He wrapped it in a square of brown paper. 'For her throat,' he said, tying it with a piece of string. 'These may not make her speak again, but who knows? If she believes? And,' he added, with a wink, which seemed almost comical to Howard, 'they taste like candy.'

'I am sorry,' Shun-ling said, lowering her eyes. 'I have no money.'

'No, no, my dear. It is my gift. Please be gracious and accept.'

'Thank you, Ah Sam. Once more we are in your debt.'

'Oh, pshaw,' he said, as he wrapped the vials. 'It is nothing. It has been my great pleasure to see you. Please remember me to your father.'

He handed the packages to Howard and Gordy. 'Ancient Chinese medicine,' he said, his face serious again. 'It works. A single application is all it will take to relieve the itching, and after that the bugs will leave you alone.'

He did not hesitate to take their money, which Howard estimated to be less than two dollars. A small price to pay if it would put an end to the unbearable itching.

The pharmacist bowed as Howard thanked him. 'My pleasure.'

'So how come you speak like a Brit?' Gordy asked.

'Well, my dear sir,' Ah Sam fixed his gaze on him with an indulgent smile that both excused the rude question while gently chastising it, 'I *am* a "Brit", as you so eloquently put it. I was born in London. I attended Oxford. After I became a pharmacist I moved to Hong Kong, which also, sir, is British.'

'Oh – I –' Gordy stuttered '– I only meant, well, the clothes, the . . .'

'All extremely good for business, wouldn't you say? A Chinaman in traditional finery?' he held out his arms, ruffling the flowing satin garment. 'This is a novelty that pleases both the Europeans and the Asians.'

* * *

While the funicular tram rose slowly up the steep mountain-side towards the Peak, Howard asked Shun-ling about Ah Sam.

'We meet him when we first come to Hong Kong, three years ago,' she answered, gazing blankly at the lush vegetation within arm's reach of the tram window. 'After we escape Japanese.'

Listening to her, Howard was suddenly struck by the realization that while they were in the shop she had spoken perfect English. Yet now she had reverted to pidgin. It occurred to him that, like the pharmacist, Shun-ling was playing a part, acting her subservient role.

And why not? She trusted Ah Sam. She had no reason to trust anyone who had bought her company.

'My sister need medicine,' she went on. 'Some other north-erners tell us Ah Sam will help. He not charge so much. Tries all time to give it to us free. But my father is proud man. Ah Sam, my father, both intellectuals. Both like talking. Ah Sam sometime find jobs for my father interpreting. Not so much any more. My father is too proud to go see him. Does not want his friend to see how far down he fall.'

Howard couldn't help but wonder at such a strange culture. Too proud to accept charity from a friend, but not too proud to sell a daughter to a stranger?

The smoke-filled dance hall above the Sun Sun Café was crowded to standing room only. Above the din of conversation the tinny sound of Glenn Miller's Orchestra playing 'The Nearness of You' came from the Wurlitzer in the corner. On the floor, the dance girls pressed close to their uniformed part-ners, their painted faces surveying the room for their next customer.

Howard left Gordy and Shun-ling beside the jukebox and pushed through the swaying crowd to fetch drinks. Spotting

Dick Baxter's tuft of orange hair, he squeezed between him and Peter at the bar. 'Hello, chums,' he said, trying but failing to mimic a British accent. 'Three beers,' he called to the bartender, his voice raised to be heard above the noise. 'And two for my friends here,' he added, leaning against the bar.

'You missed the action,' Peter said.

While they waited for the drinks to arrive the machine-gunners filled him in. 'A number of British lads got into a little tussle with the Canadians,' Dick said. 'There were fisticuffs, but it's all settled now.'

'What happened?'

Dick shrugged. 'Seems some of our boys were getting tired of watching you colonials throwing money around like there's no tomorrow.'

'Aw, they're just having some fun,' Howard said. He pulled a handful of coins from his pocket, and counted them out on the bar. 'They're like kids in a candy store right now,' he said, reaching for the beers sliding towards him.

'Well, you might want to spread the word to tone it down,' Peter said, taking the dripping mug Howard passed to him. 'There's a lot of grumbling among the ranks. Word has it that you blokes brought next to no equipment with you.' He raised his beer and looked at Howard over the foam. 'That you're relying on the garrison for almost everything,' he added, a note of challenge in his voice.

'Everything will sort itself out when our supply ship arrives,' Howard said, handing Dick a beer. 'It's on its way.'

'It bloody well better be,' Dick said, taking a sip, then wiping his upper lip. 'We don't have enough equipment and ammunition of our own, and now you chaps come with deep pockets but empty hands. No offence, mate, but many of us are wondering what good you'll be.'

'What good we'll be *when*?' Howard asked, reaching for the other beer mugs. 'When the non-existent Japanese show up?'

Peter grinned. 'No worries.' He slapped Howard on the back. 'Dicky and I are pulling your leg. Tell you what,' he said, winking at his friend. 'If either shows up – your ship or the Japanese – we'll buy the beer.'

'You're on.' Howard laughed.

Balancing the three beer mugs as he headed back across the room he found himself hoping he was right and that the equipment *would* arrive soon. Today the British Army had loaned Bren-gun carriers to some lucky fellows, but none had found their way to his regiment. During manoeuvres he and Gordy had had to take turns shouldering the guns from one position to another. And as if they weren't heavy enough, the steep terrain was a killer. Once again, Howard felt grateful for the months they had spent delivering ice in Winnipeg. Still, working his way through the dancers to rejoin Gordy and Shunling, he could feel the cramps in the back of his calves from the day's exercises.

Later, after he returned to the barracks, he sat down on his cot to write to Lucy. He would leave out any mention of the repetitive gun drills, the trench digging and battlefield manoeuvres. Instead he tried to describe the sights of this exciting city. He wrote about the tram ride up to the Peak, high above the island.

Railcars rising straight up a sheer mountainside! Right through jungles and over the roofs of houses like palaces! Really, Lucy! It's like being at the top of the world. I could even see the lights of the junks down in the harbour. Whole families live on those funny-looking boats, some never setting foot on land their entire life, we are told.

Everything I see here I see through your eyes. Would you like it? I'm guessing you would. I think you'd be amazed at some of the sights. I'm afraid all us guys are still walking around bug-eyed. The major pastime in this city seems to be shopping. I bought you a green silk Chinese dress. Don't worry, they cost next to nothing here.

Everyone smokes; even the poorest find money for cigarettes. I have a confession to make, Lucy. I've taken it up myself. Hooked on the army rations of free cigarettes. I'll quit when I get home.

I've made a friend of sorts with an Asian chap, a barber who comes to shave some of the British fellows in the mornings. I share my cigarettes with him when I come back to the barracks in the evening. Tonight I brought him a beer. He can't speak a word of English but we sat outside the barracks admiring your photograph like two lovesick schoolboys.

He didn't write about the hundreds of thousands of refugees crowding the city, about the great divide between the very rich and the very poor – Lucy would hate to hear all that. He said nothing about the bodies thrown onto the backs of the death-patrol trucks. And he neglected to mention Ah Sam, how drawn he had felt to the man, a product of two cultures. For a moment in the little store he had been tempted to share his own dreams of becoming a pharmacist with him, but had kept the thoughts to himself. He could tell her all that when he got home.

Neither did he mention the thought that had struck him as he stood on the Peak above the South China Sea. It was a breathtaking view that lost its appeal when he wondered, if Brigadier Lawson was right and an invasion from the north pushed them back to the island, where would they go from there?

19

Frankie found me. I squinted against the light spilling into the closet to see him standing in the open doorway, Dad's suit jacket folded over his arm. 'Hello, Ethie,' he said, as if there was nothing unusual about finding me sitting on Mom's closet floor with one of her blouses pressed to my face. The musky scent of her perspiration and perfume leaked out of the door with the darkness.

Frankie reached for a hanger above my head. 'What're you doing in here?' he asked.

'Sitting.' I wrapped my arms around my knees.

'Uh-huh. I see.' He hung Dad's jacket above me. 'Some of your friends are outside,' he said, taking off his own jacket. 'Why don't you come and say hello?'

I shook my head. They were who I was hiding from. Them, and all the neighbours gathered in our house. I had seen how they looked at me at the graveside. From now on I would be the girl whose mother was put into a hole in the ground. 'I don't want to see them,' I mumbled.

Frankie hung up his jacket and loosened his skinny knit tie. 'Okay,' he said, rolling up his shirt sleeves. 'But you must be stifling in here. At least come out and see Kipper – he's been looking for you.' He reached down and offered me his hand. 'He's over in the park.'

I let him pull me to my feet and lead me from the bedroom. Outside in the hallway a girl with Sandra Dee puffy blonde hair sat on the bottom stair, her chin resting in her hands. She jumped up when she saw us coming. Wide doe eyes, heavily outlined in black, watched Frankie with the same expression Kipper wore every time he stood on the kerb with his hockey stick hoping the boys would ask him to play.

When we reached her, Frankie whispered something in her ear. I felt sorry for her until she slumped against the wall and pouted. Mom would have had a field day with that forced lip. I let go of Frankie's hand, leaving him with the sulking girl, and pushed between the bodies in the crowded hallway.

Everyone talked quietly yet with urgency, as if, if they were to stop, if silence were allowed to claim space for even a moment, it would expose how empty the house was now. The hum of voices followed me. Even with all the windows open the air was too stuffy, the rooms in our house too small for all of these people.

In the kitchen the women of Barclay Street, wearing similar black cotton dresses – many with the funny little black hats they had worn to the funeral still on their heads – sat around our table. Last week their conversations had been about the rain. Today they spoke about the suffocating heat. How could they sit there like that, smoking and chatting, as if this was one of Mom's weekly coffee-parties? As if the only difference was her empty chair.

The other women, some of whom I recognized and others I didn't, busied themselves with the dishes and the food that covered every available surface. Dora Fenwick stood at the counter by the sink stirring a pitcher of lemonade. She glanced up as I squeezed between two ladies. 'Oh, there you are, Ethie,' she said. 'Would you like some lemonade? Or iced tea?'

I shrugged.

'Danny's gone home with my mother,' she said, pouring a

glass and offering it to me. 'Why don't you go next door and see him?'

I took the drink, ignoring her suggestion. I didn't want to be around Danny and his sad-eyed pity, or his grandmother, who might or might not remember my name.

Behind me the chatter at the kitchen table stopped. I felt them hovering, like a flock of black-feathered birds, watching my every move, waiting for a chance to swoop down and comfort me. If one more person asked, 'How are you doing, dear?' or tried to hug me, I knew I would scream. Why did they have to be here? Why couldn't they all go home, like my aunt and uncle had?

Dora Fenwick reached out and brushed a curl from my forehead. 'Are you hungry?' The gentle touch of her fingers brought a ragged lump to my throat. I shook my head and backed away.

Out in the hallway Frankie was leaning against the wall talking to the same pouty-faced girl. His latest flame, I guessed. I wondered how long she would last. Once, after he dumped a girl Mom had particularly liked, she had accused him of being a bit of a cad.

'I can't help it if the ladies find me irresistible.' Frankie had laughed.

Mom rolled her eyes. 'You know, there was a time when your father let his looks swell his head, too. He started fancying himself a ladies' man when we were still teenagers. But I put a stop to that. When you meet the right girl, you'll fall just as hard.'

Grinning, Frankie had kissed her cheek, then left the kitchen singing something about wanting a girl just like the girl who had married his dear old dad. He had winked at me on his way by, asking, 'Who's going to measure up to that?'

Not this Sandra Dee girl.

I shoved my glass of lemonade into her hand. Her mascara-heavy eyes did not leave Frankie's face as she accepted the drink. She raised the glass to her lips then stopped when she noticed me standing there. 'Oh, Eva, isn't it?' she said, her voice dripping with sugar.

'Ethie,' Frankie corrected her.

'Ethie. I'm so, so, sorry about your mother,' she crooned, reaching for me.

I jerked away and escaped into the living room. A veil of blue cigarette smoke hung above the heads of the men gathered there. Through a gap in the crowd I saw my father hunched on the edge of his chair, his elbows resting on his knees. Like a scarecrow with its stuffing gone, he stared at the glass in his cupped hand, while the two men on the couch leaned towards him in huddled conversation. Unlike the others in the room, who were all down to white shirts with the sleeves rolled up, the two strangers who had shown up at the funeral still wore jackets and ties.

I edged over to Dad's chair.

'I had no idea you'd settled in Vancouver, Howard,' the man who looked tall even sitting down said. 'Why haven't you ever contacted—' He glanced up and saw me. 'Hello there,' he said, sitting back.

I sat on the arm of Dad's chair. He turned his head and forced a smile that didn't reach his eyes.

'She looks just like the picture you used to carry,' the man said. 'Certainly the spitting image of her mother, isn't she?'

Dad patted my knee. 'Yeah,' he whispered, 'she is.'

The man with the missing arm cleared his throat. 'Say, did you know that Private Ken Campbell here is now Dr Ken Campbell?'

Dad glanced from one to the other, seeming relieved at the

change of subject. 'No, I didn't,' he said, 'but I can't say I'm surprised.'

The doctor gave Dad a half-smile. 'Did you ever get to study pharmacy after the war, Howard?' he asked.

'No. I took an apprenticeship as a millwright instead,' Dad said. 'How about you, Jack?' he asked the man with the missing arm. 'You stayed in Vancouver?'

'Yeah, I went to work in the fish canneries,' the man said. 'When the owner of the company found out what I'd been through, he gave me a job for life.' He lifted his drink. 'My arm may be wormshit over there because some weak-kneed politician couldn't say no to Mother England,' he squinted into his glass and gave a bitter laugh, 'but I can still push bloody buttons.' Throwing back the rest of his drink he caught my eye. 'Oops, sorry. Pardon my French, little lady.'

My father seemed to have noticed neither the man's French nor my nervous giggle. He lifted his own almost empty glass. And I smelled the fumes of the amber liquid. While my father swallowed the rest of the iced tea that wasn't iced tea the man with only one arm leaned awkwardly to the side. With his left hand he pulled out a small flask from his jacket pocket. As he filled Dad's glass Frankie pushed through the crowd. He stopped in his tracks. His face hardened into a frown. He turned away and left the house, his girlfriend following.

I looked back at my father, and saw what Frankie had seen: the empty space between my father and the world was widening.

I hadn't cried all day. Not in the limousine, not at the service. When they lowered my mother's casket into the hole in the ground, when the handful of dirt the minister threw down went skittering across the polished wood, causing Dora Fenwick to sob, I remained dry-eyed. Not because I wasn't sad, or because

I didn't want to cry, but because I couldn't. My tears were stuck somewhere behind my sorrow. But as my father tossed back his drink in one swallow, that sorrow was shattered by the fear that this time he would disappear completely into that empty space. I slid off his chair and fled out of the front door.

I stood on the porch and, vision blurred, tried to focus on the park across the street. Frankie had his girlfriends. Dad had his whiskey. I had Kipper.

'Do you know her?' someone said behind me.

I quickly wiped my face, then turned to see Irene Manson leaning against the doorway, her arms folded, watching me through her black cat's-eye glasses.

'Who?'

'The Chinese girl,' she said, nodding across the street. 'The one over there in the park talking to Kipper.'

20

I would never truly understand why I lied to Mrs Manson. Perhaps it was all the neighbourhood kids sitting on our porch steps and lawn, fidgeting uncomfortably in their Sunday clothes, avoiding my eyes. Perhaps it was because I wanted to get away from them, from her, from our house of whispering voices. Or perhaps it was simply because at the time I believed what I told her might be true.

'I only wonder because I've seen her before,' Irene Manson said, when I didn't respond immediately to her question. Without taking her eyes from me she put a cigarette between her lips and lit it. 'She usually comes in the morning,' she said, blowing smoke out of the side of her mouth. 'Shows up and just stands there, watching your house.'

The same girl I saw on Monday and Tuesday? I spun around just as someone walked out of the park and headed up the street. I looked closer. It *was* the same girl. 'She's just someone who likes Frankie,' I said, throwing the fib over my shoulder and stepping between Ardith and Debra on the porch steps. I ignored their greetings, and made my way down to the kerb where I waited impatiently while two cars crawled through the tight space left between the vehicles parked on both sides of the street. The moment the road was clear I dashed across. Kipper stood alone by the swings, waving at the girl's retreating back as if she was an old friend.

'Who was that?' I asked.

'I dunno.'

'What was she talking to you about?'

'Mom.'

'Mom!' I blurted. 'What did she say about her?'

'She wanted to know where she was.'

'What did you tell her?' I asked, but I knew exactly what he had told her.

'Heben. I told her Mom was in heben.'

At the top of the street the girl disappeared around the corner.

I looked over at our house, at the silhouettes in our front windows, at Mrs Manson going back inside. At the kids spilled out onto the porch and front lawn, looking exactly like I felt – like they'd rather have been anywhere else in the world.

I grabbed Kipper's arm. 'Let's follow her.'

My brother's footsteps were heavy at the best of times, his feet lead weights. With his slow, rolling gait, he always struggled to keep up with me. But he was not even trying. He kept checking over his shoulder.

I stopped. 'I don't want to go home until they're all gone,' I said, taking his arm again. 'Come on,' I urged. 'It'll be an adventure.'

'Okay, Ethie.'

When we arrived at the corner the girl was two blocks away. Keeping our distance we followed her all the way down to Victoria Drive where she stood waiting in line at the bus stop.

I pulled Kipper in behind the passenger shelter. 'Have you got any money?' I whispered.

Grinning, he took off his hat and turned it over. His stubby fingers dug around inside the cloth band and came out with a silver dollar.

'Wow. Where'd you get that?'

'From when I sold my paintings,' he answered proudly. 'It's for somethin' special.'

'Well, this is special. We're going to take a bus ride.'

'Okay, thass good,' he said, just as the Hastings Street bus pulled up.

The doors folded open; the line of people filed on. I waited until the girl had climbed aboard, then pushed Kipper forward. We followed the last passengers up the steps, the doors closing behind us with a mechanical sigh. Kipper handed his dollar to the driver, who tossed it into the glass box. I grabbed the change that came clinking out into the metal tray and gave it to Kipper.

'Move back,' the driver snapped, and the bus lurched forward. Kipper and I took the first empty double seat. Pretending to look out of the window, I checked the girl from the corner of my eye. She was sitting at the back behind the side exit door. I faced forward as the bus pulled into traffic.

'What else did that girl say?' I whispered to Kipper, who was busy sorting the coins in his palm.

His eyebrows furrowed in concentration. 'She said she was sorry.'

The bus passed Kingsway and then Broadway. Every time we pulled up to a stop I checked to see if she got off. But she remained, staring out of the window, as Victoria Drive became Commercial Drive.

I knew this route. Before Mom had learned to drive, this was the bus she'd taken us on whenever we went downtown. When we passed the turning to Trout Lake I swallowed a threatening sob at the memory of her comforting me the day I lost the shoes I'd thought were so important.

On Hastings Street, we passed the Salvation Army store – the Sally Ann, Mom called it when she took me there to shop for school clothes. There was one on Victoria Drive, but she refused to buy my clothes so close to home, not wanting to risk me showing up at school wearing a classmate's castoffs.

At Main Street the bus stopped at a red light. When I saw the museum on the corner I couldn't help thinking about the day we'd been there with Mom last spring. I pushed away the memory of the mummy in a glass case on the second floor.

The light changed. The bus continued to the next stop in front of the Army and Navy department store. How could it be only a few weeks ago that I'd helped Mom dig through the bins of twenty-nine-cent bras until she triumphantly came up with her size?

She was everywhere. Except with us. *Why did she go and leave us?*

I slumped against the corner of the seat, beginning to wonder why I was on this bus, why I was following the girl. What did I expect to see? Still, when Kipper poked my shoulder and pointed out of the window at the girl being swept along the crowded sidewalk I jumped up and rushed to the front doors. With an irritated sigh, the driver pushed back the lever allowing the folding doors to reopen so that Kipper and I could step off.

The downtown streets smelled of burned sugar and brewing coffee. My stomach grumbled as we wove through pedestrians on the crowded sidewalk.

We caught up with the girl at the corner, where she waited to cross to the opposite side of Hastings Street. I held Kipper back until she had set off, then led him across with the flow. I was pretty sure I knew where she was going.

Chinatown. One of Mom's favourite places. She'd loved browsing through the exotic shops, eating in the busy restaurants or watching the street celebrations. I remembered the first time she had brought us down for Chinese New Year. Both Kipper and I were terrified by the noise of the drums and firecrackers in the crowded streets. We hid behind Mom's skirts at the sight of the huge crazy dragon snaking by, until Frankie pointed out the human legs below the red-and-yellow-fringed costume. I couldn't remember Dad ever going with us.

We followed the girl down the bustling streets to where the tall buildings gave way to small stores crowded together under an array of colourful awnings, many painted with red or gold Chinese characters. The smell of hot grease and the sight of cooked ducks hanging under yellow lights in restaurant windows made my stomach growl even more.

Ahead, the girl turned into a grocery store at the end of the block. I held Kipper back for a few moments, then nudged him towards the fruit and vegetable bins that lined the sidewalk. We peered over them through the window. Inside, the girl stood talking to a man wearing a white apron. He handed her an orange.

'I'm hungry,' Kipper wailed.

'Shush,' I said, then whispered, 'We'll get something afterwards.'

'After what?' he tried to whisper back.

'After we see where she's going.'

'But why?' he asked, frowning. 'Why are we following her?' Just then the girl came back outside and disappeared into the alley beside the store.

'Just pretend we're spies, tracking the enemy,' I said, heading after her.

'But she's not a enemy. She's nice,' Kipper said behind me.

'Just pretend, okay?' I edged over to the side of the store to peer into the alley. She was gone. 'Come on.' I waved Kipper forward.

'That man gabe her a orange for free,' he said, dragging

behind, trying to peer back into the store window. 'Maybe he's Mr Fong. Maybe he'll gib us one too.'

'He's not Mr Fong.'

A weathered grey wooden fence ran down the lane beside the store. We walked to the end of it and looked into the back alley. She was not down there either. We had lost her.

I stood there wondering where to go when I noticed the wild blackberry bushes growing against the fence behind the store. At the sight of the ripe clusters I could no longer ignore my hunger. I reached between the thorny branches to pick a handful. Kipper moved along the fence, popping berries into his mouth. He stepped into a gap in the bushes. 'Ooh, pretty,' he said.

'What?' I went over to where he was squinting between the boards of the tall wooden gate.

'A little house.' He moved back to let me look. I peered through the crack in the boards. He was right. There, in the yard behind the store, was a small building, not much bigger than a child's playhouse. A tiny version of the Chinese temples I had seen in books. The red paint was faded, the steeply curved roof chequered with broken and missing tiles. The upturned eaves may have been pretty at one time, but now only flecks of gold paint remained. But to Kipper it was beautiful. 'What kinda house is that?' he asked.

Before I could answer I saw the girl climbing up an open staircase at the back of the store. I watched her go up the last few steps to a second-floor landing, unlock a door and slip inside. *She must live here.*

Suddenly I felt deflated. The game was over. I picked a few more handfuls of berries. 'Let's go,' I said, wiping my hands on my dress. 'We'll buy an orange.'

Kipper stuffed the last of his berries into his juice-stained mouth and we made our way back to the street. We looked over the neatly piled oranges in the bin at the front of the store. I chose one and was about to go inside to pay for it when I spotted the girl standing behind the counter, tying on an apron.

Kipper saw her, too. 'She works here,' he cried.

The girl looked up from the counter. I threw the orange back into the bin, grabbed a fistful of Kipper's shirt and bolted, dragging him down the street with me.

Two blocks later I stopped and waited while he dug in his pants pocket for his inhaler. 'Why . . .' he wheezed between puffs '. . . didn't we go see her?'

I couldn't answer that question. I didn't know why, and was already regretting that we hadn't.

He took another dose from his inhaler, then said, 'Let's go back.'

I looked down the street. I wanted to go home now. Maybe everyone would have gone by the time we got there. What I had told Mrs Manson was probably true. She was just another girl who had a crush on my big brother.

We stopped at the next fruit stand. I made sure Kipper had two dimes left for the bus fare, and then we bought an orange. I peeled it and we shared the segments as we walked to the bus stop on Hastings Street, taking a shortcut through Victory Square. I knew this small park in the centre of downtown Vancouver from the Remembrance Day ceremonies Mom and Dad took us to each November. Every year at the end of the service my father laid his poppy at the foot of the granite cenotaph in the middle of the park. Now, as we crossed in front of it, a man wearing old and dirty clothes lay slumped against the grey stone. I veered away from him but Kipper stopped abruptly. 'He's sleeping outside,' he said in wonder.

The man's eyes popped open and he gave a black-toothed

grin. 'Hey, kid,' he said, his voice slurring the words. 'Got a dime for an old soldier?'

Kipper reached into his pocket. I yanked him away and hung onto his hand until we reached our bus stop. While we waited, I gave him the rest of the orange; the drunk lying in the street had taken away my appetite.

The bus pulled up and I asked Kipper for the rest of the money.

He popped the last wedge into his mouth, rubbed his hands on his shirt – smearing orange stains on top of blackberry – then reached into his pocket. And came up with nothing. He dug around in both pockets, pulling them inside out. 'It's gone,' he cried, close to tears.

'It can't be.' I felt around in his pockets, even patted the one on his shirt. But he was right: the dimes we needed for the bus fare had disappeared.

'Let's go back and find them, Ethie.'

I thought of the drunk on the sidewalk. The change must have fallen out then. It would be gone by now for sure.

'It's lost,' I said, resigned. 'We'll have to walk. It's not that far.'

But it was. I don't know how many hours we walked the streets as the sun went down. By the time we reached Kingsway it was dusk. And by the time we turned onto Fifty-first Avenue to trudge up to our street, porch lights glowed in the dark. Lawn sprinklers clicked in front yards and the smell of damp grass and flowers filled the evening air.

All the way home Kipper never once complained, even though he must have been as tired and hungry as I was. When his breathing became heavy he sucked on his inhaler. Every four or five blocks he said, 'Sorry, Ethie. Sorry.' He was so sad that I couldn't stay mad at him. I was just relieved to turn into Barclay Street.

All the cars that had lined the kerbs earlier were gone and our house was dark. Not even the flicker of the television lit our living-room window. As we crossed our lawn I looked into the back yard. Frankie's Studebaker was gone. He must still be with his girlfriend. Or maybe he was out looking for us. He and Dad must be worried. Maybe they'd called the police and everyone was searching.

The living-room windows were wide open, the front door ajar. The house was silent. *Empty?* We slipped in and I flicked the switch. As light flooded the hallway I saw Dad slumped in his chair exactly where I had left him. His eyes opened. He squinted at us, then sat up. Pushing his hair back from his forehead, he asked sleepily, 'Oh, are you two still up?'

He hadn't even noticed we were gone.

21

Disembodied white gloves floated in the darkness. Luminous, they moved above Howard's blurred vision in a macabre dance. Struggling against the invisible bonds holding him captive, he knew there was no escaping the crimson horror that would follow. Jagged screams rose in his throat, jarring him awake. He found himself sitting upright on the couch, thrashing against the evaporating terror, the pleas for mercy dying on his lips.

'Dad?' A hand touched his shoulder. 'Dad, it's me, Frankie.'

Clammy with sweat, heart racing, Howard gulped at the fetid air. Willing his fogged mind to clear, he concentrated on the shadows before him. The silhouette of his son, backlit by the streetlights outside the living-room window, came into focus. And the pain of truth pulled him back to reality.

'This lumpy old couch can't be very comfortable,' Frankie said quietly.

'I've slept on worse.' He expected an argument, a gentle urging to his own bed, but instead Frankie left the room. He returned moments later with a pillow, a blanket and Howard's plaid robe. Dropping them on the end of the couch he said goodnight. At the hallway he turned back and asked, 'Are you going to be all right, Dad?'

Howard hoped the night hid the shaking of his hands as he struggled to unbutton his shirt. 'Yeah,' he said. 'Good night, son.'

In no hurry, he finished undressing, pulled on his robe and lay down again. But he kept his eyes wide open, afraid to sleep, afraid to come face to face with the horrific visions lurking behind his eyelids. And the recurring nightmare from which, without Lucy to pull him back, he might never emerge. Yet awake he was unable to stop himself sinking into the haunting memories brought on by the waking nightmare of her death. And by the appearance of the two Hong Kong veterans today. In particular Ken Campbell.

22

6 December 1941: Hong Kong Island

In the balcony of the darkened movie theatre Howard joined the collective groan at the static interruption of the film. On the screen the title character, Sergeant York, battled with the dilemma between fighting for his country and his religious convictions. But the words coming from the loudspeakers did not match Gary Cooper's moving lips.

'Attention, all military and naval personnel. All leaves and weekend passes are hereby cancelled. Repeat, all passes cancelled. All infantry are ordered to return to base, and naval personnel to ships in harbour. Immediately.'

'Well, this could be it,' Ken Campbell said, getting to his feet. Howard squeezed down the row ahead of him, apologizing each time he bumped into the knees of those staying to watch the movie. Throughout the theatre the grumbling continued over the repeated message.

'Right in the middle of the bloody show!'

'The Japs must be on the move.'

'We'll be in de t'ick of it by marnin'!'

'Ah, it's just another manoeuvre. Keep yer shirt on.'

'Yeah, what's the rush?' the soldier at the end of row asked, refusing to budge when Howard reached him. 'We can at least stay until the end of the movie.'

'Are you deaf, soldier? "Immediately" means now! Move it!'

the hulking form behind Howard barked, causing the soldier to scurry up the aisle.

Howard laughed. 'Good thing it's too dark in here to see your rank, Ken,' he said. 'Or your mug. No one would take orders from that baby face.'

'But they pay attention to my radio voice.' Ken's booming guffaw rang out as they joined the crowd streaming outside. On the screen, the turkey shooting marksman, Alvin York was coming to the conclusion that some things were worth fighting for.

During the ferry ride back to Kowloon, Howard wondered if Ken was right. Was this it? Was he about to find out, like Sergeant York had in the Great War, that it was easy to kill in order to stop more killing? Would the mettle-testing manoeuvres of the last three weeks prove to have been necessary, or was this just another drill?

Howard scanned the soldiers on the Star ferry's lower deck. Some, like Ken Campbell, stood at the rails, lost in thought, as the boat chugged towards Kowloon pier. Others alternated between complaining over the loss of passes to wild speculation on the prospect of seeing action. He recognized the bravado of youth tempered by the possibility of war. He, too, felt the quickening of blood in his veins at the notion of being tested, of finding out who he was in the face of danger. And, conflicting with those heroic notions, the chilling reality of fear.

When they arrived back at Sham Shui Po, Colonel Sutcliffe warned the men to get a good night's rest but left them as much in the dark as the blacked-out barracks were.

Lying in bed, unable to sleep, Howard wondered about Gordy. Early this morning he had left camp on a weekend pass. Had he heard about the cancellation of all leave? Tonight he was somewhere in Victoria with Shun-ling.

Over the last three weeks Gordy – who had always sworn no one girl was ever going to tie *him* down – had spent all of his free time with Shun-ling. Surprised by how quickly his friend had become smitten, Howard had been floored when he announced that he was going to rent a flat on the island for Shun-ling and her family. 'Aren't you jumping the gun a little?' he had asked.

'What's bugging your ass?' Gordy had snapped. 'I don't remember you asking my permission to marry Lucy.' He grinned, but Howard had heard the warning edge in his words.

After a moment of uncomfortable silence, Gordy said, 'You wouldn't believe what they live in, Howie.' His voice back to normal, he went on to describe the corrugated shed they called home. 'You wouldn't let a mongrel sleep in that one-room hell-hole.'

With the help of Peter and Dick, who had labelled him a 'bleedin' fool' for taking on the woes of an entire family, he had found a flat in the Wanchai district. That morning he and Shun-ling had taken the ferry over to get the place ready for the family. Her father and sister would not move in until Monday morning when Gordy had returned to camp.

During the past week Howard had spent his evenings in town with Ken Campbell. 'Us old married men have to stick together,' he said, as an excuse to avoid joining the couple. But the truth was that tagging along with Gordy and Sun-ling had become unsettling. He told himself that spending time with them only made him miss Lucy more. And he couldn't shake what had happened last Saturday from his mind.

That afternoon he had wandered through the back-streets of Kowloon alone. Not certain it would be open during the weekend, he had found his way to Ah Sam's store. At Ken Campbell's urging he had gone there to buy more of the bedbug potion. It was as good an excuse as any to visit the pharmacist.

The bell tinkled above the shop door when he entered. 'Hello, Ah Sam,' Howard said to the man at the counter. 'Do you remember me?'

Expressionless, Ah Sam had shrugged. 'You all look same to me.'

Howard opened his mouth. 'I, uh . . .' he stammered.

Ah Sam held up his hand. 'I was joking, sir,' he said, a smile creasing his round face. 'Of course I remember Feng Shun-ling's two Canadian friends. How are those insect bites?'

Relieved, Howard smiled back. 'Great,' he said. 'I mean gone. I'm here to buy another bottle of the remedy for a friend.'

Ah Sam led him to the back of the store where he collected the ingredients. Then he said, 'I trust you two gentlemen are treating my good friend Feng Shun-ling with respect.'

'Of course,' Howard replied, taken aback.

'She is a very special young woman,' Ah Sam said, returning his attention to the task at hand. 'I'm sure you understand that she and her family have been through a great deal.' As he deftly tapped green powder into the tiny vial, he told Howard that Shun-ling and her father had been trapped at the university when the Japanese overran Nanking. 'They ended up in the Safety Zone – a protected area in the middle of the city set up by foreign nationals. Germans.' He looked up and cocked his head. 'Ironic, wouldn't you say? Saved by the swastika?' Without waiting for a reply, he continued, 'They witnessed the massacre at first hand. Fleeing crowds of unarmed civilians machine-gunned, children murdered, women raped and dismembered, all in plain view.' He shook his head. 'Feng Guo-ren, Shun-ling's father, told me about two high-ranking Japanese officers who actually entered into a "friendly" wager over which of them could kill the most civilians with his sword.'

Howard listened incredulously as Ah Sam related how the victims were lined up for slaughter.

'Young, old, it made no difference, just the body count,' he said, dripping melted wax over the vial cork. 'Photographs of the officers in their bloodied uniforms, along with their scores, were posted around the city afterwards. A Red Cross worker reported that one of the officers complained bitterly because he had damaged his sword cutting a man in half.' He paused. The room fell eerily silent. Ah Sam put the vial on the counter to allow the wax to set. 'After a week, Shun-ling's father bribed two of Chiang Kai-shek's retreating soldiers to take them with them,' he said. 'They escaped through a sewage tunnel under the city wall in the middle of the night. All the way back to their village, everything had been torched and pillaged. They had a difficult time locating their own burned-out home. They found Shun-ling's two-year-old brother's charred body in the ruins. He had been gutted. Their mother was outside, her naked corpse mutilated.'

Howard swallowed the bile rising at the back of his throat. 'Her sister?'

'She escaped by hiding in the bottom of the cabbage pit. One of the Japanese soldiers had taken pity on her and spared her. When it was his turn to have her, he buried her under the fermenting cabbages. She lay there, with rats crawling around her, for days before her father and Shun-ling found her, barely alive. The poor child hasn't spoken since.'

Still shaken when he joined Gordy and Shun-ling later that evening, Howard was unable to rid his mind of the horrific images Ah Sam's words had conjured up. He felt protective towards Shun-ling, knowing that she and her family had endured the brutal reality of those visions.

In the Sun Sun, he stepped up to the bar with her and Gordy.

As the bartender turned to face them a startled Shun-ling had shrunk back in fear. 'Guizie!' she whispered. 'Japanese.'

Howard and Gordy had escorted her, trembling, down the stairs and outside.

Now, staring into the darkness, waiting for morning and Gordy to arrive, Howard couldn't help remembering that it was his arm Shun-ling had clung to as she backed away from the bar. And the look that had flashed in Gordy's eyes as he had noticed it too.

By noon the next day all soldiers, sailors and volunteers were at their battle stations. More or less. Gordy was still missing.

At the south-west end of the island, in a trench overlooking the South China Sea, Howard leaned against the sandbagged walls. In full battle gear, he had distributed what was left of his Hong Kong dollars throughout his uniform. Just in case. Lucy's picture was tucked inside the diary in his breast pocket. He was ready. But for what?

Two hundred yards below, on the narrow highway that wound around the island, nothing seemed amiss. The occasional civilian car or locals on bicycles and on foot, passed by unconcerned throughout the day. Even the small barking deer that roamed the slopes searching for elusive patches of grass ignored them. In the early afternoon an elderly British couple hiked up the road carrying a picnic basket between them.

A few feet away from Howard, Ken Campbell stood up in the trench. 'This might not be the best day for that, folks,' he hollered down.

On the road below the man stopped and leaned on his walking-stick, shielding his eyes from the sun. 'And why not, may I ask?' he enquired. 'We picnic in these hills every Sunday.'

'Haven't you heard? The colony's on high alert. I'd hightail it home if I were you. There could be an attack at any moment.'

'Preposterous! The Japanese would never challenge the British Empire.'

Howard watched in amazement as the couple stepped off the road and walked down to a ledge where they spread their blanket. The woman opened an umbrella and the two took their tea in the afternoon sun. It was the perfect day for it. Black-necked starlings swooped down and caught the crumbs thrown up to them while the sea below sparkled under a clear blue sky. Still, Howard couldn't help noticing that, as if they knew something was afoot, the flotilla of junks, sampans and fishing-boats that usually bobbed in those waters had all but disappeared.

Two hours later the couple rose, gathered their belongings and sauntered away. Howard had to admire their audacious calm as sweat trickled down his neck.

In the heat of the afternoon rumours ran up and down the trenches. The Japanese armada had been spotted in the South China Sea heading towards Hong Kong.

No worries: the two battleships, Prince of Wales *and* Repulse, *the pride of the British Navy, are on their way.*

The Japanese Army amassing at the border was growing, the numbers increasing with each passing hour. By five o'clock that evening the unofficial count was forty thousand.

No worries: Chiang Kai-shek's army is coming up the rear.

Their shipload of missing equipment had been diverted to Europe.

You can bet your ass they ain't gonna risk losing that precious cargo. Wonder what that says about us, eh?

The banter in the trenches helped to alleviate the boredom of staring at an empty sea. Still, as the sun dropped Howard decided not to pay attention to any more conflicting gossip. He would believe only what he saw with his own eyes, which at that moment was Gordy jumping out of the back of a supply truck. He climbed over the ditch and, head down, charged up the hill like a bulldog to slide into the trench beside Howard.

'Glad you could drop in.'

'Yeah, don't have much choice, do I?'

Howard was startled by his friend's unusually curt reply, but said nothing.

The supply truck distributed the evening meal. Gordy left his biscuits and bully beef untouched. Standing with his elbows propped on the top of the trench, he gazed out at the darkening sea. 'We heard talk during the ferry ride over that Japanese civilians have disappeared this weekend.' When he turned, his face was a mask of concern. 'The refugees are panicking. Shun-ling too.'

Knowing her story, Howard wasn't surprised. He wondered how much Gordy was aware of, but refrained from asking.

Gordy unscrewed his canteen cap, took a long pull, then wiped his mouth with the back of his hand. 'It's chaos in Kowloon,' he continued. 'Getting off the ferry we had to fight our way through crowds of refugees trying to get over to the island. The minute we got through, Shun-ling rushed away to get her father and sister. She wouldn't let me go with her, but I followed her anyway. I hung back and watched until I was sure they were safely aboard the ferry before I went back to the barracks to get my gear. And I don't give a rat's ass what this man's army says about me being late.'

'You didn't miss anything.'

Gordy crouched in the trench and pulled a crumpled cigarette pack from his sleeve. Silently he offered it to Howard. With cupped hands he lit both, then sat back and met Howard's eyes. 'You know, it took everything I had to come back, Howie,' he said, his voice low. 'I ain't no deserter. Yeah, I'm scared. I ain't scared of fighting or even dying. It's what could happen to her and her family if the Japanese attack.'

'Maybe they won't,' Howard said, trying to speak with conviction. 'It could turn out to be a false alarm. By this time tomorrow night we could be back at the cinema.'

At seven the next morning Howard was trying to locate the source of the distant hum, the unmistakable drone of high-flying aircraft. The sky was clear, but from the sound dozens of planes had to be approaching. *Reinforcements?* The drone turned into the synchronized whine of a squadron quickly losing altitude. Moments later, the rolling thunder of explosions on the mainland drowned his brief hope. 'Christ, they're bombing the base!' he yelled, shaking Gordy awake.

The scream of air-raid sirens, then bursts of anti-aircraft fire, came from the direction of the Kai Tak airfield. Along with the rest of their troop, Howard and Gordy crouched helplessly in their island trench, unable to see, unable to help, while a short distance across the water devastation rained down. Less than ten minutes later, the aircraft were turning away. To the east, clouds of blackened smoke billowed into the sky. Howard glanced down the trench and met Ken Campbell's eyes. His face was ashen. Still holding the radio receiver, he shouted, 'Pearl Harbor was attacked six hours ago—' He was cut off by the roar of a low-flying plane.

The lone Zero fighter passed directly overhead, the rattle of machine-gun fire reaching Howard's ears as bullets strafed the hillside, kicking up dirt and showering it into the trenches. He saw the blood-red circle on the wing tips the second before he hit the ground. There was no guessing now. They were at war with Japan.

* * *

Two days later they were sitting in the same trench, the war a distant rumble and radio reports. Things were not going well on the mainland. As Brigadier Lawson had predicted, the main thrust of the invasion had come overland from the north. The Gin Drinkers Line, manned by the Royal Scots and Indian brigades, the Punjabis and Rajputs, had been breached. The rugged eleven-mile defence line running east and west, less than ten miles north of Kowloon, had been expected to hold for weeks. In the trenches there were no longer any smart comebacks to the reports. Men were dying.

By Wednesday, Gordy's concern for Shun-ling was taking its toll: he was slumped in the trench, sweat running down his forehead.

'Boy, I'd sure welcome a chunk of that ice we delivered in Winnipeg,' Howard said, in an attempt to lighten his friend's mood.

Gordy remained silent.

'Remember how those kids used to snatch the broken chips from the back of our wagon, then run off with it as if it was stolen treasure?' he prodded. 'They really thought they had something, didn't they?'

Suddenly a truck roared up the road and stopped below their trench. A sergeant strode up looking for volunteers. D Company was being deployed to the mainland to provide back-up to the Royal Scots who, having suffered heavy losses, were withdrawing to the island. Howard and Gordy scrambled out of their trench and bolted down the hill before the request was finished. Ken Campbell was lumbering along a few yards ahead of them.

On the mainland Kowloon was burning and in total chaos. Unloading from the ferry, their truck was swamped by panic-crazed civilians still trying to escape to the island. Uniformed policemen, clubbing their way through the mob, freed the truck to inch forward. As they drove past Sham Shui Po, heavily laden looters rushed in every direction from the ransacked camp. Howard felt a twinge of regret over Lucy's green dress left in his locker – surely gone by now. He should have mailed it.

Deployed to their positions on the edge of the city, Howard and Gordy's company was left to spend the night in the polo field while intermittent explosions from bombs and mortar shells lit the smoke-filled canopy above.

The next morning, providing cover for the retreating Scots, Howard had his first glimpse of the enemy. Then, as the mass of Japanese soldiers, their faces blackened and fierce with intent, surged over the rise, screaming, '*Banzai-ai-ai!*' he had a taste of action. And found it bitter. Crouched back to back with Gordy in the sagging doorway of a bombed building he tossed his first grenade. Then another. Both duds. 'Jesus Christ,' he swore. 'We might as well be throwing rocks.' Moments later they jumped up and ran behind the exhausted Royal Scots. Shooting blindly they beat a hasty retreat with the rest of the Grenadiers, the screaming Japanese warriors at their heels.

Heart hammering, Howard watched from the deck of the retreating ferryboat as the rearguard, the East Indian units, waged hand-to-hand combat with the Japanese swarming the streets and wharves of Kowloon.

'Not exactly the myopic little men we were told to expect,' Ken Campbell panted beside him.

A wild-eyed Royal Scot sat against the deck rail talking wildly to no one. 'Jesus! They just kept coming and coming!' he ranted. 'Friggin' suicidal maniacs! The first ones threw themselves on top of the barbed-wire barricades and the rest surged right over 'em using their bodies as a bridge – couldn't shoot 'em fast enough. As soon as one fell, ten took his place!'

23

In the days following my mother's funeral the first thing I did was check the park across the street. The girl was never there. But each morning I found my father sitting at the kitchen table, his unshaven face greyer by the day. On Saturday morning it occurred to me that he, too, was watching the park. As quickly as the thought entered my mind I dismissed it. It made no sense. What did make sense were the empty whiskey bottles in the garbage.

'Howard's never missed a single day's work through drinking,' I remember Mom once insisting in a conversation with my aunt. In response Aunt Mildred had slid a pill bottle across the table. 'Just put one of these in his coffee each morning,' she said. 'He'll get violently ill if he tries to drink any alcohol.'

'Really, Mildred! Sometimes you say the most inane things,' Mom had exclaimed. 'Howard's not an alcoholic.'

'Isn't he?'

'He went through a lot in the war.'

'Many men did.'

'A drink now and then is how he copes,' Mom said, ignoring her. 'It's harmless.'

'Is it?' Aunt Mildred let her eyes travel around the room, taking in our sparse home.

'At least he doesn't beat me,' Mom replied, indignant at the implication. 'Or end up out on the street in the middle of the night fist-fighting with his sons, like some of our neighbours.

And if you think I'm going to make my Howie sick by sneaking pills into his coffee, you're crazy.'

Standing in the kitchen doorway on Saturday morning, watching Dad's hands shake while he drank his coffee, I wondered at my mother's belief in him. The night before I had woken to his anguished cries. Half asleep, I'd waited for her voice to bring him back from whatever torment had him in its grip. I came to full consciousness with the sinking knowledge that she would never do that again and that someone had to. I leaped out of bed and was halfway down the stairs before I heard Frankie's voice. Long after Dad's nightmare had ended, long after my brother climbed up to his room and the living room was silent, I had remained awake, listening, readying myself to take my mother's place.

Saturday morning he was slumped at the kitchen table again, staring out of the window. Across from him, Kipper sat with his art supplies. Wearing one of Frankie's old shirts, he concentrated on the pots in front of him. Smears of paint covered his hands and cheeks, while a dab of yellow decorated the thick forward fold of his left ear. With his tongue to the side of his mouth he mixed colours, oblivious, like Dad, to anything going on around him.

I watched him dabbing his brush between the pots until it became a brilliant red. Just as he began his slow, meticulous strokes, a housefly landed on the table. It crawled between his canvas and Dad's hand. I grabbed the fly swat from the hook by the stove and crept over. With a flick of my wrist I swept it from the table. Dad's head turned, and I saw the familiar faraway look on his face.

I often wondered what my father saw in those split seconds before recognition set in. Where was he when his eyes glazed? Could he see what was in front of him and did he have to force himself back from wherever he had gone? Did he even want to return?

His eyes followed the fly to the floor, then he raised them to look at me. 'Thank you, Ethie,' he said, and I felt a surge of pride at taking on Mom's mission to keep our house free of the flies my father loathed.

Awakened from his trance, Dad watched Kipper working on his painting. His brush moving slowly, he was filling in his outline with bright red paint.

'What's that you're painting, Kipper?' Dad asked.

I froze.

'A little house.'

'Where'd you see a house like that?'

The shrill ringing of the phone made me jump. In our home the telephone had been Mom's domain. When it rang it was almost always one of her friends. She could sit holding the receiver to her ear, chatting for hours. These days when the phone rang it was either Aunt Mildred or someone who had just found out about Mom calling to say how sorry they were. Frankie had become the official phone answerer. But Frankie was still upstairs in bed.

Dad and I stared at the phone on the wall as if it were a snake. Finally Kipper stood up and reached over to lift the receiver. 'Hallo,' he said, then listened to whoever was on the other end. 'Yes, he's here, Mr Telford.' He handed the phone to Dad, who regarded it as if it might bite.

'Yes?' he answered, holding it a few inches from his ear.

I could hear Mr Telford saying something about Kipper's paintings at the art shop. While Dad listened to him, Frankie came downstairs. He poked his head into the kitchen, then went into the bathroom.

Suddenly anxious to hide Kipper's artwork I seized on an idea that had struck me as I was getting dressed that morning. 'Let's go looking for pop bottles,' I said, trying to sound excited so Kipper would be too. Then I whispered directly into his ear, 'Maybe we can make some money to help Dad out.'

'Okay!' Kipper jumped at the suggestion. He wiped his brush on a rag. 'And maybe if we get enough, we can go to the drive-in show.'

'Yeah, that's a good idea,' I said. I picked up the painting of the red curled-roof house. 'Let's put this up in my room.'

I didn't want to have to explain why we had gone to Chinatown the other day. Maybe Dad had no idea that our boundaries didn't extend to bus trips downtown, but Frankie sure did.

24

I understood early the power of money. Or, more exactly, the lack of it.

'Too much month left at the end of the money,' I once heard Mom joke, when she ran out of cream for the ladies' coffee one morning. 'If the wolf isn't exactly at the door he's somewhere in the neighbourhood,' she added, with false cheerfulness.

Now, without her earnings, with Dad and Frankie not working for a whole week, and from the bits of conversation I overheard between them and my aunt, I was afraid money was going to be an even bigger problem now. By the time Kipper and I left the house I was convinced that if I could earn some, it would take the pressure off Dad, and maybe, just maybe, it would stop him sinking further away.

Kipper's rusty old wagon – one wheel held on by a piece of wire twisted at the axle – bumped and rattled along behind us as we made our way along the dirt roads above Marine Drive. We kicked back the weeds with our rubber boots to search for discarded bottles in the ditches. By lunchtime the wagon was filled with clinking pop bottles.

We took the first load to the greengrocer's on Victoria Drive. Kipper and I stood on the wooden floorboards while the tiny Chinese lady, her face so wrinkled it was hard to see her eyes, counted the bottles. Kipper stared intently at the penny candy in the glass jars on the counter top.

'Twenty-seven bottles,' the old woman said. 'That two cent

each, fifty-four cent.' She opened the till and handed me the coins. Taking in Kipper's expression, she asked, 'Maybe some candy?'

'Nope.' He smiled proudly at her. 'We're saving our money for our Da.'

We plodded back up the hill, Kipper's mouth and lips black as he sucked on a jawbreaker – the store lady had given us one each.

Fifty-four cents wasn't nearly enough to help with anything. It cost two dollars just to get into the Cascade drive-in theatre – if Dad would take us. I didn't know what movie was on that night. The truth was I didn't really want to go but I liked Kipper's idea of doing something, anything, with our father.

My boots felt hotter and heavier with each step up the hill. At the top we passed our street and continued to where they were building the new houses. 'C'mon,' I said, turning down a gravel alley. 'Let's see if the workers left any bottles behind.'

The unfinished houses lining both sides of the lane stood silent, abandoned for the weekend. The afternoon sun poured down on the skeleton frames. The warm air smelled of new timber and drying concrete. Ignoring the 'No Trespassing' sign I started into the first backyard, leaving Kipper in the alley with the wagon.

'What does, pros-pros-acute . . .' he called after me.

I turned and looked up at the sign he was struggling to read. 'Prosecuted,' I said. 'It means anyone caught stealing any building stuff will go to jail. But we're not stealing. They don't care about old pop bottles.'

I wandered around the building supplies stored in the yard. Among the crumpled waxed paper and rotting apple cores left by the workers I found a brown Orange Crush bottle. I could still smell the tangy scent of soda pop as I wiped off the dirt and checked it for cracks or chips.

Moving from yard to yard, I found at least one or two empty bottles at each unfinished house. In some places, they were lined up neatly as if waiting for us. Beside one pile of timber I found an empty whiskey bottle. Useless and ugly. I tossed it into a dark basement hole, feeling satisfaction as it smashed against the cement walls.

Heading back to the alley with my arms full I saw a large wooden wagon parked beside ours. Two boys stood with Kipper. One was leaning over our wagon with pop bottles clutched to his chest. *They're stealing our bottles!* I dropped mine and threw myself at the boy, knocking him down. The bottles in his arms crashed to the ground around us.

'What the heck?' he roared, as I scrambled on top of him, punching and scratching.

'Ethie, stop,' Kipper cried.

Someone grabbed me from behind. 'Hold it, Ethie.' It was Danny Fenwick. 'We were just giving Kipper some bottles,' he said, pulling me away.

'Jeeze,' the other boy swore, jumping up. 'You're crazy.' He dusted himself off, then headed down the alley. 'Keep the stupid bottles,' he yelled back. 'You look like you need 'em.'

Danny ran after him and spoke quietly to him for a while. I knew what he was telling him.

The other boy's expression changed. He glanced back at me. 'Sorry,' he called, just loud enough for me to hear.

'Yeah, me too.' I kicked at the dirt. I didn't want his sympathy. Or his bottles. I grabbed the wagon handle. 'C'mon, Kipper, let's go.'

Danny hurried back. He started picking up the bottles scattered in the alley. 'He didn't mean anything,' he said, loading them into the wagon. 'We're building a fort in the bush by the golf course. Why don't you guys come and see it?'

'No,' Kipper said, pointing to the building supplies in the wooden wagon. 'I think you will be pros-pros-cuted.'

'Because of this stuff?' Danny laughed. 'Nah. These are just old bent nails and pieces of boards the workmen leave out for us. Like the bottles.'

That was one of the things I had always liked best about Danny. The way he spoke directly to my brother. 'What do you say?' he asked him now. 'Want to come and see our fort?' Kipper said yes for both of us.

The swamps and bushes around our subdivision were getting smaller all the time. New streets filled with new houses were replacing them. But there were still acres of bush around the Fraserview golf course. Danny's fort was hidden in the trees above Marine Drive. We climbed up the rope-ladder with him to check it out.

Kipper and I spent the rest of the afternoon with Danny. Just like we used to. We hiked through the woods, wading through the musty-smelling creek to catch frogs, pulling up stinky skunk cabbages and chasing each other with them. We yelled down the new concrete storm sewer tunnels and listened to our voices echo back. Danny and I crouched low and crawled into one, pretending we were soldiers hiding from the enemy. When it was too dark to see we crawled back out to find Kipper, who had refused to go in with us. He was sitting at the opening using a stick to draw a house in the mud silt. A house with curled-up eaves. He had that Chinese house on the brain. I'd hoped he would have forgotten it by now.

Later we walked to the golf course where Danny showed us how to search for balls in the tall grass along the edge of the fairways. It wasn't much different from looking for pop bottles, but when we took the balls to the parking lot the golfers paid a lot more money for them.

Kipper was the best salesman. Danny said it was because all anyone had to do was take one look at his honest face to know he hadn't run out on the greens to steal them, like some kids did. Here was another way we could earn money, I thought, excited.

We arrived home just as Frankie was heading off to night school. He wrinkled his nose at the swampy scent of mud and skunk cabbage clinging to our clothes, and asked what we'd been up to today. Kipper told him about the pop bottles and the golf balls. 'Good plan,' Frankie said, when he heard we were going to ask Dad to take us to the drive-in. 'But you might want to change those clothes before he has to sit in a car with you.'

I set the dinner table and placed twelve dollars in front of Dad's plate. 'What's this?' he asked, when he sat down.

'It's for you, Da.' Kipper beamed. While we ate, he and I took turns explaining how we had earned it.

'And Kipper thought maybe we could use some of it to go to the drive-in movie show tonight,' I added.

Dad looked down at the pile of coins and crumpled dollar bills. 'When I was your age it took me more than a month of delivering the *Star Weekly* to earn this kind of money,' he said, shaking his head.

A paper route. 'Maybe Kipper and I could get a paper route too?'

'Maybe you could,' Dad said. His eyes flickered to the top of the fridge as he slid the money back across the table.

My heart sank. No drive-in movie tonight.

'But you kids keep this,' he said. 'You earned it.' He put down his fork. 'Well,' he pushed himself away from the table, 'what are you waiting for? Let's do these dishes and get going.'

We didn't end up at the Cascade drive-in theatre that night. When Dad checked the newspaper and saw that *Judgment at Nuremberg* was showing there, we drove instead to the New Westminster drive-in where *To Kill a Mocking Bird* was playing.

None of us saw the end of the movie. We fell asleep on the front seat of the Hudson. It didn't matter. During the ride home, curled up between my father and Kipper, I pretended I was still sleeping. I let Dad carry me up to my room and tuck me into bed without opening my eyes. Feeling him kiss my forehead as he covered me with my blanket, I began to hope that maybe it was working, that maybe helping out as much as I could would make him see how much we needed him. Before I fell asleep I remembered what Mrs Fenwick had said. She was right. The sadness, the hurt were still there, but it was all right to feel happy to go to a movie show with my father and brother, and all right to enjoy playing with friends again.

Dad must have come to some sort of resolution, too. For the first time since Mom had died he spent the night in their bed.

25

13 December 1941: Hong Kong Island

Howard pulled the thin army-issue blanket tighter around his shoulders. He and Gordy had been dispatched to this concrete pillbox overlooking the South China Sea after returning from the mainland. Except for minor scrapes and superficial wounds, the entire company had come through relatively unscathed. All present and accounted for. Except for one Private John A. Gray. Howard tried to put a face to the Manitoba farm boy, but couldn't.

He shivered. Last night's drizzle had found its way into their pillbox. Even in the heat of the afternoon he still felt damp.

'What the hell are we doing here?' Gordy burst out, for the umpteenth time that day. He was not expecting an answer this time either.

They didn't talk about it. Torturous sounds came from Kowloon, inhuman screams, so loud that they carried across the narrow body of water between the mainland and the island. They both knew what they meant.

After the last of the garrison forces had been evacuated to the island, the Japanese – in control of the colony's radio stations on the mainland – had broadcast a declaration that all Chinese women were prostitutes. The implication was that they were worth less than animals. The speaker made clear that they would be treated as the spoils of war for the conquering soldiers to do with as they liked.

Gordy clutched his head. He covered his ears trying to block out the distant cries. 'God! I can't stand it.' He rocked back and forth, cursing the Japanese, God, whoever had sent his regiment there. Then, with no warning, he shot up and headed for the opening. 'I can't sit here doing bugger-all,' he cried, struggling against Howard's sudden grip on his arm. 'We're bloody useless.'

A tremor shook the earth beneath their feet. At the same moment a barrage of artillery fire and explosions came from the north. They were bombing Victoria again. Gordy went limp, then sank to the ground and buried his head in his arms.

Howard scanned the naked terrain leading down to the one-lane road and the rugged coast below. The rocky slopes were bare, long ago stripped of any usable firewood or brush. Not even the smallest of Japanese soldiers could find camouflage there. What were they watching for anyway? The Japanese weren't on the island. Were they?

They had received the most recent news a few hours ago when a Middlesex machine-gun unit had passed. Spotting Peter Young riding on the Bren-gun carrier and the freckled face of Dick Baxter as he marched alongside, Howard had scrambled down to the road. The carrier slowed to a standstill. 'Hey there. It's the Canucks.' Peter's face broke into a wide grin. 'What are you lads doing here?'

'Seems like some Limey can't give up the idea that there'll be an invasion from the sea.'

'Humph! Not bloody likely now. The Nips are barking up our rear. They think they've already won this whole friggin' thing. Sent a delegation across from the mainland on a barge this morning. They were carrying a white banner saying "Peace Mission".' Peter snorted. 'Giving us the opportunity to surrender. Right nice of 'em, eh?'

'And the response?'

'Told 'em to bugger off, of course,' Dick answered.

'We're headed down to guard the Lye Mun Passage,' Peter said, revving up the Bren carrier. 'That half-mile stretch of water is the most likely place for the Japs to try and cross. Why don't you blokes come with us?'

'We can't leave our post.'

'Up to you.' The carrier jerked forward. 'But you won't see any action here,' Peter shouted, over his shoulder.

'Nor win any medals either!' Howard called after him.

'Heard about our battleships?' Dick asked, walking away backwards. '*Prince of Wales* and *Repulse* were both sunk off the coast of Malaya.'

Howard's jaw dropped. *Both ships gone?* He trudged up the hill, unable to ignore the thought that any hope of relief from the sea had vanished with them. Now soaking up the afternoon sun streaming in through the tiny opening he couldn't ignore his hunger. They hadn't had a hot meal in three days. Their last rations had been dry biscuits yesterday. He was beginning to wonder if their unit commander had forgotten him and Gordy. Watching the road for the supply truck, he had to admit he had been tempted to go with the machine-gunners. Anything would be better than sitting for hours in this crumbling excuse for a pillbox overlooking a barren hillside. And the sea, the empty sea, from where, he knew – Gordy, Lawson, everyone, it seemed, except Major Maltby, knew – an invasion would never come. Still, orders were orders. He would sit there until the cows came home if he had to. Until he had a direct order from his troop commander to abandon this post. An order he found himself praying for. It was not that he was anxious to be in the thick of it. He had no desire to be a hero. He could hear the distant screams of mortar shells, feel the tremor of explosions, smell the acrid smoke and cordite on the wind. He knew it was all too real. But, like Gordy, he felt the frustration of sitting there useless, doing nothing.

Six hours later, the order came with their rations. Under cover of night they were moved to a new post only to find themselves at dawn in a similar bunker with a different view of the sea.

The heavy shelling from the mainland continued all the next day and night. Air-raid and all-clear sirens screamed intermittently while he and Gordy did nothing but move from one post to another.

Finally, ordered to report to Brigade Headquarters on the Wong Nei Chong Road in the centre of the island, they caught up with their platoon on the morning of December 17th. Through a curtain of rain Howard recognized Ken Campbell – the radio equipment bouncing beneath his rain cape – on the road ahead. They rushed forward and fell in beside him. 'This is organized confusion,' Ken grumbled, rainwater streaking his face. 'No sooner are we stationed in one spot than someone radios another plan. Orders given, orders withdrawn. I'm beginning to wonder if anyone knows what they're doing.'

'Yeah, us too,' Howard said. But they were on the move. North, towards Victoria. Gordy was visibly relieved. As they hunkered down in a ditch for the night, Howard was looking forward to advancing to Brigade Headquarters in the morning. Brigadier Lawson was there. He would get the mission back on track.

The next day, at dawn, Howard's unit closed in on the Wong Nei Chung Gap. Tired, hungry, they were running on something more than food now. Last night, the Japanese had invaded – no, swarmed over the island. Just as Peter Young had predicted, they had come across the narrow passage at Lye Mun in the dark of night. Now every man in the platoon knew they could be in hand-to-hand combat before the day was over.

Howard had stopped losing sleep over what might come next.

Somewhere over the last few days of endless shelling and constant manoeuvres that had led nowhere, he had learned to grab catnaps whenever there was a moment of silence, a break in the constant scream of incoming fire. He had stopped flinching at the sound of every bullet and mortar shell, stopped thinking about killing another human being. Backing up the Royal Scots' retreat from the mainland he had seen his first enemy soldier fall a heartbeat after he took aim and squeezed the trigger. But, unlike Sergeant York, he found he couldn't turn killing into a turkey shoot. The enemy was human, after all. But in the split second before he had trained his sights on the next charging warrior, Howard had experienced a surge of relief that there was one less Japanese soldier out there who would try to kill him today.

Less than a mile from Brigade Headquarters they came under attack. The sudden burst of machine-gun fire sent the troops scrambling for cover. Howard threw himself into the ditch as the high-pitched whistle of an incoming mortar pierced the air. His hands clutching his rifle – *never let go of your rifle* – he lay with his face buried in the wet earth while soil and rock fragments rained down on him. And something else. Something soft. Heavy rain-like plops landed on his helmet, his back. He brought his hand down and squinted at the red mush smeared on his fingers. Frantically he wiped them on his pants.

Where's Gordy? He twisted from side to side, furiously searching the ground around him with his hands, his eyes. 'Gordy!' he shouted. He lifted his head to peer over the side of the ditch. There, directly above him, with bullets spitting all around him, Private Veronick stood frozen, staring at a fresh crater a few yards up the road.

'Gordy! Get down!'

But he remained standing, mumbling something unintelligible above the rattle of gunfire. Scrambling up the side of the ditch, Howard threw himself forward, tackling his friend at the waist and bringing him down. He dragged him back into the ditch and lay on top of him as another explosion showered debris. Ignoring Gordy's struggles, he turned to Ken Campbell, who was crouched a few feet away struggling with the wireless radio. He hit it with the back of his fist. 'Mortar fire coming from the north,' he shouted to the platoon leader.

The north. Holy Christ! How can the Japs be north already?

Beneath him Gordy groaned.

Pinned down for the next hour the unit could only shoot blindly at the unseen enemy. Then, as suddenly as it had started, the barrage ceased. Cautiously, one by one, the Grenadiers picked themselves up and squatted in the ditch, taking inventory. Two men missing.

'Johnson and Maxwell,' Gordy muttered. 'They were there – then gone. Nothing left but a hole in the road.'

One of Gordy's boots caught Howard's eye. 'Your foot?' he asked.

Dazed, Gordy glanced down. His right boot was split open at the sole, a blood-soaked woollen sock showing. 'Must have taken some shrapnel,' he said. 'Funny, I don't feel anything.'

'There's a dressing station up there.' The platoon leader pointed back the way they had come. 'First side road to the right. Take him there.'

'I'm okay, sir,' Gordy said.

'Go! Now! That's an order!'

The two soldiers scrambled from the ditch. Crouched low, Howard trailed behind his limping friend, expecting a hail of bullets at any second. But there was silence as they threw themselves to the ditch on the other side of the road. For what seemed like hours they crept along the edge before they decided it was safe to walk in the open.

The first harbinger of the horror to follow was the bullet-ridden ambulance blocking the narrow road. Inside, the Punjabi driver lay slumped over the steering-wheel, his face gone. Shaken, Howard and Gordy stepped around the vehicle only to be greeted by more bodies at the side of the road; all appeared to have crawled to their death, reaching for help that would never come. Below the road a jumbled tangle of corpses filled the ravine.

'Don't let them see you limp,' someone said behind them.

Gordy and Howard spun around, rifles tight at their shoulders, aimed and ready.

On the other side of the road a pile of bodies moved. A khaki-clad soldier crawled out from underneath it. Covered with dried blood and dirt, a tattered dressing around his head, he pushed himself up with his left arm. 'Private Jack Dell,' he said. 'Royal Rifles.'

Howard lowered his gun. 'What in hell happened here?'

'A massacre. Nothing but a friggen' massacre,' the Newfoundlander spat. 'They don't want no prisoners. Use any excuse to kill us.' He pointed to a nearby tree. It took Howard a moment to grasp that the apparition hanging from the branches was a corpse strung up by its heels. 'Bayoneted for nothing but the fun of it,' he said, struggling to sit up. 'The wounded, every one of them killed. Nurses, medics, all gone, marched off to God-knows-where. I played dead under my mates' bodies. They missed me – well, almost.' He held up his bloodied right arm. 'Caught it with a bayonet.'

Offering his hand, Howard pulled the seemingly weightless soldier to his feet. Standing, Jack Dell was no more than five foot six.

Howard turned to Gordy. 'Go with him and backtrack to the coast. Find another dressing station. I'm going to catch up with our unit.'

'Bullshit!' they answered in unison.

'There ain't nothing wrong with me except this bullet graze on my forehead.' The Newfoundlander held up his right arm and wiggled his fingers. 'The arm's okay. All I need is to wrap it. I can still shoot Nips with it.'

'Yeah. Who promoted you to sergeant?' Gordy growled at Howard. 'I can walk perfectly well.' And to prove it he headed back up the road, walking on his heel.

That night, they found most of their company. Too late. Brigade Headquarters had fallen. Lawson was dead, cut down leading his men in a charge from the bunker. The Japanese were in control of Wong Nei Chong Road. They had effectively split the island in two.

Skirting the mass carnage on the road and hillsides around the bunker, Howard's unit forged ahead under the cover of darkness. They reached the eastern slopes of Mount Nicholson and dug in just in time to hear a static voice coming from Ken Campbell's radio box: 'To all military forces in Hong Kong. This is Mark Young, the Governor of Hong Kong speaking. The time has come to advance against the enemy. The eyes of the empire are upon us. Be strong. Be resolute and do your duty.'

'What the frig does he think we've been doing?' Jack Dell asked.

The next night, after a heavy day of fighting, Howard had lost all sense of time. Hours had passed in minutes. That morning the platoon commander had ordered Jack Dell to St Stephen's Hospital. There was no arguing with him. Gordy escaped his scrutiny and was repositioned with Howard at Middle Gap, trying to take back the Wong Nei Chong Road.

Outnumbered, under-equipped and untrained, they were being pounded by the battle-hardened Japanese. Over the last hours Howard had witnessed, and heard reports of, more acts of heroism than he cared to in a lifetime. Grenadier Sergeant Major Osborn had been killed smothering a live grenade to save his men. Private Jack Williams had been shot down carrying a wounded mate to safety. Private Aubrey Flagg had volunteered to charge into a deathtrap with two Colt pistols and rescued an English woman and her two young daughters from a group of renegade Japanese. Even the Royal Rifles' mascot, the huge black Newfoundland dog Gander, had saved his unit by racing into the mêlée to fetch a grenade that had landed at their feet. He ran off with it in his mouth and was blown to oblivion. There were heroes of every rank, Howard was certain, but like most of his comrades he was just trying to stay alive.

He looked at Gordy, fast asleep sitting on the hillside next to him. He was something too, this bulldog friend of his, re-fusing to limp although he had had to loosen his lace to relieve his swelling foot. He was running on pure adrenalin. But how long could he keep it up?

In the pre-dawn light, his unit prepared to fall back, down the same slopes they had fought their way up yesterday. A group of Hong Kong Volunteers was trapped in a concrete bunker below. Howard's straggling unit, now less than thirty men and one Vickers machine-gun, was on its way down to rescue them. With the machine-gunners covering from above, they started their descent.

They had made it halfway down the mountainside before Howard saw the reflection of steel bayonets, and heard the bloodcurdling battle cries coming from the black wave storm-ing up the slope. He dropped to the ground. Pulling a grenade from his belt and ripping out the pin with his teeth, he tossed it, then raised his rifle to aim into the advancing Japanese. A burst of bullets from the Vickers whistled overhead and the enemy fell back. An armoured car appeared on the road below, guns blazing. The British Middlesex! The Japanese were caught in the vice, the Grenadiers pressing down from above, the armoured car coming up to their rear. Howard and Gordy rose with the rest of their troop and charged down the hill, flinging grenades and shooting into the ranks of the trapped enemy. Suddenly, a second wave of Japanese came swarming from the flanks, heavy mortar fire with them. The armoured car below took a direct hit. Howard dropped and rolled behind a knoll, Gordy close behind. To their right a dry creek bed fell away from the slope. Howard pointed to it. Gordy nodded. Together they rose and dived, rolling to the bottom. Crawling on their elbows they inched downhill.

The too-familiar smell of cordite mixed with the scent of freshly turned earth filled Howard's nostrils and an unexpected vision of a newly ploughed Manitoba wheatfield flashed in and out of his mind as they moved towards the ridge. He raised his head and peered over.

The turf-covered roof of the concrete bunker in which the Hong Kong Volunteers were trapped lay directly below. On the road, which was littered with casualties from both sides, sat a Japanese cannon with the business end pointed at the bunker door. From out of nowhere, a helmet appeared on the edge of the bunker roof. A dark figure hoisted itself up and crawled across to the ventilation pipe. He stood up, exposing himself as a Japanese soldier, who in one quick movement grabbed a grenade from his belt, pulled the pin and leaned over the pipe.

Howard had no time to think. He leapt, hitting the soldier

from behind, knocking him and the exploding grenade over the side of the bunker.

The concussion from the blast threw Howard backwards. Arms and legs flailing, he felt himself sail through the air. He thudded to the earth face down, his rifle flying from his hands. Ears ringing, eyes burning, he searched blindly for his gun. With relief his hand clamped on to the butt and he rolled onto his back clutching it to his chest.

Above, in the innocent morning sky, the last stars shone down on a world gone mad. A vision of Lucy came to him, her face so clear he could see the freckles sprinkled on her nose, the white of her teeth as she smiled at him. So this was the moment. Death was waiting out there with the dawn. If he was going to meet it, he would go out fighting, as Brigadier Lawson had. He braced himself to rise, to launch himself back to his feet and charge forward to whatever fate awaited.

He saw the glint of steel, felt the pressure against his chest before he saw another Japanese soldier straddled over him, forcing him back to the ground with the point of his bayonet. He reached down, ripped Howard's rifle from his hands and kicked it away. With a smile he reared back, his bayonet ready to thrust.

'Teiryuu!' The bark of command stopped the bayonet in mid-air. The rifle dropped to the soldier's side as he snapped to attention. Howard twisted his head towards the voice. On the road a Japanese officer stood with his feet planted wide. Behind him, screaming soldiers herded surrendering Hong Kong Volunteers out of the bunker. The officer strutted over and looked down at Howard. 'So, we meet again my friend,' he said.

Rising slowly, Howard took in the immaculate uniform, the red band and star on the officer's cap, the sabre hanging from the leather belt. It was a few moments before he realized that this Japanese officer, who was speaking perfect English, was the little barber with whom, a lifetime ago, he had shared cigarettes and beer outside the barracks at Sham Shui Po.

The sound of the battle carried on during the straggling march towards Victoria. For Howard, though, and what was left of his unit, the fighting was over. They were now prisoners of war. But they were alive, thanks to the officer who had spared Howard's life. All along the forced march north they witnessed the evidence of wanton butchery: British and Canadian soldiers left to rot in heaps in ditches, many with their arms wired behind their backs. The dead were not limited to the military. The decomposing bodies of civilians, including women and children, littered the route. On the outskirts of Victoria they came upon the corpse of a young woman so brutalized and mutilated that Howard had to turn away.

'Savages!' Gordy screamed at the guard leering over the naked body. 'You're nothing but a bunch of savages!' A gun butt slammed against his head. Howard, tethered to him by telephone wire, staggered with him.

'Shut up,' someone in the straggling group growled. 'These guys will kill us just as soon as look at us.'

'Don't draw attention to yourself,' Howard whispered, pulling Gordy upright. 'Lean against me.' Together they stumbled forward.

It was impossible to reconcile the mind-numbing carnage with the unexpected acts of kindness their captors sometimes showed out of the blue. Guards as likely to knock you to the ground with a rifle butt might offer a drink of water from their canteen, or secretly slip a prisoner a morsel of food.

And then there was the officer who had allowed Howard to live.

After the siege of the bunker, the Hong Kong Volunteers, along with the surrendering Canadians, were lined up, searched and stripped of anything of value. Howard's watch, the Hong Kong dollars in his uniform pockets and his wedding ring were quickly confiscated. Heartsick, he watched as his diary was tossed to the ground. The barber-turned-officer strode over, bent down and retrieved it. He straightened, opened the diary and removed Lucy's photograph. 'Childhood sweetheart,' he said, grinning at Howard. Then he reached into his uniform jacket for his own diary. He opened it, took out a similar photograph and held it up for Howard's inspection.

A young dark-haired woman smiled demurely from the sepia photograph. 'Very pretty,' Howard forced himself to say.

'Yes,' the officer said, his voice barely audible. He returned Howard's diary to him, with Lucy's photograph, before he moved on. That would be the last time Howard saw him.

Exhausted, filthy and hungry, the procession reached Victoria two days after their capture. Under a canopy of black smoke, the prisoners were paraded through the crowded streets behind Japanese officers on prancing stallions. The city had been pulverized: burned-out buses and cars clogged the streets. The harbour was a graveyard of half-sunk ships, burning ferries and fuel tanks. Glass and debris littered every step of the way. The Rising Sun emblem hung from pocked and shelled buildings. Banners displaying it stretched overhead. And lining the streets, terrified Chinese civilians wearing bandannas, with the same red blood circles on their arms, chorused in broken English, 'Asia for Asians! Asia for Asians.'

Frantically Gordy and Howard scanned the sea of faces. But there were so many. Their march ended at North Point, the former refugee camp, where they were herded inside the gates.

The camp had been ransacked, stripped almost bare. Not a metal cot, blanket or mattress was left in any of the dilapidated huts. Worse still, there was not a single latrine. That night Howard and the rest of the prisoners slept crowded onto the few wooden bunks, and on bare concrete floors. The following day many milled about, shoulder to shoulder, searching every inch of the grounds for anything edible. Some sat motionless, with the vacant stare of the defeated. Other swapped stories of what they had been through. Many wept for lost comrades. For the most part the Japanese ignored them. A few bored guards taunted them through the barbed wire for surrendering. Only cowards would allow themselves to be captured instead of dying in glory on the battlefield or killing themselves.

Every hour more prisoners arrived, British and Canadian. Howard breathed a sigh of relief when he saw Ken Campbell, minus his radio and helmet, walk through the gates that evening. Covered with dirt and appearing twenty pounds lighter, he joined Howard at the fence, sharing the news that a company of Royal Rifles and Hong Kong Volunteers were still fighting, making a final stand at Stanley, their backs to the sea.

Not long after the surviving Rajputs strode into camp a convoy of Japanese officers arrived. Wearing full dress uniform and white gloves, they drove up in open cars like royalty. One climbed out to strut back and forth on the other side of the fence. 'You are Asians, like us,' he called out to the East Indian troops. 'Shake our hands. Unite with us in victory. Join us in sharing an Asia for Asians. We must show our unity to the world.' The Rajputs sat on the ground inside the camp, cross-legged and silent, while offers of friendship and promises of a world free of white supremacy carried across to them. Pleas to enlist in the Japanese cause fell on deaf ears.

Finally the officers grew frustrated. Machine-guns were

brought in, set up on tripods and trained on the camp.

'Join us or die,' an officer screamed, holding his sword high in the air.

The Rajputs, who had fought a ferocious battle for seventeen straight days, stood as one. Howard watched, his heart in his throat, as they marched up to the wire fence. In silence, the proud warriors ripped open their shirts and thrust forward their bared chests.

The entire camp held its breath. Howard listened to the normal sounds of wind on the water and seagulls crying. No one moved a muscle. On both sides of the fence the two adversaries held fast. Finally the Japanese blinked. The officer spat an order in Japanese. The machine-guns withdrew.

For the next few days the Japanese ignored the prisoners.

Howard spent most of his daylight hours battling the incessant flies that plagued everyone. The only relief came with the rain. The moment it let up, though, they swarmed in dark clouds over the piles of manure left by the Japanese Army's horses and mules. Moving black carpets shrouded the decomposing bodies, animal and human, outside the camp. Merciless, they alighted on any exposed skin, crawled inside clothes, into every orifice and open cut. The stench in the camp was unbearable. Men were becoming sick.

Then, on Christmas Day, word came that Governor Mark Young had surrendered the colony. It was officially over. In the afternoon a truck pulled up at the camp gates and dumped three brown burlap sacks of rice on the ground.

'Merry Christmas,' Ken Campbell said, heaving one over his shoulder. Three sacks to feed thousands of men.

Hours later, Howard sat on the ground leaning against a fence post. He looked down at the handful of half-cooked rice in his helmet. He thought about the old woman outside the camp yesterday picking undigested grains from dried horse dung. Still, he had to eat. Slowly, slowly.

Gordy finished his ration in two gulps and continued to stare at the wide road beyond the fence watching for Shun-ling. Howard found himself praying she wouldn't come near the camp. He had seen what the Japanese could do to a helpless woman.

As much as the Japanese hated the prisoners, they seemed to hate the Chinese even more. Some of the guards took pot-shots at any who strayed too close, old or young, male or female, for the sport of it. Their superiors, if they saw it, said nothing. The starving old woman outside the camp had paid for her few grains of dung-covered rice with her life. The guards had allowed her to get close enough, then had systematically shot her legs out from under her, and then, laughing, used her body, as she tried to crawl away, for target practice.

Beside him Gordy set his helmet on the ground. 'She was a virgin,' he said, still staring at the road.

'What?'

'Shun-ling.'

Taken aback by this unexpected confidence, the intimacy of the words, Howard could not speak.

'I didn't expect her to be . . .' Gordy searched for words. 'Well, I thought . . . I don't know. I thought because her father sold her . . .' He paused. 'I didn't mean for it to happen. It just did. Grateful. I guess she was grateful.' He shook his head. 'I ain't proud of it.'

Howard remained silent, trying to ignore the burning in his gut that wasn't hunger.

'Christ. I have feelings for her, Howie. Not like other girls. It ain't pity, or lust, or even sex. It's something more than that.' He swallowed. 'I know it's been less than a month, but I'm thinking of, well, taking her home with me. Asking her to marry me, you know.'

The heat in Howard's stomach rose to his chest. 'Are you sure?'

Gordy lifted his head. 'Yeah, I'm sure,' he growled. 'I've never been more sure of anything.' His eyes held an unspoken challenge.

Howard forced himself to hold his gaze. 'Well, ah, that's swell, then,' he said.

'Yeah, swell,' Gordy said. 'Except now I'll probably never see her again.'

In spite of the mayhem on both sides of the fence, in spite of his confused feelings, Howard found his voice: 'Sure you will,' he reassured his friend. 'When this is all over you'll go into Victoria and find her waiting for you in that flat.'

'Yeah. When this is all over. Right.'

'Sure.' Even to his own ears Howard's words rang false. 'The Americans are in it now. It's just a matter of time.'

26

Dad tried. He really did. The morning after we went to the drive-in movie, he was up early. When Kipper and I came downstairs he was sitting at the kitchen table with a mug of coffee and the Sunday newspaper spread in front of him. 'Zero tide this morning,' he announced. 'What does everyone say to heading down to Birch Bay for the day?'

A few seconds of surprised silence followed his question.

'Sure,' I said, my voice deliberately flat, as if any display of excitement would shatter the possibility that it might happen.

Kipper had no such fear. 'Yay,' he cried, clapping his hands, then going over to pat Dad's shoulder, saying, 'That's good, Da.'

Dad smiled up at him, then turned to the stove where Frankie was frying bacon. 'What about you, Frankie?'

Frankie didn't speak for what felt like a long time. Eventually he said, 'Yeah. Sure.' But his voice, like mine, was cautious. It wasn't that we didn't like Birch Bay – everyone in our family loved going to the small American resort town across the border, especially Dad. After Mom bought the Hudson we would often find him checking the newspaper tide tables on a clear Sunday morning. If the tide was low, we would go off for the day to hunt for Dungeness crabs in the tidal flats of the bay. It was just hard to imagine being there without Mom.

It felt strange packing up our picnic lunch without her. Kipper and I buttered the bread for the sandwiches – peanut butter and jelly for us, baloney with mustard for Frankie, and for Dad, of course, his favourite sardines. Watching Kipper spread the peanut butter I couldn't help thinking how easily he had grown used to Mom not being there. How he seemed to accept her absence as part of our lives. I wondered if he understood that he would never see her again. Did he even know what 'never' meant? Mom used to say that, given enough time, Kipper could understand anything, figure anything out, that left to himself he would always do the right thing. 'He has wisdom beyond learning,' she had maintained.

As if he had read my thoughts, Kipper looked up at me. His wide face broke into a lopsided grin. 'I think in heben Mom's happy we're going to the beach,' he said, pressing the top slice of bread on to his sandwich.

I recognized the false cheer in Dad's voice as we loaded into Frankie's Studebaker. But during the drive, while he and Kipper talked about the crab feast we were going to have, he sounded as if he was truly present.

The trip to Washington took less than an hour. Kipper let out his usual whooping holler once we crossed the United States border at the Peace Arch. We set up at the last picnic table on the beach, then made our way over barnacle-covered rocks to the shallow pools of the tidal flats. Each time we flushed out one of the huge red crabs from the seaweed Frankie or Dad scooped it up from behind. Avoiding the huge pincer claws, they tossed the wriggling bounty into a bucket while Kipper and I cheered.

In the afternoon, we floated on the incoming tide in our black inner tubes. When we came out of the water I spread my towel over the sand and lay down on my stomach. At the picnic table Frankie told Dad he was going back to work the next day. 'Night shift,' he said. The last thing I remember before I dozed off was them talking about finding someone to come to the house once Dad returned to work.

I woke some time later to hear them discussing Mr Telford's phone call. 'Strange man,' Frankie was saying, 'to be concerned about selling Kipper's paintings when his wife . . .' he hesitated '. . . at this time.'

'Everyone has their own way of coping, I guess,' Dad answered quietly.

I opened one eye and saw him gazing out at the bay, but it wasn't his usual not-there stare.

'I think the call was an excuse to set the record straight,' he said after a while. 'Maybe he feels guilty that it was his boat, his faulty heater, I don't know. But he says he had no idea they were going there, that when Marlene grabbed her sketch pad after Lucy called, he assumed they were going to the shop.' He ran his hand over his face, then heaved a sigh. 'He told me that Lucy was having Marlene paint her portrait. A surprise for me. Asked if I wanted the sketches he'd found—' He stopped talking when he caught my eye.

Later, as the sun went down, we sat in the glow of our camp-fire, sucking the meat from the freshly boiled crabs. It was as close to normal as it was possible to be with bruised hearts. I kept my eye on Dad, waiting for him to slip away into his own world. I noticed Frankie watching him warily too. But Dad stayed with us, drinking nothing but Coca-Cola.

He kept it up for the next few days. Then, Wednesday after-noon, Dora Fenwick brought him Mom's note.

27

'I wasn't holding this back,' Mrs Fenwick said. 'I just found it last night.' She glanced down at the envelope in her hand. 'In the sugar canister,' she added, stepping in from the side porch. 'Mom's memory is getting worse.' She followed Dad to the kitchen table, but refused the chair he offered. 'I won't stay. I just wanted to give it to you.' She looked over to where I was drying dishes at the counter.

I knew that look. It meant she wasn't going to talk about what was on her mind while I was in the room. I put down the dishtowel and went out onto the front porch. Through the half-open window I could see her and Dad standing by the table. 'I struggled with whether or not to give it to you,' she said, turning the envelope over and over in her hands. 'I don't know if it will hurt or help, but I decided you should have it.' As if she was reluctant to part with it, she passed it to Dad.

He swallowed. A vein in the side of his throat pulsed as he took it.

'She—' Dora Fenwick's voice cracked. 'Lucy left it with my mother that Saturday. Probably didn't trust her to remember to tell me she was looking for me.' She fidgeted with her sweater sleeves as if she didn't know what to do with her hands now that they were empty. 'I'll leave it with you.' She went back to the kitchen door, then stopped and faced Dad again. 'We noticed the girl in the park when we were having coffee the day before,' she said, 'wondered about her standing there in the pouring rain, but until I read the note I never gave any more thought to her.'

Dad's head snapped up. 'The girl?'

'Read it,' she said, her voice barely above a whisper. 'Lucy needed a friend that day. If only I'd been home.'

After the door closed Dad collapsed on to a kitchen chair. He took the folded sheet of paper out of the envelope and pressed it on to the table, his hands shaking. The tremors moved up his arms and spread through his body as he read. 'Oh, God,' he murmured, 'I should have told her the truth years ago.'

But Mrs Fenwick was already out of the door. As soon as she had walked across the lawn, I went back into the kitchen. 'Dad?' I had to repeat it three times before he lifted his head. He folded the paper and, without another word, rose and left the room. Moments later I heard his bedroom door close. When Frankie called him at suppertime he sat at the table with us but he barely touched his warmed-over stew.

After dinner, while Dad and Kipper sat wedged in the chair in front of the television, Frankie left for the evening. I waited until I'd heard his car pull out of the backyard. Then I went down the hall and into Dad's bedroom. I closed the door softly behind me, tiptoed over to his dressing-table and rifled through the drawers. The envelope that Mrs Fenwick had given him wasn't in any of them. I started searching Mom's vanity drawers. It wasn't there either – there was nothing except some of her old newspaper clippings. Curious, I picked one up. The article was from an old *Daily Province*.

CANADIANS ON BATTLE FRONT HONG KONG
Dominion in Thick of Fighting as Japanese Attack
OTTAWA, 8 December 1941 – Canadian troops stationed at Hong Kong are in an active theatre of war now that Canada has de-

clared war on Japan and fighting has started in the Western Pacific . . .

A dispatch from London, which said it was believed the Japanese already have attacked 'some British possessions', and mention of Hong Kong among 'places attacked', served to give increased emphasis to the fact that the area where Canadians are serving is in the war zone. Names of the units involved have not been disclosed.

Why would she save this?

I quickly sifted through the rest of the clippings, stopping to study a grainy photograph below the faded headline, *Hong Kong Troops First Canadians in Combat.* The serious faces of the soldiers posing for the camera belonged to strangers.

I scanned the column.

10 December – Canadian Press War Correspondent
Canada's China forces are the envy of the Canadian corps. Canadian troops in Britain followed reports closely today for word of comrades stationed at Hong Kong.

'Lucky guys,' was the phrase heard on every side.

'And to think if I had stayed with my old regiment I'd be with them in Hong Kong now,' said a 1st Division colonel from Winnipeg who arrived in Britain with the first Contingent two years ago. 'They'll give those Jap fellows plenty of lead.'

As I placed the clipping back in the drawer I saw the faded yellow telegram. I picked it up and read the short message, addressed to Mom at Aunt Mildred's on Vine Street.

Hong Kong? My father had been in Hong Kong? I didn't understand. I sat down on the vanity stool. Even though my father never talked about it, I knew he had been in the war but not that he had been in Hong Kong. Suddenly I thought about the Chinese girl in the park. Did she have something to do with my father? Was she from Hong Kong? Did she know him when he was there? *No.* She was way too young. My mind was a jumble of questions that made no sense.

Confused, I put everything away and went outside to sit on our front porch. The television voice of Timmy calling Lassie home seeped through the open living-room window while I stared at the park across the street.

Out on the road a group of kids played kick-the-can in the evening twilight. The sounds of their laughter filled the warm summer night. Ardith waved at me to join them. I shook my head. Every once in a while, from porches and windows, came the singsong voice of someone's mother calling them in. The hot stone of sorrow in my chest became heavier at the thought that I would never again hear the familiar cry for me.

I sat with my chin in my hands until Danny Fenwick walked up our lawn. He sat down on the porch step below me, leaning against the rail as the evening sky grew darker. I tried to pay attention while he talked about normal things, like going back to school in two weeks, his new bike, but, like Dad's, my mind was somewhere else. Eventually he stopped trying and we watched in silence as the game wound down under the streetlamp.

'Did you know my mom went over to your house looking for yours that Saturday – the day she died?' I asked.

'No,' he said, nervously adjusting his glasses on his nose. 'No. I didn't.'

'Well, did you ever see a girl, a Chinese girl, over there?' I nodded towards the park.

'Hey, yeah, a couple of times. Even in the pouring rain one morning.'

I sat up. 'What was she doing?'

'Just standing there. I thought she must be waiting for someone, until I saw her . . .' He clamped his mouth shut.

'What? Saw what? What morning?'

'Nothing.'

'What?' I demanded, grabbing his shoulder.

'Gee, Ethie, I didn't mean to—'

'Just tell me. Please.'

'Then – well, I saw her on your porch, that, uh, that same Saturday morning . . . talking to your mom.'

At that moment Mrs Fenwick's voice sang out for Danny. He pushed himself up. 'I gotta go,' he said, jamming his hands into his pockets. He took a few steps, then turned back and said something else.

'Huh?'

'I asked if you wanted to come to the tree fort with me to-morrow?'

'Oh, uh, no,' I said, trying to give him some kind of smile, but knowing it wasn't working. 'Thanks, but not tomorrow.'

Tomorrow I was going back downtown. I was going to find out what that girl had to do with my family.

28

1 January 1942: Hong Kong, North Point Camp

The burial party left camp at dawn. Grey smoke rose from the Japanese funeral pyre as they approached a littered battlefield. So many dead. On both sides. Howard dug his shovel into the ground. Leaving it standing, he removed his shirt and wrapped it around his face. The perspiration and battle-soiled material did little to stop the gagging stench – a stench so thick the air felt solid – but at least it kept the flies from crawling into his mouth, his nose.

The wet earth surrendered easily, opening willingly, to accept its due.

The innocent scent of rain-drenched soil brought a split second's respite from the foul odours. With it came a flash of a rain-soaked Vancouver street. Was it really only a little more than two months ago that he and Lucy had stood on the damp grass in front of Mildred's house? Another lifetime. Another world – a sane world. Did it still exist? Was Lucy right now walking down that same street, or lying in bed in that same house, worrying and wondering if he was alive or dead?

I'm all right, Lucy. I'm all right. With each shovel of dirt he silently repeated the message, willing it onto the wind, to be carried across the ocean and into her heart. *I'm all right, Lucy.*

When the hole was deep enough, wide enough, the soldiers paired off to begin the gruesome task of placing their fallen comrades in the mass grave. Howard leaned over the first body. He swallowed, refusing to gag on the bile that rose in his throat, and gently removed the ID tag from the bloated corpse. Someone screamed, '*Teiryuu!*' Stop.

A rifle butt slammed into the side of Howard's head, knocking him to his knees. The tag was ripped from his hand and tossed into the hole. Through ringing ears he heard heated arguments breaking out between the screaming guards and the enraged prisoners trying to rescue ID tags.

Howard forced himself to his feet. If he had learned anything about his captors in the last weeks it was that they followed the rules only when it suited them. Just yesterday, after a British officer demanded more humane treatment for his men, he had been beaten bloody by a camp guard, who had spat out in broken English, 'Japan not sign Geneva Convention.' The prisoners were only alive by the good graces of the Emperor, which, Howard guessed, meant they must have some use for them – as bargaining tools, hostages for trade, who knew?

In the meantime, it was clear the guards meant to demoralize, dehumanize them in every way they could. What better way than by taking their names?

He turned back to the task at hand. Ignoring the continuous commands to hurry, the prodding of rifle butts, the odour of death, the hunger in his belly, he focused on the name on the next body's ID tag. 'Remember the names!' he shouted. 'Remember the names!'

The cry was picked up and passed from man to man as they laid their brothers to rest. *Remember the names.*

Bujold . . . Lebel . . . McGrath . . . Chalmers . . .

After they had returned to the camp Howard located Colonel Sutcliffe in the officers' section of the camp. He looked as if he had aged forty years in the last two weeks, and his once squared shoulders seemed to sag more with each reported name.

During the following weeks, at every roll call, every standing at attention for hours in the afternoon sun, at each bowing to guards, at each scream of a Japanese officer's name, Howard continued to repeat silently the names of the fallen. The internal mantra helped to blur the voices, the faces, the presence of his captors, strengthening his determination not to allow *their* names a place in his mind.

18 January 1942: ... Doyle ... Main ... Slaughter ...

He could never know all the names but he memorized as many as possible. There was little to do during the days except think about food and he wasn't going to fall into that trap. He mentally alphabetized the growing list, repeating the silent exercise whenever he was alone – even while he emptied his screaming bowels. The flies had brought dysentery. No one was spared.

Howard straddled the boards over the sea wall – the only place a man could relieve himself – at the rear of the camp. He hooked his belt over a fence post to keep his balance and squatted. He tried not to look down into the waters lapping the slime-covered rocks below. Each wave brought fresh horrors – bloated corpses and body parts undulating among the other flotsam.

He hitched up his pants. With a will of their own, his eyes glanced downward. He froze. Directly in the water below there was a human leg. A long cloth puttee trailed behind the naked calf, floating like a question mark from the top of the boot, which was still laced to a foot. A right foot. Howard hurriedly unhooked himself from the fence. He needed a long stick to fish out the boot that would replace Gordy's. Scrambling frantically to the edge of the sea wall he tried to pull up one of the boards.

'Forget it. Just wait a few hours for someone to leave the Agony Ward. They don't need their boots once they come out of there.'

Howard spun around to see who had spoken, but no one was there. The words had come from his own mind. He sank to the ground. What was he thinking? A water-logged boot? Hunger and worry about Gordy were making him delirious.

Gordy's leg was getting worse. He could no longer put any weight on it. Every morning Howard helped him to hobble outside to keep vigil by the camp fence. He refused to return to the hospital ward. Howard couldn't blame him. He had gone with him to the converted warehouse the first week for the doctor to cut the boot off Gordy's swelling foot. Small wonder they called it the Agony Ward, he'd thought, watching the doctor clean the wound and wrap it in reused bandages. No more than a shed at the back of the camp, the 'hospital' was no cleaner, no saner, than the other dilapidated buildings in North Point Camp.

There were now more than six thousand prisoners in the overcrowded huts meant to house three hundred refugees. The hospital was no better, and certainly no place for a well man, let alone the wounded or sick. Howard couldn't shake the image of them lying on makeshift beds and stretchers laid on the concrete floor, covered with blood and filth, flimsy blankets or none at all, cared for by overworked army doctors and volunteer orderlies who had little to offer but sympathy and false hope. Howard was as relieved as Gordy to escape.

The primitive conditions in the makeshift hospital were not the only reason the prisoners feared it. Howard, along with the entire camp, had heard about the carnage at St Stephen's Army Hospital. Jack Dell had made sure they did. His arm had been amputated there two days before the Japanese arrived on

Christmas Eve. Having survived one massacre, he knew what was in store. The moment the Japanese stormed up the stairs and into the wards he had rolled off his bed and lain hidden beneath a pile of linen while the killing spree went on. Now he walked around the camp telling anyone who would listen how sick and wounded soldiers had been shot or bayoneted to death. 'The blood was so deep it ran down the stairs. When the Japs were finished with the soldiers, they went on a rampage, raping and murdering the nurses and nuns.' According to him, the non-stop orgy of blood and mayhem lasted until the next day. When it was over, seventy British and Canadian soldiers were dead, along with twenty-five hospital staff. Jack Dell and the few other survivors had been forced to cremate them. And, like the burial parties after the surrender, they were denied the collection of ID tags. When Japanese officers arrived on the scene, and were told by a hysterical doctor what had taken place, they had executed the perpetrators on the spot, promising that the atrocities would not be condoned or repeated. But who had reason to trust their word? Certainly not the prisoners, who were already suffering from malnutrition and watched help-lessly while friends and comrades died every day.

Still, as Gordy's foot and leg continued to swell beneath the blackened bandages, Howard pleaded with him to return to the hospital. Gordy refused. All he wanted was to sit by the camp fence.

Howard pestered the doctors for non-existent medicine. 'Just get him more nourishment,' was the only advice they could offer.

Food – two miserable servings of mouldy rice often littered with mouse turds and maggots – became the event around which each day pivoted. Every now and then a load of foul-smelling vegetable matter, which appeared to be composted peelings mixed with grass and seaweed, was dumped at the gate and added to the rice. Howard hoped that the 'Green Horror', as the prisoners termed it, at least added some nutrition to the meagre portions. He stood in line twice a day, scraping half of his ration into Gordy's helmet before delivering it to him, but the weight fell off his friend's stocky frame at an even greater rate than it did from the rest of the prisoners, and the angry red of infection climbed up his calf.

During the second week in February, at Howard's urging, Ken Campbell brought a camp doctor to Gordy's bed. 'It has to come off,' the doctor said, after he had inspected the leg. 'Bring him to the medical hut.'

'They ain't hacking my leg off,' Gordy growled, the moment the doctor had left.

Ken, one of the brave few who had volunteered to work as an orderly in the makeshift ward, refused to listen. 'There's no choice,' he told him. 'It's your leg or your life.'

'I'll take my chances,' Gordy said, struggling to stand.

'And what am I supposed to tell Shun-ling when this is over?' Howard demanded. 'That you died because you were afraid? That you didn't care if you saw her again unless you had all your body parts?'

They amputated his leg below the knee. Somehow Ken persuaded one of the friendlier guards to supply a small vial of chloroform. Still, Howard didn't know how Gordy endured it. Waiting outside the hospital shed, his hands pressed over his ears, he could still hear the muffled screams as the doctors performed the primitive surgery. During the following days he stayed in the hut to nurse his friend, sleeping on the floor next to him each night. The moment Gordy could stand on his good leg, they hobbled out of the Agony Ward.

Howard's moment-to-moment purpose in life now was to take care of his friend. He found a peanut-oil can and helped him to squat on it outside their hut so he wouldn't have to make the trip to the sea wall. He ripped two boards from the back of their hut and fashioned a set of crutches. And each morning he helped Gordy to the fence where they sat in the shade of the guardhouse watching the wide road in front of the camp.

Over the following months, conditions at North Point grew worse. During the days there was no relief from the scorching sun. Nights were surprisingly cold. Many of the prisoners had only bare boards or the concrete floor to lie on so they slept curled up in groups of three or four, taking turns in the middle for warmth.

'When you get home, tell Lucy I kept your bed warm,' a shivering Gordy joked, as he lay wedged between Howard and Ken. 'Tell her I kept my promise to look after you.'

'You can tell her yourself.'

Even without blankets the bedbugs were rampant. Along with lice and fleas, they tormented the already tormented. Grateful that he, Gordy and Ken were still miraculously spared this affliction, Howard watched the not so fortunate going crazy with scratching. He wondered how long the effects of Ah Sam's magic potion would last.

Lieutenant Colonel J. L. R. Sutcliffe. On April 7th Howard added the name to his mental scroll. The colonel had succumbed to beriberi and anaemia. But Howard believed he had wasted away, died of a broken heart, at the loss of so many of his 'boys'. He joined the burial party to lay him to rest in the makeshift graveyard outside the camp. They had ceased playing the Last Post. It was too disheartening. There were no longer any grave markers. As soon as a wooden cross was placed, refugees came in the night to pilfer the valuable firewood. Graves were opened and robbed for the flimsy burial blankets. In time the prisoners stopped wrapping the bodies. There was not enough warmth at night for the living.

At the end of April, Howard stood at the fence watching the British regiments leave for Camp Argyle and Sham Shui Po on the mainland. Suddenly, among the thousands of straggling troops filing by, he spotted Peter Young and Dick Baxter. Their hair was longer and their bedraggled uniforms hung limp on their slight frames, but the two Middlesex machine-gunners seemed defiantly none the worse for wear. Relieved to see they had both survived, Howard called, 'Good to see you boys saw some action!'

Peter stopped and searched the crowd at the fence. He grinned when his eyes connected with Howard's. 'Yeah, we're just waiting on those medals.' A rifle poked at his side. Prodded forward, he shouted back, 'We'll see you two Canucks at the Sun Sun when this is all over. It's not for nothing that we're called the diehards.'

'It'll be your turn to buy the beer,' Howard shouted after him.

The more sadistic guards left with the British. The worst was a pinch-faced little man, who strutted about the camp like a bantam rooster. Howard would have found his sword-rattling posturing comical if it hadn't been so deadly. He often stood in front of the gate where, with false smiles and offers of food, he lured local girls across the road only to strong-arm them into the guardhouse. Their cries tormented Gordy and Howard.

If the essence of evil was taking pleasure in the suffering of others, Howard thought that the guard the prisoners had nicknamed Satan was its embodiment. Late at night he would hide in the shadows at the back of the camp, waiting for the unsuspecting to approach the sea wall. Before they could relieve themselves he would spring out and order them to bow to him. Forcing them to bow repeatedly, lower and lower, he practised jabbing with his bayonet, often inflicting wounds and taunting them as they soiled themselves. His only redeeming feature was his habit of sucking air through the gap between his two front teeth. Like a cat with a bell, the sound warned everyone that he was in the area. Howard, along with the entire camp, breathed a sigh of relief when he marched away with the British.

Suddenly, with the transfer of the prisoners, North Point was less crowded. Camp life became more organized, and Howard found himself believing his reassurances to Gordy that they would be free in a matter of months. Unfortunately the food did not improve and any complaints brought beatings or a further reduction in rations. But they had hope. For the first time Howard became aware of the contraband radio hidden between the wall studs in one of the huts. Spirits rose as real news – not the propaganda the Japanese spread – was passed from mouth to mouth.

Rumours ran, rich with hope, that relief was coming soon, but now their faith rested in the Americans. Chiang Kai-shek's phantom army was no longer mentioned.

In May the prisoners were allowed to write home for the first time, an allotted twenty-five words on a thin sheet of onion paper. There was no way of knowing if it would be sent, but it felt good to scratch his encouraging message, to imagine Lucy's joy at seeing his handwriting. 'My darling Lucy, Missing you and thinking of you each day. All is well. In good spirits. Being treated well. All my love always, Howard.' He felt no guilt at the falsity of his message.

Along with the goodwill gesture came the announcement that the Canadians were to be put to work extending the runway at Kai Tak airport. Howard and a group of twenty other able-bodied Grenadiers, accompanied by a rifle-toting guard, were ferried across to the mainland with the other work parties. From daybreak until dusk the PoWs hacked away at a small mountain. With baskets hanging from bamboo poles, coolie style, they transported their loads to the other end of the runway.

Fortunately the guard in charge of Howard's group was one of the good ones.

Most of their captors' cruelty, Howard noticed, could be attributed to loyalty to the Japanese empire, or to arrogance, or even to an adolescent-like sense of superiority. Few were as cruel as Satan. And few were as kind as their work-party guard, who treated them with a semblance of respect, feigning sternness only when superiors were present. He often apologized for 'our situation', sharing pictures of his family at every opportunity. On more than one occasion – at great risk to himself, Howard was certain – he had slipped a can of evaporated milk into the hands of someone in dire need.

While other guards at the airport continually screeched commands, urging more work out of their energy-depleted charges, he said nothing when someone in his crew stopped to rest. He did not ration water, allowing them to drink at will. And when they lined up in front of him at mealtimes he turned a blind eye to those who came back for second helpings.

At the setting of the sun, he bowed and thanked the men for a good day's work. Strange how exercise and a little respect can pick up spirits even in these circumstances, Howard thought, walking back to the ferry with the tired but somehow exhilarated band of men. Not to mention the extra rations. For the tenth time he checked the smuggled treasure in his pocket. Sprats. The tiny sardine-like fish were little more than mush now, but they would supply Gordy with a much-needed shot of protein. Nearing the docks he wondered how his friend had managed on his own today. Had someone helped him to the peanut-oil can? Had he made it to the fence so that he could keep vigil by the gate? Was he still there, watching, as he did every day, for someone he and Howard both – although they had never spoken of her since the first day in camp – hoped would never show up?

And then he saw her. Even from a distance he had no doubt it was Shun-ling. She stood by the turnstile at the Star ferry, in exactly the same spot she had waited on the first night they had gone to the cinema.

Howard edged through the tightly packed group of PoWs, not taking his eyes from her face. Shun-ling's gaze shifted between him and the guard who leaned against a lamppost smoking a cigarette, his rifle slung carelessly over his shoulder. Finally Howard stood before her, so close that only the waist-high metal turnstile separated them. At first neither spoke. He searched her eyes. Something was different. They were not the eyes of a girl. But, then, they never had been. She was only eighteen, but from the first moment Howard had felt like a boy in her presence. A twenty-year-old married boy, but a boy nonetheless. His experience in life had been nothing compared to the knowledge he saw reflected in her eyes. The last time he had seen her, he had just taken on the yoke of manhood with the army uniform, the hurried marriage vows, the marching off to war, while she had seen a lifetime's horror. But the last five months had been a lifetime. Howard was no longer innocent, no longer a boy, and their eyes met with the knowledge of adults.

With a will of its own, his gaze darted momentarily to the sleeve of her tunic top, taking in the white cloth tied around her arm displaying a blood-red sun. 'Ah Sam says we must at least make a show of support,' she said.

'He is a wise man,' Howard answered.

'And a good man,' she said. 'He took our family in. We are under his protection.'

'Gordy will be relieved to hear that.'

'Where is he?' she asked. 'I heard the Canadians were working at the airport. I hoped to see him. I—' She stopped mid-sentence. 'Is he all right?'

Should he tell her about Gordy's leg? About how much weight he had lost? About the blood and pus he saw each time he emptied the peanut-oil can?

He glanced around to see who was within earshot. 'He needs medicine, Shun-ling,' he whispered. 'Sulphur tablets. Can Ah Sam bring us some?'

'He cannot risk it. The Japanese believe Ah Sam is an ally,' she said, her voice so low he had to lean closer. 'I will bring it.'

'No. It isn't safe. Don't come near the camp. I'll be working at the airport every day now. Watch for me here.'

'I will find you.'

'See him?' Howard nodded to their guard. 'Only come if this guard is with us. Don't risk it if it's anyone else.'

The ferry horn sounded. The guard crushed his cigarette under his heel and gestured his crew forward.

'I'm happy to see you looking so well.' Howard backed away.

During their hurried exchange he had noticed that all pretence at pidgin English had disappeared from Shun-ling's speech. *Trust or necessity?*

It was only as she turned to leave, when he saw her in profile, her hands protectively shielding the telltale bulge under her tunic, that he realized why she had come looking for Gordy.

From the moment Howard brought back the news, Gordy insisted on joining the work party. The guards didn't care. Their quota was five hundred men and, able-bodied or not, there would be a minimum of five hundred prisoners on the ferry each morning.

Howard didn't know where he had found the strength, but the next day Gordy stood propped on his crutches, stirring a tub of cement on the chance that he would have a few moments with Shun-ling at the docks later. Before they left that morning Howard had stuffed all the money he and Gordy had managed to hang onto into the lining of his wedge cap. The Hong Kong dollars stashed in their uniform pockets had been confiscated at capture, but the searchers had missed the bills in their boots. The money was no good here. If they tried to bribe the guards with it, it would only be confiscated and the entire camp would be searched.

When they marched back to the ferry that night Shun-ling was waiting at the turnstile. While a tearful Gordy leaned forward on his crutches to reunite with her, Howard kept his distance. Only when the ferry arrived at the dock, and the guard began herding the prisoners on board, did he move closer. As she and Gordy shared a few final hushed words, Shun-ling deftly slipped a small package into Howard's palm. In exchange he quickly passed his cap to her. It was a relief to have the money out of his hands and to know that Shun-ling and her family would benefit from it.

After that, whenever she showed up at the ferry, Howard held back. He didn't want to hear any more of their hurried conversations than he had to. Or witness Shun-ling's speech reverting to that of a paid-for servant.

Whether it was the medicine she brought, or simply her presence, Gordy's health seemed to improve. Thrilled at the prospect of becoming a father, he made plans for their life together.

'She's going to marry me when this is over,' he told Howard, more than once, as if he couldn't believe it. 'Imagine that. She's coming back to Canada with this Peg-leg Pete.'

For weeks Howard lived vicariously, watching their brief meetings and listening to Gordy plan their future. It was testament to life going on.

'Those who survive are the ones able to look towards the possibilities of life beyond this,' Ken Campbell had said of the patients in the Agony Ward, and Gordy was proof of that.

Howard had his own dreams, but they were getting harder and harder to remember. Back in Manitoba he had not paid much attention to the mail. All the postman brought was bills or catalogues. Now, like all the others, he prayed for a letter from home. None came. 'No letter today,' the guards said, shrugging. The cruel ones mocked them, saying, 'Your families have forgotten you. They no longer care for you.' No one believed this, least of all Howard. He knew Lucy would be writing to him every day, just as she had promised. Still, it was difficult to keep faith, with only a worn photograph to hold onto.

29

Once the idea entered my mind that the girl from the park had something to do with my family, I couldn't let it go. After Kipper and I had gone to bed that evening, after Frankie had left for the night shift at the mill, long after Dad switched off the television, I lay awake planning how I would go downtown the next day.

In the morning, after Frankie had come home from work and gone upstairs to bed, I told Kipper we were going on a secret adventure. When Dad came into the kitchen, I held my finger to my lips with what I hoped was a conspiratorial look. But there was no need. As my father poured himself some coffee, then sat down at the table, I knew I could have told him that Kipper and I were flying to the moon. If he had answered at all, he would have murmured, 'That's nice,' while he stared glassy-eyed out of the window.

By the time we left the house I was so single-minded that I didn't notice the sky was grey with the promise of rain until we were at the bus stop on Victoria Drive. Kipper was single-minded too. Once we were settled on the bus and I'd let him know our destination, all he could talk about was the little red house behind the store. So, when he asked if we could go back to see it, I told him it was a ghost house. It wasn't entirely a lie. Last year in school we had learned about 'spirit houses' in Asia and it seemed possible that it might be one.

Knowing Kipper's fear of ghosts, I would never understand why I said it, except that, for some reason, I desperately wanted him to forget about it. But if I had anticipated the repercussions my careless words would cause later, I would have held my tongue.

By the time we got off the bus downtown black clouds were rolling overhead, darkening the sky above the concrete buildings. I felt the first heavy raindrops as we hurried across Hastings Street. By the time we reached Chinatown we were drenched. Rain splashed up from puddles on the sidewalks and dripped from the brim of Kipper's hat. Water streamed from the overhead awnings as we made our way down the grey streets, ducking from store to store, until we finally stood shivering between the vegetable bins in front of the one where we had seen the girl.

But once we arrived I was reluctant to enter. In my determination to get there, I had given no thought to the next step. What if she wasn't inside, wasn't working today? Who would I ask for? *A Chinese girl?*

While I hesitated, a small, stooped Chinese lady came out of the store loaded with bags filled with vegetables. I stepped aside to let her pass, but she stopped and looked hard at Kipper. 'What the matta him?' she demanded.

I hated that question. Only rude people asked it. I answered exactly the way Mom always said I should. 'He has Down's syndrome.'

'No,' the grey-haired woman answered, as if she was irritated, 'I mean breathing. He look like no breath.'

I turned to Kipper. I'd been so taken up with finding the girl that I hadn't noticed his breathing was raspy. He took out his inhaler and held it to his mouth. Pressing it down, he sucked in with shallow gulps. He took it out, the wheezing increasing, and looked at it. His face had turned a funny grey colour. 'What's wrong?' I asked, as he shook the inhaler.

'It's . . . empty,' he squeezed out. Guilt and fear flooded me. I patted his back. 'Just relax,' I stammered, trying to remember what Mom used to say to calm him. 'Concentrate on taking slow breaths.'

As he fought to pull air into his whistling lungs, customers came and went from the store. Most stared, but kept moving. Even the old lady had left us, gone back inside. Then, as panic was overwhelming me, she came out of the store again with the apron-clad girl beside her.

As the woman raised her umbrella and shuffled away, the girl bent down in front of Kipper until their eyes were level. 'Hallo again,' she said.

He smiled in recognition. 'Ha—llo,' he managed, between laboured breaths.

'What's the matter?' she asked gently.

I hurried to answer for him: 'Asthma. Kipper – my brother – has asthma. His inhaler is empty.' The words gushed out as if I, too, was in danger of running out of breath.

'Come with me.' Her soft voice was calm, reassuring. I took Kipper's hand and we followed her through the store. Without stopping she said something I couldn't understand to a man behind the counter, who nodded while he gave change for a customer.

The earthy smell in the storage room at the back reminded me of old Mr Fong's delivery truck. Stacks of wooden bins full of fruit and vegetables loomed over us in the dim light.

Suddenly Kipper stopped with a jerk. He dropped my hand and pulled back. 'What if – the – ghosts – the ghosts come in?' he choked out.

The girl turned to him. 'Ghosts?'

'From – the – little – the little—' He struggled with his breath and with the words.

'It's my fault,' I confessed. 'I told him there were ghosts in the, uhm, little house behind the store.'

The girl looked at me, confused. 'The little house?' Then understanding lit her dark eyes. 'Oh,' she said, then turned to Kipper. 'There's nothing to be afraid of there,' she assured him. 'It's just a shrine. The people who owned this store before us built it to honour their ancestors.'

'Ancestors?' he asked.

'Relatives who are no longer living.'

'Dead . . . dead people?'

'Yes, but ancestors are good spirits,' she told him. 'The family would go to that little house to talk to them, to ask them for guidance. It's like a temple. A good place.'

I watched Kipper digest the information, ashamed at my part in his asthma attack. He struggled to take a deep breath. 'Thass – good,' he said, and let the girl lead him through the maze of wooden bins.

At the back of the storage room she stopped at the bottom of a stairway. Without speaking, as if they had been communicating on some other level, her eyes asked if he could climb the steps. Kipper nodded and she took his arm. I followed while they made their way slowly to the door at the top, one step at a time, the sound of his heavy breathing and the creaking of the wooden steps echoing in the shadowed stairway.

The apartment above the store smelled of mothballs and incense. A narrow hallway led to a tiny kitchen where a woman, wearing a loose grey tunic and baggy pants, turned from the sink as we came in. At the sight of us, a frown crossed her face – a face that was an older version of the girl's. I didn't need to understand the foreign words. The scolding tone said she did not approve of our presence. But her frown turned to concern as the girl placed her arm protectively around Kipper's heaving shoulders and spoke urgently.

'You sit,' the woman ordered Kipper and me, then disappeared down the hall. We each took a chair at the kitchen table while the girl filled a pot with water, placed it on the stove, and then she, too, left the room. The only sound in the kitchen was the hiss of the gas and Kipper's raspy breathing.

Before long the girl returned with towels and handed one to me. Placing the other around Kipper's shoulders she removed his soaked hat. I cringed, expecting him to protest, but to my surprise – with the look that he usually reserved for Mom or me – he said nothing as he watched her hang it above the stove to dry.

A few moments later the older woman returned, carrying a large glass jar filled with dried leaves. She placed it on the counter and unscrewed the top. She scooped out a cupful, dumped them in the pot, then stirred the simmering mixture. When she was satisfied she moved away from the stove and said some quick, sharp words in Chinese. Then she took the girl's apron and, giving Kipper and me one last furtive glance, disappeared downstairs.

'She says he must inhale the steam for ten minutes,' the girl explained. She gave the leaves a quick stir and then, while they came to the boil, she filled a small kettle to make tea.

Watching her work, the unasked question buzzed in my head like a hornet. Why had she been talking to my mother on the day she died? How would I ask her? While I searched for the words, I examined the dimly lit kitchen, so different from ours. Black round-bottomed pots hung over the gas stove. Glass jars and ornate tin canisters lined the counters. From where I sat I could see into a small living room where lace doilies covered

the arms and backs of a burgundy couch and chair. China fig-
urines and photographs filled a knick-knack shelf on the wall.
Wooden dragons wound around a folding screen separating the
two rooms.

The same dragons decorated a porcelain bowl into which the
girl poured the boiled leaves. She carried the steaming mixture
to the table and placed it in front of Kipper. 'This will help you
breathe,' she said, sitting down beside him. She urged him to
lean forward, then draped the towel over his head to capture
the steam.

When she was certain he was settled and breathing in the
vapour, she went to the counter and poured the tea.

'I've never had hot tea in a glass before,' I said as she placed
the steaming glass in front of me.

'This is how we drink it in Hong Kong.'

'Hong Kong!' My heart started pounding.

'That is where I grew up. I live here now.' She sat down beside
Kipper.

Through ringing ears I heard her say that she had only been
in Vancouver for a month. She had come to attend university
here in September. When she said her name was Lily, I blurted,
'Lily? That's what my mom wanted to call me.'

At the mention of Mom, the girl raised her head, her dark
eyes finding mine. 'I am sorry about your mother,' she said
quietly. For an instant I wondered how she knew, then remembered the day of the funeral, the day we had followed her
downtown: Kipper had said he'd told her Mom had gone to
'heben'.

Feeling my throat close, I murmured, 'Thank you,' a response
I had come to realize in these last few weeks was enough.
Anything more was too much – for me and for whoever was
offering sympathy.

She lifted Kipper's towel and asked if he was all right.

He nodded. 'Yep,' he said, the wheeze already easing.

'Did you know my mother?' I asked.

'No. I spoke with her only once.' She replaced the towel, and added, 'She seemed very nice.'

Here was my chance. 'What were you talking to her about?' I asked, trying to keep my voice even.

She hesitated for a moment, then said, 'I was looking for someone.'

'Who? Who were you looking for?' *Frankie?*

'It's complicated.'

'Complicated?'

'Every month, all my life,' she said, busying herself with Kipper's towel, 'someone has sent money to us through a family friend in Hong Kong. This man, who was like an uncle to me, would not tell us where the money came from. Sadly our friend has died. His nephew, not knowing this was secret business, gave us the last money order.'

'But what's that got to do with my mother?'

She sat back, placing her hands in her lap. 'The address on the envelope was six nine seven nine Barclay Street.'

Kipper raised his head. 'Six nine seven nine. That's our address!' He grinned. Water dripped from his chin, but his breathing was normal again.

Lily replaced his towel and helped him to lean over the bowl again, saying, 'A few more minutes.' She stood up, took the pot from the stove and poured more of the steaming brown mush into the bowl.

'You told my mom about this? What did she say?' I asked, knowing the address had to be wrong. No one from our house had money to send to Hong Kong.

'She said it was a mistake. Then she told me to come back

to see her the next day. But there were many people at your house that morning. I did not want to intrude. I came each day and watched for her. Then I met Kipper in the park,' she lowered her eyes, 'and he told me the sad news.'

'Is that why you stopped coming?'

'Yes. I did not want to intrude on your family's grief.' She removed the bowl and took it to the sink, leaving Kipper to dry his head with the towel.

I blew on my hot tea. Kipper was right. Lily was nice. But she really didn't have anything to do with my family, after all. Like Mom said, it was a mistake. The wrong address. Part of me was disappointed. Watching her pour my brother a glass of tea, I found myself wishing she *had* been one of Frankie's admirers. Then the thought struck me: why would Mom tell her to come back? Was it because she was in a hurry, on her way out to visit her friend Marlene, when Lily had come to the door? Had she felt sorry for the girl coming to the wrong house? Like the stray cats and dogs that had found their way to our home over the years, had Mom intended to adopt her too? More likely, had she wanted Lily to meet Frankie? I smiled at the thought of Mom playing matchmaker.

Relieved, even a little sorry, that the mystery was solved so easily, I sipped my tea. Over the rim of the glass something on the knick-knack shelf in the living room caught my eye. I stood up and wandered over to look closer at the unframed photo-graph propped up on the middle shelf. Without thinking I reached for it. A burning heat grew in the pit of my stomach as I studied the familiar faces. How could this be?

'She's my mother,' Lily said quietly.

Startled, I spun around. Of course the girl in the photograph was her mother. I could see how much alike they were. But it wasn't her that had drawn my attention. It was the two soldiers on either side of her. Confused, I stared at their grinning faces. We had a similar photograph at home. But in the one we had, it was my mother's face pressed between the cheeks of the same two soldiers, one of whom was my father.

Why was he in a photograph with Lily's mother? What did her mother have to do with him? I opened my mouth to ask, but before I could form the words, Lily's soft voice shattered my thoughts. 'And my father,' she said, 'I think it's him who sends us money every month.'

And suddenly something clicked into place in my mind. Everything in me wanted to argue, '*No! That can't be.*' I glanced at Kipper, who was taking the last gulp of his tea, and forced myself to remain silent. I replaced the photograph on the shelf and said, 'We have to go now.'

I rushed into the kitchen and retrieved Kipper's hat from the stove. 'Thank you for taking care of my brother,' I said to Lily, at the same time urging him to his feet.

'I'll walk you to the bus stop,' Lily said.

'No, we'll be okay.'

'I wish to come with you,' she repeated. She opened one of the kitchen drawers, took out a pen and a piece of paper, then jotted something down. On the way out she grabbed two umbrellas from a stand in the dark hall.

Downstairs, I hurried through the store, avoiding the dark eyes of the woman who looked so much like Lily and the young girl in the photograph.

All the way back to Hastings Street Kipper walked with Lily under her umbrella, thanking her three more times for making him 'all better'. His breathing was perfectly normal now.

At the bus stop he asked, 'Will you come see us at our house?'

'I don't know,' she answered, her serious gaze fixed not on him but on me.

The bus pulled up to the kerb and the doors sighed open. I closed the umbrella, and tried to hand it back to Lily, but she refused to take it. Instead she pulled the slip of paper out of her pocket, reached through the curtain of rain and tucked it into my closed fist.

'See, Ethie?' Kipper said, leaning over me to wave through the window as the bus pulled away. 'I told you she's nice.'

'Yeah.' That was true. Lily *was* nice.

'Will she come to see us?'

I gave him the same answer Lily had. 'I don't know.' I didn't know anything right then. I couldn't concentrate. I couldn't stop thinking about how our mother had worried over money at the end of every month. And I kept seeing the mixed-up images of our father sitting at the kitchen table hunched over those envelopes and his grinning face in that photograph.

In the seat ahead of us, a teenage boy held a tiny plastic transistor radio pressed to his ear. The silver antenna pointed back at me while Frankie Valli's high-pitched voice sang about big girls who don't cry-yi-yi. Blinking back stinging tears, I looked down at the scrunched-up piece of paper in my hand. I slowly smoothed it out on my lap until I could read the neat script. 'Lily Feng. Daughter of Feng Shun-ling.' And, below that, a phone number.

She hadn't needed to say it. I had seen it in her dark eyes. The note was not meant for me. It was for my father.

30

24 August 1942: Hong Kong Island

Adams . . . Berzenski . . . Ellis . . . Payne . . . The names burned themselves into Howard's mind. The four Winnipeg Grenadiers had made their escape on August 20th, slipping away in the dark of night only to be captured three days later. That day everyone – the sick and dying included – was forced to stand, or lie, in the square. Howard stood with his head down, silently repeating his mantra of names as four guards, with ceremonial swords laid across white-gloved hands, marched from the camp.

Hours later, a shrill voice broke through his trance. Bamboo canes whipped through the air as the prisoners were forced to count off in groups of ten.

'*Ichi.*'

'*Ni.*'

'*San.*'

Each man defiantly called out his number. Howard's was eight. '*Hachi.*'

'Remember your number,' a Japanese guard shouted. 'If anyone go away, the other nine die.'

There would be no more late-night whispers of attempted escape.

The truth was there were plenty of holes, plenty of opportunities. There always had been. The Japanese, so certain that their captives would not attempt to escape, had become complacent about security.

Howard found it easy to understand why the Grenadiers had risked their lives. The small chance of freedom measured against the certainty of disease and starvation? Dysentery, beriberi, pellagra were rampant in the camp. Even diphtheria had reared its ugly head. And now there were whispers of cholera.

The four escapees had accepted the risk; they had lost, but at least they'd had a plan and acted on it. As Gordy grew stronger a similar escape plan had begun to kindle in Howard's imagination. Now that glimmer had been extinguished.

Twelve hours later the prisoners were still standing in the square under a blazing sun. The camp commanders deemed it punishment, but Howard, like the rest of the Canadians he was sure, saw it as an honour paid to the courageous four.

The Japanese officers had yet to administer the most torturous blow. At the going down of the sun, two guards carried a bulging mail sack into the yard and dropped it onto the ground before the exhausted men. Audible gasps ran through the ranks. Parched and half dazed, Howard let down his guard and allowed himself a moment of hope. The canvas bag was upended and the contents spilled out. Hope turned to horror when a guard splashed diesel oil onto the mountain of letters while the other tossed an ignited match. Tempers exploded with the flames. Enraged prisoners had to be restrained by their neighbours, who wept openly as the words of their loved ones turned to smoke and ashes and drifted away on the wind.

At the end of September the Canadians were moved back to their old barracks on the mainland. On the ferry ride over, Howard spotted *Lisbon Maru*, the Japanese freighter he had seen docked in Hawaii almost a year ago, moored in the harbour. Word passed from mouth to mouth that the converted troop-ship, waiting to sail on the morning tide, held two thousand British PoWs from Sham Shui Po, bound for work camps in Japan. Howard shared none of his suspicion with Gordy that their return to the vacated camp meant they would be the next to go. Gordy was frantic enough. For more than two weeks Shun-ling had not been at the turnstiles when they returned from the work parties.

Once again, side by side, Howard and Gordy made the familiar hike up Nathan Road. Unlike their first march to Camp Sham Shui Po, there were no Union flags waving at the bedraggled parade of Grenadiers and Royal Rifles. Instead, the Rising Sun hung from balconies and storefronts along the way. Crowds of once friendly Chinese, wearing the blood-red emblem on white armbands, jeered at the weary prisoners as they passed.

A half-mile from the camp Howard gripped Gordy's arm. 'Look!' he whispered, nodding ahead at a group of heckling spectators on the side of the road. Standing among them, cradling a grey bundle, was Shun-ling.

'Oh, God,' Gordy croaked, and jerked forward.

'Don't draw attention to her,' Howard hissed into his ear, pulling him back.

The moment Shun-ling saw them she turned the bundle round. The shock of dark hair and the tiny pink face brought an unexpected lump to Howard's throat and he found he had to restrain himself as much as Gordy as they passed – so close and yet so far.

The state of Sham Shui Po shocked Howard. There was little left of their old camp. Like North Point, it had been looted to a skeleton. The once immaculate huts were reduced to hovels.

Corrugated metal covered the glassless windows. The walls were now little more than tar-paper and stucco. But the army cots remained. Their flea- and bedbug-infested folding mats were better than concrete floors and wooden planks.

The few British prisoners left in the camp were the ill and maimed, and those caring for them, in the hospital – a replica of the North Point Agony Ward. Howard spent the first day searching for Peter Young and Dick Baxter. No one knew anything about the two machine-gunners.

Three days later the relocated contraband radio brought the news. It spread like wildfire through the camp. *Lisbon Maru* had been sunk. On the third day after she had sailed, the Japanese ship, which had borne no sign that she was carrying PoWs, had been torpedoed by an American submarine. More than a thousand British prisoners were feared dead.

Despondent, Howard absorbed the news, praying that the two Middlesex machine-gunners had somehow made it to safety.

Life went on in the new camp. And so did death. Diphtheria was taking its toll. An average of three men were dying each day. And Gordy was weakening. In his usual bulldog fashion, he refused to admit it, making jokes about playing a tune on his now exposed ribcage. One morning, when Howard suggested he should rest rather than come with the work crews, he barked, 'Who made you my mother?' The effort brought on a coughing fit. After he had regained control of himself, he looked up, eyes watering. 'You know I need those few moments, Howie,' he said. 'It's what keeps me going.'

Although the transfer to the mainland meant they were closer to where Shun-ling's family lived with Ah Sam, it also meant the loss of opportunities for stolen conversations at the turnstiles. The only contact they had now was glimpses of her standing at the side of the road with the baby during the march from the Kai Tak airfield to Sham Shui Po at the end of the day.

Then, as if the gods were bent on grinding their spirits to dust, as if deprivation and disease were not enough, the move to Sham Shui Po brought a further terror.

At first the new camp interpreter looked like salvation. As word spread that he was Japanese-Canadian, British Columbia born and raised, hopes rose. Surely he would have sympathy for his fellow countrymen. The first day the tall, rake-thin sergeant strode out to the square, his dark brown jackboots reflecting the sun, whispers rippled among the prisoners standing at attention.

'Look at the crease in his pants – you could shave by it.'

'Takes a Canuck.'

The remarks were short-lived. He came to an abrupt halt before them. Standing ramrod straight, he rested a white-gloved hand on the hilt of the sword hanging from his hip. His narrow eyes, severe under heavy brows, scanned the yard until there was silence. In perfect English, the sergeant explained his duties as camp interpreter. Then he let the troops know exactly where he stood. While he was growing up in Canada, he told them, he had been humiliated and treated like an outsider by the whites. The men soon grasped that he meant to make them suffer for what he'd experienced.

During the second week of October, after nearly ten months in captivity, Howard sat on his cot watching the men around him opening mail. Letters from home! He held Lucy's tightly. Beside him, Gordy lay on his back clutching an identical envelope to his chest. Howard would read it to him later. How like Lucy to write to Gordy, knowing he had no family to do so. And, fortunately for Howard, he would have two letters from her to relish. Carefully he lifted the flap of his unsealed envelope, wanting to savour every second of this gift.

'Shit!' Ken Campbell blurted. Similar expletives echoed through the barracks. Howard glanced up in time to see Ken unfolding his letter. The thin paper was mutilated by thick black marks. Throughout the barracks others cursed the huge spaces where words, whole sentences, paragraphs, had been obliterated by the censor's pen. While they strained to read what was left, Howard returned to his with trepidation.

He gingerly removed the thin sheets of blue onion paper. Bewildered, he pulled them apart, checking each page, the first, second, third . . . All three were intact, not a word struck out. He turned away from the others to face the door, not wanting anyone to witness his good fortune.

The letter was dated 12 March 1942.

My dearest Howard,

Are you getting snowed under with all my letters? I have no way of knowing if they are getting through. I pray every day for a letter from you. I have heard nothing. Yet I don't need Ottawa to tell me. I know you're alive. I feel your presence every day. Still, I long to hear from you, my darling. Are you well? Are they treating you kindly?

I walk down to Kitsilano Beach every evening to watch the sunset. Looking out over the waters of English Bay makes me feel closer to you somehow . . .

Vancouver is on blackout every night. How strange not to see lights on the North Shore. But everyone is doing their part for the war effort.

Not all are pleasant. The young Japanese-Canadian woman who works in Sidney's office was taken away. She and her

*entire family were rounded up and transported to an intern-
ment camp somewhere in the interior. Sidney tried to intervene.
To no avail. The way they are being treated is shameful. They
are Canadian. Her father, who fought for Canada in the last
war, is a decorated hero whose name is engraved on the
Japanese-Canadian War Memorial in Stanley Park. Still they
whisked them all away, allowing them to take only what they
could carry. Sidney stored the rest of their possessions in the
basement for when this mess is over . . .*

The rest of the letter was less serious, newsy ramblings about
Mildred and Sidney and everyday life in a rational world. Until
the last page.

*I'm feeling quite well, over the morning sickness. I lost my job
at the drugstore, of course.*

*You'd think they would get over this old-fashioned notion
that expecting women should hide their condition. Especially
while there is a war on. But Mildred is delighted to have me
around every day and pampering me like a spoiled child.*

*I'm not due until the middle of July but I'm getting so fat
people wonder if I'm having twins. I'm not. At least Sidney
doesn't think so. Although the baby kicks so much it sometimes
feels like two. It must be a boy. I hope so. A beautiful strong
boy, just like his father.*

Come home to me, to us, my darling. I miss you so.

*All my love always
Lucy*

A baby? July? He was already a father. The news was as nour-
ishing as food. More. He read the letter again, this time slowly,

savouring every word. Only after he had read it three times did he wonder how it had passed unscathed through the censors, in Canada and here. Was it random selection? Or were the censors so overworked that some slipped through? He didn't care. He wasn't about to look a gift horse in the mouth.

Suddenly the small hairs at the back of Howard's neck stood on end. Behind him the hum of conversation ceased. The hut became eerily still – the animal stillness of prey caught in a predator's stare. Hate leached through the humid air like an ominous odour. The contemptuous sound of leather soles on wooden floorboards shattered the sudden silence. Heel, toe, heel, toe. The footsteps echoed through the hut until they ended with a final click in front of Howard. The careless drone of flies filled the void left by the stillness of the jackboots at the edge of Howard's vision. He willed himself to stare at them, repeating his mantra . . . *Bacon, Baptiste, Barclay.* He let the names scroll slowly across the blackboard of his mind before he lifted his head to allow his gaze to rise to the smirking face. With studied insolence he refolded the letter and placed it in the envelope.

It made no difference. Censorship was the interpreter's job. Still, Howard couldn't help the revulsion that welled at the thought that the sergeant had read Lucy's words.

The snake-like eyes held Howard's. 'My father also fought for Canada in the last war,' he said. 'A decorated hero. I played with his war medals when I was a boy. His name, too, is on the war memorial in Stanley Park. And still we were nothing but little yellow bastards.' With a self-satisfied smirk he scanned the silent hut. 'Now you'll see what this little yellow bastard can do.'

Three days later the interpreter kept his promise, announcing that food rations would be reduced for all those men not working or not working hard enough. The push was on to finish the runway at Kai Tak airport. Those too weak or too ill to work were carried there. If they didn't get up and pitch in, their rations were withheld.

'This is ass-backwards,' Howard argued with him. 'Tell your superiors that they can't expect to get work out of men starving to death. They need more food, not less.' Unlike others whose complaints were rewarded with a lashing from a bamboo cane, Howard got away with the insolence.

'No work, no food,' the sergeant said, and strode away.

By the middle of November it became obvious that the Japanese were asking the impossible. With bodies swollen from beriberi, mouths and faces a mass of open pellagra sores, many men were losing the will to go on. The lack of essential nutrients brought on 'electric feet', leaving many unable to walk. Tormented by unbearable pins and needles shooting through their feet, the afflicted were reduced to lying in bed and weeping. Those who could sat with their feet immersed in buckets of water, ignoring Ken Campbell's pleading warnings that the temporary relief brought the risk of deadly infection or, worse yet, pneumonia.

Diphtheria and amoebic dysentery were now endemic. The efforts of medical personnel were defeated by the scarcity of drugs.

The Japanese, concerned for their own, began to wear masks and berated the helpless doctors for their inability to control the diseases. On the night seven PoWs died, Ken Campbell limped back to the barracks. As he gingerly removed his shirt Howard saw that the skin on his back was a mass of welts. 'The interpreter.' Ken groaned as he lay on his stomach. 'Thrashed every one of the doctors and medics because we're making him look bad.'

A small amount of anti-toxins were issued, leaving the doctors to play God with the meagre supply. The cases of diphtheria increased. Their departure from Vancouver had been so hasty that most of the men in C Force hadn't been inoculated. Howard was one of the lucky few. As a teenager, he had stepped on a rusty nail. The combined anti-tetanus and diphtheria shot he had received rendered him immune to the plague ravaging the camp.

Gordy was not. By the time work was completed on the runway he could barely hold himself up on his crutches. Still, he was disheartened at being confined to the camp. He refused to acknowledge the fever and sore throat, the dreaded symptoms, until he was unable to muster the strength to stand.

After the work parties ceased Howard spent his early mornings watching the furtive refugees, who were returning to scour the mud flats each morning. Since Satan had left there had been few incidents between the Chinese and the guards. Japanese superiors had clamped down on sadistic treatment of civilians. It had been more than a month since he had glimpsed Shun-ling but when Howard saw her appear with a group of scavengers in the morning mist – it brought an unexpected lump to his throat – he slipped back into the shadows. But she had seen him.

She waited until the rest of her group had disappeared over the bank. When she was alone she crouched in the vegetation at the corner of the fence. Howard checked over his shoulder for guards. 'This isn't safe,' he whispered, as he squatted on the other side of the barbed wire.

She passed a small brown-paper packet through the fence. 'For Gordy's intestines.'

He took it, knowing that the herbal medicine was not strong enough for what ailed Gordy now. 'He has diphtheria, Shun-ling,' he said, slipping the packet into his pocket. 'Can Ah Sam get serum?'

'I will come back tomorrow.' And with that she backed away and disappeared into the mist.

The following morning she brought more herbs. 'The Japanese have confiscated all the serum. This is all Ah Sam has to offer. He says Gordy must drink lots of boiled water.'

Howard watched for her early each morning. Every few days she appeared and passed precious items through the fence. She brought tiny wrapped morsels of food with the packets of herbs, news of the outside world and stories about the baby girl, named Lily in honour of Gordy's mother. The hurried visits, the relayed conversations, became as much a lifeline to Howard as they were to his sick friend.

Whatever Ah Sam's potions were, they had worked on Gordy's dysentery – Howard's too – but they had no effect on diphtheria and Gordy was getting worse.

Finally there was no choice. He was moved to the hospital shed. Howard didn't need the doctors or Ken Campbell to tell him: he could smell the truth on Gordy's breath, see it in the swollen neck glands and hear it in the cough. Still, his friend hung on, mocking death even as it stalked him. Howard stayed at his side night and day. He trickled the sterilized water Ah Sam had advised over Gordy's leathered tongue. He spoon-fed him the broth made from the herbs Shun-ling provided, only for it to be regurgitated in black phlegm. Nothing worked, and Gordy was slipping away. Every night Howard slept on the floor by his cot, leaving only to use the latrine or to check the fence at the back of the camp in the morning. But as he hurriedly accepted Shun-ling's tiny packages of hope he couldn't bring himself to tell her how dire the situation was.

One morning Howard woke to the sound of rattling breaths.

He sat up, then knelt by Gordy's cot, watching his sunken chest move laboriously up and down. His friend was now little more than yellowed parchment skin draped over bones. Howard adjusted the thin blanket, noticing the splotches of purple, the blood pooling in Gordy's remaining foot.

His eyelids snapped open. 'Howie?'

Howard searched the cloudy eyes. 'I'm here,' he said, smoothing back the hair on Gordy's skull.

The cracked lips moved with effort. 'That's still a sissy name,' he whispered, and for the briefest moment a flash of the defiant schoolboy appeared. Then his eyelids fluttered down. Watching his friend's shallow breaths, Howard found himself taking air into his own lungs in rhythm with the slow rise and fall of Gordy's chest.

In ... out ... in ... out ... in ...

And then . . . nothing.

No! No! Howard forced out his own breath willing the motionless chest to exhale.

Suddenly air whistled from Gordy's gaping mouth. Howard crawled onto the cot to lie beside him. Then, as he cradled him in his arms, he heard his friend say, 'Look ... after my girls ...'

Denial rose in Howard's throat with the jagged lump, even as he felt the life, the energy that was Gordy, fading. He swallowed. He would not dishonour him with worthless lies, would not pretend that death was not staking its claim. 'Of course I will,' he choked out.

4 December 1942: ... Gordy Veronick ...

31

Kipper and I arrived home in the middle of another downpour. Even Lily's umbrella couldn't protect us from the pounding rain splashing up from the sidewalk. Like two drowned rats we stole into the house through the basement. It wasn't necessary. Frankie was still asleep. And Dad wasn't at home. He must have gone walking in the rain. I was glad. I didn't know what I should, or would, or could say to him.

While Kipper took a bath, I changed into my pyjamas. After he got out of the tub he went upstairs. Frankie came into the kitchen as I was mixing powdered cheese into the Kraft Dinner noodles. He yawned and scratched his chest. 'So, what have you and Kipper been up to today?' he asked, reaching for the coffee-pot.

I knew it was just a question to fill the empty space in our house, in our lives, but as I watched him rinsing out the coffee-pot, I considered telling him. I really did. But what could I have said? 'We went downtown and I found out that Dad has another daughter – another family'?

Kipper came back into the kitchen wearing his pyjamas and his soggy hat.

'Nothing,' I said. Then, hoping to change the subject, I asked, 'Do you want some macaroni?'

'I don't think so,' he said, mussing up my hair. 'This is my breakfast, remember.' He turned to Kipper. 'Hey, buddy,' he said, 'you're ready for bed pretty early, aren't you?'

'I got wet,' Kipper said. 'Just like Da.'

'Dad went for a walk?' Frankie asked. He tugged a carton of eggs out of the fridge and glanced up at the half-empty bottle of whiskey.

I shrugged. 'I guess so.'

By the time we had finished eating Dad still wasn't back.

'I'm going to take in a night-school class before I go to work,' Frankie said, pushing himself away from the table. 'You two'll be all right alone, won't you?'

Weren't we always?

Kipper and I curled up on the couch to watch *Leave It to Beaver*. How I envied Beaver and Wally Cleaver's make-believe lives. Their clothes always looked brand new, their beds perfectly made, and they even had their own bathroom in their bedroom. Was anyone really that rich? Most unbelievable of all, they had a father who had nothing better to do with his time than to pay attention to them.

When the show was over I left Kipper on the couch, his eyelids drooping, and went to clean up the kitchen. I cleared the table to the sound of whistling coming from the television as Sheriff Andy and Opie headed to their fishing-hole once again. I used to feel sorry for little Opie Taylor without a mother. Now his life as an only child, with a father who solved all his problems with a few wise words, looked pretty good.

I scraped the food left on my plate into the garbage pail under the sink. Closing the cupboard door, I noticed two brown-paper bags behind the drainpipe. I didn't need to open them to know what they were. More whiskey.

Suddenly furious I grabbed both bottles and slammed them onto the counter. I ripped them from their bags and unscrewed the caps. With shaking hands I upended them into the sink and watched the amber liquid splash on white enamel. As it swirled down the drain, I lost my resolve. What was the use? He would just get more. I emptied both bottles anyway, then went over to retrieve the one from above the fridge. As I reached for it my hand brushed something on the refrigerator top. A piece of paper slid over the edge and fluttered to the floor. I bent down to pick it up.

If only I'd put that note back, unopened, unread, none of what followed would have happened. But I didn't. I unfolded it and read my mother's words.

Dora,

I desperately need to speak to you. The girl we saw in the park yesterday came to my door this morning – looking for her father!

I have reason to suspect that Howard has been sending money to her family in Hong Kong for seventeen years. I'm so confused I don't know what to think.

I told her to come back tomorrow. I need time to sort this out in my own mind before I can face her. Or him.

If ever I needed a friend it is now. Please call me as soon as you get home.

Lucy

My mother knew! That was why she was upset and had gone to see her friend Marlene. Stunned, I reread the words, then let the paper slip through my fingers and flutter to the floor. Leaving the dirty dishes on the counter and in the sink, the sticky pots and frying pan on the stove, Kipper in the living room, I grabbed the half-full whiskey bottle from the top of the fridge, and fled upstairs with it.

In my room I climbed into bed, pulled the covers up to my knees and unscrewed the top. Maybe it was like medicine. Frankie had once poured it onto an aching tooth to numb it. Maybe it would numb my brain, make me stop thinking. Just like Dad.

I tossed the cap to the floor, grasped the bottle by the neck, tipped it and swallowed a huge gulp. A shock of burning liquid scorched my throat. I gagged, and whiskey sprayed from my mouth and nostrils triggering a coughing fit that racked my body as I fought to catch my breath.

'No, Ethie,' Kipper cried. Through blurred vision I saw him rush over to the bed. 'Thass bad,' he scolded, reaching for the bottle. I hung on to it as he tried to wrench it from my hands. Half-hearted, I wrestled for a few moments, then let go. Kipper tumbled backwards, losing his hold on the bottle. It sailed through the air, an arc of amber liquid splashing over the bed and wall, then fell to the floor and rolled into the corner.

'Oops,' Kipper said.

'I didn't want it anyway.' I flung myself back, pulling the covers over me. What I wanted was everything to be the same again. I wanted my mother back. I wanted my father to be a father. I wanted what my mother had written in the letter not to be true.

'You sad, Ethie?' Kipper asked, from the side of the bed. I could hear a sob rising with his words. But I couldn't reassure him. I could only move over and pull back the covers to let him climb in beside me so we could cry ourselves to sleep.

I woke in the morning to my aunt's startled shriek.

32

'Stay here!' Aunt Mildred ordered me, and dragged a sobbing Kipper out of my bedroom. A few seconds later the gunshot crack of his slamming door ricocheted across the hall, like an accusation. At the sound of my aunt's footsteps pounding down the stairs, and her voice screaming my father's name, I jumped out of bed.

I arrived in the downstairs hallway just in time to see Dad scrambling into his pants beside his bed. 'Mildred,' he said, pulling up his zipper. 'What's going on?'

She stormed over to his bedroom doorway, her chest heaving. 'I came to take Ethie shopping for school clothes and found—'

'I'm sorry,' Dad said wearily, reaching for his shirt. 'I forgot you were coming.'

'Forgot? You didn't forget – you were just too hung over to care,' she spat. 'Too drunk to know what your children are up to.' She stood in the doorway with her feet apart, her hands on her hips. 'Christopher was in Ethie's bed! I caught him. And they've been drinking whiskey! Your whiskey. Her room smells like a brothel.'

'What *are* you talking about?' Dad asked.

'We didn't drink it,' I cried, behind her.

My aunt spun around to look at me. 'I told you to stay in your room, Ethie!'

Dad pushed past her and into the hallway.

Aunt Mildred jumped at his touch. Her eyes narrowed. 'You

weren't even here last night, were you, Howard? Look at you. Your clothes are still soaked. Out on one of your famous self-indulgent walk-abouts,' she accused his back, 'rather than being home with your children.'

Ignoring her, Dad put his arm around my shoulder. 'Let's go up and see Kipper,' he said, guiding me back down the hall.

'I'm not leaving, Howard,' Aunt Mildred warned. 'We're going to talk, you and I.'

'Suit yourself,' Dad answered, without turning. 'Right now I'm seeing to my children.'

'A bit late for that.'

'It wasn't Kipper's fault.' I sniffed, trudging up the stairs. 'He didn't do anything wrong.'

We found him sitting on his bedroom floor, slumped against the wall, still wearing his pyjamas. His tear- and mucus-streaked face lifted when Dad opened the door.

'Aunt – Mildred – says – I'm – bad,' he sobbed. 'I'm – not – bad. Am I – Da?'

'Of course you're not.' Dad knelt down and helped him to his feet. 'Never mind about her,' he said, sitting on the edge of the bed and taking Kipper in his arms. He held him until his shuddered sobs eased, then asked, 'Where's your hat?'

Kipper wiped his nose on the back of his pyjama sleeve. 'In Ethie's room.' He sniffed, attempting a smile.

'I'll get it.' Dad pulled back the bedcovers. 'You just crawl in here while I go downstairs and talk to your aunt. Okay?'

'Okay, Da.'

In my bedroom Dad's eyebrows rose as he took in the rumpled bed that hadn't been made for days, the clothes strewn on the floor and the empty whiskey bottle in the corner. The air still stank of stale alcohol. But he probably didn't notice it because he smelt the same.

'I suppose if you see this through your aunt's eyes, her shock might be somewhat understandable,' he said.

'It's my fault,' I confessed. 'I took the bottle. But I didn't really drink it. It spilled.' Suddenly remembering my anger at him, I sat down on the bed.

'Pretty nasty stuff, huh?' Dad said, sitting down beside me.

I shrugged off his hand, then sat back against the headboard with my arms folded, refusing to look at him.

'It's not your fault or your brother's,' he said. 'It's mine. Your aunt's right about that. I should have been here.' He took Kipper's hat from the bedpost above my head. 'I'll try to calm her down.' He reached over to stroke my hair. I pulled away, still refusing to look at him.

After he'd gone downstairs and into the bathroom, I crept down to sit on the step above the turn in the stairway. The step where, when I was young, I hid from Kipper when we played hide-and-seek. The one where he and I would fall asleep on Christmas Eve waiting for Santa to arrive. The same step I had sat on the night the police came into our house with the wind and rain.

Downstairs, the bathroom taps were turned off and Dad came out and went into the kitchen. The house was so quiet I could hear him lift the coffee-pot from the element on top of the stove. 'Listen,' he said. 'I know this looks—' He stopped abruptly.

My aunt's voice broke the silence. 'You – you—'

I barely heard my father's choked response: 'Where did you get that?'

'A daughter?' my aunt cried, ignoring his question. 'The day Lucy died she found out you had a love child?'

Mom's note! Not caring if they heard me I rushed down to the living room and crouched in the corner by the sofa.

In the kitchen Dad stood by the counter, the coffee-pot still in his hands, a bewildered expression on his face. 'No, that's not—'

'Lying to Lucy all those years,' Aunt Mildred was shouting. 'Sending money to China, to another family, while my sister went without.'

'You've got it all wrong.'

'Do I? Well, explain this.' She shook the paper at him. 'Did Lucy have it wrong, then? Did she go to her grave believing this – what? Untruth? Mistake?'

'Yes. Unfortunately she did.'

'Unfortunately?' she shrieked. 'Do you know how many times I gave my sister money? She never asked. Oh, no. It would have cost her too much to ask. But she took it. And we always, always, had to keep it from you. Didn't want to hurt your precious pride. And all the while you were sending money away for an illegitimate child.'

'It wasn't that way.'

Then she must have noticed the empty whiskey bottles on the counter for she asked icily, 'Two bottles a day now, Howard? I warned Lucy for years. She just wouldn't see it. You're nothing but an alcoholic.'

I was about to jump up, to run in and tell her that he hadn't drunk those bottles, that I had dumped them down the drain, when Dad spoke: 'You're right,' he said quietly, 'I am.' He set the coffee-pot down on the counter. 'But I'll quit. I'll—'

'Fine,' Aunt Mildred said. 'I'll take Ethie to live with me while you do just that. And I'll put Christopher into a good institution where he will be—'

'No,' Dad said quietly.

'What do you think Social Welfare would say if someone reported this?' Aunt Mildred asked. 'A teenage boy in bed with his little sister? A child's room reeking of alcohol? The state of this house? You? Your children would be whisked away in minutes.'

'Let's just calm down and talk about this rationally,' Dad pleaded.

'No,' she snapped. 'You sit down and listen. Someone has to take over. You're in no shape to look after this family right now.'

'We – I'll change. I'll stop drinking. We'll manage.'

'And how will you do that? Who will look after the boy during the day? Be here for Ethie after school? Who will cook for them? Or do you expect them to live on,' she grabbed a cheese-smeared plate, 'packaged macaroni?' She tossed the plate into the sink with the other dirty dishes.

'We'll find someone to come in. Our next-door neighbour says she'll speak to the woman who stays with her son after school. Dora thinks she might be willing to come here the days Frankie and I are at work.'

'Dora!' The name came off her tongue like bitter spit. 'Ha. Wouldn't she just love to get her hooks into you? And her hands on my niece.'

'It's not like that. She's – she was Lucy's friend.'

'Some friend.'

The harshness of her words made me shiver. But I suddenly realized there was more than anger behind them. Of course. The note to Dora Fenwick. When Mom had needed someone to talk to she had turned to two friends but not to her sister. As if the same thought had struck Dad, he said, 'I wish to God she *had* called you.'

'That's enough!' I heard a sob catch in Aunt Mildred's throat. 'Don't you dare blame me.'

'I didn't mean to. I know you loved her.'

Neither spoke for a few moments. 'Listen to me, Howard,' Aunt Mildred finally said, her tone softening, 'let's be rational.

Do you really have a choice? Do you really believe you're doing what's best for these children? I don't. And I won't stand by and let my sister's children suffer because you're too blind to see it. If I have to I'll take it to court and fight for custody.'

'Mildred, don't do this,' Dad said, but the words came out cracked and broken.

'I'm not threatening. I'm just telling you some truths. Somebody has to. I swear if we end up in court I'll win. Or you can let me take Ethie home with me right now without argument. Let me look after her while you get your life back on track. Let me take the boy to a place that's set up for people like him. Where he'll be safe and taken care of properly.' She took a deep breath. 'You and I both know Lucy spent hours each day teaching him, caring for him. Who will replace that? He'll get that kind of attention in a residential school. And if Ethie lives with me,' she pressed, 'you can visit her any time you like. And then, if you truly do get your life back in order, well, we'll see.'

When he made no reply she continued, 'It's time to think of someone besides yourself for a change. Think about what's right for Ethie . . . and for Christopher. And Frankie. What about him? Isn't it time you took this burden from him as well?' she asked. 'It's up to you, Howard. If Lucy could, I'm sure even she would tell you it's time to do what's right for these children.'

She clicked open her purse. 'And there's no reason for them to ever know about this,' she said, dropping Mom's note into her handbag and snapping it shut.

'It doesn't matter,' Dad said, his voice barely a whisper. 'The truth is worse.'

33

18 December 1942: Camp Sham Shui Po

Two weeks after Gordy's death Howard still hadn't told Shun-ling. He slipped out of his bunk in the darkness and made his way cautiously to the fence at the back of the camp. He scooped away the loose sand by the corner post, then crawled under the barbed wire to drop down to the ledge below. Wrapped in his thin blanket while he waited in the darkness, he made up his mind. This time he would tell her. Without warning she emerged silently from the shadows to squat beside him.

At the sight of her Howard lost his resolve. It didn't help that she had shown up with two vials of serum. 'Diphtheria anti-toxin,' she breathed, holding them up proudly. 'From Ah Sam.'

'What a great risk this must have been for your friend,' Howard said, accepting the tiny bottles. Keeping his voice low, he added, 'And for you.'

'It is worth it. He says there will be more next week. I will bring it.'

Looking into her dark eyes, so full of hope, Howard could not bring himself to tell her that it was all in vain. He would grant her a few more days of not knowing, of believing that the herbs, the potions and now the serum she had brought were helping Gordy.

So, instead of telling the truth he asked about money. 'Do not worry,' she told him. 'Ah Sam is keeping an account. He says he will present you with a bill when this is all over.'

'He believes it will end?'

'He has no doubt.'

Before she turned to retreat up the grassy bank Howard touched her arm. 'Feng Shun-ling,' he whispered 'I—' He stopped. He wasn't certain what he had meant to say. Perhaps he had just wanted to hear his voice say her name. Perhaps he had been going to tell her about Gordy, but he didn't get the chance. Staring into his eyes, she reached up and touched his lips with her fingertips.

'Howard Coulter,' she whispered, then disappeared into the early-morning shadows.

'My God, man, can she get more?' Ken Campbell asked, when Howard turned the medicine over to him.

'She thinks it's for Gordy,' Howard confessed.

Ken urged him to keep the supply coming. 'This stuff means life for a lot of men.' It was too late for Gordy but the anti-toxin would save lives. How could Howard deny them?

Reluctantly he agreed, warning that eventually he would have to tell Shun-ling that Gordy was gone. That there was no reason for her to risk coming here.

As he continued to meet her he quelled his conscience by telling himself that at least someone would benefit from his deception. But he knew that, behind all the excuses for not telling her – the need for the serum, the packets of Chinese medicine, not wanting to cause her sorrow – beyond all that there was his own need. His need not for the scraps of food she brought – which were meant for Gordy and tasted like sawdust when Howard choked them down – but for those glimpses of sanity. Those stolen moments of escape on the other side of the fence that kept him going for a few more days. When he was sitting with another human being who still had light shining in her eyes, listening to her soft voice whispering in the shadows, he could believe that some day this would be over.

She brought news of the outside world. If they had believed the interpreter's announcements of the Japanese Empire's glorious victories on land and sea, spewed out at roll call each morning, they would have given up completely. A radio was hidden somewhere in the camp, yes, but only a few officers were privileged enough to listen to it. By the time word reached Howard's ears it was difficult to separate truth from rumour.

And Shun-ling brought news of Lily, a proud mother's stories meant to be passed on to Gordy. Huddled under his blanket with her behind the fence, listening to the child's growing accomplishments, Howard allowed the stolen images to transport him across the sea.

He had yet to receive a second letter from Lucy. Their baby – A boy? A girl? – must have been born a month or two before Lily. So each time he listened to Shun-ling's shy boasting he imagined Lucy glowing with pride over a first smile, a giggle, a tooth felt on tiny gums. Such simple things that seemed impossibly extraordinary, impossibly far away. Like Lucy. An entire world away. A world that he was finding harder and harder to believe still existed. Shun-ling kept that world alive. She represented freedom, hope, life beyond this misery. So, again and again, those few moments of promise kept him silent.

And after each clandestine meeting, like a thief salving his conscience by delivering alms to the altar, he dropped the smuggled packets of hope on Ken Campbell's bed.

Attuned to the night's rhythm, Howard lay listening to the sounds of the camp, the inhaling and exhaling of the damned that had become the new normal. Above the rumble of snores from those fortunate enough to find sleep came the phlegmatic hacking, the involuntary moans and muffled weeping of those tormented by hunger, electric feet, churning bowels, fever and delirium. He prayed that tonight he would not hear the plaintive call of a dying man for his wife, his sweetheart or, more commonly – with his final breath – his mother.

Staring into the darkness, Howard waited like a blind man with heightened senses. Every once in a while moonlight broke through the cracks in the boarded-up windows. It cast shadows in the hut, broken every few moments by the silhouettes of emaciated phantoms on their way to the latrines.

Some macabre camp statistician had estimated that the average prisoner afflicted with dysentery emptied his bowels a minimum of ten times an hour during the day. The night brought no relief. And yesterday this parade of sorrow had become even more torturous with the sudden reappearance of the guard Satan. Between him and the interpreter, with his consuming hatred of anyone Canadian, anyone white, no one was safe.

The Japanese-Canadian sergeant was making good his promise. He used any excuse to punish the prisoners. Many had suffered his tortures. His favourite, forcing water down the throats of his victims until their bellies were bloated and jumping on them, made him the most hated man in the camp.

During a Red Cross inspection at the end of November, a Canadian officer had made the near fatal mistake of stepping forward to inform the delegates about the staged conditions they were witnessing. After they had left, the enraged interpreter beat him senseless with his belt buckle, bare fists and boots. Now the officer was clinging to life in the Agony Ward.

As dangerous as he was, the sergeant's ire was reserved for the prisoners. He showed no interest in the Chinese civilians.

Howard sensed he was no real threat to Shun-ling. Or, for some bizarre reason, to himself. Ever since Lucy's letter, the interpreter had treated him with an almost friendly air. Howard did his best to avoid him, which was not easy: the man was caught between two cultures, accepted by neither, and occasionally felt the need of someone to talk to. Each time he cornered him, Howard would stand with his head bowed, silently repeating his mantra. But it was not the interpreter he feared running into in the morning darkness.

Satan's sudden return was a threat to Shun-ling. This frightening turn of events made it all the more crucial that this meeting with her was the last. He must tell her about Gordy, ensure that she did not come back to the camp. He wished he could warn her to stay away. He had hoped for the torrential rains to begin – prayed for them: rain meant she would not come. But the intermittent rays of moonlight mocked him as he rose.

He wrapped the thin blanket around his shoulders and, moving carefully to avoid squeaking floorboards, made his way through the hut carrying his boots. Outside he ducked under the steps to pull them on, all the while listening for a spray of pebbles against the side of a hut, an out-of-place sneeze or three barking coughs, all signals that a guard was near. Hearing nothing, he crept toward the fence, hugging the barrack walls.

Clouds scudded across the sky, providing cover to slip between buildings and bringing the faint promise of rain. The island was on blackout, making darkness total when the clouds shadowed the moon. At the back of the camp Howard crept along the Japanese officers' garden. A sliver of moonlight revealed movement among the potato plants. He froze. A few feet away, on the other side of the first row, a hunched back moved, a head lifted, bulging eyes stared up from a skull-thin face. Just another prisoner scrounging. Howard let out his breath. A silent greeting passed between him and the apparition. There was something familiar about the prisoner's startled face. Seeing Howard, he grinned and held up a dirt-covered fist, thumb in, the signal that the way was clear. Then he went back to his digging. It was a dangerous activity, leaving the plant tops to grow while stealing tiny potatoes from the roots. Dangerous, and eventually there would be hell to pay, but that was the soldier's business, Howard thought. Suddenly he connected the grinning face with the young soldier he had seen on *Awatea*'s bow, the man-child taunting the Japanese on the *Lisbon Maru* a lifetime ago. He might or might not have been the same boy – no, not boy: there were no boys left here.

The garden poacher lifted his head and held out his hand to display his treasure, then popped the worms into this mouth and chewed them with relish. Hunger made it possible to eat almost anything. Howard had recognized parts of rats, snakes, mice and insects – even maggots – mixed with the rice. He had learned to choke back the welcome protein. He had not yet been reduced to eating worms. A fist of guilt punched his gut. He fingered the wrapped square of chocolate in his pocket. The last piece left from his share of the Red Cross parcels distributed during the humanitarian inspection. He had saved the final square, a Christmas gift – now a parting gift – for Shun-ling.

But he couldn't turn away from the young soldier in the garden, from the eyes speaking of death, and the soil surrounding the mouth like cake crumbs. Howard took out the carefully hoarded chocolate square, leaned over and dropped it beside the other man.

A few minutes later he squatted on the sandy ledge below the fence to wait for Shun-ling. The clanging of a bell-buoy drifted up from the bay, with the sound of water lapping on the tidal flats. The same innocent sounds he recalled from his first day in camp, more than a year ago now. *A year.* One entire year spent in this hellhole. 'Home by Christmas' was no longer heard around camp, replaced by 'Home come next spring.'

The moon appeared suddenly in the water below, her light streaking across the harbour, exposing the illusion of freedom. So deceptively near. So impossibly distant. How tempting it was to climb down to the bay and wade out with the tide. To swim away, take his chances with the sampans and fishing-boats bobbing there. But the nine other men who would be punished, perhaps executed, if he did not return kept him still. And Shun-ling. He must stay here to warn her.

And suddenly there she was, crouched, moving soundlessly along the ledge towards him. Howard felt the blood pounding in his ears at the sight of the cotton dress she was wearing, the blue and white floral pattern shining brightly – too brightly – in the moonlight. He lifted his blanket to cover her as she squatted beside him, so close he could smell the spicy-sweet scent of her perspiration. She pulled the dress down over her knees, and slowly raised her eyes to meet his. The same dangerous moonlight reflected on her oval face shone in her dark eyes as she silently searched his face. Without warning she placed her hand on his cheek. 'Howard,' she said. It was not a question or a statement. It was an entire conversation in a word.

Startled by the warmth, the comfort, of her palm, he felt himself leaning into it. But there was no time. He must tell her this very second. He reached up to touch the back of her hand, pressed it to his face and held it there briefly. 'Shun-ling, you must listen,' he whispered. 'It's—'

The last thing he remembered before the rifle butt struck his temple was the hiss of air sucked between teeth.

* * *

Gravel bit into his knees. Wire cut into his neck and wrists. At the edge of his vision, familiar dark brown jackboots came into focus, the polished toes inches from his temple.

Through the high-pitched ringing in his ears he heard muffled cries from the guardhouse. Shun-ling. The wire around Howard's neck and binding his hands behind his back cut deeper with his desperate struggling. 'Let her go,' he begged the motionless boots, fighting the blackness that threatened to return. 'She's done nothing. She's just a refugee, a scavenger from the mud flats.'

The boots moved, slowly circling their prey. 'She has nothing to do with me,' the interpreter answered. 'She is *his* prize for thwarting your escape.'

'I wasn't—' Howard clamped his mouth shut. There was no explanation without implicating Shun-ling. From the guard-house the sounds of her frantic resistance and Satan's harsh retaliation grew louder.

'Animals!' Howard growled.

'The punishment for attempting escape is death,' the inter-preter said. 'What am I to do with you?'

In answer a bamboo cane whistled across Howard's back. Again and again. He fought to keep conscious through the searing pain, but the swirling darkness took over.

As he came to, something heavy thudded to the ground. He opened his eyes to see Shun-ling lying face down, spreadeagled, her head within arm's distance of his.

'A warrior!' Satan said, giving her limp body a kick. 'She fought well.'

She raised her head, her tangled hair falling to the ground. The moment her eyes met Howard's, her bloodied lips parted in a defiant smile.

'Shun-ling,' he whispered, searching her unflinching eyes.

From above them came the chilling sound of steel sliding from a scabbard. 'A warrior deserves an honourable death,' Satan crooned.

'Leave her,' Howard screamed. He twisted towards the interpreter's jackboots. 'Stop him. For God's sake! In the name of your father – a Canadian hero – I beg you, please. Spare her.' He lowered his head to the ground. 'Here, here,' he pleaded, stretching out his neck as far as the wire would allow, offering an easy target. 'Please.' He squeezed his eyes shut, willing death to meet him on the razor edge of a sword. His muscles tensed at the whisper slicing through the air. Cold steel met flesh with a thud. A surge of warm liquid splashed over him, the sharp metallic smell filling his nostrils. A soundless cry rose in his throat.

The bamboo cane slashed across his back, forcing his head up. Howard struggled to keep his weighted eyelids closed. A second blow deepened his determination. He would not bear witness, would not allow the horror that he knew waited beyond the red veil to take shape. The blows continued until, no longer able to control himself, his eyelids snapped open, to see the unimaginable vision – the slumped torso, the ragged neck spilling blood. And on the ground the unseeing eyes of Shun-ling looking up from between her outstretched arms. Arms reaching for, almost touching him.

The first heavy raindrops fell with the white gloves that landed on the ground by Howard's cheek. Satan walked away carelessly, sucking air between his teeth, as the interpreter tossed aside the cane. 'You deserve no such honour,' he said, then turned on his heels and left Howard alone to beg the weeping heavens to let him to die. As the torrential downpour washed the blood-soaked earth, he surged in and out of consciousness. He awoke in the grey light of dawn to witness

Shun-ling's remains being dragged outside the camp gates and dumped on the road. Moments later a group of refugees appeared in the drizzling haze and carried her away.

34

My father gave me away. *He gave me away!* Like a puppy or a kitten he'd grown tired of. He didn't want me. It was as simple as that. He didn't want Kipper either. It was only Mom who had wanted us all this time. Now that she was gone we were in the way. A bother.

'For a while,' was how Dad explained it when he came up-stairs and sat on the edge of my brother's bed to tell us. Kipper, in true Kipper fashion, accepted it, trusted Dad when he said that the place he was going to was like a sleepover school, where he would learn lots of new things, make new friends. And he could come home every weekend if he wanted to. Well, after the first month. 'Think of it like summer camp,' Dad said, when Kipper's lip began to tremble. 'You always wanted to go to summer camp. And if you don't like it you don't have to stay.'

'Okay, Da,' he said, sucking back his lip.

Dad looked up at me standing by the door with my arms folded. 'It's not for ever,' he promised.

'Ha!' I turned my back on him, stomped across the hall into my room and slammed the door.

After he went downstairs, after I heard him leave the house, I threw open my closet and yanked everything out. Clothes, skipping ropes and games, shoeboxes full of carefully saved treasures, all went flying to the floor. I grabbed my prized stack of comic books from the shelf and, one by one, tore them to shreds. When Aunt Mildred pushed my bedroom door open again, an unsolvable jigsaw puzzle of anger lay scattered at my feet.

She raised her eyebrows, but said nothing about the mess. 'I found a suitcase that Christopher can use,' she said, holding up the old one from the basement. 'You just take what you can pack in your overnight bag, dear,' she added, as if this was a holiday and she wasn't taking us away from our home.

After she went to Kipper's room I threw clothes and underwear into the little suitcase I usually took when I went to stay at her house. I left everything else behind with my childhood. But I took my secret about Lily with me. I folded and refolded the wrinkled piece of paper with her name and phone number until it was so tiny it couldn't be folded again, then stuck it behind the lining of my suitcase. If my father didn't want us, he wouldn't want her either, I told myself. Or maybe I was more afraid that he did.

I crawled back into bed, pulled the covers over my head and waited for Aunt Mildred to tell me what to do next. I woke to her calling upstairs that it was time to go. Before I left my room I took Kipper's painting from the wall above my bed. I came downstairs with it tucked under my arm, just waiting for her to complain. But she led me out to her Volvo, opened the trunk and placed my things inside without a word.

'Where's Kipper?' I asked, looking into the empty back seat.

He was gone. They had come and taken him away already. 'It's best this way,' Aunt Mildred explained.

Best? I didn't even get to say goodbye. I couldn't help it, I started to cry. 'I want Frankie,' I sniffled.

'Frankie will come to visit,' she said, opening the passenger door and guiding me into the car.

During the drive to her house I sat on the front seat as close to the door as I could get. I had nothing to say to her. Nothing to say to anybody. I wondered if it was possible to stop talking for ever. There was nothing worth talking about any more. I didn't think there ever would be again.

Aunt Mildred took one hand from the steering-wheel and reached over to touch my hair. 'Tonight we'll shampoo and untangle this mop,' she said. 'Then I'll braid it for you in the morning. I used to do that for your mother, you know. When she was a little girl, I braided her hair every single day.'

I pulled away from her touch.

My aunt and uncle's house was huge. A house of antiseptic smells and soundless footsteps. 'Too big for two people,' Uncle Sidney had said, on many occasions. Even with three it was still too big. The front hall smelled of old wood and furniture polish. The moment we entered I marched across it and up the wide oak staircase. Aunt Mildred called after me that lunch would be in an hour.

Upstairs, I tossed my suitcase into the corner of the room. I leaned Kipper's painting against the wall and threw myself across the bed.

Ever since I could remember I had had my own room at my aunt's house. A room she had decorated just for me, all in pink. I'd loved it. I'd loved the rows of dolls that looked down from the shelves above the bed, dolls she'd brought back for me from her holidays all around the world. Now I climbed up on the bed and reached up to run my hand along the shelves, sweeping them all away. They tumbled down, another remnant of childhood, in a confused heap of porcelain arms and legs on the floor. I gathered them up, shoved them into the bottom of the closet and slammed the door. Then I slumped down at the vanity table. Twisting a long strand of hair into my mouth I stared into the mirror. Hair just like my mother's. I'd heard it all my life. I got up, opened my bedroom door and went across the hall to Aunt Mildred's sewing room. I searched through all the drawers until I found what I wanted. Back in my room I sat in front of the vanity mirror. I took a clump of hair and lifted the pinking shears. As my curls fell to the floor I smirked at the thought of my aunt's shocked face when I sat down at her dining-table.

35

'What did she do?' Frankie demanded. 'What could she possibly have said, or done, to persuade you to let her take them?'

Hunched over the table, Howard stared into his coffee mug. 'It's not for ever,' he mumbled. 'It's just until I get straightened out. It's the right thing to do.'

'The right thing? The right thing for who? You?' Frankie asked, his words brittle with a sarcasm Howard hadn't believed him capable of. He strode across the kitchen and snatched the mug from Howard's hands, spilling cold coffee across the table as he raised it to his nose.

It was only coffee, but Howard suspected that the evidence of his visit to the Legion earlier was still on his breath. Just one – he had needed just one drink to help him through this day, to keep him away from the house while she had done the deed for them both.

'Yes, for me, for you, for everyone right now.' His head jerked up as the mug slammed back down on the table. 'It's not for ever,' he repeated. With a will of their own, his eyes flickered to the top of the refrigerator.

'Christ!' Frankie swore. He shook his head, turned away and walked over to the kitchen door. With his hand on the knob, he spun back to face Howard, who flinched at the rage – rage kindled by pain – he saw smouldering in his son's face. 'I've always wondered why Mom had such a blind spot about your drinking,' he said, his voice low. 'Why she never forced you to choose between the booze and her.' He blinked as his eyes filled. 'I guess I have my answer. She knew which one you would have chosen.'

'No,' Howard whispered. 'Never.'

Frankie's jaw hardened. A tear spilled onto his cheek. He swatted at his face to brush it away. Then, with no warning, he rushed over, grabbed Howard by the shirt and yanked his face so close to his own that Howard could see a purple vein pulsing on his forehead. 'Do you know what?' he screamed, spittle spraying from his mouth with each word. 'I wish it was you! I wish it was you instead of her.' He choked on a sob, then released Howard's shirt with such force that he fell back and hit his head against the window-ledge.

'So do I,' he murmured, to Frankie's retreating back.

The slam of the door echoed in the silent kitchen, leaving Howard's ears ringing. He pushed his hands through his hair. His head hurt to the touch: a hammer pounded inside his skull. Even his eyeballs ached. His mouth was a dry canyon.

He rose and, with shaking hands, searched the cupboards under the sink. Finding nothing he headed to his room and frantically checked under the bed, rummaged through the dressing-table drawers. Nothing. He pulled the closet door open.

The fragrance hit him like a sucker punch. He sank to the closet floor, grabbed a handful of Lucy's clothes from the laundry basket and pressed them to his face. He breathed in her essence, which filled a craving alcohol never could. After a while he became aware of the soothing rhythm of rain falling outside the bedroom window. He wiped his eyes on his sleeve and checked his wristwatch. Then he stood and made his way through the silent, impossibly empty house. He took his leather jacket from the front hall closet and pulled it on. Outside, he stopped on the bottom porch step, tilted his head back and let the rain wash down his face. Then he lifted the matted sheep-skin collar and headed up the street.

Unlike when he'd set out in the rain yesterday – waking in the dark of night to find himself lying on the waterlogged grass above Lucy's grave, not knowing how he'd got there or how long he'd been there – he knew where he was going. He walked past the liquor store on Victoria Drive and past the Royal Canadian Legion on Fraser Street. He kept going until he reached the address he was looking for on Oak Street. The address he had been unable to push out of his mind. The one Ken Campbell had given him on the day of Lucy's funeral. He stopped in front of the building, took a deep breath, then walked around to the basement entry.

In the room downstairs heads turned at the opening of the door. Howard stopped, feeling suddenly paralysed, unable to cross the threshold. He heard a chair scrape across the concrete floor, a lifeline thrown to a drowning man. He stepped forward, reached for and clung to its back. Understanding faces waited. He squared his shoulders, opened his mouth and said, 'My name is Howard Coulter. And I am an alcoholic.'

36

17 January 1943: Camp Sham Shui Po

Howard waited in line for Ken Campbell to finish swabbing the throat of the prisoner in front of him. Like the rest of the PoWs, all fat had long since disappeared from Ken's face, leaving no trace of the once cherubic cheeks. His hulking form had dwindled away to beanpole limbs held together by knobby joints.

'What the hell are you doing here?' he demanded, when Howard stepped forward and opened his mouth. 'Don't be crazy, man,' he said. 'You'll never make it through the voyage. You've got malaria. You can barely stand up.'

'Yeah, but I don't have diphtheria, and that's all they care about. Swab my throat.'

Ken glanced over his shoulder at the guards wearing white face masks to oversee the screening operation. 'Look, this is just a numbers game with them,' he said, his voice low. 'They need six hundred and fifty bodies, slave labour for their shipyards and coal mines. They expect some to die on voyage. You'll be one of them.'

Howard wrapped his arms around himself to still a fresh volley of chills. He nodded at Jack Dell, who was leaning against the hut doorway. 'What about him?' he rasped. 'You tested him. He'll go with only one arm?'

'That little Newfie's tougher than nails,' Ken said. 'He'll survive anything. You won't.'

'Swab my throat.'

Ken unwrapped the little stick reluctantly. 'I know exactly what you're doing.'

Two days later Howard woke bathed in sweat. He struggled to rise but a heavy hand pressed against his chest, holding him down. 'I've got to get up,' he groaned.

'No one's stopping you,' someone said from a distance.

Howard forced his head up, his eyes focusing on the morning shadows. There was no hand, no one near him. Freed from the imaginary restraint he pushed himself to a sitting position and threw his legs over the side of his cot. He needed to get up. But why? He searched his fever-racked mind. Across the room Ken Campbell was bent over his own cot, wrapping his few possessions in his blanket.

That was it. The ship would sail for Japan today.

'I'm going with you,' Howard said, reaching down to grab his boots.

'Sorry. You're not.' Ken gave the knot in his blanket a final tug.

'Oh, yes, I am.'

Hoisting his makeshift bag onto his shoulder, Ken walked over to him. 'Your diphtheria swab came back positive,' he said, standing above Howard.

'Bullshit!'

'Prove it.'

A coughing fit took hold of Howard. 'I've been immunized,' he rasped, catching his breath. 'And you know it.'

'Going on that boat would be your death sentence. And *you* know that.'

But Howard wasn't listening. He struggled to stand. 'You falsified my test? I'll—'

'You'll what?' Ken asked. 'Report me?'

Howard was beaten.

Ken put a hand on his shoulder. 'The difference between life and death in this place,' he reminded him, 'is the ability to see beyond what we have to do to survive here, to see beyond this animal existence to a future as human beings. You've lost that ability. I've watched you defying the guards, practically begging them for beatings with your insolence, taking latrine duty when you don't have to, volunteering in the hospital, giving away food. But you're doing it all for the wrong reasons, man, and I'll be damned if I'm going to help you to die.'

'Everybody dies some time,' Howard said, but he couldn't meet Ken's eyes.

'Yes, and in the end a man is defined by what he's willing to die for. Think about Gordy, all the men we've buried, even the girl – each willing to risk it all for something. What? Love of country? Love of another human being? It's all the same. Even the Japanese are willing to die for something bigger than themselves. Are you less than that?' He dropped his hand from Howard's shoulder and stepped back. 'Find your purpose again, my friend. Don't let me come back from Japan when this is all over and find out you died for something as small and self-serving as guilt.'

37

I missed Barclay Street. I missed my old school, my friends. Most of all I missed my family. I blamed my aunt. And my father.

For two weeks I refused to see him. The first time he came to visit I fled upstairs and locked myself in my room. I lay across my perfectly made bed, pressed the fluffy pink pillows to my ears, and pretended I couldn't hear him on the other side of my bedroom door calling my name.

The next evening Aunt Mildred came upstairs when, again, I refused to come out. 'That's enough, Ethie,' she said, her insistent pounding overtaking my father's soft knock. 'Open the door.'

'Don't force her,' my father said. 'I'll come back tomorrow.'

I slid down the bedroom wall and sat by my door, listening to his footsteps recede.

It became an evening ritual after that, him waiting downstairs while my aunt came up and tried to talk me out of my room. After she had gone away I stood behind the frilly curtains in my fancy new bedroom, wearing my beautiful new clothes, and watched my father walk back to his car in the street below.

Frankie came and tried to reason with me. 'Dad's trying, Ethie. He's really trying.' He explained about Alcoholics Anonymous and the meetings he had gone to with Dad. 'I was angry at him too,' he said, 'but I know he's doing his best.'

I wanted to believe Frankie when he said that eventually we

would all be together again, that this wouldn't be for ever. But Dad had said that too.

I almost told him then. Almost told Frankie about this huge secret of our father's, now mine. I wanted to ask, 'If Dad had lied to Mom, never told her about Lily, why should we believe anything he said?' But I kept it to myself, stuffed it down inside. And I didn't know why.

I didn't know who I was any more. When I looked into the mirror every morning I didn't recognize the person looking back at me. It was more than the haircut, which Aunt Mildred's hairdresser had done her best to fix. At my new school I felt older than the kids in my class. I gave them, and the whole world, the cold shoulder, the silent treatment. Especially my aunt. I did everything she asked me to, but spoke only when spoken to. I gave her nothing more. And, worst of all, I stopped calling her 'Aunt', relishing the hurt I saw in her eyes each time I addressed her as 'Mildred'.

One Sunday morning, two weeks after I came to live with them, while she was busy gathering windfall plums from the tree outside, I lay sprawled on the living-room couch, staring at an empty television screen – just like my father. Suddenly Uncle Sid was standing before me, a large photograph album tucked under his arm. I hadn't even noticed him come into the room.

'Can I sit with you, Ethie?' he asked.

I sat up and moved over to make room for him.

He settled beside me and placed the album across his lap. 'I thought you might like to look at some old photographs of your mother and father,' he said, smiling at me. 'You know your mom lived with us while your dad was away at war, don't you?'

I nodded. He opened the album and pressed the thick black pages flat. The breath caught in the back of my throat at a photograph of my mother sitting on my aunt and uncle's front porch steps with her chin in her hands.

Uncle Sidney removed the snapshot from the corner tabs that held it in place. 'I can still remember her sitting out there waiting for the mailman,' he said, handing it to me. 'For more than two years it was the same every morning. She sat out on the steps, or if it was raining, inside in the hall, hoping for a letter to come sliding through the slot telling her that your father was alive and well. He fought in Hong Kong during the war,' he said. 'Did you know that?'

I bit my lip and shrugged, studying the picture of Mom.

'For the first two years after the battle,' he continued, 'there was no word. I tried to pull strings in Ottawa to get a list of casualties and prisoners. But they didn't have a complete accounting. Your mother knew, though. She never doubted for one minute. On New Year's Day that first year, she came downstairs and told us she had heard your dad's voice in the middle of the night. Clear as a bell, she swore she'd heard him telling her he was all right. When a letter finally arrived from the War Office, the postman wouldn't drop it through the slot. Instead he knocked at the door and placed it in her hands.'

He turned the page. 'The *Admiral Hughes*,' he said, pointing to a snapshot of a ship approaching the docks. 'The American troopship that brought your father home. We went to the pier with your mom to pick him up.'

I searched the faces of the soldiers waving from the decks.

'Your dad isn't in any of those snapshots. I didn't take one of him that day. After four years in a prison camp he came down the gangplank little more than a rattling skeleton. Your mother and aunt wouldn't let him go to the veterans' hospital. We brought him home and, between the two of them, they nursed him back to health.' He looked down at me. 'I know your aunt's ways can be harsh sometimes,' he continued, 'but she was once a very competent and compassionate nurse. Your father would be the first to testify to that.' He thought for a moment. 'Perhaps it would have been better if she had remained in practice. But we hoped to have a family. Then your mother came to live with us. After the war, well, Mildred just didn't have the heart to start all over again.'

He turned his attention back to the album and pointed out a photograph of them all at the dining-table taken the first Christmas after my father returned. 'He came home craving sardine sandwiches. Did you know that? He just couldn't get enough of them. Or anything, really.' He chuckled. 'One night, without thinking, your aunt served rice for dinner. After she'd set it on the table she suddenly remembered and apologized. "I guess you had your fill of rice over there," she said, taking the bowl away. But your dad told her to leave it. "The problem was we never got enough of it."'

I knew he was telling me all this about my aunt and my father because he wanted me to understand them better, but I was barely listening. I was stuck back at the words about my father spending four years in a prison camp.

16 August 1945: Camp Sham Shui Po

It was over. Wearing nothing but a grey loincloth and the tattered remains of his shirt, Howard stood in the hospital-hut doorway watching, through a haze of drizzling rain, as American cargo planes passed over the camp. Billowing parachutes filled the grey sky, carefree flowers drifting towards the ground. Drums and crates of all shapes and sizes swung beneath them, many cracking open on impact to reveal the life-giving supplies inside. Canned food, chocolate bars, cigarettes and medical supplies littered the ground in and around the camp. The Yankee display of abundance and generosity, after what seemed like a lifetime of need, left Howard, like many of the prisoners standing in the square, momentarily stunned. Others chased after and fell upon the bounty, stuffing chocolate into their mouths and trying to load their arms with cans of peaches.

When the cargo planes had departed, the sky filled with fighters dipping and diving in a show of victory and strength. American eagles at play on the wind.

Howard couldn't help but compare this aeronautic display to that of the antiquated fleet that had welcomed the two thousand eager young Winnipeg Grenadiers and Royal Rifles to Hong Kong four years ago. Now fewer than four hundred Canadians remained in Sham Shui Po to cheer on their liberators. More than a thousand of their comrades had been shipped to Japan in the last two years. How many had survived to see this day?

Months ago, the hidden radio had brought news of the end of the war in Europe and the stepping up of the battle in the Pacific. The American armada had control of the seas. Japan was under blockade, her citizens starving. Low-level firebombing of Tokyo had left fifteen square miles of the city in ashes, one hundred thousand dead.

It's just a matter of time now. Hang on. Hang on.

On August 13th the Japanese guards had laid down their arms. Before they disappeared from the camp, the friendly little guard who had led the work parties at the Kai Tak airport, his face a mask of suffering, had confided in Howard that a bomb, *one bomb*, had destroyed an entire Japanese city. Two days later a second had demolished another.

Could it be true? Saved by the deaths of hundreds of thousands of civilians? It didn't matter what side you were on, Howard thought, this war had cut through the souls of men and exposed their animal hearts. But it was truly over. This heavenly display was final proof.

He didn't know what he'd expected to feel when this moment came. *If* it came. But he felt strangely empty. No excitement, no exhilaration. A void of emotion.

Overhead, white papers spewed behind the fighter planes. Like giant snowflakes, they filled the sky and fluttered down while wings dipped in victory. Then, one by one, the American planes flew out to sea, some passing overhead so low that – even through the curtain of rain – Howard could make out the pin-up girls painted on the fuselage, and the pilots' grinning faces above. Suddenly a dark bundle flew out of a cockpit. It tumbled through the air and thudded to the ground not five feet from the hut where Howard stood. He walked over and retrieved the bomber jacket from the mud. Sinking to his knees he wrapped it around his trembling shoulders. As the warmth enfolded him, he felt something in the inside pocket. He reached in and removed a folded piece of paper.

'Notice to Allied Prisoners of War.' The leaflet, identical to those falling around him, confirmed the unconditional surrender of Japan. The notice instructed the internees to remain inside the camp until humanitarian and health officials arrived. The Pacific Fleet, the British and Americans, were on their way. The notice was signed by A. C. Wedemeyer, Lieutenant General, USA.

He looked closer. Something was written in pencil at the bottom. A lump came to Howard's throat as he read the scribbled message. 'Greetings from Wing Commander Gregory Jonas, of Little Rock, Arkansas. Welcome back to freedom, and a better world.'

A better world? Freedom? Was it possible?

Howard touched his shirt pocket, feeling the reassurance of the letter he kept next to his heart. A letter received shortly after the last group of Canadians had been shipped to Japan almost two years ago.

Since Shun-ling's death Howard had refused to speak to, or even acknowledge the existence of, the Japanese-Canadian interpreter. He had endured, no, welcomed beatings over this insolence. After Ken Campbell had left for Japan, Howard had languished for months, rarely leaving his cot. Then one morning he had woken to find the interpreter standing above him, a blue airmail envelope in his hand. Something inside Howard cracked when he saw the familiar handwriting. In that moment nothing mattered except the letter. Not life or death, not even hate. He reached out for it.

The sergeant leaned closer, tempting him with the nearness of Lucy's words. 'Say my name and I will give it to you,' he offered. 'Just my name.'

And Howard felt the screaming of his soul, the torture of his dry throat, as he strained to give voice to the man's name. And found he could not.

He turned on his side. In the silence that followed he heard the angry intake of breath. He waited for the snap of a belt buckle across his back, a boot kicking him from his cot. None came. Long moments later he heard the sound of his tormentor storming out of the hut. Howard never saw him again.

In the end it wasn't hope for the future or dreams of freedom that kept Howard alive. It was the uncensored letter the interpreter had dropped onto his cot.

He had memorized every word.

15 December 1942

My darling Howard,

As always I pray this letter finds you safe and well. I still have received no word but I feel you in my heart, and hope you are getting at least some of my letters . . .

Sidney and Mildred promise to take lots of photographs of Frankie's first Christmas. Can you believe our son is almost six months old? I can hardly believe it myself and I see him growing every day. He looks so much like you, my darling . . .

Promise me you will do everything it takes to get through this. We – how strange and wonderful it feels to say 'we' and not just 'I' – we need you. Come home to us.

Your loving wife
Lucy

39

'I always suspected that the reason your father liked Birch Bay so much was because of the way the Americans treated the Canadian survivors on the way home,' Uncle Sidney said, turning the page of the photograph album. 'They went from being treated like animals to being treated like gods.'

The next two pages were all snapshots of Frankie as a baby and a toddler, either with my mother or my aunt or both. I had seen many of them at home, but I remained silent, trying to absorb this new information about my father while Uncle Sidney went on.

'Frankie was three and a half years old when your dad came home,' he said, 'and for all that time your mother and aunt raised him together. I'm sure for a while he wasn't even aware which one was his mother. He called your mom Mommy, and Mildred was Mum-Mum. Your aunt adored him. It was very hard on her when they moved out. Me, too, I must admit.'

He smiled down at a photograph of Dad holding Frankie on his bony knees. 'From the moment your father got off the boat, that boy could see no one but him. He became his shadow, barely left his side. After they moved out of our house, every time we went to visit them Frankie would become distraught at the sight of your aunt, frightened she was there to take him away from his father. It was a long time before he stopped running to hide each time she appeared at the door. It broke her heart.'

I snorted and sat back, folding my arms.

'I know you're angry at her right now, Ethie,' Uncle Sidney said quietly, 'but I just want you to understand her side. She loved her sister – your mother – deeply, and she loves you just as much. And, right or wrong, she truly believes she is doing what is best for you, for Frankie and . . .'

'And Kipper?' I demanded.

'Yes, in her own way she does,' he said. 'I may not agree with her, but I do believe she did what she thought was right for him. When Kipper was born your aunt could only imagine a life of pain and heartache for your mother. She tried from the very first day to persuade her to give him up. Fortunately, neither she nor your father ever considered it, not even for a moment.'

'Why can't she love him, too?'

'I think she doesn't know how to. Some people are afraid of differences. Your aunt's one of them. I always hoped that, given enough time, she would see beyond his differences. Who couldn't love Kipper once they knew him?'

She doesn't even try to know him, I thought, but before I could say it, heavy footsteps pounded up the front porch, followed by my aunt's voice calling my father's name.

I jumped up from the couch and ran into the hall. The front door flew open as I arrived at the stairway. I put my hand on the banister, glancing quickly over my shoulder at my father standing in the doorway. Aunt Mildred rushed up behind him. 'Howard, I thought we agreed you'd call first.'

He ignored her and stepped inside. His gaze settled on me. Something in his eyes stopped me in my tracks. 'It's Kipper,' he said.

40

Once again Frankie's memories had to fill the gaps for me. Each day after Aunt Mildred took us away, he said Dad marked an X on the calendar by the phone. One more day of sobriety. One more day without his family. The days dragged by in excruciatingly slow motion, most ending the same – with the sting of my silent refusal to see him.

'She's as tenacious, as stubborn, as her mother,' he told Frankie, 'but the silence she learned from me.'

'Give her time,' Frankie said. 'She'll come around.'

At work Dad used the lunchroom pay phone to call Sunnywoods every day. Kipper's new home had a thirty-day no-family-visits policy to give new residents a chance to settle in, according to Aunt Mildred. 'How did I ever agree to not seeing him for a month?' Dad chastised himself over and over again.

The receptionist at the home came to recognize his voice, transferring him without comment to the director. At first Mrs Crossly answered his questions with polite indifference. Yes, Christopher was adjusting nicely. No, he was not homesick. Asthma? I'll look into that. No, they could not visit until the thirty-day period was up – rules were rules, best not to confuse the boy.

After the first week her smooth answers to Dad's queries became clipped replies. After ten days she was making strong suggestions that his constant calling was unwarranted. Then, on Friday, her voice brittle with impatience, she reprimanded him for all the time-consuming telephone calls that were, in her opinion, only for Dad's benefit, and doing no one else any earthly good. She hung up, leaving him with the firm message that they didn't expect to hear from him again until the thirty days were up. Until then, 'If there's a problem we'll call you.'

The call came at ten o'clock on Sunday morning.

Fear clutched at Frankie's gut when Dad's face darkened after he'd answered the phone. 'No, he's not here. What do you mean *wandered away*? When? . . . He's been gone *all night*? We'll be right there,' he shouted, slamming down the phone.

The heavyset male worker who opened the massive doors at Sunnywoods looked to Frankie like a bodyguard in some rough-neck bar. Grim-faced, a ring of keys clanging against his hip, he led them across the main entry and down dimly lit hall-ways. The metallic echo of doors locking behind them followed them through the empty corridors.

In the director's office, Dad and Frankie remained standing while Mrs Crossly stayed seated behind her desk. Frankie felt instant rage at the bizarre fact that this woman, who had known since yesterday that Kipper was missing, had taken the time to apply makeup and style her perfectly upswept hair without a strand out of place. He listened incredulously to her describing the situation as if it were a minor inconvenience.

'Why in God's name did it take you so long to call me?' Dad demanded.

'We fully expected him to come back at any minute,' she said. 'We were so certain that he was just hiding in the building somewhere, sulking.'

'Sulking?'

'Well,' she sniffed, 'he had been reprimanded, uh, restrained, as it were. For aggressive behaviour.'

'Aggressive?' Frankie snapped. 'Kipper?'

She ignored him, addressing Dad. 'Yes, the boy bit one of our workers.'

'My son has never bitten anyone in his life.'

'I assure you, he has now. At any rate,' she continued, 'the staff spent all afternoon and evening searching the building and the grounds. As I said, we were certain he would show up. When we hadn't located him by dark, we notified the police. There wasn't any point in calling you at that hour. What more could you have done?'

'I could have found my son before he spent a night alone God-knows-where,' he said. 'I want to talk to the staff. To all his friends here.'

'The police have already done that. And I won't allow you to bother our people any further. Your son has caused enough upset already. The boy's just too independent for his own good.' She stood up and walked to the door, dismissing them. 'I'm certain they'll find him. Certain that when he's hungry enough he'll either show up here or wander on home. I suggest you go there and wait. If he comes here, we'll call you.'

'Well, there's one other thing you can be certain of,' Dad said. 'He won't be coming back here.'

Outside in the parking lot a young man stepped out from the hedge behind Dad's car. 'Are you Kipper's family?' he asked, approaching them, his shoulders hunched.

'Yeah,' Frankie answered. 'Who wants to know?'

The man's eyes darted nervously between them. 'I work here,' he said, his gaze settling on Dad. 'Well, for now anyway.' He checked over his shoulder, then stepped closer. 'I just want you to know that Kipper didn't wander off,' he said, his voice low. 'He ran away. We found an open window in the basement laundry. He must have climbed up to it and crawled out.'

'The director said he had been restrained. Exactly what does that mean?' Dad asked.

'I didn't tell you this. They tied his wrists to the bedpost at night to stop him sucking his thumb.'

'What?' Frankie said. 'Kipper hasn't sucked his thumb for years.'

The man winced at the volume of Frankie's voice. 'Well, he did here,' he said. 'A few nights ago we were checking the dorm rooms before lights out and found him gnawing at his restraints. One of the workers went to tighten them and Kipper bit his hand by mistake.' His eyes darted up at the building, then back to Dad. 'Do you have any idea what they do to the residents here who bite?' he asked, then added quietly, 'Your son did.'

After the young man slipped away, Dad stared up at the three-storey building, at the whitewashed exterior shining in the morning sun like a lie, at the shadows behind the barred windows.

'How,' he wondered aloud, 'in all the times I've driven past here, could I, *of all people*, have failed to see this place for what it is?'

Only then did Frankie notice the ashen faces in the windows. From a distance it was impossible to tell whether they were young or old, male or female, whether they were real and not some trick of the light. But he couldn't shake the image of the haunted eyes staring down from the shadows.

Dad pulled the car door open. 'Kipper didn't *run away* from here,' he growled. 'He escaped.'

41

Aunt Mildred didn't object when Dad said he was taking me with them to search for Kipper. 'If anyone can figure out where he might have gone it's you, Ethie,' he said, as I laced up my running shoes with shaking fingers. 'I've always thought you had a sixth sense about your brother.'

I grew more and more frightened listening to him and Frankie explain to Uncle Sidney and Aunt Mildred what had happened. What would Kipper do, alone at night? Worst of all, he didn't have his inhaler with him.

Frankie pulled it out of his pocket. 'A guy who works there gave it to us in the parking lot. He said the director wouldn't let Kipper carry it around. She believed it was a "crutch". That his asthma attacks were psychological.'

'My God!' Uncle Sidney swore. He reached for the inhaler, examined it, then handed it back.

'I could cheerfully have wrung the woman's neck,' Frankie said, putting it into his pocket.

'The idea occurred to me,' Dad muttered.

I finished tying my shoes and jumped up.

'Bring a jacket or sweater,' Dad said. 'There's no telling how long we'll be.'

I grabbed my jacket from the hallstand.

Aunt Mildred's face filled with panic. 'We'll come with you,' she piped up, her voice barely a croak.

'No, that won't be necessary,' Dad said, opening the door.

'But—'

'Mildred.' Uncle Sidney's voice carried a warning. He gave Dad's shoulder a quick squeeze. 'Just tell us what we can do to help, Howard.'

'Go over to our house. Someone should be there. Just in case.'

I sat on the front seat between Dad and Frankie as we drove down Marine Drive towards Sunnywoods. The home was near the border of Burnaby and New Westminster, only a few miles from our house. Dad thought if I saw exactly where Kipper had started out from we could figure out where he would go from there.

Frankie stared out of his window at the muddy waters of the Fraser river below the road. 'Do you think he would have gone near the river, Ethie?'

My stomach lurched. I couldn't think clearly. *No. No. Why would he?* 'I don't think so,' I whispered, not even wanting to consider it. 'We never went down there.'

After we passed Victoria Drive the winding road became familiar. I squirmed in my seat, twisting to scan the dense bush on our left.

'We saw Danny Fenwick when we left,' Dad said. 'He's going to get some of his friends to help search the neighbourhood. Can you think of any other places Kipper might have gone?'

'The golf course,' I blurted. 'We went there searching for golf balls. Danny has a tree fort in the bush there.' Excitement made my words run together. 'Maybe he went there. Maybe he slept in the tree fort last night.'

We turned at the next intersection. I directed Dad through the maze of new streets, half-built houses and empty lots above Marine Drive. I pointed to a dirt road leading down to the forests surrounding the golf course. 'Danny's fort's down there.'

Dad swerved onto it, our tyres kicking up gravel as we straightened out. Coming over a rise in the road, a sudden flash of light reflecting from a mirror below blinded me for a second. The Hudson slowed to a crawl, then stopped with a jerk. The clearing in front of the forest looked like a parking lot. The afternoon sun glistened from the windshields, grilles and hoods of all the vehicles parked there. Frankie leaned forward, peering out of the window.

'Those are our neighbours,' Dad said.

He threw open his door and we rushed towards the crowd gathered behind a pickup truck. Dad was right: Mrs Fenwick, the Mansons, the Jacksons, the Blacks, everyone from Barclay Street, everyone who had been at Mom's funeral, was there. Even the boy I had fought with over the bottles was laying his bike down in the grass and joining the group.

Dora Fenwick saw us coming and hurried to meet us. Danny had spread the word about Kipper through the neighbourhood, she told us on the way to the truck. Ardith's father, who was a fireman, was organizing the search of this area. The crowd parted silently to let us through to where Mr Price was spreading a map on the truck's tailgate. He and Dad shook hands silently.

Danny suddenly appeared beside me. He squinted and pushed his glasses back up on his nose. 'I thought he might have come to the tree fort,' he said, his face a mask of disappointment, 'but I just checked and it doesn't look like anyone's been there.'

All afternoon we combed the forest, clearings, creeks and ditches. Search parties trudged through the tall grasses, thistles and snarled undergrowth. They looked in all the unfinished houses. As word spread throughout the day more and more people arrived to help. The mill where Dad and Frankie worked shut down for the day, and the employees came to help. Many golfers left the fairways to join us, using their clubs to beat a path through the bush. We flushed out frogs and squirrels, found discarded tyres and a stray dog, but no Kipper.

Late in the afternoon our group came to the opening of one of the concrete sewer tunnels.

'Where do these lead?' Dad asked.

'Eventually to the river,' Mr Price replied.

'Ethie?' Dad turned to me.

'No. He wouldn't go in there,' I insisted, perhaps too strongly, because he knelt down and looked into my eyes.

'He really wouldn't?' he asked gently. 'Or you hope he wouldn't? Have you ever played in them?'

'I did. But Kipper didn't.' Mom always said that, left on his own, Kipper would always do what was right. I knew first hand that that was true. 'No,' I said, looking into my father's anxious eyes. 'For sure he wouldn't go in there. He wouldn't even go in with me. When Danny and I played in them Kipper stayed behind.' *Stayed behind and used a stick to draw houses in the mud.*

'The art shop!' I cried, my heart suddenly pounding. 'Maybe he went downtown to Marlene's art shop.' Of course! It made perfect sense. He'd gone there with Mom so many times. I was certain he knew the way.

Dad stopped at the first phone booth on Marine Drive. Through the open window I listened to him talking to Mr Telford, insisting that he meet us at the shop right away.

'No, it's got nothing to do with his paintings,' Dad said impatiently. 'Kipper's missing and he may have gone there.' His jaw clamped shut, the muscles working as he was interrupted yet again. 'Listen to me,' he said, lowering his voice, enunciating each word slowly. 'We'll be there in about twenty minutes. If you don't meet us, I swear I'll break down the Goddamned door.'

When we arrived in the alley behind the shop Mr Telford was standing by his car. Dad threw open his door and jumped out before the Hudson's engine sputtered to a stop. He pointed to an open overhead window at the side of the building and two overturned metal garbage cans below.

'Jesus Murphy!' Mr Telford said. He pulled a key from his pocket and walked towards the door.

'Hurry,' Dad yelled. The second the lock turned he pushed past him. Frankie and I followed on his heels, with Mr Telford switching on lights behind us. We rushed through the building, frantically searching each room, the storefront, closets, bathrooms, calling Kipper's name.

Frankie and I stopped at the art-room doorway. 'What's this?' Frankie yelled, rushing into the dimly lit room.

Mr Telford switched on the overhead lights. 'Well, well, it appears someone *has* been here,' he said.

Frankie squatted down to inspect a bundle of paint rags under the art table at the back of the room. 'Looks like somebody used these to sleep here,' he said. As he lifted the edge of one, a large black sketch pad fell out from the folds and slid across the floor, face down.

Mr Telford picked it up. 'It's Marlene's,' he said. 'The sketches I was telling you about,' he said, handing them to Dad.

Dad's chest and shoulders sagged inward, as if the air had been sucked out of his lungs. He slowly closed the book, but not before I'd seen the pencil drawing of my mother's face. Then something clicked in my mind. 'Dad,' I said, tugging at his arm. 'Dad, I know where he is.'

42

The rays of the setting sun bounced off concrete buildings and the darkening downtown windows. A red glow in the western sky promised fair weather tomorrow. There was no such promise for the coming night. I didn't need Dad or Frankie to tell me that time was not on our side. If we didn't find him soon, Kipper might spend another long night alone, without food or – I shivered even to think it – his inhaler.

Frankie drove. He didn't slow for amber lights or even red ones, racing the Hudson down Granville Street. 'If the police come after us,' Dad had told him, when we scrambled into the car, 'keep going. We'll explain later.'

Now he sat beside me in the front seat, encouraging me to continue my stammering confession of why I thought we'd find Kipper behind a Chinatown grocery store.

'I think he went there to talk to Mom. I told him – we told him – it was a place where people went to speak to dead relatives.'

'We?'

And the whole story spilled out – about the girl in the park across the street, about following her downtown the day of Mom's funeral, and about the little red house in the yard behind the store. 'Kipper couldn't stop talking about it. He wanted to go back to see it. He even started a painting of it. So the next time we went downtown I told him there were ghosts in it.'

'Next time?' Dad said, surprise clear in his voice. Frankie, too, glanced at me, eyes wide, then went back to concentrating on the road.

'I'm sorry,' I stammered, 'I know . . .'

'It's okay.' Dad patted my knee. 'The next time?' he prompted me.

I lowered my head and explained haltingly about Kipper having an asthma attack when we arrived at the store. 'But his inhaler was empty. The girl took us upstairs to the apartment where she boiled some leaves to help his breathing.' I burst into tears without looking up. 'I shouldn't have said that about ghosts,' I wailed. 'I shouldn't have taken him there.' Dad pulled me into his arms and I sobbed against his chest.

'Everything will be all right,' he murmured, holding me close. 'We'll find him.'

Then, after a few moments, he asked quietly, 'Ethie? What was the girl's name?'

I sat up and wiped my eyes. 'I forget her last name.' I sniffed. 'She wrote it down with her phone number on a piece of paper. But I left it in my suitcase at Aunt Mildred's. I know her first name though. Lily.'

Dad's body went still, as if he had stopped breathing.

'I'm sorry I didn't tell you about her.'

'It doesn't matter now,' he said, his voice catching. He cleared his throat. 'The only important thing is finding Kipper.'

A few blocks later, I blurted, 'She has a picture of you, with her mother. I saw it. Lily thinks . . . she thinks . . .' I lowered my head again.

'She thinks what?' Dad prodded. 'It's all right, Ethie. You can tell me.'

'She thinks you're her – her father,' I whispered.

The car swerved. 'What?' Frankie said, and regained control.

Dad lifted my chin. 'Ethie, look at me,' he said, wiping the tears from my cheeks with his thumb. I lifted my eyes to meet his. And the empty space between us was gone.

For the rest of my life I would remember the blue of my father's eyes that day. And the light I saw in them. The sadness was still there behind that light, the anguish over Mom, the fear for Kipper, but as my father's eyes held mine I knew that light included me.

'I have one daughter,' he said gently, 'and that's you, Ethie. I'm not Lily's father.'

'But – but what about . . . what about the money you sent her every month?'

Once again Frankie glanced at us, but he remained silent.

'It's a long story,' Dad sighed, 'and I promise I'll tell you both – some day. But right now let's concentrate on finding Kipper.'

We heard him before we saw him. The moment we pushed open the wooden gate behind the store we heard the ragged struggle of shallow breathing.

Dad made it across the yard to the little house in three quick strides, with Frankie and me right behind. We found Kipper curled up in the corner of the tiny porch, his eyes closed, his wheezing lungs fighting to drag air over a swollen tongue. Dad knelt down and lifted him into his arms. Kipper's eyelids opened slightly. A weak smile lifted the corners of his cracked lips. 'Hi, Da,' he said hoarsely. 'Mom said you would come.'

Dad pressed his lips to Kipper's grey face. 'You were dreaming, son,' he whispered. Cradling him, he shifted to let Frankie squeeze in with the inhaler. Holding it to Kipper's open mouth, both he and Dad took deep breaths with each pump, as if it would somehow help release the medicine into Kipper's congested lungs.

'I'll get Lily,' I said.

43

The meeting – Dad's sudden collision with his past – was blurred by Kipper's laboured breathing.

'Bring him upstairs,' Lily urged, as soon as she saw him. In the kitchen above the store, the same woman who was there last time stood at the gas stove, once again spooning leaves into a pot of boiling water. She gestured with a tilt of her head towards the sitting room.

As Dad and I settled on the couch, with Kipper wedged between us, Frankie asked to use the phone. Lily led him into the hall. While he called the police and Uncle Sidney to let them know we had found him, I watched Kipper leaning against our father like a limp rag doll.

How could he have walked so far without anyone noticing him? Dressed in baggy engineer's coveralls and a grey shirt, his shaved head nicked and scabbed, he looked like the men who worked in the fields of the Fraser valley prison farms.

Lily came back into the sitting room with towels and placed them on the coffee-table. She held one up and Kipper lifted his head to let her drape it over his shoulders. As she did so, Dad smiled at her wistfully. 'You look exactly like your mother,' he said quietly.

Suddenly shy, Lily lowered her dark eyes. Behind her, the woman in the kitchen glanced up as she poured the steaming mixture into a bowl on the table. Over the mist, her eyes met Dad's.

'Shun-qin?' he asked.

She nodded wordlessly, then returned to her task. A moment later she replaced the pot on the stove, carried the bowl into the sitting room, set it on the coffee-table and returned to the kitchen.

Lily reached across to tent the towel around Kipper's head. He smiled up at her, then leaned over to breathe in the steam.

'I see you're an old hand at this.' Dad laughed.

'Yeah, Da,' Kipper's muffled voice came from beneath the towel. 'This will make me all better.'

'Fifteen minutes he be good as new,' the woman in the kitchen said, setting glasses of tea on the table.

'Shun-qin,' Dad said, startled, 'you can speak.'

'You raise child, you must learn speaking.'

As Kipper's breathing cleared, I sipped my tea and looked around the room, at Frankie sitting ramrod straight, completely bewildered, at Lily kneeling on the floor beside the coffee-table, hovering protectively over Kipper, lifting the towel every once in a while to check on him.

'Thank you for helping him, Lily,' Dad said, suddenly breaking the silence. 'This time and last.'

She met his eyes, acknowledging his words with a shy smile.

'Your mother brought herbs to your father in the prison camp in Hong Kong.' He took a deep breath, as if measuring his next words. Then he went on: 'Unfortunately they were too late for him. But many other soldiers, including me, owe their lives to her smuggled medicines.'

He glanced up at Shun-qin standing in the kitchen doorway. 'How is our friend, Ah Sam?' he ventured.

'Gone,' she answered. 'Many months now.'

'I'm sorry to hear that. He was a good man.' He turned back to Lily. 'I saw you in the park,' he said. 'Then I convinced myself it was my imagination, that I was seeing things. For years after the war I thought every Asian woman I saw looked like your mother.' He was silent for a moment, then asked, 'Was it Ah Sam who gave you my address?'

'No. His nephew. He didn't know it was a secret.' She looked down at her hands, then back up at Dad, her dark eyes swimming. 'I am sorry I went to your home that day. I brought bad luck to your door. Perhaps if I had not spoken to your wife. If—'

Dad's face turned pale. 'No.' He held up his palm as if to halt the flow of Lily's words. 'No,' he repeated. The sorrow in that single word filled the silenced room.

44

The expression on Lily's face brought a lump to Howard's throat. He had lived the last seventeen years waking up to the same look. Seventeen years, which had passed by in a fugue of regret. *If. If only.*

If only he had told Shun-ling about Gordy before that night. If only he had stopped her coming to the camp. And now the added torment of knowing that if only he had told Lucy these truths years ago she would never have been on that sailboat.

He looked into the eyes of Shun-ling and Gordy's daughter and knew he owed it to them to ensure that she did not suffer a similar burden of guilt over a superstitious notion that her presence had brought tragedy to his house. 'No,' he said, shaking his head. 'Lucy's death was an accident, a terrible accident. You did nothing to cause it, and could have done nothing to prevent it. If she could, she would be the first to tell you that it was Fate – heaven's unchanged heart, she called it.' Saying the un-planned words aloud, he realized he, too, would have to find a way to hang on to them. He would have to do more than repeat the words of a memorized prayer and find a way to accept the things he could not change.

At that moment he noticed an unframed photograph propped up on the corner knick-knack shelf. He rose from the couch and walked over to look at it. 'May I?' he asked. From the corner of his eye he saw Lily nod. Feeling her watching him, he took down the old sepia photograph from the shelf. He stared at it, allowing the memories to surface, while somewhere a clock ticked in the silence. He turned to face Lily, holding up the picture. 'This man,' he said, pointing to Gordy, 'was your father.' He looked over at Shun-qin. 'Did you not know that?' he asked her.

'No,' she said. 'I only know one man is father of Lily – one man Shun-ling's friend.'

Howard turned back to Lily. 'Your father's name was Gordy Veronick. He was my closest friend. We grew up together. He loved your mother, and you, very much.'

Lily's dark eyes filled with tears. 'He died?'

'Yes, I'm sorry.'

'But it was you who sent money while I was growing up?' she asked, brushing away an escaping tear.

'Yes,' he said. 'I made a promise to your father.' Then he added, 'And I owed it to your mother.'

'That debt is paid.' Shun-qin spoke from the kitchen doorway.

'Never.'

'What my aunt means,' Lily said, 'is that we no longer need financial help. Ah Sam helped her make very good investments. Enough to afford to come here, to buy this store with our second uncle, and for me to attend university. That was why I went to your house. To thank you.'

'I want to go to our house too,' Kipper wailed, from under the towel.

Frankie shook himself as if he was waking from a dream. He leaned across to Kipper and squeezed his arm. 'You bet,' he said. 'I miss my roommate.'

Lily returned to Kipper. 'I think that's enough.' She removed the wet towel, replaced it with a dry one and patted the moisture from his head. 'My hat,' he cried, reaching up to his shaved scalp. 'They took my hat away.'

'I'm sorry, son,' Howard said, putting an arm around his shoulders. 'First thing tomorrow, we'll buy you a new one.'

Lily rose from the floor and disappeared down the hall, returning moments later with a cap. 'Here, Kipper,' she said. 'You may have this one.' She handed it to him. 'It's a very special hat. It was my father's.'

Startled at the sight of his old army cap – the one he had used to pass money to Shun-ling at the ferry – Howard opened his mouth to correct her. But something stopped him. Why take this memory, and the generous gesture, from her?

Smiling through his tears, Kipper tugged the wedge cap over his grey scalp. 'A special hat?' he asked.

'Yes,' Shun-qin said, her eyes fixed not on Kipper but on Howard. 'My sister told me hat belong to man who had her heart.'

45

Kipper and I climbed into the back seat with Dad for the drive home. 'They were going to pull out all my teeth,' Kipper said sleepily, once we were settled. 'Thass bad, isn't it, Da?'

'It certainly is,' Dad said, putting his arm around us both and pulling us close.

Kipper yawned. 'You said I could leave if I wanted,' he said, leaning against him. 'And I did.'

'You certainly did.' Dad chuckled. Hugging us both a little tighter, he promised Kipper he would never have to go back to Sunnywoods. 'From now on,' he said, 'this family sticks together.' But by then Kipper was asleep.

I melted into Dad's side, thinking about what he had told Lily of her family, that Gordy Veronick had no one left in Canada that he knew of. 'Your father and I were like brothers, though,' he told her, 'and I promised him I'd look out for you. So even if you don't need financial help any more, I can still be there for you, be your Canadian uncle, if you'll let me.'

'Dad,' I whispered in the darkness of the back seat, 'I really like Lily.'

He kissed the top of my head. 'I'm glad, honey.'

In the rear-view mirror Frankie's eyes crinkled in a smile. A few blocks later he broke the humming silence in the car, saying, 'You never told Mom.' It was a more of a statement than a question, but I waited for the answer.

'No,' Dad said, his voice low.

'Why not?'

After what seemed like a long time, Dad said, 'I don't exactly know. At first after I came back I just couldn't talk about it. The more time passed the more impossible it seemed.'

When we stopped at the next light Frankie turned around. 'I think she would have understood,' he said.

'Yes, she would.'

It was late when we turned onto Barclay Street, almost midnight. We drove slowly past our neighbours' houses. Porch lights glowed above every door.

Kipper woke. He sat up and rubbed his eyes. 'Home again, home again, jiggety jig.'

'Yes, son,' Dad said. 'Home again.' The car slowed down and I stiffened at the sight of the one parked in front of our house.

'Uncle Sidney wants to check Kipper over,' Frankie said, pulling up to the kerb behind Aunt Mildred's Volvo.

Across the street the curtains moved in Mrs Manson's window. She appeared on her porch the moment Dad helped Kipper out of the car. 'Glad to hear you found him,' she called. 'Everything all right, Howard?'

'Yes,' Dad answered, over his shoulder. 'He's just tired. We'll see you tomorrow.' Halfway up the sidewalk he stopped and called back, 'And thank you, Irene.'

In the living room Kipper sat on the couch while Uncle Sidney listened to his heart and lungs, then checked his throat, eyes and ears. I stood at Dad's side, clinging to his arm and avoiding Aunt Mildred's eyes. When he had finished his examination, Uncle Sid patted Kipper's knee. 'He just needs a good sleep,' he said, standing up. 'So do you all. We'll be on our way now.'

Aunt Mildred stepped forward. 'Come on, then, Ethie,' she said.

I clung tighter to Dad. Frankie helped Kipper to his feet and they stood beside us.

'She's staying,' Dad said, hugging me to his side. 'Tonight and for good. So is Kipper. This is their home.' Aunt Mildred opened her mouth, but before she could speak, Dad held up his hand. 'Look,' he said, 'I believe you mean well, and I know I owe you a debt of gratitude I may never be able to repay, but I won't pay with my family. If you want to fight me on this, go right ahead, but I won't back down. Not this time.'

'But how can you possibly cope?' she demanded. 'What will you do?'

'We,' Dad corrected her. 'You mean what will *we* do. *We* are a family and will do whatever it takes to stay that way from now on. Now, you can be a part of that *we* or not. It's up to you.'

'But—'

'Mildred,' Uncle Sidney interrupted, 'just stop right now.' He looked at Dad. 'She won't fight you, Howard, I promise. And we'll help in any way you'll allow us to.'

'Thanks, Sid.'

Suddenly Aunt Mildred crumpled into Dad's chair, her hands over her face. 'Oh, God,' she sobbed. 'Now I've lost all of you.'

Kipper stepped over to her and laid a hand on her trembling shoulder. 'We're not lost, Aunt Mildred,' he said, patting her. 'We're all right here.'

46

In the years that followed, there were good times and bad, the *yin* and the *yang*. At first the sad times greatly outweighed the happy ones. There were many mornings, which we will all admit to, when the thought of getting out of bed to face another day filled with Mom's absence felt just too painful to bear. During those periods we learned to concentrate on putting one foot in front of the other, watching warily for the lurking dark holes of despair we sometimes slid into. It was Kipper who saved us, who helped us to climb out of those holes, get our footing and move on. Whenever too much time passed without anyone mentioning Mom – because sometimes it hurt too much just to say her name – he would shatter that unspoken agreement of silence by recalling a special moment with her or repeating one of her many favourite quotations, reminding us that, in a very real way, she was still with us.

There were times when my father struggled, probably more than we ever realized. But after a while I would stop worrying every time he put on his bomber jacket and come to believe that he took his long walks in the rain more from habit than necessity.

It wasn't always easy, I'm certain, but he kept his word. As far as I know he never took another drink. And over time he kept his promise to share his past with us, enabling me to record his story all these years later.

After the war, in the spring of 1947, my father was asked to return to Hong Kong to testify at the war-crimes investigations. He refused.

Following those investigations, the captain of the PoW ship, the *Lisbon Maru*, was found guilty of giving the order to batten down the hatches and remove the ventilation chutes during the ship's sinking. He was sentenced to seven years' imprisonment for his part in the loss of 846 British prisoners deliberately trapped in the hold. The Middlesex machine-gunners, Private Peter Young and Private Dick Baxter, had been among the lost.

Even without my father's testimony the Japanese commander of Hong Kong's prison camps and the camps' medical officer were found guilty of 'callous disregard for human life'. They were both sentenced to hang. Their death sentences were later commuted to twenty years' imprisonment.

The interpreter, the camp sergeant at Sham Shui Po, a Canadian citizen, born and raised in Kamloops, British Columbia, was given no such reprieve. The sergeant – whose father's name is engraved on Vancouver's Stanley Park war memorial, which honours the thousands of Japanese Canadians who fought for Canada during both world wars – was found guilty of high treason on 21 April 1947. He was hanged three days later.

The camp guard known as Satan was never brought to trial. The day after Japan surrendered, his bloated and beaten body was washed up in the mud flats below the camp. 'War leaves no soul untarnished,' was all my father would say.

Dad has never remarried. He and Kipper still live in our old house on Barclay Street. A number of years ago they built an art room behind it. The two of them spend hours together out there, Kipper with his paintings and Dad building frames for them.

My brother Frankie has often accused me of being a sucker

for happy endings. And I must admit there was a time when I fantasized about my father falling in love with my mother's friend Dora Fenwick. But when I was fifteen years old, Mrs Fenwick married a man from the telephone company.

Then I imagined that some day he would marry Shun-qin, with whom he became friends. But that was all they ever were, good friends. Like Danny Fenwick and me. After the events of that summer Danny was once again my best friend. He was also the first boy I ever kissed. But in high school we realized that we didn't want to ruin a perfectly good friendship with dating. Danny moved to Calgary, Alberta, not long after we graduated. I still get a Christmas card from him and his wife every year.

Frankie ended up going to university, became a teacher and married. Better late than never, according to Aunt Mildred.

Years ago, our father made peace with her. We all did. Something happened to her after that summer. She took Dad at his word that she could become part of the *we* that was our family. It was she who found our housekeepers while we were growing up, often volunteering to look after us herself when Dad had to work an overtime shift. The first time she invited Kipper and me to stay at her house overnight I was shocked and reluctant to go. But the moment we walked into her living room and I saw the painting Kipper had given her and Uncle Sidney hanging on the wall above her fireplace, I knew it would be all right. The painting of the little red house – where Kipper insisted he had talked to Mom – seemed so out of place in the formal room that it looked odd even to me. But it still hangs there today.

After Aunt Mildred started spending time with Kipper, she made it her business to learn all she could about Down's syndrome, as Mom had. Slowly she realized that it was not an affliction, but only a part of who Kipper was. I swear my aunt's

face softens every time she looks at him. And every once
while I catch a flash of Mom in her green eyes.

For years now, every weekend when the sun is shining, Dad
and Kipper have set up his latest canvases at the open air art
market in Stanley Park.

Today I sit cross-legged on my blanket in the park, just steps
away from the Japanese-Canadian war memorial, and close my
notebook. On the grassy knoll above, Lily leans back in Frankie's
arms to watch their ebony-haired son play catch with his Uncle
Kipper. Yes, that's right, Frankie and Lily fell in love and married.
He can't blame me for that storybook ending. Or perhaps he
can. I don't mind. From the moment they met, Frankie admits
it was inevitable. Lily, who is now a pharmacist, became part
of our family after all. Nothing could have made my father
happier.

Now he sits in a lawn chair by the path, chatting with my
husband and Uncle Sidney while keeping an eye on prospective
buyers viewing Kipper's paintings. I glance at my brother.

Kipper is slowing down. His heart is failing. Panting heavily,
he hands the ball to his nephew. 'I have to rest my heart now,'
he says to little Gordie, and makes his way towards my blanket.

Perched on Aunt Mildred's knee, my daughter watches as,
slowly, he slumps beside me. Her eyebrows knit with concern.
'Why does Uncle Kipper have to rest his heart?' she asks.

'Well, honey,' Aunt Mildred says, brushing back a copper curl
from Lucille's serious forehead, 'that's because his heart is
bigger than other people's.'

Kipper grins up at her. 'Aunt Mildred,' he says, 'now that's
just braggin'.'

In October 1945 the surviving members of Canada's C Force made their way home. Four years earlier, 1979 eager young Royal Rifles and Winnipeg Grenadiers had sailed out of Vancouver harbour in answer to Britain's request for reinforcements to shore up the Hong Kong garrison. Of the 557 who did not return, 289 died during the eighteen-day battle for Hong Kong. The remaining 268 perished in the PoW camps of Hong Kong and Japan.

Lacking equipment and perhaps training – but not heart – the all-volunteer infantry were the first Canadian troops to engage in armed combat in the Second World War.

And they were the last to come home.

Acknowledgements

My thanks to agent Jane Gregory, and editor Stephanie Glencross, of Gregory and Company, and Jane Wood of Quercus, for your encouragement and patient guidance through the edits as well as your continuous faith in this project.

I would like to acknowledge the Hong Kong Veterans Commemorative Association for their dedication in maintaining and sharing their database of information and 'C' Force memorabilia. Any errors here are mine, and liberties taken in timeline, scenes, or dialogue attributed to historical figures, are solely for the sake of the story.

This story is a work of fiction. The characters, with the exception of historical figures – including Brigadier J. K. Lawson and Lieutenant J. L. R. Sutcliffe – are also a product of my imagination. Unfortunately the Battle of Hong Kong in 1941, and the subsequent internment of the allied survivors, is not.

I wish to extend my deep gratitude to these Hong Kong Veterans who so generously took the time to share their memories with me: Aubrey Flegg, Dick Wilson, Robert (Flash) Clayton, and Jan Solecki. True gentlemen all, in whose eyes I saw the truth of Dwight D. Eisenhower's declaration that 'no one hates war more than the soldier who has lived it, who has seen its brutality, its futility, its stupidity.'